# A Deadly Service

*by*

**Neive Denis**

# Copyright

Cataloguing-in-publication data
Creator: Denis, Neive, author
Cataloguing-in-Publication details are available from the National
Library of Australia www.trove.nla.gov.au

This is a work of fiction. All characters and events are purely the
imagination of the author. All locations are fictitious. Any resemblance
to a particular location, or anyone, living or dead is coincidental.

ISBN: 978-0-9953533-2-9 (paperback)

Cover design:  T A Marshall, Mackay, Queensland

# Contents

## Also by the Author

*An Ancient Solution*
*Missing!*
*Connections*

# Acknowledgments

Writing reputedly is a solitary activity. In my experience, it is not. While the hours pounding the keyboard happens is a solitary pursuit, even when it occurs in a crowded space. However, the process of producing a book depends on many others in so many ways. Any number of people has provided support, encouragement and inspiration along the road to publication of this book. Heartfelt thanks to all of you.

In particular, I must thank Tom Marshall for his patience and forbearance in developing cover designs, and Rowena for taking the time to review the writing. Special thanks to the 'Glass Tarts' who politely suffer my deliberations about writing. Lastly, my deepest gratitude to my long-suffering husband who has been nothing but patient and supportive as he struggles to comprehend what motivates me to spend the hours at my keyboard.

# Chapter One

Ahh, bliss. Saturday spent stretched out on the couch with a good book, a coffee, and with the good citizens of Millhaven behaving themselves so there is nothing to investigate. Damn! There is always something comes along to stuff things up.

"Hello, Whittington Investigations. How can ..."

"Sonoma Whittington?"

"Yes, this is Sonoma ..." If I get lucky, I might actually get to finish a sentence.

"Something horrible has happened to Mum."

"Who is this?"

"It's Kate. Mum is dead. Can you come? We need your help."

Kate. Kate? How many Kates do I know? This one sounds vaguely familiar. My mind raced for a few seconds before recognition clicked in: Therese Melrose's daughter Kate. Okay, if that's correct, Kate's mother, Therese Melrose, is dead. That thought released a rush of images from my memory banks, not necessarily pleasant ones. My initial reaction was to be 'too busy' to get involved, but profession-alism stepped in and I endeavoured to piece together the story... no easy task as it turned out.

Not surprisingly, Kate was incapable of providing a coherent account of what happened. She handed the task over to a friend, Sandra, who just happened to drop by. Extracting the story from Sandra proved a long-winded affair. After about half an hour, I had managed to cobble together the basics of Therese's demise.

My notes showed: about mid-morning, Kate found her mother's body in the ground floor granny flat of the family home and called the Police. The Police declared it a domestic accident. The family couldn't accept that verdict and wanted a second opinion... hence the call to me. There were two things I couldn't figure out: why did the family think there was more to the death than the Police's verdict indicated, and how come Sandra, who lives in Millhaven, was so well informed so soon after the event.

1

I still wanted to decline. In what now seemed like another lifetime, Therese was my boss. It hadn't been the happiest relationship. She was a contributor to my decision to quit the Public Service. However, although I do okay as a private investigator, I'm not so affluent that I can choose which jobs to take and which ones to turn down. This one might not have a lot of appeal, but I had no other jobs scheduled for at least another week. I weakened and agreed to drive to Ralston in the morning, and spent the day wondering if I might regret it. The prospect of the early morning four-hour drive from Millhaven to Ralston didn't thrill me either.

Ralston at 10.30 on a Sunday morning is not exactly a hive of activity. Tirandi Street is even quieter. Number 53 was towards the far end of the street. Sandra said she would be at the house when I arrived. I assumed the small sedan parked in the driveway belonged to her daughter, Emily. Sandra Inneston met me as I fronted up to the entrance.

"Sonny, thank God you've come. This 'Therese thing' is really – *really* – horrible." Strange way to describe a friend's death – a Therese thing , I thought, but I didn't get a chance to comment as Sandra rushed on. "I know you're not one of Therese's greatest fans, but you have to look into this... please. Poor Kate is almost out of her mind. You remember her husband, Ken? He's trying to hold it together, but he's not in much better shape than Kate."

Before going upstairs, I had a quiet word to Sandra. "I need for Kate and Ken to tell me in their own words exactly what they know about what happened to Therese. I do need to talk to you as well, but I need to talk to Kate and Ken alone." Sandra nodded and took me upstairs.

"Hello Kate. I'm Sonny Whittington. We've spoken on the phone a few times in the past. It's sad we finally get to meet under such tragic circumstances." In spite of her best efforts, Sandra couldn't help herself and kept interrupting and prompting while I spoke to Kate. In desperation, I suggested Sandra might make us all a cup of coffee, including one for Ken who had retreated to his office earlier in the morning. I could see him beavering away on his computer.

"Is it okay to sit here and talk?" Kate nodded. "Where are the kids? There are three aren't there?"

"Yes, the three of them spent the night with their best friends, the Andersons' kids. We'll pick them up this evening. They don't know about Mum yet, and we want to keep it that way until we know exactly what happened."

"Okay, take your time, but tell me everything that led up to your finding your mother yesterday. Include every little thing you remember, it might be important although it seems insignificant."

"Uhmm …oh, I don't know where to start."

"Start from yesterday morning. What happened when you first got up?"

"We slept in until very late and had to rush when we got up. Our instructions were to be at the school at 9.15a.m. to collect the kids…"

"Why were you collecting the kids? Where had they been?"

"On a school camp; the bus was to drop them back at the school at nine o'clock."

"Maybe we should start the story from the night before. What happened on Friday night?"

"Friday night was our last kids-free night, so we went out to dinner with the Andersons and another couple. After dinner, we went to the Andersons' for coffee and the night dragged on to the early hours of the morning. We're not used to late nights – not that late anyway. We slept in way past our usual time and had to rush to be at the school by 9:15 to collect the kids."

"I thought school camps usually finished on Friday. How come this one didn't finish until Saturday?"

"The school camp was at the outdoor education centre on Crispin Island. The island had another group arriving on Saturday. Like everyone else, the economic downturn has hit them hard. When the school made the booking, the island offered us an extra night at cost only – basically, just the cost of meals – to stay until Saturday morning. We agreed, and the island saved themselves and extra boat trip. After the bus dropped the kids back at the school at nine o'clock, the staff organised the kids and their luggage ready for the parents to collect them at 9:15. The parents had a strict timetable: be there at 9:15, and all kids to be collected and gone by 9:30. It was only supposed to take a few minutes to collect your kids and be gone."

As with many well-laid plans, this one fell foul of Murphy's Law. The bus ran late, a mix up occurred with the children's luggage, and the anticipated few minutes turned into well over an hour. Kate continued the story from when they arrive back home.

"We spent about half an hour listening to the kids' tales from their week away. Then the kids grew concerned that Grandma hadn't come upstairs to welcome them back. They pooled their meagre pocket money to buy her a small gift from the camp's souvenir shop and were anxious to give it to her. Poppy ..."

"Who is Poppy?"

"She's the middle child of our three, the only girl and somewhat a favourite of Grandma's. Poppy dashed down to the granny flat. I heard her bang on the door and call out several times. She didn't appear to be getting any response. I decided to go down stairs to investigate, but met Poppy, looking very disappointed, at the top of the stairs. She said she thought Grandma was either still asleep or had gone out. Mum never slept that late. She was a poor sleeper, but always got up early."

"Was her car at home?"

"Yes, it was where it's parked now."

"When you came home after your night out, was the car there then? Apart from the car being there, are you sure Therese was at home?"

"Yes, the car was there when we went out and it was still there when we came home... and, yes, she was home. I remember there was a light on in the flat."

I was surprised that neither of them felt it necessary to investigate a light in the granny flat at that hour of the morning. Kate explained that part of the arrangements for the whole family to live in the one house was that they didn't interfere in each other's lives. Therese would have been annoyed if they checked on her. If she woke up during the night, she usually got up and read reports, or whatever, to catch up on her work.

"Okay, so after Poppy gave up on Grandma, then what happened... you went to investigate?"

"I asked Poppy to do something for me in the kitchen. Then I grabbed our key, and went down to the flat. The light we saw the night before was still on. I knew something was wrong for that light still to be switched on. I let myself in."

At that point, Sandra came in with coffees and looked about to settle herself at the table where Kate and I were sitting. I gave her a hard look and shook my head. She understood my signal, and went to the office to sit with Ken. However, in that time for Kate, the memory of what she saw on entering the flat came flooding back. She broke down and was unable to continue for a few minutes. It took a while to piece together the rest of the story. Later, Ken corroborated her account of what happened after that.

Kate rushed out of the flat and yelled to Ken, who started down the stairs with the kids bouncing along behind him. Before they were half way down, Kate stopped them and sent the children back upstairs. Curious and concerned about what might have happened to their grandmother, the children retreated up the stairs only a little way and then stopped. Ken claimed the sight of his wife, ashen faced and leaning for support against the wall near the door of the granny flat, spurred him into action. Kate struggled to tell Ken that Therese was dead. He sent the children back to their rooms before doing anything else.

From the doorway, Ken surveyed the scene in the flat before joining Kate who now sat on the bottom step. He took charge, firstly phoning the Andersons to arrange for them to keep the children overnight, and then sending Kate upstairs to supervise the packing of overnight bags. He wanted the children away from the house as soon as possible, and before the Police arrived. That in place, he called the Police.

"You said the Police declared it a domestic accident. Did they share their reasoning for that verdict?"

"They believed she rose suddenly from the couch, became dizzy and fell over, crashing onto the glass coffee table and hitting her head on the tiled floor."

Sandra came to collect our coffee cups, causing another pause in my questioning. Kate complained of a headache earlier and took a couple of pills of some sort. She now looked exhausted. I didn't want to push her any further. Rest probably was the best thing for her, but I needed to check one thing before suggesting it. "As the Police don't believe there are any suspicious circumstances involved, I assume your mother's flat is not considered a crime scene. I didn't see any crime scene tape as I came past, so I am assuming it is okay to access it."

"Yes. We can go in, but they suggested we keep it locked until they send the special clean-up people around. They said to expect a few days delay and, unless we really needed to go in for something, it would be less upsetting for us if we left it locked."

"I think you should take yourself off to bed for a while. I need to look at the scene, but Ken can let me in. Besides, I need to have a chat to Ken." There was no argument, and she got up to leave.

I was on my way to talk to Ken when Sandra, looking a bit upset, emerged from the kitchen and called me over to her. She took a call on her mobile while she was rinsing the coffee mugs, so I assumed that was what had upset her.

5

"Geoff has told me I have to go home now and not get involved in all of this. I explained how Emily decided she would like to spend a couple of days in Ralston to do a few things, and we now thought we might stay until about Tuesday. It didn't do me any good. He insisted I be home by tonight. We'll have to go back to get our bags and check out and all that, and then head off. I don't know what got into him, but he seems none too pleased about it all. I'm sorry I can't stay to help you out with this; even just to stay and support Kate a bit."

"Don't worry about any of that. Besides, Kate and Ken probably need some time alone to come to terms with what has happened. I'll keep an eye on Kate for as long as I'm here."

"I know Kate and Ken don't have a lot of money, but I will pay you at least to take a look at what happened. Therese was a good friend to me when Geoff was out west. Would you like a retainer now? I could give you a cheque, or will you just send me progressive accounts as your investigation continues?"

My initial thoughts were that confirming the Police's findings probably wouldn't take me more than a couple of days. I had packed accordingly. I convinced her we would sort things out after I talked to people and gained a better idea of what happened. In the meantime, she should go home as her husband insisted. "Okay, but I will want to know what's going on and what you find out. I'll call you from time to time."

However, if she was going to leave Ralston, I needed to talk to her before she left. I suggested I accompany her and Emily when they went downstairs and that we have a chat in private down there somewhere. Sandra went to the office, said goodbye to Ken and rescued Emily from the magazine she had read while parked in the office since they arrived at Tirandi Street.

Keen not to delay Sandra's departure, I didn't waste time on niceties and began my questions. "How come you and Emily were here so soon after Therese was discovered?"

"I spent a week out with, Emily. You know, my daughter is an chemical engineer working out on the gas field at Moxton. She was driving me home to Millhaven today and then going to spend a week or so at home with us and maybe catch up with some of her old school friends. We planned a late lunch in Ralston before heading up the highway to Millhaven. As we came into the city, I heard a piece on the radio about a new exhibition that opened last night in the Ralston City Gallery. We decided to have lunch and afterwards take in the exhibition. It would be too late after the exhibition to head up the highway, so we opted to stay in Ralston overnight rather than finishing the trip home in the dark."

"So, you changed your plans and went to look at the exhibition?"

"Yes, after lunch we went to the exhibition. It was a bit disappointing and didn't keep us hanging around for too long. Afterwards, we organised accommodation and I rang Therese to ask her to join us for dinner. Kate answered instead. She was in an awful state. I managed to work out something happened to her mother and went round to see what I could do for Kate."

"If the Police believe it to be an accident, what makes you think I will find something different? There most likely will be and autopsy in due course, which will confirm the Police's findings."

"Sonny, you haven't looked at anything yet. Therese was eviscerated … or, that's how I interpreted what Kate told me. Kate does not believe what she saw in that flat is consistent with an accident. I urged her to ring my good friend Sonoma Whittington, the private investigator, who would get to the bottom of what really happened... and that's why you're here."

After waving Sandra and Emily off, I went back upstairs to talk to Ken. He confirmed Kate's version of his involvement after she found her mother's body, but added a little extra information.

"I made the calls to the Andersons and the Police from inside the flat. I didn't want the kids to hear. While I was waiting for the kids to pack their bags, I took a whole lot of photographs of the flat with my mobile phone. I know it sounds a bit ghoulish. It occurred to me there could be a coroner's inquest at some stage. We might have to give evidence. The photos will help refresh our memories if that happens, as I know both Kate and I are going to be trying hard to block from our memory what we saw in that flat if we can."

"I don't think it was ghoulish. I am amazed you could think so clearly given the situation," I replied, trying to think of what to say to reassure him.

"Kate doesn't know I took them and I would prefer it stayed that way unless she needs to see them."

I agreed and asked him to let me into the flat. Ken grabbed the key off the hook and led the way down the stairs. He unlocked the door and stepped aside to let me into the granny flat but remained resolutely outside. He shook his head when I motioned for him to come in too, but asked to have a chat to me later – away from Kate. I nodded and he closed the door behind me.

I dropped my bag on the floor near the door and pulled on gloves before groping for a light switch. One glance and I understood why he hadn't wanted to join me. I stood in an open plan area containing kitchen, dining and lounge spaces, with a door in the far corner probably leading to the bedroom/bathroom part of the flat. Files and folders littered the dining table. They seemed strewn about haphazardly. Everything else appeared perfectly tidy and normal, except for the corner where the couch was located. It backed up against the bench that separated the small kitchen from the rest of the room.

The remnants of a long, narrow coffee table lay piled against the external wall near the couch. A cheap rug, bordered on two sides by the couch and the coffee table, now lay in a bunched up heap. It sported an enormous bloodstain, which crept beyond its edge and onto the ceramic tiled floor. An additional stain appeared to be coffee or tea, and a broken coffee mug lay amongst the wreckage.

I quickly went around the room looking at and photographing everything. That completed, I headed for the door. A growing uneasiness made me stop near the door for a minute or so. I swivelled my head around slowly, again surveying the room. Nothing stood out, but something started to gnaw at my gut. Perhaps this wasn't an accident, but it wasn't obvious why my gut should suggest that.

Ken was sitting on the stairs when I exited the flat. He picked up a large envelope from the step beside him and handed it to me. "I printed out a copy of all my photos for you... thought they might be useful somehow with your investigation," he added a shrug. "Kate's asleep. I wanted to give them to you while she wasn't around."

I could have hugged him, but settled for profuse thanks. I will look at them later. It doesn't matter if they are good or not. If they show the body in situ, they will be better than anything I have to work with so far. As I stuffed the envelope in my bag, we heard a noise upstairs. Kate was awake again and came looking for us. I went upstairs to talk to her, leaving Ken sitting alone on the stairs.

Sandra said, when she rang to ask Therese to dinner, Kate answered the phone. That seemed strange, so I queried whether it was normal practice for that to occur.

"No, not normally, but Mum used to switch her phone through to us if she was going to be away. I remembered she mentioned someone was coming to see her on Sunday. Oh, that's today isn't it? She didn't say who or what for. It all seemed a bit hush-hush really. I thought it might be something to do with this investigation, or whatever it is that she is involved with at work. I didn't know if they were meeting here or at the office, but I thought, if whoever the person was rang before they arrived, I could tell them what happened and save them the trip to the house. So I switched Mum's phone through to us upstairs."

Kate said she still felt lousy and was going back to bed for a while. There wasn't much else to ask Kate except whether the children would be around tomorrow. I wanted to look at the flat again and it could be difficult if the children were at home – and being kept in the dark about what happened to Grandma. She assured me the children would be going to school as normal. I took my leave and she headed back to the bedroom.

Ken remained sitting on the stairs where I had left him. I regained my earlier seat on the step below his. "Kate's gone back to bed. If you have a few minutes, I have a couple of questions." He indicated I should continue. "What's all this stuff about some hush-hush investigation? Do you know anything about it or who this somebody is who's supposed to come to see Therese today?"

Ken stared at some indeterminate spot ahead of him and shook his head before looking back at me. "I don't know, but there is – or was – something funny going on. I still work in the same department as Therese but I'm located in a different building now. A couple of years ago, they added a mezzanine floor to the engineering training building and created offices up there for all the engineering apprentice trainers. It's a more convenient location for our offices. Last Monday, my car was in being serviced. I slipped over during the morning to ask if, on her way home, Therese could give me a lift to pick it up. Her secretary told me Therese was away for a few days, and made it clear she wasn't going to elaborate when I commented I wasn't aware Therese was going on leave. As I was walking out, one of the blokes in the office sidled up to me and asked if I knew what was going on, as there were all sorts of rumours flying around. I didn't give him the satisfaction of an answer and just kept walking... but, well, I had heard whispers myself. None of them made any sense."

"What sort of whispers?"

"Nervous speculation, more like. There has been a rash of forced redundancies and a couple of other witch-hunts over the last 12 months. People speculated that, whatever it was that was happening now wouldn't do anyone any good."

I quizzed him about Therese's absence the preceding week and any other unusual behaviour he noticed. He genuinely didn't seem to know anything more, but willingly volunteered a couple of nuggets of information.

"She arrived back here on Thursday afternoon late and was unpacking her car when I arrived home from work. As I walked up to her, she struggled to pick up a large box of what looked like files. I offered to carry it in for her. She quite abruptly told me she could manage, and seemed deliberately to stand between me and the box. It seemed like she didn't want me to see what was in it."

"Did you see enough to be able to describe what was in the box?"

"No, not really; files, a couple of biggish folders, and there seemed to be a pile of pages held together with a big clip lying on top of everything else – you know, like a report or some other large printout."

"Did she say anything else or offer any explanation?"

"I was a bit taken aback by her manner, but I asked her to come up for dinner with us. I said there would be only Kate and I, so it would be quiet. It would save her worrying about food when she had just arrived home. She changed her attitude a bit but declined the offer, saying she needed to complete a substantial report. She needed it drafted by the weekend because someone was coming to review it with her before she presented the finished thing on Monday – that's tomorrow. Then, she picked up the box and went inside, letting me know the conversation was over. I wonder where the presentation was supposed to occur and what will happen now. Her secretary, Liz Cranston, would probably know more."

Some other obscure ideas occurred to me as Ken spoke. I was about to run them past him when the sound of tyres on the driveway followed by footsteps crunching the gravel towards where we sat on the stairs halted discussions. Our conversation interrupted, the unexpected visitor put both Ken and I on high alert. Half expecting the mysterious *someone* to appear, we were surprised and exclaimed in unison, "Emily!" as she came into view around the corner of the building.

"Sorry, guys. Didn't mean to startle you," she said with a lopsided grin. "Dad was determined Mum should get the hell out of Ralston. One of his staff is attending a meeting in Millhaven tomorrow and was driving up today. Dad arranged for him to collect Mum and take her with him, 'so I could have time in Ralston to do what I wanted and drive up when I am ready'; how considerate of him!" Ken and I shared an enquiring glance in response to her sarcasm.

She plonked herself down on the bottom step. "Look I'm … uhmm … I hope you don't mind if …well, you know … if I sort of hang around and maybe I can give you a hand somehow, Sonny. You know I am a chemical engineer, and I did do some post-grad forensic

10

science subjects while I was waiting for funding to come through for my doctoral studies. I was thinking of doing more forensics. This might be the catalyst I need to get started."

What could I say? There were probably a host of things I could have – should have – said. Instead, I settled for a lame assurance that another set of eyes might be useful; although I wasn't sure there was anything to investigate. Reassured she wasn't going to faint on me, I handed her a pair of gloves and opened the door to the flat. Taking the gloves, she raised her eyebrows enquiringly.

"Just in case! No point after the event regretting we contaminated the scene."

After closing the door behind us, I grabbed her arm and held her back as we stood just inside the flat and while I groped for the light switch with my free hand. "Just stand here for a moment and survey the room before you start looking around." Then as she started her prowl around the room, I said, "Look all you want, but please don't touch anything yet." I was impressed. She took her time, made some notes, and didn't react badly to the grisly couch corner.

As we exited the flat, my stomach growled loudly. "Yours or mine?" Emily asked. I claimed it. "I haven't had lunch and it sounds like you haven't either. Maybe we should go and eat something before we try to do anything else."

It was a long time since breakfast. As it was mid-afternoon, I told Ken we might not be back today, but should be back in the morning after the children went to school. I threw my bag into my car, before joining Emily in hers. There was little conversation as we drove to the local suburban shopping mall in search of food. I wasn't at all sure we would find much to eat at this hour on a Sunday afternoon and was delighted to find a place still open.

We sat near the window overlooking the park and ate our salads in silence. It wasn't until coffee arrived that we felt sufficiently refuelled for conversation. Emily chatted about her work, and asked how I had managed the transition from public servant to my now somewhat different existence. As we chatted, I realised I hadn't booked any accommodation for the night.

"We are... that is, I am staying at the Regency down on the river. It's quite nice, reasonably priced and breakfast is included in the tariff. Why don't you see if they have a room available?"

She found the phone number on something in her bag and I tried my luck. They had one room available. Did I mind it being on the 11th floor? Hell, I didn't mind what floor – so long as I didn't have to climb the stairs to get there! We drove back to Tirandi Street where I retrieved my car and followed Emily to the Regency.

One of those early brick hotels, the Regency managed to survive a complete makeover without losing its external charm. It survived total gutting and refurbishing internally. As part of the refurbishment, a 13-storey tower addition to the back of the hotel now occupied the area that once housed the stables and more recently the guests' carpark. Purchase and demolition of the neighbouring building created a new parking lot, and somehow they managed to create a basement carpark as well.

In the elevator on the way to our respective floors, we arranged to meet in the hotel's restaurant for dinner around seven o'clock. It was now almost five o'clock, and I desperately wanted a shower and some time to make sense of all the notes I made during the day. Surprise! My 'room' turned out to be a suite with a shoe box sized area containing a kitchenette, dining setting, and with a small lounge area at the far end. It had an adjoining large bedroom with ensuite facilities. The whole décor was red, black and white, and *very* nice.

# Chapter Two

A shower was tempting, but there were important things to do before I could freshen up. All my mental notes and observations needed recording properly before I lost or overlooked anything. A small bench attached to a wall in the lounge area served as a desk, so I set up my laptop and started work. With all my notes transcribed, I turned my attention to the photos I took in the flat. A quick look at them and I decided I needed a printed copy.

At the last minute before leaving home, I packed a small printer, although I didn't think I would need it for this job. Another quick trip to my car to get the printer, and then I set it up to print my photos while I showered. As I stood under the stinging blast of warm water, I let my mind wander back to my days as a public servant and my association with Therese. It all seemed so long ago now. Although I knew there were good times and good friendships along the way, I didn't think on that time in my life as a happy one.

After graduating from university, I went straight into a job with the State-owned museum – and straight into becoming a Public Servant. While I enjoyed my time there, I outgrew the job and looked for something offering a bit more challenge. That precipitated my move to the Department of Vocational Education Training and it Central Queensland Institute of Technical and Further Education (TAFE), and my new job as a trainer. I enjoyed teaching but the sameness of the job, year after year, became monotonous and I moved into a management position at the same institute. A couple of years before I quit, the institute appointed a new director: Geoff Inneston.

Geoff transferred on promotion from a small western institute and located his office on the Millhaven campus. About six months after his appointment, he needed a new head of campus for the institute's Ralston operations. His ever-obliging colleague and second in command at the western institute, Therese Melrose, got the Ralston job. Although based in Ralston and head of that campus, she also was the senior manager of the institute's School of Humanities. It was in that latter capacity, that Therese became my boss.

Time seemed to evaporate as I stood under the shower. I suddenly remembered a phone call I toyed with the idea of making before dinner. Out of the shower, dressed and feeling a bit human again, I checked my photos printed okay, before checking the clock: ... just enough time for a quick phone call before heading down to the restaurant.

"Hi Liz. This is a voice from the past. It's ...."

"Sonny! You're right. It is a blast from the past. How are you? Where are you?"

"I'm in Ralston at the moment. I heard you are still Therese's assistant. How many times is it now that you have threatened to resign?" Her familiar deep-throated chuckle rumbled through the phone. She had been Therese's assistant for many years. Although something of a love/hate relationship, together they made a formidable team. Liz and I were mates and it was a standing joke between us that, at least once every few months, Liz would resign because she 'couldn't stand Therese'. Therese would laugh it off and refuse to accept the resignation.

"Liz, I really need to talk to you but I don't want to do it over the phone. Is there any chance we could meet before you go in to work tomorrow, or maybe you could slip away soon after everyone settles in for the day? I'm staying at the Regency, or we could meet at that little coffee shop where we used console each other after a lousy day."

"Come in to the office. I'll shout you a coffee."

"No, Liz. I don't want people to know I'm around and, more importantly, I don't want anyone to know I've contacted you. I know it all sounds a bit dramatic. To some extent, I suppose it is, so please don't mention anything to anyone."

We agreed she would slip away from the office around nine o'clock the next morning and meet me in my room at the Regency. With that task taken care of, I headed for the restaurant. It was a few minutes before 7.00 o'clock. I planned to have a drink while I waited for Emily. However, as I entered the restaurant, Emily walked away from the bar, drink in hand. At a table beside a high-vaulted mullioned window set in the hotel's front wall, we watched the boats on the river as we sipped our drinks. The restaurant soon filled, preventing any opportunity to talk 'shop' safely. We confined ourselves to inconsequential chatter, but arranged to meet in my room after dinner to go over the day's events.

On leaving the restaurant, I went to my room while Emily went to collect her notebook from her room on the fifth floor. A knock at my door changed my plans for the night. I expected to let in Emily. My visitor came as a shock.

"Liz..." Liz Cranston, in the jeans and tee shirt she had worn all day and looking a little embarrassed, stood outside my door.

"I hope you don't mind. I couldn't wait until.... Well, the truth is, something about your call made me feel uneasy. I knew I wouldn't be able to sleep. Better I know what's going on tonight rather than spend all night wondering about it. Can I come in so we can talk about it now?"

We sat in the lounge chairs. I started hesitantly, looking for the right words, but then decided simply to launch into it. "Look, Liz, there is no easy way to do this so I'm just going to say it. Liz, Therese is dead."

"Dead? What happened? When ... was it while she was away last week?"

"No; Friday night sometime. Kate and Ken weren't home at the time. They asked me to take a look."

"What about the Police? Surely, they looked into it. What did they say?"

"They labelled it a domestic accident."

"I fail to see why they – Kate and Ken – would see any need for you to look into Therese's death, if the Police already have determined there's nothing to investigate." She tossed her hair and shot me a challenging look to match her tone.

"I'm sorry, Liz. It seems I got it wrong in contacting you. There's no point in our continuing this conversation but, just so you know, Kate and Ken don't believe it was an accident. Of course, that might be just a reaction to the whole thing but, until they have a second opinion – mine apparently – they can't move on."

"No, no. I'm sorry, Sonny. That didn't come out right. I was shocked, that's all. If I can help..."

That's more like the Liz I knew. I gave her the bare bones of what the Police said, and stressed the importance of not discussing the matter with anyone – even if Therese's death was made public in the immediate future. There were things only she could help with, so I asked her to check on Therese's recent phone calls, particularly if there were any over the weekend on her office phone. The installation of a VOIP phone system began around the time I left the department. I installed the same system in my own office. The system kept a record of outgoing, incoming and missed calls as well as voicemail messages. Liz would be able to access these on Therese's phone.

After fetching my notebook, I spent a few moments thinking through what questions she might be able to answer tonight. The investigation Therese was working on and the report she supposedly was presenting tomorrow seemed a good place to start. Some information on how security now operated at their building would be useful too. She contemplated some spot on the floor in front of her for a whole minute or more before speaking, and then didn't answer my questions.

"Sonny, the Police's version can't be right. It was only a couple of months ago she said she hadn't felt this well in years. She changed her doctor. The new bloke did a whole lot of tests; she had two or three days in hospital at the time. He took her off all the medication, and started her on a completely new regime. She hasn't had a dizzy turn or been light headed in months."

Okay, that was interesting, but even more interesting was her avoidance of the question about the investigation and the report. Might be wise to leave that for the moment, I think. Good decision. When she continued, she went straight to the question of security operations.

"Now, about security; over the weekend, the place is completely locked down and security guards are rostered for two shifts per day. Coverage is from 7.30am to 10.00p.m. If anyone came looking for Therese over the weekend, it would be logged. Jim – you remember Jim, the security guard?" I nodded. "Jim was supposed to work day shift yesterday and today, but the bloke who was rostered for afternoon shift today called in sick. Jim is covering his shift until 10.00 tonight. After tonight, Jim probably won't come back in again until mid-morning tomorrow. I'll try to catch up with him when he comes in."

"You'll need to think about how you are going to ask questions about any visitors looking for Therese without arousing Jim's suspicions." An almost imperceptible nod accompanied by almost a smile in reply.

"You might remember, back in your time with us, I was friends with Jim and his wife. His wife died, not long after you left, I think. I tried to support him a bit through that time and then, 12 months later, my mother died and he was there for me. We've grown quite close since then, although we keep the relationship quiet at work."

Our relationship looked as though it was back to normal, so I took a punt and revisited the issue of the investigation and the report.

"I'm not playing silly buggers, Sonny, but I don't know anything about any investigation. She wasn't working on anything that I was aware of."

"Could Therese have worked on something – something big, perhaps – without you knowing about it?"

"Not likely; she would need my help. She isn't any more computer literate now than she was when you knew her. There certainly wasn't any mention of presentation of a report or someone coming to see her about it. Of course, it might not be a presentation. It could be that she was supposed to *submit* a report… but on what and to whom, I don't know."

In my experience, a number of investigations – witch-hunts more like – occur with monotonous regularity in the department. Misappropriation of property, travel rorts, and staffing numbers frequently come under scrutiny. I reminded Liz of these and added my thoughts about them. "I doubt it had anything to do with staff numbers and workloads. In recent times, the media has had a field day with the department's latest round of slash and burn redundancy initiatives. Did this institute have many redundancies? There was plenty of dead wood who should have been considered."

"There were about 15 or 20 across the institute. The majority were from the Ralston campus."

"Any bad reactions? Anyone particular bitter enough to want to take it further?"

"No. It was a good package. Most of them couldn't wait to grab it and go. There was a handful of reluctant starters who needed a little extra persuasion. It was a case of, take the good package now, or face redundancy in the near future with no package on offer and only normal entitlements available. There was anger and bitterness in some cases, but not to that extent."

"Uhmm, what about missing equipment? No abnormally high number of entries in the 'Damaged, Lost or Stolen Register' lately? No major items appear to have walked out the door in recent times?"

"No, I don't think so. Pretty much the usual rate of stuff lost, stolen or strayed. None of those usual investigations are happening at the moment and, if they were, I would be involved in pulling together the information."

After a couple of moments silence between us, another thought flashed through my mind. "What about compliance audits? There has been a lot of stuff in the media lately about the government clamping down on training providers – mainly private providers I think – about not meeting compliance requirements. It seems the government finally woke up to something we griped about for years: training providers who take the money and award the qualifications with not much training happening in between."

"Nothing unusual in that area either. If there were, our internal auditors, Jan and Chris, would be involved. They haven't been. I'm fairly close to Jan. Even if I weren't involved in that sort of investigation, she would tell me about it, but I would probably know it was happening anyway."

Both of us were approaching mental exhaustion status. There was not much else I could achieve tonight. I walked Liz to the door to see her out, and opened the door to something I had forgotten about. Emily was standing there, her notebook in one hand, and the other hand poised to knock on the door. "Sorry it took me so long. Mum rang. Dad's out at some work type dinner so she decided she wanted to chat," she explained.

So involved was I with Liz, I had forgotten Emily was coming. As they passed one another in the hallway, I introduced Emily as my 'associate' to Liz Cranston – and we all tried not to look too wrong-footed by the incident. With Liz gone, Emily and I set to work listing what we knew and what we didn't know. The latter list turned into a long list of questions to which answers would be useful.

At the top of the list was the question of the whereabouts of Therese's laptop, work mobile phone and iPad. We studied Ken's photos and mine for a while, but it was getting late and we were both fading fast. After arranging to meet for breakfast at 7.30 next morning, we abandoned work for the night.

Breakfast was a leisurely affair, not having to return to Tirandi Street until after the children had gone to school. Afterwards, we scanned the local papers available in the dining room for any mention of Therese's demise. To my relief, it hadn't warranted a mention. Then we lingered in the dining room, planning our day until it was a safe time to go back to the flat. Ken met us when we arrived and unlocked the flat but, before going in, I wanted to check Therese's car. With gloved hand, I tested the car's passenger side door: unlocked.

Ken looked stunned. "She always locks it!" Mental note to self: look at the car again later.

Emily led the way into the flat. We dumped our bags near the door and headed straight for the dining table with its conglomeration of files. None of the contents appeared clipped into the folders. Loose pages spilled out of folders everywhere. They looked rifled through.

We agreed the clear space in the midst of it all was about the right size for a laptop. If Therese worked on the laptop at the table, she would probably plug it into the power outlet on the wall behind her. A check of the outlet found it turned on but nothing plugged in.

Emily started searching cupboards and drawers in the living area for the laptop or phone, while I made for the bedroom end of the flat. At the door leading to that end of the flat, I paused to study the key rack screwed to the wall, before returning to my bag for my camera. While over at my bag, I checked the lock on the main door. Now that is interesting.

Key rack photographed, I searched the bedroom. It didn't take long. Not much to search here: a built in wardrobe along one wall and a couple of bedside tables. No hidden laptops or anything else of interest found. In fact, not very much found at all. Therese must have been feeling the financial pinch. There wasn't even much in the way of clothes in the bedroom. I wandered back to the kitchen and found Emily on her hands and knees, wriggling her way backwards out of a corner cupboard. Nothing here either apparently, so I continued wandering back towards the dining table.

Once upright again, Emily stretched her back and, a few moments later, called me back to the kitchen. "Have a look at this." She pointed to an area at the end of the bench near the fridge occupied by a small capsule-type coffee machine and a milk frother. "These looked a bit incongruous with the sterility of the rest of the place so I pulled them forward to look behind them. There is only one power outlet at this end of the bench. Use of this coffee making gear requires two."

I peered behind the coffee machine and saw the power board hidden there. The board had three leads plugged into it, not the expected two. I raised my eyebrows at Emily and reached for the third power lead. "That looks like a mobile phone charger." Only the plug end was visible, as the lead itself had fallen down the gap between the bench and the fridge. More photos, and then I jotted down details of the charger from the maker's label.

"How about a coffee?" Emily chirped.

My reply was a bit short as I thought she was being smart-arsed. "As if; but I have to admit I could do with one about now."

"Well, let's go sit outside and have a coffee." I looked reproachfully at her over the top of my glasses. She continued smugly, "I have coffee in the car and a couple of mugs."

She and her mother packed a thermos of coffee and a couple of travel mugs before leaving Moxton for the trip to Millhaven. Emily washed it all and, before we set out this morning, refilled the thermos using the free coffee making supplies in her hotel room. We sat on the bottom step and savoured the coffee – and the break from ferreting through Therese's belongings.

"I want to look through Therese's car, Emily, but you might check out the laundry and the bathroom. I doubt you'll find a laptop, but see if there's anything that strikes you as unusual."

The glove compartment of the car hadn't closed properly. Its contents looked as though they were pulled out before being pushed roughly back into the compartment. Whoever rifled through the contents used enough force to engage the catch. A corner of the owner's logbook protruded a little and caused the door to gape slightly at one end when it closed. More photos. There was nothing else of interest in the car, so I abandoned my search.

On my way into the flat, a thought struck me. I doubled back to the car. After opening the boot, I folded back the carpet and lifted the cover off the spare wheel well. Emily came up behind me, startling me as I stood staring into the well. She peered over my shoulder and exclaimed, "What a mess!"

Ken, on his way to the rubbish bin with a bag of trash, stopped to peer into the spare wheel well with us. He let out a low whistle. "She would not be happy to see that. Therese was a wee bit particular about this car."

"She wouldn't have been able to drive it around like this," Emily commented. "All that stuff would roll around in there and rattle something terrible."

I turned to look at them both. "I think it only got like this after Therese was no longer likely to drive it anywhere." It was time to ask questions and share suspicions. "Ken, I think we need to talk to you and Kate. Is now a good time?"

We sat around at a small outdoor setting just outside Therese's laundry. Emily and I with our packets of sandwiches and bottled water, and all of us perched on the most uncomfortable wrought iron chairs I have ever encountered. "Did the Police remove anything from the flat on Saturday?"

Kate considered for a moment and shook her head. "Don't think so."

"Okay. Ken, as you work for the department, could you ring the police officer in charge and ask if they removed Therese's laptop, mobile phone and iPad? Explain they belong to the department. You need to hand them back but can't find them anywhere at the flat. I expect he'll tell you they didn't take them. Why would they when it wasn't a crime scene? Sound a bit concerned if you can, and just mention that her work keys also need to be returned and you can't find them either. Throw in that they are usually in her handbag but her handbag seems to be missing as well. None of this is likely to get you any useful response but it might start them thinking, and will open the door for me if I need to go talk to them about my findings."

"What are your findings?" Kate demanded, now sitting bolt upright.

"Relax, Kate. We are still investigating, but there are a few answers I need."

I asked about what keys normally hung on the key rack. Neither one was sure but, with some pointed questioning, information was forthcoming. Yes, the car key and her flat key normally hung on the rack along with the key to the upstairs section of the house and a number of other small keys.

Did Therese go out on Friday? They didn't think so. Both Kate and Ken took a flex day off on Friday and stayed home all day except for about an hour or so in the morning when they went to the supermarket. After some thought Ken said, "No, she didn't. She didn't go out while we were home and she hadn't gone out while we were away. Remember, Kate? My mate rang back with that phone number I wanted just after we got home. I put my notebook on the bonnet of Therese's car while I wrote it down. The bonnet wasn't warm, so her car hadn't been driven."

I queried what usually was on the coffee table, the one now a mess of broken glass and bits of wood. They weren't sure but thought she didn't keep anything there, but might leave a report or something she was reading there if it was an ongoing thing.

"Do you have any photos showing what that corner of the room looked like before this happened? Given its present state, it's a bit hard to picture what it looked like previously." They couldn't think of any but Kate offered to look through their collection. Emily puckered her brows and looked at me enquiringly but, to my relief, said nothing until we were alone later.

"What's with all the strange questions, Miss Marple?" she asked when we returned to the flat. "What's so intriguing about the keys, the car and the coffee table?" She giggled. "That sounds a bit like an adult version of one of the Tales of Narnia. You know, the one about the lion, the witch and the ... uhmm ...wardrobe wasn't it?"

"Uh huh. Someone once said – or wrote – or something: *the hardest part of an investigation is identifying what's not there.* We have a l-o-n-g list of what's not here. The car key and flat key are not on the rack, but the key for upstairs is there, along with what looks like luggage keys. The report she was supposed to be finishing off – perhaps that's the big bundle of paper with the clip on it that Ken saw – is nowhere around. She didn't go out on Friday. Well, not during the day anyway, so she didn't take it anywhere, unless she slipped out with it after Ken and Kate went out for the evening. These missing items need adding to the list of those already identified as unaccounted for: laptop, phone, iPad and handbag.

"R-i-i-ght. So, what's the fascination with the coffee table?"

"Look at the couch. Would you watch TV from there?"

"No. I mean, you could see it from there but, if you were going to watch TV, you would sit in one of those lounge chairs positioned in front of it."

"Agreed. To me, that corner looks like a place to sit and read – newspaper, magazines, work stuff – except, the lighting is terrible over there. There's a light in the kitchen and one in the dining area, but neither lights up that corner very well. It would be a terrible place to read, particularly at night."

"Maybe she just needed somewhere to park the couch and that's where it fitted."

"Maybe; come and give me a hand to have a look over there."

Roughly stacked up against the wall, the bigger pieces of broken glass and wood were where the Police put them to get out of the way while they carried out their investigation. Without scattering it about too much, we carefully lifted the debris away from the wall.

"Bingo! See there's a power outlet down there on the skirting board, and it looks like it is turned on."

"So-o-o…." Emily started, but a knock on the door interrupted her before she could say any more.

Kate waited outside with a photo in her hand. "This is about the best I could find. Mum took it of Poppy when she came down to show off her costume for the school's fancy dress ball. The couch and stuff is in the background. I don't know if it's any use to you."

"Oh, yes. Thank you. It's great. May I keep it for a day or two?" She hesitantly agreed, but stressed she wanted it back. "Definitely," I promised. "What time do the kids come home from school?"

"Ken is going to pick them up shortly, but they won't be home for another hour and a half or so. The boys have soccer practice and Poppy has a ballet class."

"That's okay. We're done here for the day, so we might head off. Is it okay if we keep the flat key overnight, rather than having to keep bothering you to let us in?" Kate simply nodded.

My phone rang and I walked away to answer the call. It was Liz. We arranged she would come to eat with us tonight. I told Emily about Liz coming for dinner and asked if she wanted to join us.

As I was locking the flat, Ken came down the stairs on his way to pick up the kids. He came over and spoke quietly. "They rang earlier to say the autopsy is scheduled for this afternoon and the report should be available sometime early tomorrow. They'll let us know when it's available."

"Ken," I started slowly, trying to choose my words carefully. "You know you can always ask for a second – independent – autopsy to be done?"

"Thanks, but why would we want to go down that track? Once it's done, it's done. Why would anyone want to get it done again? Leave her in peace. Besides, I wouldn't know how to go about it, or who to get to do it."

"That's okay, and this one might say exactly what's needed to eliminate any doubts. I was only thinking of Kate's peace of mind. If she is still concerned after seeing the report, it is an option that's available."

"That won't be necessary. I've got to go." He marched off to his car leaving me pondering his abruptness.

Emily, having loaded her stuff into her car, wandered back to see what was going on and was within earshot just in time to hear Ken's final retort before he strode off. She cocked an eyebrow at me. "What's his problem?" I could only think of some inane comment about the stress of the situation probably leaving him a bit frayed around the edges.

On my insistence, we took both cars when we left the hotel this morning as I thought it would free up Emily to go off and do those things she planned to do while in Ralston. As we climbed into our respective cars to leave Tirandi Street, it occurred to me that I should talk to her about her plans. We met again at the coffee shop we ate at yesterday. There wasn't a lot of conversation initially. I guess we both pondered the day's outcomes in silence. Our coffees arrived, and I took advantage of the interruption to ask Emily about what she planned to do while in Ralston.

"Nothing; I really didn't want to go home for the week. I already knew one of my old friends was overseas and the other one let me know she wouldn't be in Millhaven for a couple of months. There is a symposium on at the university here in Ralston, so I used that as an excuse to stay on to attend. I didn't have any intention of attending. It has second-rate speakers peddling old information. This is much more interesting than either the symposium or going home to Millhaven."

"Devious and creative: good qualities in an investigator. How creative can you be about what to have for dinner tonight? Liz is coming, remember, and I thought we might eat in my rooms. So, do we want room service or take-away?" We agreed on take-away, which Emily would organise and deliver to my table around seven o'clock.

There was nothing more to say or do, and I was keen to get back to the hotel. My immediate concern was my laundry situation. I only packed enough clothes for a couple of days and, while I could get through tomorrow, I would have nothing clean for the next day. My instinct was telling me I would be here for another day or two yet.

It was still early when I arrived back in my rooms. I rinsed out some underwear and hung it to dry in the bathroom on one of those travelling clothesline things that seems to reside permanently at the bottom of my suitcase. After that, it was time to add today's bits and pieces to my case notes. I had barely enough time for a short jog along the Esplanade and a shower before answering a knock at the door.

Liz stood there. Her hair still damp from her post-yoga shower, a rather large tote bag over her shoulder and bottle of wine in hand. I picked up a couple of bottles of wine from a bottle shop on my way back to the hotel. We probably could manufacture significant headaches from the alcohol supply now on hand. Emily, laden with food, arrived a few minutes after Liz and we got down to the serious business of eating. No one mentioned Therese throughout dinner, and Liz and I kept Emily and ourselves entertained by recounting stories from our earlier days together in the Department.

While Emily and I cleared away the wreckage that had been dinner, Liz rummaged in her tote bag and produced a sheaf of paper. As we managed to demolish only one bottle of wine with dinner, we were upright and reasonably coherent. The table cleared and Liz's papers at the ready, the late night session of the investigation into Therese's death began.

# Chapter Three

Liz neatly arranged her stack of papers as Emily and I again settled ourselves at the table and then looked expectantly at her. Instead of launching into a report of what she found out as expected, Liz resolutely clasped her hands on top of her papers and looked hard, firstly at Emily and then me.

"Right! Exactly what is going on? You tell me Therese is dead but, so far, there hasn't been as much as a murmur about it from the Department or the Director. You assured me he did know... and yes, Emily, I know he is your father."

Emily dismissed the comment with a wave of her hand. I took a deep and audible breath as I tried to compose a response. Liz's tone left me in no doubt she was angry. The defiant Liz I encountered yesterday had reappeared. Before I could deliver any kind of response, she continued.

"You say the Police determined it was an accident, yet you seem determined to make it something else. You seem determined to suggest Therese's death – if she is dead – is associated with something shady. Sonny, I know there was no love lost between you and Therese, but why are you trying to sully her name like this? Therese was – is – a friend as well as a colleague, and I am not going to help you develop some fanciful notion that she was involved in something so bad it got her killed."

"The reason I came to you, Liz, is because of your relationship with Therese. There is no question about her being dead. Emily and her mother, Sandra, will attest to that. I'm not surprised there has been nothing in the media. The Police think it was a domestic accident; no news there. I don't know why the director hasn't released some statement to staff but I can think of a couple of possibilities. One of those is that he is aware I've been brought in to look into her death, and he might be waiting for the outcome of my investigation before saying anything."

"Oh, come on, Sonny. Don't you think you might be inflating your own importance just a bit?"

"No, I don't, Liz. I believe that is a possibility, although it might not be the correct reason he hasn't said anything. The other possibility is that he is concerned about the image of the institute. TAFE institutes have attracted a lot of mud in recent times, from the government, in the media, and from the public. Mud sticks, even though it might have been generated because of only a couple of rogue operators."

"He is still going to have to tell staff at some time. How does waiting make it any different – any better?"

"I can't answer that. I don't know what his thinking is. However, if you don't want to help with this investigation, I accept that. After all, I am concerned about involving you in something that could turn out to be dangerous for you. However, it's your choice. You apparently brought with you material you consider might be relevant. It's decision time. What are you going to do with it? You are free to leave – and take your paper with you – if you choose to."

Liz bit her lip and deep furrows formed between her eyebrows. The only sound I heard for the next few moments was my own heartbeat. Her deliberations complete, Liz finally withdrew her hands from on top of the pile of paper and slowly pushed it across the table to me. Without meeting my eyes, she posed her original question again, "What is going on?" I tried to exhale slowly and not too obviously. I hadn't noticed but I seemed not to have breathed much during her tirade.

"We don't really know, Liz. I can tell you that, for me, the whole situation has developed a distinctly bad smell. My instinct is telling me there is something very rotten under all of this. I am even more adamant there should be no way you can be connected to me or my investigation... and Emily, I am more than a little concerned at your involvement as well – that is, apart from what your father's reaction might be if he finds out."

I saw Emily's expression set hard and fully expected an argument, but I also saw a fresh flash of doubt in Liz's eyes, so I pressed on before either could cut in. "I'm not trying to be melodramatic. I don't believe Therese's death was an accident. Before I start espousing hypotheses, I need to dig a lot deeper; gather definite information. Maybe whatever you've managed to find out will help."

She relented. Her ruffled feathers somewhat smoothed once more, she pulled the bundle of papers back to her and, as she handed us each document form the stack, recited details of what it contained. They covered all the information she had managed to gather for us during the day.

She obviously spent a long coffee break with her mate Jim, the security guard. There was quite a lot to report from their discussions. As Liz mentioned previously, Jim worked multiple shifts on Friday and over the weekend to fill in for others who did not report for work for whatever reasons. He confirmed Therese did not come in at any time after Friday morning, and there was no record in the log of her coming in after hours on Thursday evening either. She had not advised security she would be coming in, or that anyone else would be likely to come looking for her over the weekend. No one rang in on the general number enquiring after her during that time.

"There's more from Jim, but I'll come back to that later," Liz said as she selected another sheet from the stack. "I went through her office with a fine tooth comb. I didn't find anything. Well, it was more a case my not finding things that I should have found there."

"There's already a long list of missing things," Emily interjected. "We'll just add yours to the bottom of it."

"Hmmm," I murmured in agreement. "Go on please, Liz, and we'll try not to interrupt unless we absolutely can't contain ourselves." I gave Emily a warning look. "What sorts of things were missing?"

Liz read from her list: laptop, phone, iPad, files, a notebook that doubled as a diary, and a box containing a pocket recorder and a few tapes. Most of these we knew about, but the notebook and pocket recorder were interesting. Why would she keep a physical diary when all staff used electronic diaries? And a *pocket recorder?* I hadn't seen anyone in the department use one of those in years before I left. Liz couldn't shed any light on their significance, other than, they had always been in Therese's drawer and now they weren't ... and we knew they weren't at the flat.

Next were the lists of phone numbers. Liz listed from the VOIP directories on Therese's phone all the incoming and outgoing calls made over a period of slightly more than two weeks. She also correlated the missed calls directory with the incoming calls. Once these directories reach capacity, they simply drop off the oldest records and add the new ones. This meant the period covered by the directories at any one time depended on the amount of traffic on a particular phone. As Therese was away for most of the week prior to her death, the directories held information mostly from the two weeks prior to her absence. During her absence, Liz diverted all Therese's incoming calls to her own phone.

Bless her. Where she could identify it, Liz added the caller's name next to each number. As expected, many of the numbers belonged to members of Therese's staff or other people within the department. A few were from her daughter and grandchildren, but that still left quite a few unknown numbers. To allow interrogation of the lists, I asked Liz for an electronic copy. She delved into the cavernous tote bag and, after a bit of scratching around, triumphantly held up a USB stick before pushing it across the table to me.

Liz's brow furrowed as she picked up the next pages from the pile. "Therese emailed me not long after she disappeared. I'm sorry, I think of it as 'disappeared' because, from my point of view, that's what she did. Anyway, she emailed me a list of information she wanted me to gather from various sources. I was to list it only as a series of facts. She wanted it emailed to her no later than lunchtime on Thursday, and I had to do it *quietly*.

Some of the stuff she wanted took a bit of finding. I don't have access to some of the sites I needed and had to use her login on occasions to find the information she wanted. A lot of it was just figures about all sorts of things, and some of it was dates and places. Here's the stuff I put together and emailed off to her about mid-morning on Thursday."

She handed me the three pages she was holding. I gave them a cursory look before turning them face down on the table. "I'll come back to these later, if that's okay, but you carry on with the rest of your stuff for now," I said. Although I only glanced at the pages, something caught my eye. I didn't want to interrupt Liz's flow of information and, maybe, something else she had to share might eliminate the questions now occupying the forefront of my mind.

Liz produced a small notebook from her bag. She flipped through pages until she found what she was looking for. "While I was quizzing Jim about Therese coming in on the weekend or anyone looking for her during that time, he got a bit curious about what was going on. Told him I was concerned Therese still wasn't at work and I was trying – quietly – to find out what might be going on. He hesitated for a bit but eventually told me him and Keith – you remember Keith, the other old security guard? – observed something strange involving Therese a couple of weeks ago."

Liz checked the details of Jim's story in her notebook for a moment or two while I sat mentally encouraging her to get on with it. She piqued my interest and I wanted details. Both Jim and Keith were ex-Police and went into security almost as a second career in later life. Old habits never died. They still carried a notebook in their top pocket and religiously noted anything they considered 'unusual'. Such notations never appeared in the security logs, as the incidents were not security issues as such, just 'unusual' incidents. After what seemed like far too long, Liz began to recite Jim's story.

"On Wednesday a couple of weeks ago, at about mid-morning, Jim was checking one of the pumps in the little pump shed at the rear of the gardener's greenhouse. If you remember, a tall hedge screens that ugly pump shed from general view. Out the corner of his eye, he caught sight through the hedge foliage of someone rushing out into the carpark. It was Therese. She stopped as she entered the parking area and looked about as if trying to find something or someone. A car parked in the far corner flashed its lights once and Therese rushed over to it."

I made a note, 'car details' but, not wanting to distract Liz from her story, said nothing. She glanced over to see what I was doing but continued unfazed by it.

"As she got to the car, a bloke got out and stood beside it. Their conversation seemed heated. They both appeared agitated. After only a brief period, the man got back into the car and slammed the door. He started the car, gunned it sending gravel everywhere, and took off through the back entrance. Jim says Therese had to jump away as the car took off. Afterwards, she stood there briefly – sort of looking a bit stunned – before heading back into the building. As she passed the greenhouse, Jim said Therese looked upset. He is sure she didn't see him, as he was hidden by the hedge."

I took a break from frantically scribbling notes when she finished, and studied the tabletop for a moment or two while I considered the merits of the information. The story didn't end there. There was more to tell, and Jim and Keith believed it was all part of the same saga. It seems Keith also noted what he considered to be 'strange goings on'. During the ensuing week or so after the carpark incident, on four separate occasions, Keith observed Therese drive off in her car during the day. She didn't have a bag or anything else with her as far as he could see, and she wasn't gone for long. On three occasions, she was gone only 10 or 15 minutes but, on the last occasion, she was gone for more than half an hour.

"I wouldn't call ducking out of work for a few minutes occasionally strange," I ventured carefully. "We all worked long hours and often through lunch, as you well know, Liz. If you needed something from the shops, you ducked out whenever you could find a few spare minutes. Therese might simply have gone to the pharmacy to collect her medications or something."

"Without her bag … and coming back empty handed as well?" Liz queried. "The last time she went out was on the Friday before she disappeared."

We discussed Jim and Keith's observations, positing all sorts of scenarios as possible explanations for Therese's actions but without coming up with any plausible answers. I asked if Jim noted any details of the car Therese went to meet in the carpark. Liz stared off into the distance as she recalled her conversation with Jim. "What did he say about the car…?" she mused. "Oh, yes, I remember. It was a dark blue sedan – European possibly – and he couldn't see clearly enough to read the plates."

The question was a long shot that hadn't paid off. I drew a line through 'car details' in my notes. After flicking back through the pages to find the document I wanted, I took Liz back to something she mentioned earlier. "In this information you pulled together and emailed to Therese, there's a page I don't understand." I spun the page around so she could see what I was querying. Emily stood up and leant over so she could read as well.

"To me, it looks like a list of names, dates and places. Is this something to do with travel?"

"Y-e-s, but it was a bit different this time. The details she wanted are not what she normally would require if she were investigating staff travel."

"Hmm, I don't know some of these names, but I suppose that's not surprising. I've been gone a while, so I'm sure there's been plenty of new people since I left."

"No, that's not the case. Our institute's people who are on the list are names you would know. The other names – the ones you probably don't recognise – don't belong to this institute. This was one of those situations when I had to use Therese's login. My access to that sort of information doesn't extend beyond this institute's data. Therese's login allows her access to all of the department's travel information. That's where I had to go for some of that stuff."

"There hasn't been any travel rort investigation going on that you're aware of?"

"No. In the department's current financial situation – not to mention our institute's budget restrictions – it's almost impossible to get approval to travel at all. There's a blanket clamp down on all travel."

Now that is interesting. Of course, it is possible that some people have travelled in spite of the travel ban and this has triggered an investigation. Still, it would be only a minor investigation as opposed to a major undertaking. Here I go again; my investigation is producing more questions than answers.

Emily tried unsuccessfully to stifle a yawn. It was getting late and Liz, having delivered her information, was keen to leave. I promised to keep her informed and stressed how any contact with me must remain deniable. I was starting to get an uneasy feeling about how bad this might become and didn't want Liz sucked into the mire.

We said goodnight to Liz at the door, but Emily hung back and waited until after I closed the door. It was obvious she was keen for a post mortem of the day's events. I was keen for bed and hoped she didn't want to stay too long. We briefly discussed Liz's information before Emily asked what we were doing tomorrow.

"Tomorrow you are going to your symposium or whatever else you planned for your time in Ralston. It is important your mother, not to mention your father, knows you are doing exactly what you said you were going to do. No doubt, your mother already knows you were with me at Kate's place today. That's easy to explain without raising too much interest at home. It would not be good if they became aware you continue to be involved. Anyway, tomorrow I have an appointment with Langborne."

"Langborne? Who is that?" she queried.

"Detective Langborne; he led the police investigation at the flat. If the autopsy report is available tomorrow, I might be able to trade information with the detective and, dare I say, maybe get the chance to politely suggest his findings could be wrong."

Emily began to protest, but I held up my hand to stop her and said quite firmly, "Tomorrow I have my work to do and you have to do what appears normal from your parents' point of view. Now, I need some time to myself to sort through what's been gathered so far."

She left, but not quite happily. This gave me time before I turned in for the night to go through the material Liz gave me on the memory stick. I need to be on top of my game when I meet Langborne in the morning. I rang earlier in the afternoon to make an appointment with him but, when I finally reached his extension, he made it clear he was too busy and not interested in talking to me. I stewed over his attitude for half an hour or so before deciding to try a different tack. This time, instead of asking to be put through to him, I rang the precinct and asked the lass who answered whether she might be able to give me an appointment with Detective Langborne.

When I rang earlier, Tracey answered the call. This time it was Susan. Good, there would be no recollection of my previous call. I was terribly smarmy: knew how busy he must be, just wanted a few minutes, wouldn't take too long and would be ever so grateful if he could spare the time. I wondered how obsequious the ditzy female I was portraying should appear to be. I didn't want to lay it on too thickly. It worked. She was most obliging and gave me a half hour appointment for 10.30 the next morning. She didn't check with him before doing so and I detected almost a note of malicious glee as she confirmed the time.

Tuesday morning was grey and wet. The heavens opened during breakfast. I was pleased to retreat to my room to finish the report I was putting together to give Langborne, rather than having to go out and brave the weather. When the rain eased to a light drizzle, I elected to walk the few blocks to the Police Station. It was easier to walk and risk getting a bit damp than endure the frustration of trying to find a parking space in the city heart area at that time of day.

A young constable showed me through to Langborne's area. He simply announced me as 'your 10.30 appointment, Detective Langborne,' before disappearing rapidly back to the front desk area. Langborne looked somewhat startled, and blinked at me a few times as if trying to work out how I had managed to arrive at his desk. Why is it that a first impression is hard to shake? Long ago, I discovered most of my first impressions were accurate. I have no doubt my first impression of Langborne will not change.

The old adage about 'not judging a book by its cover' didn't apply in his case. In the space of a couple of heartbeats, he created a clear impression: insipid. While waiting for him to respond to my arrival in some way other than surprised, I stood looking down on a colourless young man. It was hard to judge his height but, from what I could see of Langborne from behind his desk, he was short and of slight build.

Not his height nor his clothes, but his face was responsible for that first impression. His pale grey eyes blended into pale skin displaying only a hint of a tan. His face was 'soft' and topped by white-blonde hair in a latest style that owed more to a hairdresser's deft touch and a bucket of product than a barber's skill. Against the softly tanned complexion, his pale eyebrows, lashes and pencil line moustache appeared stark white. While his countenance lacked colour, the man's character proved devoid of charm as well.

Langborne gruffly indicated a chair across from him and demanded, "What did you want to see me about?"

I tried my sweetest smile but felt it bounce back at me. "Therese Melrose," I said quietly. "Her family asked me to look into what happened so they can put the whole thing to rest with a clear conscience."

"Nothing to look into; it was an accident," he enunciated clearly and emphatically, with a slight pause between each word as if he was talking to someone a little deaf, or perhaps intellectually disabled.

I tried again – sweetly, "They just want to be sure it couldn't be anything else. You see, there are some unusual – curious, perhaps – issues associated with her death. I was wondering whether the autopsy report showed up anything interesting. Is it available yet?"

"No. What's it got to do with you anyway?"

"Well, the family has asked me to act on their behalf, and I thought we might be able to trade information."

"There is nothing to trade. It was an accident. You know where the door is. Leave now. I'm busy."

Such a courteous dismissal! I opened my mouth to remind him that I wasn't supposed to wander through the station unescorted, but thought better of it. With my tongue clenched firmly between my teeth, I rose gracefully and exited the room. A short way down the corridor, when out of Langborne's view, I stopped and leant against the wall while I attempted to regain control of my temper, my breathing and my blood pressure.

"I hope this doesn't mean you're in Ralston now, does it?" a familiar voice demanded.

"Only briefly," I replied as I turned to look into those well-remembered incredible blue eyes. Ben Richards, tall, trim and as good looking as ever, stood a couple of metres behind me in the corridor. Was that a slight flutter I felt? It shouldn't be surprise me. The sight of him always evoked that response in the past.

"You know you are not supposed to wander through this place on your own."

"You seem to be a bit short on tour guides today."

"Did you come to see me?" he asked with a mock wide-eyed eagerly hopeful look.

"No. Langborne."

"Langborne? What on earth did you want to see him about?" He genuinely looked stunned.

"Therese Melrose."

"Therese Melrose...," he said slowly, with a slight shake of his head.

"It probably doesn't ring any bells for you. Langborne was handling it."

"So, what about her?"

"He determined it was an accident."

" ...And you wanted to acquaint him with the error of his findings?"

"No. I wanted to trade information."

He laughed openly, took my arm and began guiding me to the Station's exit. He maintained a firm grip on my arm as we chatted lightly and shared a bit of a giggle while wending our way slowly through the rabbit warren that served as Ralston's city precinct. We stopped just short of the door and, as we stepped aside to allow another couple to enter, he said quietly, "How about we catch up for a drink this evening, if you're free?" It seemed like a good idea. He suggested 6.30 at a newish place I hadn't heard of, gave me directions on how to find it, and we parted company.

A downpour was happening outside. I made my way back towards the hotel, taking advantage of awnings on the buildings along the street to stay dry. As I approached the end of the block, my spirits sank. The next block consisted of all new buildings. None provided street coverage. Damn. Why does modern have to be impractical? No awnings on the new buildings meant no cover over the footpath – which meant I would get very wet.

It continued raining heavily. I decided to avail myself of a coffee shop I was passing. From my window-side table, I watched the rain and reflected on the previous hour or so. It was amazing how easily Ben and I slipped into the thrust and parry banter that had been a hallmark of our relationship. Relationship? Friendship? Probably more like 'almost a relationship'. So many years ago now, it would be easy to remember it as more than it really was.

With the downpour over and my raisin toast and coffee disposed of, avoiding the puddles was the challenge that lay ahead. Despite my care in weaving my way around the puddles on the footpath, I misjudged one and arrived back at the hotel with one soggy wet shoe. As I hadn't brought much of a wardrobe with me, there was no option but to stick with the wet shoe. I retrieved my car from the basement car park and set out for Tirandi Street.

Kate, looking wrung out, came down the stairs as I opened the door to the granny flat. "How are you holding up?" I asked for want of something more inspired to say.

"Okay I suppose."

"Did Ken go into work today? I see his car is gone."

"Er, no, he had a couple of errands to take care of and then he was going fishing. The tides are good today or something apparently. He won't be back until after he picks the kids up from school."

Uh huh. That was a weak attempt at covering up something. Maybe he needed to escape the stress of the last few days and the effect it's having on the pair of them. "Any further news on the autopsy report?"

"Nobody has contacted us about it yet."

Kate seemed to be hovering and I had the feeling she wanted to talk about something. "Is everything all right, Kate? You seem a bit anxious about something."

She shook her head initially, and then changed her mind. "Can I talk to you for a few minutes? Something has come up and I don't understand it at all."

We sat on the stairs together and I waited patiently while she composed her thoughts.

"You know Mum bought this house, although none of us had much cash at the time. She borrowed most of the money for this place. She expected to sell the house she owns out west, the house she got as part of her divorce settlement. There was a bit of work needed doing here: a new roof and setting up the granny flat. That increased the debt even further. The arrangement was for us to pay her a small rent. We couldn't afford much at the time. After a while, when the house out west hadn't sold, she started renting it out to help meet the loan repayments on this place."

"I do remember her talking about how tight her financial situation was at the time, but you all needed somewhere to live and this seemed like an ideal option."

"That's true, but things have been tight financially for all of us since she bought the house. After my youngest started school this year, I went back to work. That helped ease things a bit for us. Then mum announced that, seeing as how I was working now, she was putting the rent up, and she did."

Kate kept her eyes lowered while she spoke and, the whole time, focused on worrying a fingernail to death. I encouraged her to continue with what was on her mind. "Are you concerned about how things will stand now that she is gone?"

"No, it's not that. It's ... uhmm .... well, I got a bit of a shock today. There was an envelope from the bank addressed to mum in today's post. I thought I should open it and put it with anything else to go to the solicitor in case it's part of the probate stuff. It was bank statements. Sonny, Mum has a lot – a lot – of money in one of her accounts."

At last, she raised her eyes to look at me. It was obvious she was looking for confirmation that I understood what she was saying. Rather ineptly, I simply murmured, "Okay."

She went back to worrying the fingernail and continued. "I rang the bank manager, explained what had happened, and asked for any other statements to be sent for inclusion in the probate process. I specifically asked about the loan account. He told me Mum paid it off ages ago, but never sought to release the mortgage. He is sending over details of her other accounts."

She looked up at me, the fear in her eyes unmistakable. "Sonny, what is going on? Where did all this money come from, and why did she keep telling me how broke she was?"

All very interesting, but I had no answers for her. I asked her to give me a call when the other statements arrived. She could call me at any time, but I probably wouldn't need to go back into the flat after I finished what I came to do today. She nodded silently and started back upstairs. I called after her that I would bring the key to the flat up to her when I was finished.

After switching on the lights, I went straight to the couch corner of the granny flat. We now had quite a few photos of the couch and that corner of the room, but we had not looked at the couch itself. The cushions were out of place. It didn't look like their disarray would have happened as part of the scenario Langborne suggested. Gloved up, I carefully lifted the uppermost cushion in the pile. Nothing to see there; photographed the couch minus the first cushion.

Lifted the second cushion. Bingo. The cushion concealed part of a typed page. About the top third as well as a piece from the bottom of the page were missing. Damage at the bottom of the page mainly involved the margin area and resulted in the loss of only a couple of words of the text. None of it looked like intentional surgery on the document. It looked like the damage was accidental. More photographs, including a tricky close-up shot to record all the text on the remnant part of the document. To ensure I had a good record of the document's content, I also recorded myself reading the text on my phone.

Another photo recorded the fact that a check of the third cushion revealed nothing. With the couch dealt with, I took a few moments to survey the room one last time before taking the key upstairs to Kate. Her swollen eyes and red nose told the story. She was still sniffling as she took the key and hung it on their key rack. I took my leave and went back to the hotel to take advantage of the limited laundry facilities provided for hotel guests.

Freshly laundered clothes in a pile on the bed, I debated whether to retrieve the iron and ironing board from the wardrobe to finish the job or leave it until the morning. My phone rang, providing me another reason to procrastinate. It was Emily telling me apologetically that we wouldn't be having dinner together tonight as she had arranged to go on somewhere with a couple of others from the symposium. Somewhat relieved by the news, I admitted I also made other arrangements, which might – or might not – involve dinner.

Forget the ironing. I had an hour or so to record today's outcomes before meeting Ben.

# Chapter Four

There was a light shower when I was about to depart. It looked as though it was clearing so I delayed a few minutes until it stopped. As it was only about three blocks to *La Cantina,* I opted to walk rather than drive. I didn't know the area I was going to, or about the availability of parking areas nearby. As I exited the air-conditioned environment via the Regency's automatic doors to enter the real world outside, the humidity almost bowled me over. Too late and too lazy to change my mind and go back for my car key, I trudged on, avoiding puddles as much as possible.

The place wasn't hard to find. Should have driven. Fronting the place was a large carpark area currently with only a few vehicles. Inside, *La Cantina's* décor was in keeping with its name: wood panelled walls, distressed timber tables and bar, and even the waiters wore uniforms styled on the theme. I don't know what the place was in a previous life but, in the refit, they retained three old-style booths at the far end of the seating area. Ben Richards waved from the furthest booth.

It was a quiet night. A waiter was at my elbow within seconds. Ben was already scotch in hand and, from the peat fumes wafting my way, I guessed he was familiar with the bottle of fine single malt I spied behind the bar as I walked in. I decided to play it safe and ordered a white wine. We clinked glasses and got down to the business of catching up on about five years' worth of what we both did during those years.

"You first," Ben invited. "The last time we caught up, as I recall, you were about to go overseas."

"…And you were about to take up a transfer out of the district on your way up the rankings ladder," I replied before continuing. "I had long wanted to go to the UK and do some further studies at one of the universities there. James… you remember James Harris, my boss at the time?" Ben nodded and I carried on. "Anyway, James encouraged me to go, so I enrolled in a couple of archaeology subjects and off I went. Loved every moment of it, and even spent some time on a dig on one of the Greek islands. As it was all coming to an end, I got a bit nervous about what I was going to do when I arrived home, and questioned whether I wanted to remain a PI for the rest of my life."

"You didn't consider staying on and working over there?"

I laughed. "No. The UK is full of much more qualified archaeologists than I, and it always was my intent to return to Millhaven – at least for some period of time in the first instance." I went on to tell of James' battle with cancer which saw him spending less time in the field and more time at home doing the administrative stuff. "Then James went to Canada to visit his daughter and was gone for a few weeks. I ran the agency while he was away. He didn't last too long after he returned and never took much part in the business after that."

I described my shock when told James left the business and his property – house, car, boat; the lot – to me. "He left a fair swag of money to his daughter, but also left what he termed 'operating capital' to me. I don't know what he thought my operating costs were going to be, but the amount of cash was staggering. About 18 months prior to James' death, we entered into a partnership and changed the business name to H & W Investigations. I suppose the bequest shouldn't have surprised me, but I didn't expected it"

"For about 12 months, the business continued to operate out of our office at James' house, while I lived at my place. After that, with probate finalised, common sense took over. I rented a shoebox-sized office in town, moved everything out of James' place and rented out his house. As part of the new arrangements, I also changed the business name again to Whittington Investigations. …And here I am, still doing what I was doing back then. Your turn now; what have you been up to since we last saw each other?"

He described what had been a swift rise up the rankings, which involved a number of transfers to various locations along the way. He concluded by saying he had been in Ralston for about 12 months and was in charge of Homicide as well as 'another small section'. Curious description that. I chose to note but not comment on it. However, it did seem strange he chose not to identify the 'small section' by its title.

By the time we were up to date on each other's life story, the kitchen had kicked into operation. The aroma wafting through the place had my stomach rumbling. Turns out, it was a tapas bar and something of a regular watering hole for Ben. He ordered for both of us. The various small plates of food arrived in what seemed like an endless procession. Finally, we were on the last dish. I struggled to find room for it, but somehow managed to do it justice.

We carefully avoided talking shop as we ate our way through the menu, concentrating mainly on small talk. Ben brought me up to date on mutual acquaintances. However, with the last of the food disposed of, it was inevitable shoptalk would happen. I led the way. "What's with your mate Langborne? What's the arrogant little turd's problem?" I asked.

Ben took a long swig of his drink while considering his reply. "Langborne, the wonder boy...," he began, "New to being a detective and new to Ralston. He's only been here about six months and it didn't take us long to work out he was useless. You remember Pete Messell?"

Pete had been a detective for many years and was one of the best around. He used to be one of the crew at Millhaven and was useful to me on a couple of occasions. A big burly bloke who generally stood for no nonsense, he exercised a wicked sense of humour after a couple of drinks. Yes, I remembered him well.

"Pete's my senior officer in Homicide now. I told Langborne that Pete would mentor him until he found his way around the place and caught up on the local culture. Six months later, I don't think he has learned anything. At least once a week, Pete asks me to assign Langborne to someone else. We don't usually let Langborne out alone except on the occasional minor case. You've discovered the reason. That's why I was more than a bit surprised when you came to talk to him."

Ben studied his drink briefly before continuing. After a couple of drinks over dinner, we were both now drinking iced water. It was obvious he was wrestling with himself about how much more to say. I remained silent. Eventually, he continued slowly and carefully.

"Ralston saw unprecedented carnage over a 72-hour period last weekend. I don't think any of us ever experienced anything quite like it before. Apart from the deaths, a number of other serious crimes also occurred. I was away at a conference for most of the previous week and planned an R&R weekend there before returning yesterday. A phone call during breakfast on Saturday put an end to all that. I was on the first available flight to Ralston, and arrived back here just after lunch. It was a case of all hands on deck to deal with the workload. Your Therese Melrose situation was a part of that growing workload."

He shrugged and gave me a half-apologetic look as he delivered his final comment. I nodded silently to indicate I understood where he was coming from, and refilled both our glasses from the carafe of water.

"I'm not saying Therese's death was not important. However, records show the person who called it in quite clearly described it as a possible domestic accident. Therefore, Pete felt justified, given everything else that was going on, in sending Langborne to deal with it. Langborne confirmed it was an accident, and it went to the bottom of the priorities list. By Monday morning, the morgue was filled to capacity. Further compounding the situation, the coroner has been off since last Thursday with that flu bug that's going around. He's due to return tomorrow."

Ben continued his insight into the Langborne/Melrose saga. He explained that, in the absence of the coroner, they 'borrowed' one of the doctors from the hospital. "The bloke gained a bit of experience doing autopsies while he was at the hospital in a small western town. His role was basic in accordance with his limited experience, and confined to the initial examination and collection of routine samples for despatch to the laboratory for analysis. In straight forward cases – like a heart attack for instance – in the absence of other conflicting indications, he could sign off on the death certificate. He worked according to the priorities set by the Police."

While I understood what Ben said, it didn't sit well with me. A combination of circumstances hardly justified Langborne's attitude or his refusal to consider any other possibility. I suspect Ben detected I was about to argue the matter.

"Yes, Melrose's autopsy was at the bottom of the list. However, Langborne had approval for a few days off this week and was due to start leave this morning. I bailed him up yesterday before he left work and told him he was not going anywhere until he cleared the outstanding work off his desk. There were about six outstanding case files to close, including Melrose's case. With the exception of Melrose's, he had nothing outstanding for any of the weekend cases, and should have been able to close them all. To do that, he needed to include the autopsy reports where relevant. Therese's was the only case needing an autopsy report, and her autopsy was a long way down the list."

"Okay, I understand the procedures involved here, but I'm not sure I see the relevance, other than sorting out the Melrose case was dependent on an autopsy that was some way off being done."

"As I said, Langborne needed that autopsy report to be able to go on leave, and he just happened to have some advantage with the fill-in coroner. Langborne and the good doctor's daughter are an item and they were heading off for those few days together. The office was tipping that a ring with a large rock attached would be involved in their getaway."

"You said Langborne had been here about six months. An engagement so soon is a bit slick, isn't it?" I asked.

"Under normal circumstances perhaps, but the girl is neither very bright nor much of a looker. However, she is independently wealthy. Some inheritance from a grandparent provides her with a substantial allowance, and the good doctor is very well heeled – well, not the doctor himself so much as his wife. Are you getting the picture?"

Loud and clear, but I restricted my response to non-verbal in order to keep interruptions to a minimum.

"Anyway, Langborne was told not to go anywhere until he cleared his desk and, if he did leave without doing so, not to consider returning. He was still beavering away when I left the precinct this evening, a feat never before heard of. I digress. In order to close Therese's case, he needed the autopsy report. I imagine he prevailed upon his prospective father-in-law to rush it through, which he did. I saw it this afternoon. The report confirms the injuries were consistent with an accident and in keeping with Langborne's findings."

"Rubbish!" I exclaimed rather more loudly than necessary, and attracted myself a few startled looks from the bar area. "Oops, sorry. That's just not possible and, if Langborne at least took a look at the stuff I brought with me today, even he would have to agree that couldn't be the case."

"Good to see you haven't mellowed any since we last met," he said with a grimace.

"Look," I said, inhaling hard to flatten my demeanour a bit. "If someone fell and hit their head sufficiently hard to sustain a fatal injury, what part of the skull would be damaged?"

"Could be the temple area or ..."

"No, if they landed flat on their back. Which part of the back of the head would most likely hit the floor?"

He indicated on his own head the most common point of impact and then, in the universal questioning gesture, held out both hands, palms up, towards me as he waited for me to explain where I was going with this discussion.

"I assume then that you don't think the brain stem or C2/C3 area is likely to be the point of impact?" I asked more calmly now.

"Not physically possible I shouldn't think, unless the neck area struck something on the way down, breaking the neck."

"Have you got time? How about coming up to my room?"

He chuckled loudly. "How long did I wait for just such an invitation all those years ago!"

"Fat chance – and it would have been pointless. You were still dealing with the trauma of the break-up of your long-term relationship with … uhmm, the blonde, whatever her name was… and I was too recently widowed. So, do you want to have a look at the stuff I've got or not? Oh, bugger. It's raining again."

"Did you walk here? Where are you staying?"

"The Regency, and yes, I walked."

"Good thing I've got wheels. At least we will remain relatively dry. Come on, I'll drive us there."

'Relatively dry' was the right term. We were more than a little damp from rushing to the car and from the car into the hotel, but it was better than walking. Ben sat at the table with the report I prepared for Langborne while I opened a bottle of wine left over from the previous night. Drinks taken care of, I flipped through the report to the enlarged image of Therese's head wound.

Ben studied it for a few moments. "Hmm, her neck might have been broken when she hit the coffee table. Although it is strange, there is no other injury to the back of the skull from contact with the floor. She's a big lump of a lady and would have made heavy contact."

"Don't be rude. But you're right, she was fairly weighty." I flicked through to another photo. "The only problem with that theory is that she hit the coffee table with her right arm and maybe her shoulder. See the injuries to the arm. I'll bet, after all this time, there should be clear bruising visible to indicate where she contacted the table. Did the autopsy report refer to it at all?"

He shook his head but didn't speak for a while as he scanned the document, stopping to examine each photograph. I watched his look grow increasingly troubled. He eventually asked quietly, "Can I take this with me?"

Of course, I wanted him to take it and read it. I found a plastic laundry service bag in the cupboard and placed the report in it to keep it dry. I let the silence between us linger for a brief moment before speaking softly.

"Ben, this was no accident. More importantly perhaps, there is something very sinister behind all this, which I can't put my finger on yet. Something sinister in the background involving others and I think it's something big."

"Sonny, I've spent enough time with you in the past to have learnt to trust your instinct, but please don't go making more out of this than it is." He sighed. "I know you think otherwise – and I will look into it – but be prepared to accept it as nothing more than an accident." I started to protest but he cut me off. "I know how it is with you. When you get involved, life gets complicated. Like I said, I will look into it because I have learnt to heed your instinct."

"Thank you. I came prepared to confirm it as an accident, but too much is telling me otherwise."

He rubbed his hand wearily across his face and drew in a long breath. "It might – *might* – tie in with something else that happened. No, I can't talk about it. Let me look into some things. I might be able to give you something in a few days. How long are you going to be in town?"

Bugger; that's frustrating, but I know better than to push for more. "There isn't anything else I can do here now, except wait for some other information, which might arrive in the next couple of days. I made appointments a couple of weeks ago to see potential clients tomorrow. I'm booked on the morning plane back to Millhaven tomorrow but I'll be back here on the afternoon flight. It will depend on this other stuff when it comes through, whether I have more to do here or I pack up and go home."

"Don't disappear without letting me know, please. I don't know if I will have anything more by Thursday, but I would like you to hang around till the end of the week if you could."

That sounded promising. It also sounded like a bit more than a simple request. Regardless, I didn't think it wise to refuse, so I agreed and we arranged to meet up again by the end of the week if not before. After locking the door behind him and putting what was left of the wine in the fridge, I realised I felt far too hyped to go to bed. Maybe I was reading too much into his words, but I felt sure things had taken a turn for the better.

If I couldn't sleep, I might as well iron those clothes still awaiting attention in a pile on the bed. About half way through the ironing, the room phone rang. Emily was checking in. She enjoyed her night out and, contrary to expectations, the day proved 'reasonable'. Most importantly, when her mother gave her the third degree over the phone about what was happening, she was able to say she didn't know, as she hadn't seen me. She added that she was going back tomorrow for the second day of the symposium. Things were definitely looking up. I didn't feel the need to tell her about my travel plans for tomorrow. We said good night after only a couple of minutes of conversation.

*****

The plane didn't leave until just before nine o'clock this morning so I had another leisurely start, deliberately breakfasting late to avoid Emily and her predictable barrage of questions. I was in my office in Millhaven by 10.30 and spent the time opening the mail until my first appointment at 11.00. There were a couple of calls to return but I would do that when I was back in Ralston. The Coopers were on time. We discussed the work they wanted done and I gave them a brochure with the scale of fees before sending them off to think about it. They had a wayward daughter they wanted shadowed to see what she did, with whom and where she went.

The second appointment wasn't until 1.00pm, so I ducked into the coffee shop two doors down the street for a coffee and sandwich before she arrived. The woman arrived a few minutes late but was quite to the point about the work she wanted done. She believed her husband was playing away with someone else and she wanted the evidence. He was overseas for the next week or so visiting equipment suppliers in Germany for his firm. I wouldn't be able to commence surveillance until he returned.

As neither of the jobs required an immediate start, it allowed me to remain in Ralston with a clear conscience for a bit longer. My flight to Ralston left at 3.30p.m. I only had time to collect a few bits and pieces before returning to the airport. My phone rang while I was waiting in the departure lounge. It was Kate. After trying a few times to ring me at the hotel, she decided to try my mobile.

She was clearly upset and wanted to see me now. I explained the situation. I would not be back in Ralston until just after 4.30pm and, by the time I got back into the city and collected my car, it would be at least five o'clock at the earliest. Did she want me to come then?

"No. No, don't do that," she shouted over the phone. "I'll give you a call in the morning to organise a time and place. I don't want Ken to know."

Okay, so the plot thickens. More intrigue to cope with tonight. I thought something might be amiss when she gave me the lame excuse the day before about Ken going fishing. While there was nothing to suggest he shouldn't go fishing, it was the notion of his disappearing off for a day of fishing that somehow didn't gel with the current state of affairs in that household.

With time to kill at the airport before my flight boarded, I found a pay phone in a quiet corner and rang an 'associate' in Ralston. Years ago, when he operated out of Millhaven, I managed to extricate him from a sticky situation with the Law. It resulted in something of an ongoing unholy alliance between us. I had occasion to call upon his services a couple of times since then. I needed them again now. We quickly discussed the nature of my requirements, and the cost. It was a brief conversation. There was no evidence of it to be found on my phone should anyone have reason to look.

Arriving back at the Regency, I collected my parcel from reception, the weight of it somehow reassuring as I carried it up in the elevator. Back in my room, I opened the parcel, unpacked the Glock, stripped it, checked it thoroughly, reassembled it and loaded the magazine. It was the same model as my own, currently residing in my safe back in Millhaven. I am licensed to carry a weapon but usually don't, and generally don't have any reason to carry one. However, a couple of messages on my mobile phone indicating the potential shortening of my life expectancy tended to suggest a weapon might come in handy. As it is near to impossible to bring a weapon back from Millhaven on a plane, I called on my 'associate' for assistance.

I met Emily in the restaurant for dinner and allowed her to dominate conversation with a running report on the symposium (turns out it was better than anticipated) and her night out with her new friends. She is going back out to the university tomorrow to have a look at the post-graduate research project with which one of them is involved. She indicated she probably would head home to Moxton on Friday morning 'unless I needed her here'. I assured her there was little more to do in Ralston, and I too probably would head home on Friday. The meal over, I excused myself, citing notes from my busy day to sort out. In truth, I didn't have much to do, but I didn't feel like company.

It was still early. I was restless and needed to be busy. Forced myself to type up notes from today's interviews and check emails, but that didn't take up too much time. Surfed the TV channels. The only vaguely interesting thing was a cricket match underway somewhere, and we were losing badly. Tried reading an eBook but couldn't concentrate, and ultimately gave up looking for things with which to amuse myself. It was still too early and I was too restless to go to bed.

However, I realised that, up until then, there hadn't been time to just sit and contemplate this case.

After arming myself with a glass and the remainder of the bottle of wine from the fridge, I turned off the lights. The nearby streetlights filled the room with a soft glow. I settled in one of the lounge chairs, sipped the wine and let my mind wander. Something was ringing a bell somewhere in the deep recesses of my mind but I hadn't been able to bring it to the forefront of my thoughts. The lack of visual distraction worked – or perhaps it was the wine.

My mind kept coming back to the granny flat. It didn't matter how hard I tried to focus on other aspects of the case, the flat kept nagging my subconscious. I let my thoughts drift to Kate, her impending visit tomorrow, and the strange conversation a couple of days ago about her mother's bank statement. No doubt, it was further information from the bank and not Ken's fishing trip that prompted tomorrow's meeting. Her comment about not letting Ken know what she was doing, while intriguing, also was a bit troubling. The stress of the last few days had the potential to destroy what appeared to be a solid relationship.

Just then, something Ben said on Tuesday night came clanging into my thoughts. I felt my antennae twitch. There was something about the flat. What was it? What had I missed? What the hell is my subconscious prodding me about? I sat until I felt my eyes starting to droop and my brain was telling me it had done too much exercise to be of any further use tonight... of course, it could have been just effect of the wine.

# Chapter Five

I opened one eye and squinted at the clock. There seemed to be a lot of daylight around. Not surprising perhaps, considering I had slept well past my usual get-up time. That's what engaging in mental gymnastics for half the night does to you. Dressed, and with breakfast out of the way, I filled in time waiting for Kate's call by fiddling with my case report: adding more details here and there and making other sections more succinct.

Her call came just after 10.00 o'clock as she was leaving her solicitor's office. We arranged to meet at a coffee shop just out of the city heart and on her way back to Tirandi Street. I didn't want her coming to the hotel, and it seemed like she wanted this to be a covert meeting. When I arrived, she was sitting at a corner table wringing the life out of a paper napkin. This was not going to be an easy meeting. She was as nervous as a kitten, and I feared she was on the verge of tears. I don't cope well with tears.

My earlier assumption was correct. The extra material the bank gave her was almost beyond her comprehension. The number of accounts and amounts of money involved were staggering. She put all the pages back into the large envelope and handed it to me.

"This is your copy of everything. I've given the solicitor the originals. Please look through it all carefully, Sonny. I think there is another story in there," she said, pointing to the envelope, "And I want to know what it's all about. Don't worry about the expense. I spoke to the solicitor. He said your expenses could come out of Mum's estate as they related to establishing the cause of her death and, therefore, were critical to the probate process. He gave me this cheque for you as a retainer and towards your expenses to date."

I did a double take at the amount, but composed myself and asked for the solicitor's details so I could send a receipt. It would more than cover everything for this week. However, I was more interested in finding out Kate's thoughts on the secondary story that she believed was a part of the story of Therese's death. I need her to open up to me honestly and fully, without losing her to her emotions. The envelope

48

lay on the table. I put my hand on it and asked what her thoughts were on what story the envelope's contents might tell. She is stronger than I thought.

"I don't know, Sonny," she said sadly and shook her head. "I don't even want to think about what it looks like to me. Please see what you think. I'd be happy if you said there was nothing there...." After a short pause, she looked directly at me and finished the sentence, "... But I don't think that's the case."

Her lip started to tremble, and I feared the tears were about to cascade. She pushed back her chair and jumped up. Snagging her bag off the back of her chair, she turned to leave. As an after-thought, she turned and said, "Don't let Ken know about this. You'll know why when you look through that stuff."

Back at the Regency, I spread the photocopies out on the table. There appeared to be statements for five bank accounts. I picked out the statement for the loan account, which covered the purchase of the Tirandi Street property. No recent transactions. The statement showed the loan paid out some time ago – and quickly – as Kate indicated. It was interesting that, after a few initial standard looking payments, subsequent payments occurred in hefty chunks and at random intervals rather than according to a regular schedule. I put it aside. While it posed a few questions, the lack of recent transactions provided no useful insights.

The next statement was for the 'Rent' account. Its transactions indicated this was the account that received the rent payments from the Tirandi Street property (from Ken and Kate) as well as from her previous home out west. Rents appeared paid in by automatic bank transfers. There was a third regular payment also in to the account, but the transaction details weren't particularly helpful. What caught my eye were the regular transfers out of the account.

While this could be a legitimate move to maintain the account balance at some desired level, that didn't seem to be the situation. The week after rent went in from Ken, an amount equal to half that payment went out of the account. Its destination was an account at another institution, and the account name didn't provide any clues as to its owner. However, the 'in and out' ritual on alternate weeks was in place from the start of the statement. I guessed it was likely to have been in place long before that – probably from early in the life of the account.

I let out a low whistle as I looked at the balance shown on the next statement. This must be the one Kate mentioned on Tuesday.

Her shock was justified. It was a lot of money. The account, given an obscure 'trading company' type name, was an extremely busy account. Many payments out; far fewer payments in, but payments received were in big – really big – lumps. A 'light bulb moment' happened.

There appeared to be payments from this account to another account similar to one I had just seen somewhere in the pile in front of me. I went back to the statements I had looked at. No, I was mistaken. It was a similar account name, but not quite the same as the one receiving funds from the Rent account. I needed to go through this statement carefully, but opted to look at the remaining statements first.

Having forced myself to put it aside, I picked up the next statement. It looked like some form of general purpose account. Therese's salary went in each fortnight, and a whole raft of payments went out for utilities, fuel for her car, medical and pharmaceuticals, and groceries from one of the large supermarket chains. Nothing immediately attention grabbing here.

A telephone account lay at the bottom of the pile. Therese linked her home phone and her personal mobile on the one account. Wow! This was one hefty phone bill. The list of calls went on and on, and seemed evenly distributed between both phones. A quick scan of the pages revealed some of the numbers featured frequently and appeared throughout the period covered by the account. My trip to Millhaven yesterday was worthwhile. I now had just the tool with me to interrogate this phone account.

While it is relatively simple to find the phone number belonging to a known name by searching the internet or phone book, it is not a simple matter to find out who belongs to a known phone number. A service that does that is available on the web – at a cost. It isn't a viable option if there are many numbers to check. On my office computer, I have a program that allows a reverse search. The user only keys in a phone number in order to identify whose it is. A hot and heavy but brief relationship with a Senior Sergeant resulted in my acquisition of a copy of the program. While in Millhaven yesterday, I copied the program onto my laptop with the intention of running Liz's list of calls from Therese's work phone through it. Now I had an even more impressive list of numbers for it to work on. In fact, it would make sense to start right now.

Data entry took quite a while but, by three o'clock, I had sorted and printed the information from my program. My pulse stepped up a notch as I scanned the list on my way to add it to the other papers on the table. This was one scary list. Some of the names on it were not considered to belong to fine upstanding – decent – citizens of this part of the world. Ben was not answering his phone. I left a message asking him to call me – urgently.

That was one list of numbers sorted out. Now for Liz's list. This was much quicker as she already had identified many of the numbers. I entered the unidentified numbers into my program and printed off the resultant list of information. The newly printed list didn't immediately ring any alarm bells. The names the program revealed for this list didn't appear significant and, overall, the whole list looked reasonably innocuous.

I took the laptop to the table, ready to start entering all of the transaction details from the big account statement into a database. The phone startled me when it rang. I told Ben briefly I had additional information I thought would interest him. He said he would come sometime after six o'clock. That gives me little enough time to get my head around it all before he arrives. However, I had seen enough to agree with Kate. There was something going on… and I detected a sinister overtone to it all.

My room phone rang again: Liz. "Liz, I thought I made it clear there should be no way you could be connected to me."

"It's okay. I'm ringing from Jim's home phone. He suggested it. When I'm walking my dog, if Jim is on late shift, I stop by his place to feed his dog. That's what I'm doing, but I also thought of a couple of things after our meeting."

"Did you want to meet up somewhere or can we deal with it over the phone?"

"Over the phone is fine. I'm not sure it's important anyway, but Jim thought you should know."

Good on Jim; I grabbed a notebook and she began. She provided information about three people, one of which I was tempted to ignore almost immediately. The other two men sounded much more interesting. The first story stemmed from the upheaval in the TAFE system the previous year and the events it precipitated at the Ralston institute.

"As part of a streamlining initiative, the institute decided there should be only two schools instead of the previous three. The School of Engineering studies was safe, but the other two – the School of Business Studies and the School of Humanities – were to combine into one large school and become the School of Humanities. In a bid to appear to make the process transparent, the existing three Heads of Schools had to reapply for the jobs under the new arrangement. Only two of them could be successful and applications were not open to others or outsiders. The Head of Engineering got his old job back – or 'retained' his job, if you prefer to think of it that way. Therese became Head of the new School of Humanities. That left the third bloke without a position of any sort within the institute." Liz paused. I took the opportunity to ask a question.

"There's nothing new in that as many ex-TAFE staff will attest. If it runs true to form, after a couple of years or so, they will decide the new school is too large for one person to manage, and will split it into two schools again. So why have you singled out the bloke who lost his job for special attention?"

"He was extremely bitter, as you might expect, and couldn't find a position at any other institute or within the department. His very vocal claim was that the whole thing was rigged, and that Therese received 'special' treatment as a mate of the director. He took to drink, his wife ran off with some other bloke and he went broke. Anyway, long story short, he took to ringing Therese at all hours of the day and night, sending her threatening texts and emails, and even took out a notice in the paper making libellous claims against Therese and her association with the director. Therese took legal action. When he didn't stop, the Police went to talk to him and he tried to run them down. One officer ended up with a broken leg. The bloke found himself in court, continued to hurl abuse at everyone and ended up in jail. He got out two weeks ago. There is some suggestion the whole business has left him psychotic."

Liz gave me his name and a few other details… which I would pass onto Ben to look into. Somehow, in spite of everything, I didn't see him as a strong suspect for Therese's death. Ben might prove me wrong. That left one other person Liz had suggested might be worthy of consideration. I asked about that third person.

"I don't know a lot about this one. It all stems from something that happened sometime before Therese moved from out west to Ralston. All I know is that the man held Therese somehow responsible for the death of his son. He gave her a hard time before she left there and stepped up his attack a notch after she moved here. It became a Police matter, but I don't know what the outcome of it all was. By the time I started working for her, it was already in the hands of the Police. I know it flared up to some degree a couple of times after that but I think solicitors and Police dealt with it."

That's another one who doesn't grab my attention as a likely suspect, but still is probably worth a look. I thanked Liz and agreed to keep her in the loop as much as possible. By the time her call ended, there was little enough time left before Ben might arrive. I went back to Kate's pile of paper and went straight to the thing I was about to look at when Liz rang. The alarm bells this financial statement raised continued to clang all through Liz's phone call, making it difficult to concentrate on what she was saying. I cleared my mind and focused on the statement in my hand.

I couldn't remember Ken's middle name, doubted I ever knew it, and wished I did. Payments from a couple of the accounts were going to another account shown as *KLN Trading. It* was the statement for KLN Trading that grabbed my attention. I separated it from the rest of the pile and studied it. What was Ken's middle name? A little voice in the deep recesses of my mind kept suggesting KLN were Ken's initials.

Nothing about this pile of paper, and this statement in particular, looked good. Kate might well be justified in being so distraught. The odd white lie in a marriage might remain hidden, but this was looking like a monumental deceit. I continued to study the statements until a knock at the door brought me back to the here and now. As I made my way to the door, my mind struggled with what appeared to be unfolding. A voice in my head kept screaming, what was Therese doing? What had she gotten herself involved in?

Ben was at the door, bag of take-away food in one hand and bottle of wine in the other. There was no contest about what to do first: eat before the food went cold. I gave Ben my lists of phone numbers and bank accounts to read while I organised appropriate equipment for the despatch of dinner. Not wanting to interrupt his preliminary scan of the data, I opened the wine and poured us both a glass before dropping onto a chair opposite him.

"Phew!" he said as he looked up at me. He pushed the papers out of the way and studied a spot near the centre of the table for a moment before taking a long swig of wine. It was obvious he was mulling over the information gained from his brief scan of my lists. I kept quiet for a few moments, but soon reached the point where I could no longer remain silent, and cleared my throat to speak. He beat me to it.

"You probably should know this whole Melrose thing has exploded. I told you the Coroner would be back this week. He came in for the first time yesterday while you were back in Millhaven. I asked him to take a look at Therese's body first up and to treat the whole thing as urgent." He took another sip of wine before continuing. "She is now officially confirmed as a homicide."

A surge of excitement charged through me. "Anything else you'd like to share?" I asked cautiously.

He looked across his glass and shrugged, apparently having decided it was okay to share more. "The head wound couldn't possibly be caused by her head hitting the floor: probably caused by a blow from a cylindrical object about 100mm to130mm in diameter," he recited mechanically. "The glass shard in the abdomen was inflicted by a downward thrusting motion that ended with the piece of glass left in situ."

I leapt up from the table and went to the pile of paper and photos I had accumulated. After ferreting out the photo Kate gave me of the couch area, which showed a lamp on the coffee table, I returned to the table and stood beside Ben.

"Yes, okay, nice photo, but what's the little girl got to do with anything?" he asked a bit shortly.

"Look beyond Poppy. See the lamp on the coffee table. It's not in the flat now, but I think the base of it might just about be the right size to have inflicted the head wound." I hoped I hadn't sounded too triumphant. The lamp appeared to have a cylindrical ceramic base that was patterned all over, and had a dark glaze. I estimated it at probably about 400mm or so tall. There was some sort of fancy fitting between the base and the shade.

"Hmmph," he grunted in response. "I'm almost not game to ask, but what's your take on this whole thing so far? Keep it brief, please," he added with a sigh, and it occurred to me he was looking a bit worn out tonight.

"I'd prefer you came up to speed with everything before I start espousing my theories. By the way, is there a little woman at home somewhere waiting for you? We can do this some other time during the day instead of now, if it suits better."

He laughed aloud and those blue eyes twinkled. "There is no little woman anywhere, but thank you for asking."

"You're looking a bit ragged. I'm sure you have already had a long day," I hurried on, "But, if you're okay, I'm happy to work on."

That settled, we moved to the lounge chairs and started discussing facts and theories developed so far. The soft buzzing of my room phone rudely interrupted the flow of discussion. My car was parked in the hotel's basement carpark. The caller was one of the valets. My car security alarm was sounding and it wasn't responding to the remote when they tried to turn it off.

"Don't go near it! Stay right away from it! Clear the area if you can," I shouted down the phone. My hand was white-knuckled from gripping the phone so tightly.

"What!" Ben demanded. Standing beside me, mobile phone already in his hand, he no longer looked tired; now highly alert.

I swallowed hard. "My car's been tampered with. I received a couple of death threats yesterday. The valets...." I was talking to myself. Ben had moved away from me and was talking softly but rapidly on his mobile phone.

"Explain! Quickly!" he demanded from across the room.

Do you remember the bloke we used to call Boris?"

"Boris? Boris? Oh, that mad inventor bloke; what's he got to do with anything?"

I quickly explained that some time ago there were a number of incidents in other countries involving explosive devices placed on targets' cars. They exploded when the ignition was turned on, killing all on board. This awakened some creative streak in Boris' mind and he invented a small device to fit as an add-on to a vehicle's security alarm system. If it detected even a small change in the vehicle, such as something placed in the engine well or attached to the undercarriage, it triggered the car's security alarm. The only difference in such an instance is that the security alarm will not respond to the remote control. There is no way to stop it yodelling. With this characteristic, there is no mistaking the situation as something as simple and innocuous as a bump or a bird landing on the vehicle as having triggered the alarm.

"He wanted to fit it to a vehicle as a trial to see if it worked, and asked if he could fit it to mine. I think his motivation was more than that. I looked after him a bit after his family deserted him. It was probably some sort of thank you gesture on his part. You know: something to keep me safe. I never really thought about it. Boris made quite a bit from sales of the device. There was no interest in Australia, but the gadget sold well in some overseas countries."

"So how do you turn it off – deactivate it?" he demanded.

"I don't know. I don't think he ever showed me."

Sirens were growing louder as I tried to continue the explanation, but Ben had bolted out the door and was disappearing rapidly down the corridor shouting over his shoulder at me, "Stay there. Do *not* come down to the basement."

"Stay here! You must be joking. That's my car down there," I announced to an empty corridor. Overcoming the initial inertia, I grabbed my room key, locked the door and raced down the corridor to the elevators. There was a brief moment of hesitation in front of the elevators. I was a long way up. Would it be quicker to race down the stairs or wait and take the elevator? I pushed the button while trying to decide. One elevator was in use, but a 'ping' announced the arrival of the other one moments after I pushed the button and had taken a couple of steps away.

I disembarked on the first floor and quickly but quietly made my way down the stairs to almost the exit to the basement carpark. Common sense suggested it wasn't wise to make a grand entrance, so I backed into the shadows a few steps from the bottom. The scene was like something from some sci-fi TV show.

Bulky green mounds moved cautiously around my car, while others pushed cars out of the garage. There already was a clear space around my car, but they continued moving vehicles out. I realised those bulky green mounds were bomb squad personnel in full protective gear. One of the green mounds moved over to talk to Ben. I saw him look in my direction before making some further comment to Ben.

The lighting in the stairwell was poor. I pushed myself back against the wall as hard as I could in an effort to become invisible in the shadows. It didn't work. Ben was striding toward the stairs – and me. He did not look too pleased.

"What the hell are you doing down here?" he demanded with more fury than I had ever seen him display in the past. I knew he would be angry, but I was unprepared for this.

"Er. Umhh," I stammered, desperately trying to get brain and mouth to co-ordinate. "I wanted to see what was happening to my car," I finally blurted out lamely.

"You were told to stay upstairs. Don't you ever do as you are told? You could have been killed," he barked.

"So could you!" I retaliated sharply. Feeble response, but it was all I could manage at the time. No doubt, plenty of much cleverer responses would come to me later.

Contrary to my intention to remain aloof and unmoved by our encounter, I winced as Ben grabbed me by the arm and propelled me up the stairs. This was not going well at all. I had to do something to diffuse the situation and, more importantly, let Ben get back to doing his job.

"Whoa. Hang on, Ben. I'll go back to my room if you promise to come and tell me soon as you know what is happening with my car. I need you to find out what's going on." I planted my feet and resisted all attempts to move me further. Well, that seemed to work. He stopped dragging me up the stairs and the vice-like grip on my arm relaxed a little. I was a little unnerved by whatever was going on with my car. The twinge of apprehension in the pit of my stomach was making me less than co-operative. I kept my feet planted, stuck my chin out and refused to budge.

"Okay, but do not come back down here until I have spoken to you. Understood?" I nodded, applied my best attempt at a chastened look, then turned and started up the stairs again, without assistance this time.

Incapable of settling to do anything, I paced the room for what seemed like an eternity. In reality, it was probably about 15 minutes before Ben knocked on my door. Whatever the news was, at least he looked as though he had cooled down a bit.

"They found a funny little device. Nothing like they had seen before. It wasn't explosive. It looks designed to snuff the engine after the vehicle is driven for a while by not letting the exhaust gases escape properly… a bit like shoving a potato up the exhaust pipe." He might have looked calmer, but the tension hadn't disappeared from his manner or the way he delivered the information.

"I don't understand what they – whoever *they* are – hoped to achieve. I think I could understand the use of some sort of explosive device, but I don't understand this. Does it mean they didn't intend to injure or maim – just frighten? If that were the case, it worked. That thought made me grimace.

"No, you can't dismiss it so lightly. The guys tell me it would create a very slow build-up of gas by only partially impeding the exhaust. It would take a while before it stopped the engine. I think it was designed to take effect when you were down the road a bit on your way home, probably somewhere along that long deserted stretch of road way outside the city limits."

I thought about the stretch of road in question. There was nothing but fenced cow paddocks bordering the road for about 40 kilometres – no houses in sight and a complete dead spot for mobile phone reception. I felt an uneasiness stirring. I turned to Ben and opened my mouth to speak but he cut me off before I could say anything.

"It's likely they knew you were planning to leave Ralston tomorrow. It would be difficult to do away with you while you were here in Ralston. Broken down on a lonely stretch of road on your own would be a different matter. Were you planning to leave Ralston tomorrow?"

"Yes. I told reception I would check out tomorrow. I was going to see if I could catch up with Kate before I left, but I hoped to be on the road by lunchtime." I made a mental note that I hadn't rung Kate earlier this evening as intended. "How would they know I was leaving tomorrow? As it turns out, the car might have died in the middle of suburbia on my way to Tirandi Street. They needed to know I was leaving in the morning, and not know about my intention to visit Kate, or the plan you think they had for me would not work."

"Good question... and one we are working on getting an answer to. In the meantime, you *are* checking out tomorrow, but you are not staying here tonight. So, how quickly can you get all this stuff packed up?" He described an arc with his arm indicating all the office gear scattered around the lounge area.

"I don't really fancy sleeping rough tonight, so what have you got in mind? And I think the hotel staff might get a bit nervous if they see me traipsing backwards and forwards to my car with all this gear when I am not checking out till tomorrow."

"Your car is not here. The squad disabled the alarm system to stop the noise. They took it back to the precinct to give it another going over and to reinstate the alarm system. Don't worry about people noticing you are moving out. We have that covered. Now, for God's sake, start packing."

Well, packing wasn't going to take too long. The few clothes I brought went into my bag, quickly followed by my wet pack and the hotel's complimentary toiletries, which I felt might come in handy. With the bag parked in the kitchen area ready to go, I slipped the laptop along with its associated bits and pieces into its bag. I was zipping the bag closed when there was a knock at the door. I spun around to face the door, a bit apprehensive about what might be outside. Ben opened the door and three squad members, now minus their safety suits, marched in.

"Come on, keep packing," Ben rallied me into action again, while indicating my bag and the laptop case to one of the men.

One of them picked up the bags and headed out the door. A second one snatched up the printer box as soon as I managed to put the printer and its cable roughly into the box. This only left the bag in which I carried paperwork around. I gathered up all the paper I had strewn around the place and shoved it roughly into the bag. All the while, I found myself thinking it would be good if I knew where I was going and for how long I would be there.

The last of my stuff disappeared out the door. I did a quick scan of the place before coming back to the kitchenette area. We managed to attack the wine but not the food before the rude interruption by my car. Ben packed the take-away containers into the carrier bag they arrived in and was searching for the screw cap for the wine bottle. It had fallen into the carrier bag.

Food and wine now packed, he glanced around the room and said, "Get your purse or whatever and let's get out of here." I locked the door behind us and followed him down the many flights of stairs at breakneck speed to the basement carpark. At the bottom of the stairs, conveniently parked there for a quick get-away was his car. The other guys and my gear were nowhere in sight. I noted no hotel staff were anywhere in sight either.

# Chapter Six

It didn't take me long to work out that we were heading towards Police Headquarters. While I'd managed to work that much out, I was more than a bit keen to know what my final destination might be. As we approached Headquarters, I couldn't stand not knowing any longer. "Thank you for taking me to Police Headquarters but I don't really fancy spending the night in the cells."

I looked across at Ben hoping for an answer of some sort, but he remained 'eyes front' and silent as we drove through the entrance and around to the back of the building. He didn't speak until we were crossing the brief expanse of gravel on our way to the building's back entrance.

"I'll explain shortly. Do you suppose this food will heat up okay in a microwave?"

"I don't know," I snapped in frustration. "Where are we going?"

"It is easier to show you first and then explain – hopefully over some food and wine." With that, he pushed the button for the elevator and we started on our way to the top floor.

Ben exited the elevator first and led the way down a dogleg corridor. Part of the way along it, I realised it actually was some sort of walkway spanning the police complex's entrance driveway below. It led from the Police building to the adjacent one. When it reached the other building, the walkway formed a T-junction with another corridor running from the front to the rear of the second building. At this junction, we turned right and followed the corridor to where it terminated abruptly at a back corner of the top floor of that second building. A door stood open and lights and airconditioner were on.

The squad members who had carried my gear from my hotel room to their cars were leaving, and said good night as they walked past. The last member, who I took to be their leader, gave Ben a nod as he passed and said, "All clear." From the corridor, I could see my gear stacked neatly in an area at the far end of a room, in what looked like a small lounge area beyond an even smaller kitchenette. Ben stood aside and ushered me in.

It was small, tidy, simply furnished and with a similar layout to the rooms I had at the hotel. I wandered through on a familiarisation tour: small kitchenette, lounge/sitting area, bedroom and ensuite facilities. No free toiletries in sight. Just as well I liberated the supply from the hotel.

"Do you know how to drive a microwave?" Ben greeted me as I returned to the kitchen to find him unpacking the take-away containers. "There must be wine glasses here somewhere," he muttered as he opened various cupboard doors.

The microwave proved to be a standard model and didn't present any challenges. We soon found ourselves seated at the kitchen bench, which also served as a breakfast bar. We had an assortment of hot take-away food spread out along the bench and wine glasses in hand. I hadn't felt like eating, but the smell of the food won me over. The crispy things were no longer crispy, but my appetite didn't really care. They still tasted good.

"Okay, Ben. Talk to me, starting with, what is this place?" I demanded as he shovelled food into his bowl. He paused shovelling briefly to take a deep breath and collect his thoughts, before beginning what turned into a long story that lasted late into night.

His explanation of the place to which I appear to have relocated began with a brief history lesson. "Some time ago, the Police Department leased the whole of this top floor from the Government agency that occupied the rest of this building. That's when the walkway between the two buildings was constructed. Then, in more recent times, a combination of restructuring of the local Police operations and relocation of some of the Police technical facilities out of the city heart left the Police with a whole lot of extra space they didn't need for day to day operations. However, at around the same time, the agency occupying the rest of this building needed a little more space. Compromise resulted in erection of a wall dividing the top floor into two halves from front to back."

A couple of sips of wine and a few more mouthfuls of food and he continued. "This half of the top floor – the side closest to and running parallel to the Police building – was retained by the Police Department, while the other half reverted to the tenants of the rest of this building. The Police Department divided their section in two. The front part – that's the part at the other end of the corridor outside – houses my 'Special Squad' and this back section became an apartment for use by specialist officers called in to help with difficult cases."

"Why was something needed for them? "It all looks very new and unused," I said.

"Yeah, I think they used it only once or twice after it was set up. We used to have a problem. Whenever we had a serious crime and had to bring in specialist to help out, there was always some big event going on in town and accommodation was scarce. Sometimes we had to billet the special officers with one of us for a few days because there was no accommodation available anywhere else in town for them. Since the formation of my Special Squad, there hasn't been occasion when we needed to import expertise."

"Were the bomb squad people who dealt with my car tonight part of your Special Squad?"

"N-o-o," he replied cautiously before deciding to explain. "They are members of the Army Bomb Squad stationed at the Army base just outside of town. A select group of them spent the last month training with our men on dealing with the kind of extreme situations we might encounter. That's why they were here at the precinct tonight when I needed them, and not out at their base. Can I help you set up your computer and stuff?" He asked, none too delicately changing the subject.

"No. No, thanks, I don't think I'll bother as I'm probably only going to be here overnight – or as long as it takes for them to get my car mobile again," I replied with just a hint of doubt starting to invade my mind. "Ben, isn't bringing me here tonight a bit over the top? I was going to leave town tomorrow anyway, so surely I could have spent tonight at the hotel."

"No, I couldn't guarantee your safety at the hotel. And no, you will not be going home tomorrow," he answered quite firmly. "I'm not sure ..." he began, but I cut him off before he finished.

"I came here for what I anticipated would be a couple of days to look into Therese Melrose's death for the family, and I did that in the first couple of days I was here. Kate then asked me to look into a few anomalies, which I did. All that information I now have passed on to you. I have done more than originally intended. There is nothing more for me to do here, and Kate isn't going to pay me to do nothing. It's now up to you to progress the investigation into Therese's death. Besides, I do have a business to run and clients waiting for me in Millhaven."

Time to get tough, I decided. "Unless you can give me a damn good reason to stay – or you arrest me for something – I am going home tomorrow straight after I talk to Kate again. Please make sure my car is mobile again by then." My ultimatum delivered, I stood, hands on hips and jaw set as I looked at him defiantly. There were a few butterflies flapping around in my stomach. Knowing Ben of old, he was just as likely to arrest me for something in order to win the battle of wills.

"Oh, for God's sake, Woman; I am trying to keep you safe – keep you alive even. Sit down. Would you just try doing as you're asked for once? Although … now you mention it, arresting you might be the easier alternative."

Taken aback by his comment for a brief moment, I quickly mustered some of my former bravado. "If I knew what was going on, Ben, I might understand what you are trying to do, and why – and who knows, I might even feel inclined to co-operate."

Ben sighed deeply, wearily rubbed a hand across his face as he wandered down to the lounge area and dropped onto the couch. "Okay, fine. Let's talk. You had better see if there is anything to drink in that fridge. We're going to need it before we are finished." With that, he leaned forward, hands on knees, and focused on the floor.

I assumed he was gathering his thoughts, so I quietly checked the fridge while allowing him time to do so. There were the remnants of a bottle of white wine and a couple of bottles of soda water. I took the wine and one of the bottles of soda water to the coffee table, figuring that, if we made spritzers, the wine would stretch far enough to see us through the next conversation.

After pouring drinks, I perched on the edge of my chair in anticipation, but Ben was still off somewhere else and didn't begin the awaited conversation. I prompted him. "Ben, I don't know …," I began and then decided to change tack. I began again, "I think this thing –whatever this thing is – started well before Therese's death. I don't think your concerns for me stem just from her death. Maybe, if I understood how her death fits into the bigger picture of whatever is going on, I'll be able to understand and appreciate what you are trying to do for me."

He contemplated me for a moment or two before drawing a deep breath. "Okay, you're right. The thing is an ongoing investigation that, I suppose, really started about three months ago." His narrative was off and running and I held my silence so as not to interrupt the flow of words or the thought processes behind them. His story began not three months ago, but about two months ago.

At Metropolitan Branch headquarters for a three-day training program, when they had to break into groups for some of the activities,

Ben found himself grouped with a couple of men from the Metropolitan Squad. The three of them got on well and spent non-class time socialising together. Inevitably, conversation came round to what they were working on at the time. It only took a few minutes for them to realise that, although none of them yet fully understood the cases they each were working on, there were significant similarities between Ben's case and the ones the Met boys had. After a few moments pause and a sip of wine, Ben continued his story.

"About a month previously, the long-serving and highly esteemed Director General of a Public Service department apparently committed suicide. There were all the usual comments from those interviewed: nobody could believe it; there was no evidence anything was wrong. His behaviour was normal except in the last week or so before his death, when he was a bit more prickly than normal, but that was excusable as it was budget preparation time. The department took a beating in the current financial year, resulting from the Government's restructured funding arrangements."

"Staff was lost, and more were likely to be sacrificed if increased funding wasn't forthcoming in the new financial year. However, an increase in funding was going to be difficult to justify. The same throughput of work was occurring, but the reduced staff numbers meant the remaining staff had increased workloads. The workloads would increase further if staff numbers were reduced further due to a lack of funds to pay them."

I nodded. There was nothing new in this story. I knew from former colleagues that the same situation currently existed throughout the Public Service. No point in telling Ben something he already knew, so I didn't say anything and Ben continued.

"Consensus among those interviewed was that the Director General was under a strain and felt personally responsible for the jobs of his staff. That explanation initially seemed plausible. The newly elected Government's restructure of the Public Service saw many public servants lose their jobs – on short notice in many cases – and it triggered a rash of suicides. However, interviews with close family members painted a different picture in this case. The man was planning to retire. They believed he might already have discussed with his superiors likely termination dates and payouts. This new insight appeared to raise the Met detectives' curiosity levels somewhat but not significantly so."

That's strange. The whole thing smelled off to me and I was only hearing the story third-hand. I supposed the Met detectives, better informed than I am, made their assessment of the situation accordingly. Not my place to question their findings – not yet anyway – so I let Ben's story continue uninterrupted.

"Since the case was considered a suicide, it didn't attract a high priority, and it was a couple of weeks later before the detectives got around to talking to the Minister who the man answered to. The Minister's comments got the detectives' antennae twitching. He confirmed there had been discussions regarding the Director General's possible retirement. The proposed timing was fortuitous, coming in the budget preparation season as it had."

"It's always fortuitous at budget preparation time if someone puts their hand up to jump ship. That's one less salary they have to find, and his replacement – if there is one – being new to the job would receive a much lower salary." I couldn't help myself. The comment was out before I realised it. Ben looked reproachfully at me. I apologised and invited him to continue.

"There were some high level discussions surrounding the amalgamation of a couple of departments within the Public Service. A quiet investigation of what each of the departments did clearly indicated opportunities for streamlining and amalgamation."

"Same old, same old," I commented. "It's the way the Public Service has always been. Streamline and amalgamate, then empire building sets in anew, and more departments are created." Oops, I did it again. "Sorry, Ben, please go on." Another dark look, but he continued.

"Nothing concrete was in place yet as Cabinet was still working on the details. Not the least of those was which of the two existing Directors General should go as part of the amalgamation. When the approach for a possible retirement occurred, the Minister jumped at the opportunity, and suggested a redundancy instead. That would effectively rid them of a potential surplus employee as well as providing the incumbent with a very nice redundancy payout."

"They would have to offer the unwanted employee a redundancy anyway, so the move would not save money, but it would quietly avoid a difficult situation, and potential bad publicity," I observed.

"Quite possibly; anyway, the discussions ended with the Minister left to seek approval for the redundancy and to confirm the payout figure. In fact, they had scheduled a meeting to finalise arrangements for the day after the man died. The Minister admitted to being perplexed by it all, but said he just accepted it as 'one of those things'."

I digested Ben's information for a few moments before admitting, "The sequence of events is intriguing to say the least."

"Intriguing, yes, but still nothing to suggest it was anything but suicide until about a week prior to that training program the detectives and I attended. A Cabinet Secretary died in an apparent vehicle accident that happened on a long, lonely back road – a long way out of the metropolitan area and a long way from his home."

"Was he from the same department or associated in some way with the Director General who supposedly committed suicide?"

"No, no connection. The man's family was holidaying on the coast. He was to join them on the weekend and spend the following week with them finalising arrangements for their daughter's forthcoming marriage to a lad from that area. His wife told the other family it wasn't clear when her husband would be joining them. It depended on whether he could get away at a reasonable time on the Friday night, or if he chose to wait and drive down on Saturday morning. He did arrive very late on the Friday night but, soon after breakfast the next day, announced that he had to return home, citing some sudden work issue as the reason."

"Oh dear, that probably didn't go down well with the future in-laws."

"Who knows? His wife believed he would go straight to his office, so she waited until Saturday evening to check if her husband was okay. There was no answer when she rang their home. She assumed he was working late and elected not to ring him at work in case she interrupted something important. The family went to dinner with the daughter's intended in-laws as planned and returned to the hotel quite late. The wife tried phoning her husband again next morning, but they slept in and it was late when she rang. When there was no answer, she though he must have already gone to work. She admitted she was angry when he left. She was angry that, as usual, she was left to deal with sorting out all of the wedding arrangements."

I shrugged. "Never mind being left with the wedding arrangements. She would have been embarrassed by his absence and how it looked for her daughter."

"You're right. She admitted she was embarrassed: what must the future in-laws make of his absence? The wedding arrangements and his absence were a concern, but that wasn't all. It annoyed her that it never occurred to her husband to let her know he had arrived home safely, what was happening, and whether he would be returning for the rest of their stay at the coast."

"As I said before, not a good impression to create for the future in-laws. Still, I would have expected the daughter to be the more upset than the wife. After all, she will be joining the other family and, no doubt, she would like her father to at least show some interest in that process," I mused.

"Sunday morning, the detectives were called in to investigate a fatal road accident along the back road to a hinterland farming area. A farmer taking a truckload of vegetables to the produce markets in readiness for Monday's trading came across the grisly scene of a burnt out sedan on the side of the road. They found the driver still in the car, but too badly burnt for immediate identification. The car's plates indicated it was a government vehicle. That left the detectives stymied until the next day. Monday morning, they contacted the government's carpool attendant to determine who booked the car out for the weekend. Three cars went out of the compound that Friday evening without their details entered into the system. If the attendant has left for the night, late leavers are responsible for entering into the system details of the cars they take."

"Fairly standard departmental practice," I confirmed.

"At about 5.45pm on Friday, a freak storm, with strong winds, hail and then heavy rain swept over the metropolitan area. It caused a power outage lasting about five minutes. It also fried the department's main server. Computer systems remained down the whole weekend. It wasn't until Sunday night that the IT team was able to get them up and running again. Anyone leaving after the storm on Friday was unable to book a car out on the system."

"What would you call it: luck, fate, coincidence…?" I asked.

Ben just grunted and ignored the question. "The last entry in the booking system was by a senior staff member at 5.20pm. None of the three cars taken after the storm were returned to the compound on Monday morning. There were three staff not expected back at work on Monday, and the attendant assumed theirs were the three unreturned cars. As it turned out, two staff were having a few days of leave, and the third staff member was undergoing some medical procedure on the Monday before taking a couple of days off to recover. The detectives tracked down the three staff members – all alive and well – then started hunting for the dead man's dental records as a means of identification."

"I imagine that would be difficult without any leads on a possible victim to start with. Where do you start such a search? Until someone is reported missing, there wouldn't be any easy way of narrowing down which dentists to contact for dental records, would there?"

"That's more or less how it happens. It was Wednesday before they finally had a breakthrough and were able to identify the driver. By that evening, his family were located and informed of the tragedy. Their first response was there had been a mistake. He had gone back into work. He had no reason to be so far out in the country so it couldn't be him."

"What about his work colleagues – his secretary or whoever – didn't they miss him?"

"He wasn't missing. Remember, the man was supposed to be spending the week at the coast with his family. The staff member's secretary confirmed the man left immediately after the blackout. Not knowing how long the storm might last, they both packed up and started to leave. They were out in the main corridor when the power came back on. Her boss made a short phone call on his mobile just prior to leaving the office and, as they walked out together, he commented that he would be driving straight to the coast after he collected a car. The secretary left in her car and her boss continued on to the car compound. That was at about 5.55pm. She had no idea what he was doing out in the hinterland area. There certainly wasn't anything work-related happening to take him out there."

"How long does it take to drive to the coast these days? From memory, I'm thinking something like a bit more than an hour is a reasonable time, or maybe a few minutes more given it was a Friday night and there had been a storm," I suggested.

"If the secretary's times were right, her boss should have arrived at the hotel on the coast by seven o'clock or a few minutes later if traffic was heavy. He did not arrive until around ten o'clock. Traffic Branch advised there were no snarls or accidents to delay traffic on the highway that night, and that traffic leaving the city was light after the storm. Their home security system showed no activity at the house after he left for work on Friday morning, so he did not go home before leaving for or after returning from the coast. The preliminary coroner's report indicated the accident occurred late on Saturday night. What happened during the gap in that timeline was a mystery."

Ben was starting to trip over his tongue. He paused and waved his empty glass at me for a refill. After drinking about half a glass, he continued.

"The detectives took another look at the car. Forensics found accelerant inside the car consistent with that in the car's fuel tank.

There was some minor panel damage to the front end, mainly to the area around the headlight and part of the grill on the passenger's side. The detectives revisited the accident site. On the way to the site, one of them rang the carpool attendant and asked for a check on the damaged car's fuel card."

The car had ended up on the correct side of the road but nose first in the drain running beside it. Damage to the car was inconsistent with the way it ended up in the drain. There was nothing around for the car to hit and no skid marks leading up to the crash site. It was not surprising that the vehicle remained undiscovered for some time, as the road now only services two mega-sized farms. While the detectives were walking the scene, the car pool attendant rang back. The car got fuel at 9.40p.m. on Friday night – at a service station a long way from the hotel where the deceased was supposed to be staying.

My mind did its own calculations as Ben spoke. "That timing is a bit odd, don't you think? It wouldn't take him until then to drive to the coast. He must have had something else to take care of before refuelling and going on to the hotel," I suggested.

"CCTV footage confirmed the car and the identity of the driver. It also showed the car entering the driveway from the south and heading north towards the hotel after refuelling. They weren't so lucky establishing what he did between leaving the hotel Saturday morning and ending up in the drain on Saturday night. The carpool attended solved some of the mystery a bit later. An interstate transaction on the fuel card came through. Fuel was booked on the card around midday on Saturday, from a service station about an hour's drive over the border."

That didn't make any sense and I said so. "He wouldn't have needed fuel again so soon unless he had driven quite a distance. Perhaps he drove some distance further south before turning around to head for home again, and stopped for fuel before crossing the border back into Queensland."

At this point, Ben looked up and waved his empty glass at me again. He had continued recounting his story of these two incidents, with only sips from his glass punctuating the flow of words. I wanted the story to continue as quickly as possible, but there was a hitch. "Sorry, wine's gone. We're on straight soda water now," I said as I waved the empty wine bottle at him in reply. Well, there wasn't much in the bottle to start with, and I had kept our glasses topped up as he talked. He grimaced in mock horror but beckoned me to fill his glass.

While he drank, I continued speculating. "So, basically, your newly-found friends had two dead people with no apparent reasons for their deaths. Fascinating, but what has it got to do with you, me or Ralston – or Therese Melrose?" I asked as I eyed him over the top of my glass.

"As I said, we were discussing cases over drinks and dinner after the first day of training. I was telling them about my case up in the Gulf country," Ben stopped for another sip and I jumped in.

"What case up in the Gulf? Therese spent quite a few years up in that area before coming to Ralston. Ken and Kate did too. Is that case somehow connected to her death?" I felt a surge of adrenalin as I edged forward in my chair. "Come on, how does it all tie together?" He drank some more, delaying continuing his story – and probably just to test my patience. After what seemed too long, he started to tell me about his case.

"It was about five weeks ago now. A senior public servant, one of the few public servants in the Gulf area, died when his light plane crashed. While there's nothing exceptional about a light plane crash killing its pilot, this pilot was fastidious to the point of obsessive about looking after his plane. You know the sort: pedantic about maintenance, pre-flight checks, the whole bit. He became a bit of a joke among the other flyboys up in that area. All of them are careful, and so they should be when their lives depend on it, but this bloke was considered beyond the pale."

"I guess they have to be, given the remote location and the lack of facilities and support available," I ventured.

"Apparently, the guy travelled a lot visiting the various remote centres under his jurisdiction. On top of that, there were trips to State headquarters for various meetings, as well as to other major centres along the coast. He used to drive everywhere initially but, with the public service staff cuts, he found himself trying to do everyone's job and spending more time driving than working. As a further complication, for a large part of the year, it's almost impossible to drive anywhere up there due to the wet weather and the state of the roads. There are commercial flights in and out of the area but not to where he needed to visit. For a while, he had an arrangement whereby he hired a light plane and the department paid for it. He couldn't always get a plane when he wanted one. As a pilot with an open license and hundreds of flying hours behind him, he wanted the independence of his own plane. He bought one and the department paid running costs when he used it for work."

I nodded. I could understand someone doing just that.

Ben continued. "About 12 months after that, the crash occurred. Light plane crashes are common. However, the air crash investigators found the crash was due to a mechanical problem: a split fuel line. Nobody who knew him believed that."

"I don't remember seeing anything about that in the media," I said, casting my mind back over everything I'd seen or read over the last few weeks.

"No. It made it into the local newspaper, but I don't think it made it into the media outside his home area."

"S-o-o, I'll ask again, how does this tie in with your friends' cases or Therese's death." So far, I couldn't see any connection.

"Okay, I'm getting to that. If you stop interrupting, I'll get to it. You wanted to know what this *thing* was all about, so sit there and listen and you will get to know all about it."

Patronising sod, I thought but bit my tongue and smiled sweetly. "Sorry, please go on." It worked and Ben continued.

"When I knew I was going down for the training program, I rang the air crash investigation mob and asked if their final report was ready yet. They said it would be at least another couple of weeks but, if I was in their area at all, I should call in and they would go over some stuff with me. I flew down a day early and went to see them." Ben went on to explain how they suggested their investigation was now taking a different stance on the cause of the plane crash.

"By then, they were reasonably confident the fuel line had been slit, not split ... well, actually, a combination of both. They explained it looked as though the fuel line was slit, but not right through, leaving a thin layer of the internal wall intact. Once the plane was in the air, the fuel pressure built up in the line causing the thin section of the internal wall to rupture. With the engine starved of fuel, the engine died and the plane crashed. They warned it was only a theory at that stage. They were still waiting for some additional laboratory tests to confirm the theory. I was hoping to get their final report sometime this week but is hasn't arrived yet. If their theory is right, it fits more consistently with what we know of the pilot."

"Okay, so now you and your mates have three suspicious deaths. ... or, perhaps more correctly, three deaths that don't really add up." I had to admit as intriguing as they were, I couldn't see where it was taking us in relation to my Therese Melrose investigation. I sat quietly for a few moments hoping Ben would go on with the story, but he seemed to be deep in thought. I topped up his glass of soda water and that seemed to bring him back to the real world.

"Uhmm, yes, Therese Melrose…," he mused. "What do you remember about what was going on in Ralston the weekend of Therese's death?"

Now it was my turn to sit and think for a few moments. What did I know? Not very much I thought, since I wasn't in Ralston at the time. Was there something important happened? A vague memory hammered for attention and made its way to the front of the queue. "I remember reading something in the newspaper about some bloke committing suicide and, from snippets of conversation I heard in the hotel restaurant, I gather he was some sort of big noise here in Ralston. Some sort of local businessman I think."

Ben clapped his hands in mock applause. "The man owned a travel agency. Please note, not a public servant this time. He was well heeled. Had a posh house, flash car, yacht in the marina, and was philanthropic. Local sporting bodies, community projects and charities all did very well out of him."

Those bodies Ben counted off on his fingers as he spoke. After downing more soda water, he went on painting the picture of this generous soul while I kept trying to remember more of the newspaper article.

"His speciality was organising trips for various groups. You know the sort of thing: the lady bowlers want to do an interstate bowling safari, he organises the bus, accommodation, various games of bowls, throws in a couple of free entry coupons to a show or something, and provides the tour with a host – hostess, tour guide, whatever you call them – to look after everything during the trip. He always manages good prices and doesn't object to a few changes made during the planning process. So, basically, he was everyone's hero."

"And then he died," I added flatly.

"Yes, and the local newspapers ran his suicide story on page one. We managed to get them to correct the story."

"I don't remember seeing that," I said as I ran my mind back over what I recalled from newspapers over the last four days.

"Oh, so you missed the three line article on the second last page of Wednesday's edition?" Ben asked sarcastically.

"Apparently so... what did I miss?"

"That it was a domestic accident. The man was up a ladder hanging a painting on the mezzanine floor level, when he fell from the ladder, went over the railing and landed on the entrance foyer's terrazzo floor below. You can see how it was an accident and not suicide, can't you?" Ben looked at me wide eyed in anticipation.

"Uhmm, was he really hanging a painting? Something tells me that is not exactly what happened."

"Give the lady another glass of soda water. There was no painting, but there was evidence of a struggle up on the mezzanine. Strange that, given he was home alone at the time. His wife has been overseas visiting their children who both live in Europe now."

"So you added him to your list of 'funny' deaths. And I'm guessing you've added Therese to that list as well now." I was aware of a twinge of unease starting to make its presence felt. I didn't know why exactly but I felt that, if Ben continued with his story, I might discover exactly why I should feel uneasy. I told myself I did need to know, and I should steel myself for it.

"Yes. Therese's name is on the list, and I have no desire to add yours to it as well, or anyone else's for that matter."

"Ben, this is a very disparate group whose only connection appears to be the unlikely circumstances of each of their deaths. However, I suspect you and you Metropolitan mates believe there is a stronger link than that, or you wouldn't be so concerned about my safety. What do you think is at the bottom of all this?"

"I can't really say...," he began hesitantly. I cut across him.

"Can't or won't?" I shot back. It was getting late. I was getting tired.

He took a deep breath and sighed. "No, I can't. We don't have enough evidence yet to be sure. The fact that they risked messing about with your car in such a public arena suggests you are getting too close to the truth. I have no doubt it is in some way linked to organised crime – and all the money in Melrose's accounts tends to support that – but how and in what way I don't know. I believe we are close to cracking it. In the meantime, I don't think it is safe for you to be anywhere but here. So, for once in your life, don't give me a hard time and just do as I ask," he demanded.

I agreed. There didn't seem to be any other intelligent option. It was late and my kidneys were awash with soda water. Ben said he was going down to his office to check on something and told me to get some sleep. We said our goodnights and he left. I didn't feel settled enough to sleep so I cleaned up the kitchen and tidied up before heading off to take a shower.

Convinced I still would not be able to sleep, I dug out a book to read in bed. I didn't manage two pages before my eyes closed.

# Chapter Seven

The strange surroundings I glimpsed through half-open eyelids had me disoriented. It shocked me into becoming fully awake. I scanned the room. Recall of the previous night and my relocation flooded back. I relaxed, closed my eyes again and let my mind explore those memories. While pondering information gained from discussions with Ben, I noticed there wasn't a clock in the room. A check of my watch on the bedside table brought me bolt upright in bed. It was way past my usual get-up time, but the comfortable bed lured me back. I lay back, eyes closed, for a few moments before realising I was drifting off again. After mentally prising myself away from the temptation, I staggered, yawning and stretching, in the general direction of the kitchen. Coffee would be good, and I needed to investigate what else might be available for breakfast.

I stifled a scream. As I entered the living area, I saw, out of the corner of my eye, movement at the far end of the lounge. My strangled shriek caused increased movement. From under a rug on the couch, Ben emerged with a silly grin on his face.

"What are you doing here... and how long have you been there?" Relief and anger together produced a volatile mixture. I now knew the couch folded out into a bed – a futon actually by the look of it. I wasn't going any closer to find out.

"Well, at long last I can say I spent the night with you." The grin became even wider as he propped himself up on an elbow.

"You did *not!* You might have spent the night on the couch, but you did not spend it with me. You still haven't explained why you stayed here. Besides, I saw you out last night. So, when did you let yourself back in?"

"We could discuss it over coffee. I could do with a cup about now." He was still grinning.

The heat was beginning to dissipate. It would dissipate even more quickly if he stopped grinning at me like that. "Me too; I'll put some on to brew." I had stopped yelling at him. While waiting for the coffee, I explored the fridge and cupboards. "You can have cereal or a full English breakfast. Take your pick. However, if you choose the full English, you will be preparing it yourself."

"Coffee, cereal and juice will be fine."

We perched at the kitchen bench with our breakfast. After a few sips of coffee, I again tackled Ben about his overnight sojourn.

"I went down to my office and worked for a while after I left here, but I had a niggling feeling about something. In the end, I decided I shouldn't ignore it. So I came back up here about an hour or so after you saw me out."

"This niggling feeling of yours sounds a bit ominous. Is it something I should be aware of?"

"Look, I do have to get down to my office shortly, or they are all going to start wondering why I'm not coming to work today. I'll give you the bare details now and will fill you in on the rest of it later today, or this evening, or whenever. Before I do that, what are your plans for today?"

"Uhmm, I have to ring and try to set up a meeting with Kate. Apart from that, I don't have any firm plans."

"Can't you just deal with Kate over the phone? I'd prefer you stayed here and didn't go out."

"No. I am going to try to have a meeting with her and, unless you have me under house arrest or something, that's exactly what I'm going to do. Now, how about you tell me why you are so concerned. Concerned to the point where you felt compelled to stay here last night."

"Okay, but don't read too much into this just yet. Basically, I have a sneaking suspicion I might have a rotten apple in my barrel."

"A what...? One of your officers is up to something funny?"

"Yeah, that about sums it up. There have been a couple of little things, nothing in themselves, but enough to make me wonder if something not quite right is going on within my team."

"That's a serious doubt to have. But why would it impact on me?"

"As I told you last night, outside of my special team, less than a handful of people know about this flat. More importantly, I supposedly was the only person, outside of the three special guys who brought your stuff up here, who knew someone would be here last night and who that person would be."

"So there wasn't any need for you to be concerned."

"In theory, yes, but my gut told me otherwise and I heeded it. I decided to spend the night. At about four o'clock this morning, someone tried to pick the lock on the door to this flat."

"Eh? Bloody hell!"

"I was ready for them had they come through the door, but they couldn't get it open. It seems like the effort spent in sourcing those special locks was worthwhile. We will discuss this later today but, in the meantime, there are a couple of things I want to put in place."

I felt stunned and not too inclined to argue when he outlined the way he wanted things done. Of course, he made it clear his preference was for me to stay in all day. Somehow, to me, that no longer seemed to be the safest option. I checked my watch. By the time I cleared away the breakfast debris, it would be a reasonable time to try calling Kate. I wanted to catch her before she went out if that was on her agenda for today, but I wanted it to be after Ken left for work. Where to meet was the other problem. I still didn't have a car, and I couldn't bring her here. It needs to be somewhere close by. There's probably less chance of something unpleasant happening if we stay close to the Police precinct.

Kate answered on the second ring. She didn't have much planned for the day but she was about to take the kids to school.

"Good. Can we meet up sometime this morning? There is some stuff to discuss, and a couple of things I'd like you to do if you have the time."

"After I drop off the kids, I've got a solicitor's appointment at nine o'clock. That should only take about half an hour, but it is his first appointment of the day and he never seems to start work on time. Maybe if we plan for ten o'clock, it will leave me enough time to do a couple of other things before we meet. Do you want me to come to the hotel?"

"Er, no; there is a coffee shop a few doors down from the Police Station. It does lovely continental pastries. We could meet there."

"Oh, yes. I know the one. I'll meet you there at 10.00."

Ten o'clock gives me some time to kill before I need to set off for the coffee shop. To help get my head around the things I was going to ask Kate to do, I decided to take another quick look at all the account statements she gave me. I needed more information, but it had to be Kate, or her solicitor, asking the questions as none of the financial institutions were likely to pass on any information to me.

I started shoving all the papers into my bag ready to head off to meet Kate. A knock on the door brought everything to a halt.

Immediately on high alert, I stood riveted to the spot... and totally devoid of common sense. It took a few seconds for common sense to kick in. Get them to identify themselves I told myself, and opened my now very dry mouth to call out. Ben took the initiative and saved me the trouble.

"Sonny, is it okay if I come in?"

"Yeah, come on in. I'm decent."

"That's disappointing," he responded as he came into the room.

"I'll ignore that. What brings you to my door at this hour of the day?"

"I thought I had better check up on what your movements were likely to be today. Just in case... well, you know what I mean."

"I'm meeting Kate shortly. I was about to leave when you arrived. I haven't any other plans after that, so I suppose I'll come back here."

"Give me a call when you are on your way back, or come to my office, and I'll bring you back up here."

"Can't I come back up here by myself?"

"Well, actually, no. It's complicated. I'll explain later. If you are ready to go now, we could go down together."

I rifled through the contents of my bag and found everything I needed there. We rode down in silence. Just before we reached the ground floor, he asked where I was meeting Kate. I gave him my intended destination. He nodded but appeared to be considering my answer. At that point, the doors opened and he extended his arm to hold them open for me to exit first. I made for the front door and headed out onto the street.

The city had come to life for the day by the time I hit the pavement. At least it wasn't raining today. The sound of the traffic was almost overwhelming after the silence of the apartment, and the smell from the chicken diner across the street teased my taste buds all the way to the coffee shop.

It was a few minutes before ten o'clock. Relieved to find the place deserted, I selected a table at the back of the shop, away from the counter and the front windows. A waiter arrived at my elbow the moment I sat down. After indicating I was waiting for company, I commented on the lack of customers in the place. He assured me it would liven up after 11.00 o'clock when patrons start arriving for brunch or lunch. Perfect. Kate and I should be able to speak freely without concern about eavesdroppers.

Kate rushed through the door, stopped and looked around, spotted me and made her way to our table. She threw herself onto a chair facing me and dumped her bag on the floor.

"Sorry I'm late. I got held up everywhere I went this morning."

"You're not late. Relax, take a few deep breaths. I've only been here a couple of minutes. I've been sitting here taking in the tantalising smells of baking pastries coming from the kitchen."

"Coffee and something that smells so good would go down well right now."

The waiter bustled over and took our orders. While he clattered and fussed with the coffee machine, I focused conversation on general topics: how was Ken? How were the kids and had they settled back into school okay? All interesting, but not important. I didn't need to ask how Kate was coping. She looked drained and it was obvious she wasn't sleeping well. Running out of 'polite nothings' to talk about, it was a relief when our orders arrived and the waiter retreated to the kitchen, leaving us alone in the shop.

With the account statements spread out on the table, I launched into my thoughts and questions about each of them. Kate said little during the process, just nodding occasionally and offering 'I don't know' type responses a couple of times. It was time for the hard questions.

"Do you think Ken knows anything about these accounts or how much money Therese had in them?"

"No. No, I'm sure he doesn't know anything. I haven't shown him anything or told him about the accounts. No, I'm sure he doesn't know anything because, a couple of days ago, he commented on how our finances would improve when the estate finally settled. I questioned him and he said we wouldn't be paying rent anymore as the house would be mine."

"Yes, I see your point. By the way, what are his initials?"

"KLN: Kenneth Lawrence Norris. You don't think that KLN Trading account had anything to do with Ken, do you? There was a mountain of money in that account. More than we've earned in our lifetimes." She shuffled through the pile of papers on the table and pulled out the statements for the KLN Trading account. "Look at it," she demanded. "There's no way that could be Ken's."

"Take it easy. I'm not suggesting it is. What we do have to do, however, is find out exactly who does own it, how it was set up and who can operate on this account. That's part of what I wanted to talk to you about."

"I'm sorry. I just don't know what to think anymore."

"What I need you to do, as executrix of Therese's Will, is to approach each of these institutions seeking information on how the accounts were set up and details of any regular periodic transactions. You could use the excuse that anyone involved needs to be advised of the change in circumstances and, if any account is held in more than one name, the other party needs to be contacted as soon as possible."

"Okay, I can do that."

"It is possible you might run into resistance in some quarters. If this happens, explain to your solicitor what we are trying to do, and ask him to try to obtain the information. If that doesn't work, let me know and I will suggest to a friendly detective I know that he applies for a warrant to get the information."

"There are so many accounts, and I have no way of knowing if this is all of them. The solicitor is going to run one of those 'notice to creditors' things in the newspaper early next week. Maybe that will flush out any we don't already know about – or stuff we might prefer not to know about."

We discussed other minor details of Therese's death. The opportunity arose to ask about the missing property: the laptop, phones, and handbag. I suggested she ask Ken about the department's missing gear, and if he thought the department might seek restitution. "You could take the approach that, if the department was likely to seek payment for its missing property, you need to let the solicitor know so it can be taken into account when winding up the estate."

"He hasn't mentioned anything, but I will ask him."

"There is another aspect of this case I find intriguing. When we checked the flat, there were no personal papers anywhere, no cheque books, no bills, nothing personal at all. It was as though it was a display home and nobody actually lived there. Any ideas on how this can be?"

"I hadn't noticed but, now you mention it, I can't remember ever seeing anything like that in the flat. There was always work stuff lying around. You know the sort of stuff: files, piles of signing and reports to read, but nothing personal."

"There wasn't even a file containing receipts and other papers needed to complete a tax return at the end of the financial year, and no bank statements. Is there likely to be anywhere else she could keep that sort of paperwork?"

"Nowhere that I know about; she wouldn't take anything to her accountant until tax time, and there isn't anywhere else she could keep stuff."

"Do you know who her accountant was?"

"No. I know the one she used to use, but she changed accountants last year. I don't know who the new firm is."

"Okay. That looks like another job for your solicitor. See if he can get copies of her last couple of tax returns. They might help shed some light on where all the cash came from, and whether any it was being declared."

Kate scribbled a note of everything required. I stopped speaking to let her catch up. She put down her pen, sat back and flicked through her notes, nodding a couple of times as she did so. Apparently satisfied, she closed the notebook and laid it on the table.

"Right, I think I'm okay with all of that. I'll ring the solicitor straight away to see if I can get another appointment. Sonny, this whole thing is getting more and more confusing. I'm thinking I didn't know my mother at all. I feel so useless not being able to answer the most fundamental questions about her life – well, answer any of them with any certainty at least."

I signalled for the waiter and asked if we could have some water. The meeting had gone longer than anticipated. We had consumed two large coffees each and, after all the conversation, I was feeling parched. The water arrived and we waited until the waiter refilled our glasses before speaking again.

"I'm sorry about dumping so much to do on you. If there is a problem with any of it, let me know and I'll try to work out how to get around it."

"No, no. Thank you. I want to help and I want to know. I want to understand what was going on in her life. What was going on that could have gotten her killed. Do you know if they have a ladies' room here? My kidneys are awash."

Our friendly waiter pointed Kate in the right direction. I quickly dug my phone out of my bag and rang Ben, and hoped he would answer. It rang a few times and I was beginning to feel a bit desperate by the time he answered.

"Sorry, Sonny, I was on my other phone. What can I do for you?"

"Ben, I think I have a problem. You remember I was meeting Kate at that continental coffee place just a couple of doors away from the Police Station?" I didn't wait for an answer and ploughed on. "I think the place is being watched. I noticed a car parked on the other side of the street just after I entered the shop. It parked illegally in a No Standing zone. Anyway, a short while later, a Parking Officer came along and tried to move it on. There seemed to be some sort of brief argument before they eventually drove off. They were gone for maybe ten minutes or so. Kate arrived just after they drove off, so I don't think they saw her arrive. We are sitting right at the back of the shop, so they shouldn't be able to see us from the street. They have parked – again illegally – opposite the coffee shop. I don't want them to know Kate was here, but I don't know how to get her out of the place without them knowing, and I don't want to alarm her."

"Stay put. Don't do anything, but try to keep her there for a bit longer. I'll deal with it."

The call barely ended before Kate arrived back at the table. She made move to pick up her bag to leave. I asked her if she could spare a few more minutes. She wasn't in a hurry and sat down again. I told her I had a couple more things to ask her, but asked her to wait while I went to the ladies' room first. While a trip to the toilets wasn't exactly pressing at this time, it would give me a few minutes to think of what else to talk to Kate about. I lingered as long as might be credible before returning to the table.

As I made my way back, I noticed a commotion going on across the street. The Parking Officer had returned and was trying to issue a parking infringement notice. The $100 fine associated with it probably was of little consequence to those in the car. However, one man, who I assumed to have been an occupant of the car, appeared to have taken umbrage at the situation. He was pushing and shoving the Parking Officer as he attempted to write out the ticket. Just when the aggression level appeared to be escalating, a friendly uniformed police officer wandered along and intervened.

Seated back at the table with Kate, I began a new line of conversation. "Kate, I don't really know too much about Therese's life – or yours for that matter – before you all moved to Ralston. I can't help thinking whatever is at the bottom of this whole mess might have its roots in a time and place before Ralston. I've no idea what I'm looking for but it might be useful if I knew something about that time."

Kate blinked at me a few times as she pondered what I said before replying, "You might be right, but I have no idea where to start. It was all pretty ordinary." Then the moment was lost. Kate looked up slightly startled as Ben slid onto the seat beside me. He had not arrived via the front door. He hijacked the conversation.

"Good morning ladies. Kate, where did you park your car?"

"…In that big public carpark at the end of this block. Is everything all right?"

"We are just being very cautious at the moment," I answered, hoping to sound convincing. The look of alarm that settled across her features tended to suggest I hadn't managed to achieve that.

"Time to go, ladies, and we will be departing via the kitchen," Ben said as he stood up and motioned for us to join him.

Everyone stopped work and watched us as we processed through the kitchen with Ben in the lead. There were only four people in the kitchen. An elderly man, who I took to be the owner, nodded silently to Ben as we passed. The kitchen opened onto a narrow lane running through the centre of the block. It provided access to the rear of the buildings on either side of the block for deliveries and garbage removal. An entrance to the lane was about half way along on the other side of the block. The smell of food long past its prime greeted us as we stepped into the lane. Industrial bins dotted the length of it. Immediately opposite the rear of the coffee shop was the rear of a large department store. It had several bins, all with crushed cardboard cartons and other packing materials protruding from their open tops. Further down the block, closer to the carpark where Kate left her car, were a number of eateries. No doubt, the more pleasing aroma of food cooking emanated from that end of the block.

A woman met us outside the backdoor. Ben introduced her as a plain clothes Police Officer, and explained she would be escorting Kate to her car. He also instructed Kate to use the back exit when leaving the carpark and to take the long way home via the main highway instead of the much shorter route through the city. Both officers were becoming anxious about us standing around in the lane, so I hurriedly said farewell and sent Kate on her way.

"Kate, I think we should go. Given all we don't know about what happened to Therese or why, it is best if we aren't seen together for a while. Keep in touch by phone and let me know how things go with the solicitor. It's probably best if you call me. That way I won't risk ringing you when the kids or Ken are around."

She nodded her understanding as the officer shepherded her away. Ben took my arm, spun me around to face the opposite direction, and we headed back to the Police precinct at a fair pace. We entered the precinct via a door in the precinct's high brick perimeter fence at the far end of the lane. Silence prevailed as he took me up in the elevator and delivered me to my 'quarters'. Once inside, he announced he had ordered in salads for lunch. My watch indicated it was very nearly lunchtime and I silently marvelled at how my life had become a continuous whirl of eating take-away food and drinking coffee – and the odd glass of wine or three.

Ben lowered himself into a lounge chair and said, "Now tell me the whole story, blow by blow from when you left here this morning until you rang me."

I took the chair facing him and focused on a spot on the opposite wall as I let my mind rewind the morning's events. I completed my report and he sat for a few moments, elbows on knees, and contemplating the carpet. Finally, he sat upright and began his interrogation of my story.

"So you didn't see the car until you were sitting in the coffee shop?"

"I'm not sure. I have a feeling it might have been cruising the street when I stepped out onto the footpath. I wasn't really taking any notice at that stage. It was just a car driving down the street. However, in hindsight, I'm almost convinced it was one of the few vehicles on the street at that time. I can't be sure. It might have been just some other black SUV I saw."

"I don't think that's likely. To me, it's obvious they knew you were here."

"That thought occurred to me as well: the work of your 'bad apple' perhaps? Wouldn't I be safer somewhere else? Maybe I should make like the proverbial Arabs and roll up my tent and steal away in the night to some other undisclosed accommodation."

"I agree – not with the bit about the Arabs. The suspect member of my team might have been the catalyst for today's events. From this afternoon, I'll have something in place that will neutralise the problem for a while. I don't agree with your idea of moving somewhere else, but I intend to put it about that you will be moving to some yet undecided new location. I'll tell you about it over lunch, which should arrive in about half an hour or so. See you then."

Ben departed, leaving me to take stock of the day thus far. I had given Kate quite a bit to do but, if the information I asked for was forthcoming, we might be able to start to make sense of things. I suppose it really came down to a question of how good her solicitor was. Asking her about their lives before Ralston had been a bit left field, but it was all I could come up with at the time. Of course, now I remember the story Liz told me about a problem with some bloke from that part of Therese's life. Pity I couldn't remember it when I was with Kate. I might have gotten more details from her.

It now occurs to me that this is something worth pursuing: Therese's life before Ralston. What do I know of it? Not a lot, I don't think. Maybe it is worthwhile documenting what I do know so I can identify where the gaps are. At least that way I'll have more idea of what to ask Kate the next time I talk to her. I grabbed a notebook and started scribbling, listing facts I knew, or thought I knew, and noting questions that arose as I thought about them. A knock at the door interrupted the thought processes. Lunch had arrived.

The Caesar salad with calamari was excellent. We despatched a goodly portion of the meal before allowing conversation to intrude. "This is good, Ben, but I am going to have to run up and down the fire escape a few times to run off all the food and wine I've consumed lately. Tell me about this plan of yours."

"The whole of my special task force is going out to the Army base this afternoon. They will be there for a couple of days – or maybe more – getting further first response and fitness training. I've made it known that I am able to spare them now for a few days, as there won't be any investigations happening in the foreseeable future. I told them that the Metropolitan detectives who have similar cases are coming to Ralston. We will be comparing notes and sifting through information to determine if there are any real links and, if there are, how to progress jointly from this point forward."

"Are they coming, or is that part of the yarn you have concocted?"

"Oh, yes. They definitely are arriving on this evening's plane. The 'yarn', as you call it, got a bit of a response too. One of the team was very interested in how we were going to accommodate them 'seeing as how there was some woman staying in the visitors' unit'. I explained that it wasn't a problem as she was going home today."

"Am I?"

"What?"

"Going home?"

"Don't be daft, of course not. But there was only one person who showed any interest in what you might be doing."

"Did he have 'rotten apple' emblazoned across his forehead?"

"…Didn't need it. His life is now being closely scrutinised by a couple of very hardnosed internal investigators."

"So, am I moving out?"

"No."

"Where are these other detectives going to stay?" I could hear alarm bells. Apart from the fact that it would be a wee bit crowded with three of us in here, I was reasonably certain I didn't want to shack up with two blokes I didn't know.

"A friend of mine is the senior partner in the accounting firm whose offices back onto that lane we walked along earlier today. He has an apartment on the top floor that he doesn't use, not since he got married and built his wife the mansion to which she felt entitled. We have used the apartment before on occasions. The Met boys will be able to exit the building and come into the precinct via the lane without being seen."

Ben gave me a keycard for the elevator. Without it, the elevator won't access this top floor. "You might need this to go down to the front door if you order in food or anything. It works the same as the room electronic keys they use in hotels and motels these days. Every time a keycard is used, there's a record in a log, which only I can access. This card is in my name but I will be able to distinguish between your trips and mine. I won't be checking up on you, but it will provide a good reference point if anything goes wrong. Anyway, I have to go. I'll leave you to enjoy the rest of your day."

With Ben gone, the reality is, I now face an afternoon of doing God knows what to occupy my time. Relying on other people to gather information for me is frustrating. I am not used to working this way, hanging about waiting for others to get me information. No good sitting here gnashing my teeth about it though, best I find something productive to do. I could spend some time going over those phone lists. Maybe something will jump out at me.

Concentrate, Sonny. Look for patterns, any unusual contacts. Damn, that's my phone. Oh, well, all interruptions are welcome at present. Kate: just letting me know she managed another appointment with the solicitor last thing this afternoon while the kids are at football practice and dancing lesson. Only a few minutes later, the phone rang again.

"Hi Sonny, it's Emily. Where are you? Are you still in Ralston?"

"Contrary to plan, yes, I'm still in Ralston."

"Great. I have all of next week off and I'm about to leave to drive to Ralston; should be there about six o'clock this evening. How about we catch up for dinner? Are you still at the same hotel?"

"How can you have more time off? You've only just gone back to work after your last lot of time off."

"I work a roster remember, and things are pretty quiet here at the moment. Global markets are slow and stockpiles are high, so the mine owners have decreased extraction rates for a while. There is nothing much more than cleaning and maintenance operations happening just now. Anyone with accumulated flextime or leave is encouraged to take it. Therefore, I have all of next week off. So, are we on for dinner?"

"Er, give me a call when you get into Ralston and we will work something out. By the way, I've changed accommodation. I'm not at the hotel any longer. I'll tell you all about it later."

Now I have given myself a problem to ponder. I don't suppose I can bring Emily up here, but I'm not supposed to leave the precinct. Somehow, I don't think there will be compliance. Ben didn't mention anything about dinner tonight and he is likely to be busy with his visitors after they arrive. I do have to eat, so I guess I'm just going to have to make my own arrangements.

# Chapter Eight

As arranged, Emily rang to say she had arrived in Ralston and was ready to eat. I still hadn't sorted out how this was going to work, with me supposedly confined to quarters, so to speak. However, it turned out not to be a problem. The aroma of onions and garlic wafting from the restaurant further down the block had assailed my nostrils for a while before she rang. My taste buds were now insisting on something Italian.

Emily explained the apartment she booked for the week was in a multi-level building in Byron Street, adjacent to a two-storey public carpark. A section of the upper floor of the carpark was for the apartment block guests' cars. Sometimes things just fall into place. The rear entrance to the Police precinct was on Byron Street. The carpark Emily mentioned was where Kate parked earlier today, and the restaurant I had in mind opened onto Byron Street. We arranged to meet at *Dominic's Pizza & Pasta* in about 20 minutes.

When we departed the coffee shop via the rear lane earlier today, I noticed the restaurant. It backed onto the lane, and was the only one with a sign over its rear door. I could use the lane again to get to the restaurant virtually unseen. There is a driveway into the lane not far beyond the restaurant. From the lane, it would require only a short walk along the footpath to enter the restaurant's front door. If I left now, I could spend some time checking out the area before making the final dash along the footpath to the eatery. Shoes on, hair combed, a quick check to make sure I had the elevator keycard, and I was out the door. I felt a bit like a teenager escaping through a bedroom window for some forbidden assignation.

It was a very black night, and the lane was virtually devoid of lighting except for a brightly illuminated patch towards the other end, somewhere near where I thought the restaurant was. A narrow vehicular entrance/exit to the lane separated an insurance company's office building from the precinct's high perimeter fence. I would use a similar access way at the other end of the lane to get to the restaurant.

I slipped through the heavy wooden side door in the precinct's fence and waited in the shadows for my eyes to adjust to the darkness.

As I waited, a vehicle's headlight appeared at the far end of the lane. I moved quickly to my left and crouched in a patch of deeper shadow beside an industrial rubbish bin. The lights came along the lane towards me. I flattened myself against the building's rough concrete wall in an attempt to lose myself completely in the shadows. Above my elevated pulse rate I heard the car drawing closer. My heart increased its percussion.

I couldn't duck back through the precinct gate as the vehicle's headlights now brightly lit that area. If the worst scenario happened, this was not a good place for a shoot-out. I extracted the Glock from my bag and slid back the slider. I was taking a few deep breaths to steady myself when the lights turned away. Intrigued, I peered around the bin, and saw the car's taillights disappear out the exit and onto Byron Street.

I stood up and leant on the bin for a few moments while I tried to regain normal breathing and pulse rate. Having decided the best tactic was to move down the lane as quickly as possible, I set off, pausing only briefly in the shadow of each bin I encountered before moving on. I was about half way down the lane when another vehicle drove in from the far end. It pulled up at the rear of Dominic's restaurant. The driver went inside.

It seemed like a good idea to keep moving while I had the lane to myself. I was almost opposite the restaurant when a longhaired youth, loaded with parcels of some sort came out, got into the car and drove off down the lane. As it drove past, I read the sign on the side of the vehicle. Apparently, Dominic's delivered and a number of pizzas were now on their way to various hungry customers.

After a few minutes, no further vehicles having entered the lane, I continued, entered the driveway and stopped just short of the footpath. More waiting around in the shadows. I waited, checking out the passing traffic for anything that looked even vaguely suspicious. At that point, my greatest danger appeared to be the untimely arrival of another delivery driver who became curious about some strange woman standing here in the dark. One deep breath and I was out on the footpath, past the intervening shop and into the restaurant.

It was early so there were few diners yet. In an earlier life, the place probably was a milk bar or café. Although modernised with an appropriate 'Mediterranean' décor, it retained two of the original booths at the rear of the dining area. Both featured dark stained timber and red vinyl covered upholstery. I chose the one with the best view of the street. Emily arrived only a couple of minutes later and I waved her to the booth. We opened the night with general small talk and studied the menu as wait staff brought cutlery and wine. We ordered a shared platter of fresh asparagus with hollandaise sauce for entrée, and for mains, Emily chose a vegetarian lasagne and I ordered fettuccine carbonara.

When eventually left to ourselves, Emily could control herself no longer. "What's happening with the case? I thought you would be back in Millhaven by now."

"Ah, yes. Well, so did I, but things became 'curiouser and curiouser' – to quote the White Rabbit or whoever it was – and they have also taken a bit of a nasty turn."

"I thought it was established that Therese's death was murder and the Police had taken over the case."

"True. However, Kate brought me some new intriguing information and I needed to dig around in it a bit before I felt confident about passing it on to the Police. It seems I managed to prod a few nerves along the way. There was a strange incident with my car, and today I appeared to be under surveillance by some pretty unsavoury looking people."

Kate's eyes widened. "Go on. Don't stop there. What sort of incident?"

A brief intermission followed for entrees' arrival and wine glass refilling. Then, as concisely as I could, I gave Emily a rundown on Kate's new information, the car incident and my relocation to my present abode. She sat silently throughout, only nodding or shaking her head at various intervals. Emily had only picked at her food and I had eaten little. It is difficult to talk and eat at the same time. I noticed wait staff eyeing off our table.

"Perhaps we should finish the asparagus before we go any further, don't you think?"

"Eh? Oh, yes. Let's eat while I try to digest all you have told me so far." She raised her eyebrows enquiringly. "I'm sure there is more to tell."

I simply nodded, and wondered how much I should tell. "The wait staff will descend upon us again in a minute, so perhaps we should discuss something more innocuous until things settle down again. How are your parents? Are you going to head up to Millhaven to spend some time with them this week?"

"No, not a chance; visiting home is not high on my priority list at the moment, although I am a bit concerned about things there."

"Are they all right? I haven't heard from your mother, not since the day after she went home I think. I admit I'm a bit surprised, as I expected her to be badgering me for updates."

"I don't think she is allowed."

"Eh? What do you mean by 'not allowed'?"

"I don't know exactly. I haven't heard from her this week, which is most unusual. However, my sister said Mum was concerned about the way our father is behaving. It would appear he has become very irritable and dictatorial. I always thought he was a domineering old sod, but Mum would always disagree. She puts this change down to his job as the director. You know the mantra: so much stress from Public Service job losses and budget cuts, blah, blah."

"Yeah, and while those things have always been there, the situation under the new Government has become worse. There would be more pressure on directors these days," I offered as explanation.

"Yes, I can accept all that, but there's more to it than that. Those are work-related issues. My concern is for the things that are happening at home."

"Such as…?"

"Well, for starters, apparently mum has been told not to talk to me about the Therese thing. On the couple of occasions she rang me after she got back, I'm told he quizzed her – more like interrogated her – about what was discussed. Bloody cheek of him! He's scrutinising the phone account and she thinks he is checking her emails. If she goes out, he wants to know where to, why and who she has spoken to."

"If it is as you say, it is worrying. You don't think your mother might be reading more into it than there is?"

"No, I think there is something going on. Even the last time she rang me, there was something … I don't know … something furtive almost about the brief conversation we had."

"Would it not be better for you to go home and look into it, rather than staying here and avoiding the issue?"

"No. I love them both, but my father and I clash all the time. He is always trying to tell me how to live my life, how to do my job, telling me to get a promotion, questioning why I haven't got married. If I went home, I've no doubt I would end up making the situation worse."

"I am starting to feel concerned that our association might be contrary to improving your situation with your family. I'm certainly not the one to be giving you advice, but I would suggest you give your mother a ring sometime and see how that goes."

Our main course dishes arrived and the wait staff withdrew. After a couple of mouthfuls, Emily's curiosity kicked in again. "Back to more important matters: tell me about today's incident with Kate."

I explained the purpose of the meeting in the coffee shop and the factors leading to my asking Ben to rescue us. It also gave me the opportunity to stress how, for her own safety, she should not be seen with me. She had walked from the apartment to the restaurant and I held some niggling concerns about her walking back alone at the end of the night. Perversely, she was convinced she would be perfectly all right and refused to discuss it further.

We discussed the information I asked Kate to arrange for her solicitor to gather for me, and I whined on about my frustration at not being able to chase it down myself. The zabaglione she ordered for desert finally arrived. I wasn't having desert so, while she ate, I continued to whinge about going home and the other clients who expected my return by the following week.

The evening flew. It was nearing ten o'clock, and we had reached the point where it was obvious we were talked-out. We said our goodbyes and Emily left. I ordered a coffee and settled our bill when it arrived. The shop between the restaurant and the entrance to the lane was undergoing renovations. As I drank my coffee, I noticed the level of noise from saws and hammering had increased considerably since my arrival. I also noticed two tradesmen's vehicles parked in the entrance to the lane. It was so narrow I was surprised the two could park side by side. However, I knew it would allow little room for me to slip quickly and quietly down that driveway and into the lane.

What I needed was an opportunity to leave inconspicuously. There had been no black SUV or anything else worthy of my attention, but I held the belief that one can't be too cautious. A rowdy group of young ones in the front corner of the restaurant were celebrating the birthday of one of their number with obligatory cake with sparklers, and loud rendition of 'Happy Birthday'. They started to leave. I trailed out after them. To my relief, they were heading in same direction. As we oozed along the footpath as a constantly changing mass, I moved to the inside of the group. By staying close to the shop fronts, I hoped to look like one of the group while remaining inconspicuous.

We were about 50 metres along the street when a stunning red-headed girl in the group asked if everything was all right. My constant checking the street for traffic had caught her attention. I gave her my best smile... and lied. "Yes. I'm just visiting and was wondering what else might be in this street."

"Only the nightclub over the road just up ahead of us. That where we're heading. Is that where you are going as well?"

"Me? Oh, no, I'm just going to walk off my meal and then go back to my room. I've had a big day."

I almost choked mid-sentence as a black SUV cruised past. It continued on, the bright lights out front of the nightclub partially illuminating the interior of the vehicle as it drove by.

We only walked another four or five metres before the leaders of the group wheeled off and headed across the road. I hung back as they all straggled off the footpath and onto the road. As the last of them moved to the edge of the footpath, I slipped into the doorway of the nearest shop. It was a reasonably dark recess only faintly lit by the soft lighting woven through the window display of various bits of female apparel. I have no idea exactly what was in the window. My attention remained glued to the taillights of the SUV as it continued along Byron Street.

From my darkened recess, I watched it until it turned the corner at the top of the street. Then I took off at a flat out sprint – not easy after an indulgent Italian meal. My thinking was that, if I went down the entrance driveway to lane, I'd be out of sight from the street and I could enter the precinct again through the side door. I was within three metres of the driveway. The lights of a car coming out of the lane shone out onto the street. A decision on the fly required. I'm too exposed. I can't stop and wait for it to pass. Summoning every bit of pace I could muster, I charged across the driveway in front of the startled driver, and kept running the extra 20 metres or so along Byron Street to the back entrance to the police precinct.

As I dashed through the entrance, I scanned the area. To my right, the courtyard was well lit, and there were a number of patrol vehicles nosed up against the perimeter fence. The left side of the courtyard was in shadow. I headed left, still running hard. On this side, a few vehicles were parked front-on to a long, low brick building running at right angles to the main building.

The shadows along the side of the building were my friends. I kept well back in them as I weaved my way along the side of the building until I came to an open doorway. In almost complete darkness, I raced in through the doorway, immediately banging into something metallic and then almost tripped over something on the floor. My hand stretched out in front of me to save myself from falling, found something that felt like a large drum. It was metal and wasn't likely to bite, so I slipped around beside it. I tried to regain control of my breathing. So much eating and drinking certainly hadn't done anything for my fitness. It made me pleased I'd settled for a two-course meal and not indulged in dessert as well.

Uncertain what to do next, I took a few moments to gather my thoughts, and to work out where I was. My memory of the layout of this back end of the precinct suggested this might be the vehicle workshop. The smell of oil and fuel assailing my nostrils tended to confirm the assumption. I stiffened. There was a slight noise and I thought I glimpsed a shadowy movement at the doorway.

"Sonny, Sonny, are you in here?" Ben's voice loud and clear through the dark stillness of the workshop.

"Thank you for announcing my presence."

Quieter, only a stage whisper this time. "What are you doing in here? What the hell are you up to?"

"Trying not to be seen."

"Why not come into the station? Why hide in here?"

"I would have had to cross a fair stretch of well-lit courtyard to get to the back door."

"Why was that a concern?"

"...Probably had something to do with a black SUV cruising Byron Street. I think it was the same black SUV that caught our attention this morning."

"Did they see you?"

"No, I don't think so. But, the SUV had four occupants: two in the front, and two in the back – with rifles."

"Rifles! Are sure?"

"Yes. I saw very clear silhouettes of the rear passengers as the car passed the nightclub. It was lit up by those searchlight things out the front of the nightclub."

"Come on. Follow me and stay close."

He ran towards the station end of the workshop. I followed as precisely as I could at about half a pace behind him. He seemed instinctively to know his way through the dark workshop. Although I followed so closely, I on the other hand, managed to bump into several things along the way, including something large, metal and immovable. I yelped. He hissed 'keep up' as he punched in a code to open a door in the end wall of the workshop. We rushed through into a brightly lit hallway in the main station building.

Ben shouted for me to follow him as he continued running down the hallway. I watched him disappear into a side room, but I wasn't following him. I stopped to inspect my damaged shin. A fair sized egg had developed on it. It probably wasn't life threatening, so I hobbled on down the hallway to find Ben. I heard him before I found him. He was barking orders over the radio. "... Just saunter around as though you are out for a stroll. Don't draw too much attention. Maybe wander over to the nightclub to check out the crowd."

"We're at the nightclub now. Good crowd in tonight. ... Sir, black SUV ..."

There was a brief pause before the same voice crackled over the radio again. It recited a string of letters and numbers. I assumed they were from a vehicle's plate. Ben told the voice on the other end of the radio to hang around the nightclub for a few minutes before wandering back to the station. Then he spoke to the duty officer sitting at the desk beside him. "Run a check on that registration for me."

"...On it; it's coming through now. It's a hire vehicle registered to Elite Hire Cars."

"O-o-h, so it's one of Barney's. Email that info to me, please."

"It's on its way."

"Thanks. Ah, when Smith and his partner get back, could you ask them to hang around for a bit until I get a chance to have a chat to them."

That taken care of, Ben turned to face me. I groaned inwardly. Here it comes. "Come on. You're going back upstairs."

I smiled sweetly and fell in behind him. We rode the elevator in silence. Ben strode ahead, opened the door and ushered me inside before shutting the door behind him with probably a touch more force than was required. Oh, yes. This is not going to be pretty.

Ben went through and plonked down on one of the lounge chairs. I stopped in the kitchen and filled a plastic bag with ice cubes from the fridge. I was tying the bag around my calf when Ben noticed I hadn't joined him.

"What are you doing?"

I explained about my shin.

"You will probably end up with a good bruise out of it. Now, suppose you sit down and tell me exactly what you were doing out on the street tonight. I put you here so we could keep you safe ... just in case you've forgotten why you are here."

"Emily came to town, and I needed dinner, so we met up at Dominic's to eat and chat."

"I want details of this evening, and I mean everything, from the moment you left this apartment till I found you in the workshop. Every detail, even if you don't think it's important. Is that clear?"

I tried to look suitably chastened and nodded. Then I began the long story of my night out. The tale progressed slowly, punctuated by many questions from Ben. I finished my report and he sat silently mulling it over. I decided to break the silence.

"It was good to have someone not involved with the case to talk to, especially as she already knew about the early stages of it."

"Yes, but did you gain anything useful from the risk you took?"

"Hmm, I'm not sure. A little voice in the back of my mind is telling me I did, but I can't work out what it was. Maybe if I sleep on it, it will become clearer in the morning. By the way, it was a bit of luck getting the registration number of that SUV."

"Luck didn't have anything to do with it. Sergeant Smith saw someone dash through the back entrance. They had just come in from patrol, and were sitting in the car chatting before coming into the station. At some point, as you ran along in the shadows, he caught a decent glimpse of you. He rushed in to tell me the 'Private Investigator woman' was behaving strangely and had disappeared into the workshop. I sent Smith and his partner out to wander casually around in Byron Street, but to keep an eye out for a black SUV. It drove past as I was talking to them on the radio."

"So, who is Barney?"

"Barney?"

"When the Duty Officer told you who owned the vehicle, you said it was one of Barney's."

"Oh, Barney Fellowes; he owns Elite Hire Cars. I'll have a chat to him in the morning."

It was getting late and I hoped my earlier mention of sleep might give him the hint to leave. I became a bit concerned when he didn't appear in any hurry to move. Then I remembered.

"Hey, don't you have someone hanging about waiting for you downstairs?"

"Hell, Smithy. I forgot all about him. I'd better go."

"You're not going to spend the night here again are you?"

"Thinking about it … or maybe taking the keycard off you."

I was about to protest, but he intervened.

"Relax. No, I'm not staying here tonight. However, I do want an assurance that you are not going to leave this apartment until I see you again. Do I have your word?"

"Okay." There wasn't any argument worth having. All I wanted right now was a shower and sleep. At last, Ben made a move to leave but not before once more seeking reassurance that I was not going to leave the apartment.

The shower was good, but sleep eluded me. I tried reading but found myself too buzzed in some way to become sleepy and abandoned the idea. There probably wasn't anything worth watching on TV at this hour of the night – almost morning – but it might help me switch off. The least offensive thing I could find was a rerun of the 1953 movie, *Shane*. I watched it, mind in neutral, for about an hour before I felt my eyelids starting to droop. This time I felt confident sleep would not be elusive. Wrong again. The moment my head hit the pillow, I was awake once more. Okay, I'll get up again and do something; anything except watch TV.

I hoped reciting the evening's events in detail to Ben would bring to the fore whatever nagged me about my conversation with Emily. It hadn't worked, but it did strengthen my conviction that I had missed something. When all else fails, make notes. Sometimes the process of documenting events helps clarify the details.

That process took the best part of an hour. Then I read over my notes slowly, thinking about each statement of fact I had recorded. I skimmed over the comment I recorded about using small talk to fill in while the wait staff cleared the entrées and brought our main courses. Then I chastised myself. If you're going to detail something, you need to detail it. There's no point in skimming over it.

What did we talk about? Somewhere I could hear a little bell ringing, urging me to look deeper. Think about what we said. I turned to a new page in my notebook and started to document that part of the evening's conversation. It started as dot points that I then fleshed out until it felt I was trying to record it verbatim. Convinced I had recorded it all, I sat back and reread my transcript of that part of the evening's conversation with Emily.

It was obvious I was far too dismissive of the comments about her father's behaviour. I should have pressed her for more details. Had she simply given me a summary of what she knew, or was that the extent of her knowledge of the situation at home? I shared her opinion of her father as far as his domineering was concerned but, to my mind, the way he was treating Sandra was no surprise. He always treated her as being insignificant in the overall scale of things. I think they got on well. It was evident she idolised him and was loyal to a fault. In the last phone call I had from her, she said her husband told her to stay out of the Therese 'thing'. In hindsight, I now suspect she might have neglected to mention that his instructions included severing contact with me. I was certain my suspicions were right: she had made her last phone call to me covertly.

What was he playing at? Sandra loved gossip but was always circumspect – perhaps cautious is a better word – about what she passed on. I came to know her reasonably well during my days with the Department, and classed her as a friend, not one of my closest, but a friend nevertheless. She had trouble settling in and making friends after moving to Millhaven. Her forthright manner and, on occasions, rather astringent tongue probably contributed to the situation. An extremely intelligent, well-educated woman, she married young, and settled for various lesser jobs to help support and educate her daughters while her husband carved out a career in the Public Service. Both girls obtained post-graduate degrees and had done very well for themselves in their chosen fields.

During my time with the Department, I avoided any social contact with her husband. After all, he was the Director, and I didn't want to appear to be brown nosing. Apart from that, I didn't particularly like him. He came across as affable and caring, but underneath, was as hard as hell and not to be trusted – to which many former, now ex-Public Servants would attest. His focus was always on self, his image, and pleasing his superiors at any cost. However, that aside, his current behaviour as Emily tells it is way out of keeping with my assessment of him.

I needed to quiz Emily to determine how much she knew. Had she given me just a summary of the situation, or was there something more specific, perhaps something she didn't realise was important? At the end of my notes, I started jotting down questions to ask the next time I had opportunity to talk to her. She must be encouraged to ring her mother soon – Monday would be good, when her father was at work. That he was one of the anointed few as far as his superiors were concerned became clear soon after his appointment as director. As such, he probably had suffered a lot less in the Public Service's current difficult times than other department directors.

Emily's comments pinpoint the time for the supposed change in his behaviour as immediately after Therese's death. Therese was one of his two deputies – and his favourite – but his reaction was out of keeping with the situation. Given the circumstances, it is particularly strange that his wife should be on the receiving end of his behavioural change. Have there been similar restrictions imposed on department staff members as well? I might ring Liz again, if she will talk to me.

There could be little doubt Therese's death hit the director hard. They were more than colleagues. They were good friends. She could get around him when nobody else could. In spite of that, his treatment of her reduced her to tears on more than one occasion. They worked together out west and, in most people's minds, he was instrumental in her getting the Ralston position. He wasn't a director when he was out west. His move to the coast secured that promotion. This much I knew. What else did I know about his time prior to his moving back to the coast? I started mining my memory banks, revisiting old conversations with Sandra, and exploring long forgotten gossip.

Geoff took a western posting as Deputy Director of a small sub-section of the Department as a step on the way to landing a director's position at some time down the track. The appointment was supposed to be for a couple of years, but lasted four years. This might have been due to a lack of vacant director's positions over the intervening years. However, during the period of his western appointment, he often undertook special projects for the Director General. As they entailed travel and work in other regions, Therese filled in for him as Acting Deputy Director in his absence.

Despite Therese supposedly having gone through the normal recruitment process for the Ralston job, she never was fully accepted – or trusted – by the majority of the institute staff. They saw her appointment, and those of a couple of other former western staff, as 'jobs for the boys' rather than merit-based. Many saw Therese as the Director's man on the inside. Millhaven campus staff was prone to accusing her of lying. If I were generous, I would say she was proficient at swimming with the tide … and the tide frequently changed direction. I experienced being told to do something, only to have her deny it later when she found it to be contrary to the Director's thoughts on the subject. Her best description might be: a well-practised Public Servant who had learned how to achieve a long career in the Department.

All of this brings up that western connection again. Maybe I was more astute than I realised when I asked Kate to give me some background on their lives prior to Ralston. I must pursue that line at my first opportunity.

There was nothing more I could do for the moment, so I reclined my lounge chair and lay back to mull over what I had gleaned from the last couple of hours' work. I was aware of a developing faint prickling of apprehension (why, I wonder), and more than a hint of the thrill of the chase as my eyelids grew heavy. At last, sleep no longer deserted me.

# Chapter Nine

Old habits die hard, particularly well-practiced ones. Despite only a few hours' sleep, I awoke at my usual time – still in the lounge chair and stiff all over. I swear various bits of me creaked and cracked as I extricated myself from the chair. Upright and finally mobile, I went in search of something to wear today. No decision required. I was down to my last set of anything clean. Oh, well, it looks like bike shorts and a tee shirt today. Just as well I am not going anywhere other than this apartment. The time had come to make the acquaintance of the washing machine and dryer hidden in a sort of cupboard arrangement just off the bathroom.

Nothing too complicated confronted me, so I dumped in the first load of washing. Fortunately, I still had some laundry detergent left from the laundry I did while at the hotel. While the first load washed, I got dressed and remade the bed that I had messed up for nothing the previous night. A large part of my shin over and around the lump was now deeply coloured, and the pain from the jarring at every step reminded me of last night's escapade.

The first load finished. I dumped it in the dryer and started the second load in the washing machine before heading to the kitchen in search of breakfast. There was cereal (which I didn't feel like), croissants (which I'm not fond of for breakfast) in the freezer, and enough of everything for a full English. Confident I could not handle a full English breakfast, I settled for toast and coffee.

I retrieved the phone records I intended to look at yesterday. Studying them was better than staring at the wall while I munched my toast. Perched at the breakfast bar, I spread the phone records out along the length of the counter. With no idea of what more could be gleaned from them, I was hoping something previously dismissed as unimportant would take on new meaning, and perhaps scream at me. I started with Therese's work mobile and her office landline accounts. All numbers on these accounts had names against them. There was the odd private call amongst them (doctor, hairdresser, Kate) but most were legitimate work-related numbers. Some numbers appeared more frequently than others – for example, the Director's number – but they were consistent with the demands of the job.

As I skimmed down the first page of her office phone account, the last number on the page caught my eye: Mitch Johnstone. Mitch was a Millhaven-based staff member. Therese was not his line manager and it would be contrary to protocol for her to be ringing him in anything but exceptional circumstances. I sat staring at his number. Mitch's details came to mind: probably mid- to late-50s now, finally made the lowest rung of the management ladder at least ten years ago and not progressed further since.

A bit too fond of booze and women, he was not a particularly good manager either. My assessment of him was that he was not overly bright. I always thought he got his present position by being the only person to qualify for the internal appointment at the time; sort of example of a 'last man standing' situation. We had worked closely and affably together for a number of years, but he often required guidance and direction. I flicked over to the next page and quickly scanned the names of those called. Interesting; Mitch's name appeared twice on that page.

Almost certain an 'ah hah' moment was about to occur, I grabbed a highlighter pen and searched through to the end of the account, highlighting all calls to Mitch's number. Most were to his work number, but there were three to his home number as well. Final assessment: Therese called Mitch far too many times for it not to be an important factor. In view of this, Therese's work mobile phone account was worth a look as well. Surprise, surprise! Mitch's number appeared a few times on that list too.

This then posed questions. Was there something happening at Millhaven that required Therese's involvement? Had she called other Millhaven staff and, in particular, higher ranking management staff? I was pondering this – and whether to get up and make more toast – when my phone rang. It was Emily and she seemed to be in the mood for a chat.

Her first concern was whether I got home safely the previous night. Better to lie than face a barrage of questions about last night's events. Her mind at ease on that score, she moved on to the next question: would I like to accompany her to a show tonight? Three or four of her friends were in a play staged by a local amateur theatre group. Part of her reason for coming to Ralston was to take in the show. It wasn't too hard to decline the invitation, citing my current confinement as an excuse.

The conversation then turned to some of the issues we discussed over dinner. She had devoted considerable thought to some specific points of our conversation. What could she do on Monday to assist me? It was clear she wanted to be involved again and was keen to plan that involvement. Some convincing was required before she accepted that, apart from ringing her mother, there was little to do until Kate's solicitor managed to get hold of further information. While we chatted, it occurred to me to ask her about her father's time out west. I knew she had visited a few times over the four years he was there, but I suspected she wouldn't have much useful information to contribute.

She agreed to think about it and make note of any names or events she remembered from that time and place. During our conversation, I managed, one-handed, to remove the clothes from the dryer and replace them with the load of wet ones from the washing machine. On my way back to the kitchen, I dumped the dry clothes on a lounge chair. With Emily's call ended and the few breakfast things washed, dried and put away, I returned to the phone lists. The frequency of calls to Mitch Johnstone had tweaked my curiosity about other calls she made.

It seemed the most effective way of determining the frequency of calls to the various names on the lists was to combine all the information into one list and then sort it by name. I booted up the computer and started copying and pasting. I had just completed the task and was admiring my handiwork when my phone rang. I recognised Ben's number.

"Good to see you are up and about – and still where you are supposed to be. I'll be up in about 15 to see you."

Fifteen Minutes! Just about time to lose the pile of underwear off the lounge chair and tidy up a bit before he arrives. I took the washing through to the bedroom, folded it and put it away. The dryer stopped its monotonous racket and I retrieved its load of clothes. Some I folded while the bits needing ironing were stowed in the cupboard out of sight. A quick straighten up in the kitchen and lounge area, and I was ready for Ben's visit. With still a few minutes to spare before he arrived, I returned to my new combined list of phone calls.

A sort by name took only moments. I checked the entries for Mitch Johnstone and discovered I had missed a couple during my previous search. Good. That proves the effort of creating this new combined list was worthwhile – and it showed Mitch Johnstone was a popular lad.

My phone was on the kitchen counter when Ben rang. I had the paper copies of the various phone lists in my hand as I answered it and, during the brief conversation, I placed the lists in a neat pile on the end of the counter. I remembered them and went to retrieve them. That's when Ben arrived, accompanied by two strangers. I stared at the group. I didn't think strangers at my door were a part of my safety plan. I was about to voice this when Ben cut in. "I brought muffins. Hot from the bakery," and he and his companions marched in, with Ben leading the way with the bag of muffins held aloft like some standard-bearer.

"Good morning. Do come in," was all I could manage, with just a hint of sarcasm thrown in for good measure.

"This is David and Greg. They are the two Metropolitan detectives I told you about," Ben announced. "How about coffee so we can get stuck into these muffins while they are still warm? That shin is coming along nicely I see."

"Hope we haven't interrupted anything," David – or was it Greg – said apologetically.

I had lost interest in being peeved by then so, as I made the coffee, I reassured them they were welcome. We retired, armed with coffee and muffins, to the lounge area. I noticed one of the Met blokes was clutching my phone lists that I had left on the kitchen counter. Do help yourself, I thought. He placed them on the floor by his feet as Ben launched into the reason for the visit.

Before rescuing me, Ben spent the earlier part of last evening with his counterparts comparing notes about their individual cases. Their discussions resumed earlier this morning and, apparently, they were now convinced a strong link existed between all their cases, and hence the visit. They wanted to know how much more I could contribute that might be of import to their investigations.

"I don't think I have anything more to add. I've handed over everything I uncovered to Ben. I'm hoping I might get more information this week, but I'm not at all confident."

The one (I'd now worked out he was Greg) with my phone lists bent down and collected them from the floor. "These look interesting, and I see you've highlighted some entries; any particular significance?"

"I was skimming through them over breakfast and a name that I thought strange to find on the list jumped out at me. I decided to check if it was an isolated call, or whether it appeared elsewhere on the lists."

"If it is the one highlighted, it appears to have been called a few times."

"Yes, and there are another couple that I missed on the way through." I explained my reservations about Therese's calls to Mitch Johnstone. They had stirred my curiosity about the frequency of calls to other numbers on the lists.

"A combined list would be useful for that," Ben suggested.

"I had just finished creating one when you rang this morning. I sorted it by name, but haven't had a chance to look at it since, except, I did check up on Mitch Johnstone's entries. That's when I found I had missed two."

David looked at Ben expectantly and said, "That could be useful."

I moved to the computer and printed a copy of the combined list.

"Just one copy will do. I'll slip downstairs and make photocopies for all of us." Ben assured us it wouldn't take long and I called after him to make a copy for me as well. A spare copy might come in handy at some stage.

While Ben was away, his colleagues tried their hand at light conversation. Light conversation that consisted primarily of questions about what they clearly saw as some sort of strange hobby on my part: how long had I been a private investigator? How did I ever get involved in such stuff? What *real* work did I do to support myself? Then finally, they confided that their trip north had been 'valuable'. The latter accompanied by knowing nods and looks but no indication of how it proved valuable. I smiled sweetly and told myself, that's fine guys, but I will get details of how valuable just as soon as I get Ben alone again. Ben's return ended my enforced politeness.

Unfortunately, the exercise in polite conversation during Ben's absence did waste time and prevented me from getting on with examining the list of phone numbers still up on my computer screen. It seems Ben had never done the module on how to use a photocopier. Some time was lost after his return in making sure everyone had all the pages and in the right order. While the blokes sorted themselves out, I went back to scanning my computer screen.

Oh yes, chalk up one for me. It was a petty victory, but those arrogant males who treated my occupation with such disdain were going to find it hard going without my knowledge of many of the names on that list. Most of the calls were to staff members or contractors the department used on a regular basis. Best described as routine calls Therese would make in the normal course of her job. Nothing interesting there. Some, like those to Mitch Johnstone, might appear okay, but it was a knowledge of who they were and the frequency of the calls that raised questions in my mind. There was a whole raft of other names. While I recognised some, others I had never heard of. Some of this contingent of names triggered serious alarm bells for me.

Some of the ones that received a lot of calls were names I only recognised from the newspapers. Their owners were not among the finest upstanding citizens of this State or country. It's true, there was nothing proved in many cases, but some of those names were associated with various less than salubrious activities over the past few years. So intently had I been perusing the list that I wasn't aware someone was speaking to me.

"Sonny, Sonny! Would you mind joining us back here on earth for a few minutes?"

I tore my eyes away from the screen to see all three men looking at me. "Sorry, Ben; I was having a quick look at the list now that it is sorted. What were you saying?"

"We were commenting on the heavy traffic on some of those numbers."

"Hmmm yes, but in some instances they would have been routine work-related calls. They probably could be discounted although ... uhmm ... there might be some unusual activity in there that wouldn't immediately be obvious." Ben opened his mouth to comment, but caught my steely glare, and decided against it.

All three returned to flipping over their photocopied pages. After a brief period, Ben broke the prevailing silence. "Christ, look at the time. Don't you blokes have an appointment down at the harbour in about ten minutes? Better make a move I think, or you are going to be late."

Everyone consulted their watches. The two Met guys rose together and made to leave. "Thanks, Ben. We completely lost track of time. It is important we don't get this interviewee offside before we begin."

Ben walked out with them. I found myself alone in the apartment and feeling more than a little offside with the world. I cleared away the remnants of coffee and muffins before going back to the phone list. This time I took the photocopy Ben left for me and sat at the breakfast bar, accompanied by a pen and a collection of coloured highlighters.

I took a deep breath and started at the top of the list. First things first: identify all of the routine work-related numbers that don't appear to have abnormal call frequency. This proved slow going as I was determined not to hurry and to thoroughly consider each name before forming any conclusions. Was the person called only called on a regular work number? Was the frequency of calls reasonable given the person's association with the department? The first three names on the list I assessed as being okay. I was about to do the same for the next name when something in my subconscious made me pause.

There was nothing obviously abnormal, but something kept telling me there was. After considering it for a few heartbeats and still not seeing anything that could be cause for concern, I fetched the computer and brought up a calendar for the time involved. Ah hah! Why was Therese calling this quite unimportant administration assistant on weekends, and at around midnight on other occasions? Definitely not normal. I highlighted the entries and made a note in the legend I was developing, that the colour used to highlight these entries signified they required further investigation as suspicious calls to staff members. I returned to the first three names and subjected them to further scrutiny.

The first one I decided was definitely okay. I was about to tick off on the second name as well when a vague memory struggled to get my attention. That person I knew was a staff member and had been with the department for many years before I joined it. He was still there when I left, but I vaguely remembered there was something about him. I logged onto the internet and typed in his name, and got heaps of irrelevant information for my trouble. I revised the query to include the name of the department as well.

Oh, yes, Sonoma Whittington, you are hot today, albeit a bit slow, but hot, nevertheless. On the screen was the information my mind was trying to recall. The man was employed by the department for many years, initially out west as a storeman and then on promotion to Ralston. Then, about three years ago, he transferred back out west to be their purchasing officer. Why would Therese have been phoning him so often recently? He was no longer a part of her staffing. I noted the query beside the man's name on the copy.

After counselling myself sternly about thoroughly studying each name before making hasty decisions, I moved on to the next name on the list. I hadn't progressed too far through the list when I a loud knock at the door startled me. I sat upright and froze, hesitant to answer the knock as no one was supposed to know I was here. Ben's voice relieved the tension of the moment.

"Sonny, it's me, Ben. Open the door, please." He entered carrying a carton that smelled heavenly. "I wanted to have a chat to you and thought we might as well do it over lunch."

I glanced at my watch; time had gotten away. It was a late lunch, but I hadn't felt hungry until I smelled the chicken Ben brought. Crumbed chicken bits and salad dished out, we sat at the kitchen counter to eat. It became clear that it was up to me to initiate the chat Ben had suggested. "You wanted to talk to me? What about?"

"Firstly, I wanted to let you know you are no longer here."

"Oh, good. Have I gone home by any chance? It still feels a bit like Ralston Police Precinct to me."

"You moved out last night actually, just before your escapade on Byron Street."

"Okay, maybe you had better tell me about it. I would hate to miss out on the details of my flit to freedom."

"Not freedom exactly. We used a police officer that's about... You know what she looks like. She's the one who walked Kate to her car yesterday."

"She's a pretty stunning natural blonde. I don't think she would fool anyone that she was me."

"She is about the same size: add a dark wig, jeans instead of uniform. In low light, no one would pick the difference."

"So where have I gone because, apparently, I haven't gone home."

"No. Just to a hotel a couple of streets away. The policewoman went in with a bag and a trolley with a couple of boxes out of our storeroom, hung around for half an hour, and then came out – minus the wig and in uniform – to be collected by a patrol car and brought back here. We have another couple of officers staying in the hotel room in case anyone comes looking, or hotel people are persuaded to talk about who is staying there at the moment."

"So I remain quarantined here?"

"This way, only you and I know you are still here."

"... And your mates from the Met Branch."

"They don't count."

"... And your 'rotten apple'."

"Ah, yes, for the moment, but he will find out tomorrow that you have relocated."

"Anything else I need to know about that or about my night time flit?"

"Maybe tomorrow night I'll have more to tell you."

He gave me a look that clearly said 'subject closed'. His attention turned to the phone list I was working on.

"That's a useful tool you created. It's probably going to take a while for us to make any sense of the information, but it could shed light on a number of things I've been thinking about."

"Your illustrious colleagues thought it valuable."

"You didn't like them?"

"Supercilious sods. Where do they get off, treating me like some ditzy female?"

"Ah, but they don't know how much work you've done on this case. In fact, they don't know anything about you."

"Oh, so you didn't see any need to explain who I was or what I have contributed?"

"Perhaps it is better they don't know. Anyway, we haven't discussed my cases yet or any of the information that's been put together. That's scheduled for later this afternoon."

"I thought you spent time swapping notes with them last evening and again this morning."

"Yes, we have spent quite a few hours together, but it was spent cross-referencing and correlating information about their cases. While they are both from the metropolitan area, they each have different cases they are working. This is the first chance we've had – even for them – to get it all together and look for connections."

"So, where have they disappeared off to now?"

"They picked up some information that led to a couple of names here in Ralston. They're off interviewing a couple of people. We'll get together again later this afternoon when they have finished their interviews."

"Aren't these people they are interviewing of any interest to you?"

"Maybe; don't know yet. We have been keeping an eye on them. This way, we will get information without having to show our hand by interviewing them ourselves."

"So you won't be around this afternoon or this evening."

"No. I thought we – all four of us – would have dinner together."

"What, up here... seeing as how I can't leave?"

"We are all up here at the moment."

In response to my confused look, Ben went on to explain the layout of this part of the precinct. The apartment I am in occupies only about a third of the area the Police lease from the neighbours. The remainder of the area is set up for Ben's Special Task Force. Ben offered to show me the rest of the floor. I didn't feel comfortable with the idea, so he contented himself with describing it to me.

"There's an office area that holds seven desks and all the other usual office paraphernalia, small kitchen and bathroom the same as this apartment, and a combined ops/briefing room that can hold about ten, or 12 people if they're friendly. It also has two other rooms: a small sitting room with TV and a crash room.

"Crash room?"

"A room where officers can 'crash' – catch some sleep – if they are on call or there is a lull in an ongoing investigation. It can sleep three comfortably and there is a trundle bed as well. The sofa in the sitting room also folds out into a bed if required."

"I didn't realise it was so complex. I imagined it as just office accommodation for the Task Force."

"I had spoken about the set-up when I was with the Met guys during that course. When we were organising this get together, they were keen to stay here rather than in a hotel. It wouldn't have worked if the Task Force officers were around. That's why initially I arranged for them to stay in the apartment belonging to that accountant friend of mine. However, when I had to send the team off to the Army camp to isolate them for a bit, it cleared the way for David and Greg to stay here. So, you do actually have neighbours … and we are going to have dinner together somewhere up here."

Ben's phone rang halting further conversation for a few minutes. He finished the call and sat in silence studying the counter top for a few moments. He seemed to be mentally wrestling with something. I assumed it related to the phone call. After apparently having made a decision, he slowly slid his eyes to me and hesitantly began speaking again.

"Looks like you won't be entertaining us for too long this evening. Just had confirmation that an operation we have been trying to put in place is right to go tonight. I'll be involved and, depending on how their interviews went today, Greg and David might want to be in on it as well."

"Do I get to know any more than that?"

"Not really, but I can tell you it has something to do with your favourite black SUV."

His wide grin evidence he was enjoying having stirred my curiosity. I was about to protest being kept in the dark about it when it was something so closely related to me. However, his phone rang again, precluding any comment.

"The other two are on the way back from their interviews. I'll go down to the other end and do some prep work for tonight while I wait for them to arrive." He picked up his phone, checked he had left nothing behind and, on his way out the door, spoke over his shoulder. "Keep working on that phone list, it could be valuable."

With a wave, the cheeky sod was gone. Keep working on the list! What else was I going to do here alone for the rest of the afternoon? Of course, I could iron those things I washed this morning. Rather than make a decision, I dawdled over cleaning up after lunch. My mind was intent on pondering what tonight's operation might be about. I had meant to ask Ben what he found out from Barney about the hire of the black SUV. Somehow I forgot, and now there was to be some sort of operation based on that vehicle. With my mind so busy trying to probe things it didn't have any information about, it seemed wiser to do the ironing next. The present mental gymnastics would only be a distraction if I tried concentrating on the phone lists.

The ironing completed and put away, it was time to tackle the phone list. In spite of my resolve to work my way systematically from the top of the list, I caved in to temptation and flicked through pages, stopping briefly to examine various names on the way through. A lot of work was required. Just checking the department staff names to determine if calls made to them were likely to be genuinely work-related would take time. However, my attention kept wandering to other outsiders' names on the list. It wasn't unusual for anyone to make non-work related calls to people outside the department, but some of the names on this list were scary.

Some names I recognised from their alleged association with unsavoury activity. With the recognition of each name, my concern grew. Why would Therese be in contact with such people? My conviction that a part of Therese's life was involved with something 'no good' strengthened. A number of questions were banging on my forehead for attention. What possible 'no good' had she gotten involved in? How, if at all, did it relate to her job and/or the department? How had she managed to continue to carry out her job while this 'something else' was going on in her life? ... And the big one: what had occurred to warrant her death? Another question kept trying to butt in, but for a time, I kept it at bay. Was Therese's death linked to those other 'strange' deaths Ben and his colleagues were investigating?

I realised I didn't know how Therese had been performing at work in recent times. Nobody volunteered any comments to suggest anything had been out of the ordinary, but I hadn't asked that actual question. Some specific questions to her secretary might identify any changes in behaviour. I made a note to ring Liz Cranston on Monday, and then changed 'Monday' to 'sometime over the weekend'. I didn't much like the idea of intruding on Liz's weekend, but she might be more inclined to speak freely then – and I didn't want to ring her at work.

Back to the phone list and those names; no good sitting here wondering about them. I need to know why I recognised them and how. I suspected they were infamous rather than famous. An internet search for the first couple of names produced any number of entries, all containing disturbing details of their owners' careers. "Shit, Therese, this is organised crime we're talking about," I proclaimed aloud to an empty room. "How the hell did you get involved? Why?"

Details noted beside both names, I sat stunned, staring at the details I recorded. Instead of moving on to the next name on the list, I stood up abruptly and strolled to the kitchen ostensibly to get a glass of water but, in reality, I needed to tear myself away for a moment. I stood with my arms folded tight and contemplated the glass of water, that I didn't really want, abandoned on the kitchen counter. Why was the information so overwhelming? I knew whatever was uncovered would be bad, shocking even. Perhaps I knew, but hadn't accepted it, hadn't comprehended the implications – or hadn't wanted to.

Therese was never a friend, but she had been my boss. Our relationship had not always been great. Therese landed a job – by dubious means in some people's minds – that appeared from day one to be beyond her capabilities. She broke just about every rule in the management handbook. In the end, I decided I couldn't stand her lack of management skills – along with other goings-on within the department –any longer. I quit. In spite of all this, it is still unnerving to find myself confronted by such suspicions about someone with whom I was closely associated. I told myself to get over it, get back to work and to get professional. I wandered back to the computer and sat down again. A check of the time had me on my feet again and on my way to the bathroom.

Based on Ben's few comments about the operation they were running tonight, I figured dinner might be early, so it would be over before the operation began. Of course, it could be late – maybe even very late – if he delayed dinner until after the operation. Either way, I was now showered and changed, and presentable for dinner whenever it happened.

There wasn't long to wait to find out. Dinner was early. Ben called through the door, "You ready for dinner?" I opened the door expecting to admit all three of them armed with food. Only Ben stood there. With a flick of his head, he gestured towards the other end of the corridor. "You're dining out tonight."

With me trailing behind, he set off for the Special Task Force's area. He escorted me directly through to the kitchen where David and Greg were busy with food. The aroma was wonderful. My knowledge of Ralston was increasing: the Adam's Ribs place in the mall did take-away packs. If its food tasted half as good as it smelled, it was a place worth remembering. Ben and I loaded ourselves up with plates, cutlery, glasses and bottles of mineral and tonic water. We set off in convoy for the briefing room, with Ben leading the way and David and Greg bringing up the rear carrying the food. The table was laid quickly and everyone got stuck into the food, which included sides of vegetables, a salad and sauces.

Silence prevailed until quite a bit disappeared off plates. Ben was tense, the food was wonderful, and David and Greg had amended their demeanour to something much more acceptable. Conversation was sparse and stilted, and Ben checked his watch several times. Everyone ate quickly, and I assumed that was due to the timing of events planned for later tonight. I joined in the fervour that prevailed. The food despatched, everyone sat back well satisfied and indulged in light conversation.

Ben ended the moment. "Time to make a move, boys."

"If you guys need to go, I'll stay behind and clean up before I go back to my place," I volunteered. I saw Greg look at Ben and raise his eyebrows questioningly.

"You can stay here if you like," Ben said. "You and Greg can clean up and then you can sit with Greg in the ops centre. David, are you right to go?"

If I want to…? No second invitation required, thank you. Ben and David left immediately. Greg and I gathered up plates and containers and headed for the kitchen. With everything clean and tidy once more, Greg led me back to the briefing room. He opened a concertina door at the far end to reveal a small operations centre set-up. I stood back not sure what I was supposed to do.

"Grab a chair and make yourself comfortable. This is where we are going to be parked for the next couple of hours at least."

I did as instructed and placed the chair towards one end of the desk where he indicated. He wandered off and shortly after I heard the toilet flush. He returned and started turning on bits of equipment, and did a radio check with some unknown voice out in the ether. Without looking at me, he said, "You might want to take a toilet break before things start. That way, you won't have to get up and leave in the middle of things. Do you know where it is?" That was a good idea but, no, I didn't know where the bathroom was. Greg gave me directions, although I was confident I could have located it on my own.

It seems like an anti-climax, sitting here in the operations centre in silence waiting for something to happen. I want an idea of what is going to happen so I can keep up with events when whatever it is does get underway. However, Greg is preoccupied and fiddling continuously with sheets of paper, knobs, the microphone, and everything else on the ops desk in front of us. He is in his own world and I don't dare disturb it. Therefore, I will behave and continue to sit patiently while trying to picture what the next couple of hours or so might hold.

# Chapter Ten

The waiting felt interminable but it was only 15 or 20 minutes before the first sounds of activity broke the silence. Strange voices and other noises filled the small room. It all seems like general chatter to me. I wish I knew what is supposed to happen. That way, I could associate the sounds with the activities taking place. An unknown voice announced 'it was just leaving now', and then Ben's unmistakable voice announcing that it was *GO*. He then spent some time checking that various persons were in place.

Greg came to life. He sat bolt upright at the desk, pen in hand, and focusing intently on the dials in front of him. He started some sort of recorder the moment he heard Ben's voice, and now checked the sound and quality readings on the machine.

For a while, there was only the same voice giving what sounded like progress reports along a route through the city. To my dismay, I realised the route in question started not too far from the Police precinct, and very close to the hotel to which I supposedly had relocated. Then Ben's voice again.

"Team 2, what is your situation?"

"About 50 metres back from the right hand junction of Hibiscus Road and The Esplanade."

"Start up and wait for Team 1's signal to move."

"… On stand-by."

Then silence for a couple of minutes, before the earlier voice resumed the commentary.

"Approaching the marker now," it announced. "Team 2, move out."

There was the unmistakable roar of a motor bike for a few moments before it could be heard idling. Then, over the sound of the bike, the sound of what I had come to recognise as Team 2's voice. It stood out from all the others. It was female. There is something vaguely familiar about the voice, but I can't quite place it.

"I have the target. Taking up the tail."

"Team 1: abandoning pursuit and turning into Hibiscus Road. Proceeding west along Hibiscus Road." This was the first voice, the one that guided us out of the city and onto The Esplanade.

More silence for a few minutes before the radio came to life again.

"Team 2: approaching the roundabout. Reducing speed."

We heard the revs drop as the motorcycle slowed.

"Team 3 in place. Have visual on target." A few seconds pause and then, "Team 3 entering roundabout. We have the tail."

There appeared to be some sort of relay occurring involving Teams 2 and 3. Then Team 1 picked up the baton, announcing it now had the tail. Another few minutes passed. Greg sat tense and unmoving. Shortly, Team 1 announced it was approaching Ground Zero. Then there was Ben calling for situation reports from all of his teams.

"City slickers Leader to Base; we are in position. Please relay."

Greg murmured, "David's team," and relayed the message to Ben. He barely finished speaking when 'Renegade Leader' asked him to relay a similar message.

After only another minute or so, a jubilant update:

"Team1: target is entering ground zero. Team 1 proceeding along The Esplanade."

A further brief silence.

"Team 3: target has parked out front. Team 3 proceeding along The Esplanade."

"Bravo 1 (Ben) to Base: Inquiry time."

Greg relayed the message: "Base to Cityslickers Leader: inquiry time."

There was the throb of a large motorcycle, followed shortly after by David's voice.

"Cityslickers Leader entering ground zero."

The engine noise died and was followed the loud 'clunk' of the stand being engaged. Next, we heard the unmistakable crunch of boots on gravel, more than one pair of boots perhaps. An image flashed onto our big screen. It showed David, with his helmet off, walking through a lobby towards a counter.

His shapely companion, in skin-tight leathers unzipped almost to the point of indecency, was removing her helmet. I gasped as a shock of long blonde hair tumbled out from under the helmet. Greg grinned silently. It was that gorgeous looking police woman again. She struck a few slutty poses while managing to look completely bored with proceedings. Then followed David to the counter and slipped her arm around his waist.

A conversation with the female receptionist ensued, during which the receptionist consulted a computer screen a few times. David had his microphone turned off, so none of the conversation was audible. Finally, with a look of disappointed resignation, David and his companion turned and walked away from the counter and disappeared from the screen. At one point, just before he was out of camera range, David looked straight at the camera – wherever it was located – and gave an almost imperceptible nod. It was so slight, I wasn't sure I didn't imagine it. I hadn't imagined it, and Greg had been watching for it.

Greg was on the radio immediately he saw the nod. "Base to Bravo 1: Cityslickers Leader indicates success."

After about a minute of listening to its powerful engine, we heard the bike stop, and David gave his report. "The fifth floor of ground zero contains two suites. Both suites are booked in the name of Richard Green, supposedly a film producer. The suites are for himself and his crew. The party comprises five individuals who reputedly are checking out potential locations for a movie. The target vehicle is with this party and is parked in the guests' carpark at the front of the building. There is a second vehicle associated with the party, a silver grey Mercedes, currently parked next to the target vehicle."

After scribbling furiously as David gave his report, Greg relayed it to Ben. By this time, my little grey cells had deduced 'ground zero' probably was the Coral Cay Resort, which is located just off The Esplanade and overlooks the bay. I had driven past it once or twice. It looked expensive. This is not the tourist season, so there shouldn't be too many other guests. Confirmation of my thoughts came via another unknown voice that reported only another five guests currently registered, and three of those were attending some function in the city this evening. All five had rooms on the second floor.

Ben called for a report on their current positions from all of the teams. David's Cityslickers team was in position behind the resort. The Renegade team occupied positions along the front of the resort, among the shrubs between The Esplanade and the resort forecourt. I saw Greg tense – even more, if that is possible – and his knuckles whiten as he gripped the edge of the desk. When all teams had reported in, Ben asked everyone to stand-by. He was now in full command.

"Assault Teams 1 and 2: Prepare to enter on my command." I listened to him count backwards from five, and I jumped when he shouted, "Go!" Then teams began reporting in.

"Assault 2 in position."

"Assault 3 in position. Elevators deactivated."

The Ben again, "On my command: 3 – 2 – 1, Go! Go! All teams expect action."

This was worse than losing the picture but not the sound at some crucial point in the plot of a TV show. I found myself leaning forward towards the microphone – though what that was supposed to achieve, I don't know. Then, the faint sounds heralding some sort of action floated into the room. Within a few heartbeats, we were live to the action.

There were the sounds of heavy breathing and muffled footsteps, and then images once again flashed on the screen. They looked as though they might be coming from a helmet camera or something similar as they flittered around wildly on the screen. It occurred to me that, if you were prone motion sickness, watching the show playing out on our screen would do you no good at all. Although I continued to watch the screen, my mind apparently wandered off somewhere else.

I jumped, taken by surprise by a loud crashing sound followed by much shouting. The images on the screen were moving faster and had become more erratic. It was difficult to make out details, but it looked like the camera was moving down a hallway. I caught a glimpse of a patterned carpet and the toe of a boot, all accompanied by heavy breathing.

Then the shooting started; just a few shots… hand guns by the sounds of it. I glanced sideways at Greg. He seemed a few shades paler than previously and his breathing had become noticeably shallow.

"Fuck! It's going to be a fire fight." He was staring at the screen.

Suddenly a new sound joined the chorus: the repeated 'crack' of shots being fired in quick succession.

"Shit! Automatic weapons," Greg rasped, barely audible over a loud scream from the radio that filled the room.

I could hear my blood pounding in my ears, and I was starting to feel a bit detached from reality. Breathe, Sonny, I told myself, deep breaths; breathe normally. In, out, in, out; that's it. I realised I too had become very tense, and was now sitting on the edge of my chair, panting in shallow breaths. It would not do to distract Greg at this time by passing out and ending up in a scrambled heap on the floor. Although, he probably would ignore me and let me lie there.

The room echoed with more shots, more swearing, yelled orders – and abuse, heavily accented abuse. We saw a fleeting image of bloody clothing, a shirt I think. A man, sitting against a wall, holding his side as blood oozed through his fingers. How long did it go on? It felt like ages. I suspect it was no more than a few minutes.

Images began to slow their movement across the screen. They took on greater clarity and definition. The sounds died away. There were no more shots, no more swearing or abuse. The sound of spoken commands, soft footfalls, and a few other soft muffled noises replaced the previous confused racket. On the screen, a door along the hallway flew open. A loud accompanying crash echoed through the radio.

We watched a somewhat dishevelled overweight man in handcuffs propelled through the door and into the hallway. Judging by our brief glimpse of his face, he was not too happy about the situation and was reluctant to be accommodating. His reluctance was of little consequence. Two uniformed officers dragged and shoved him towards the elevators, which now stood open.

Ben's voice cut across the now much quieter scene.

"Sit rep! Assault 1: situation report. *Assault 1!*"

A slight pause and then the response, "Assault 1: area secured. Five prizes, three wounded. One friendly wounded."

Greg's hand flew to the phone. Somehow, he seemed instantly to connect to someone. The radio captured and held my attention.

"Bravo 1: All teams stand down. I repeat, all teams stand down."

"Bravo 1 to Base." A couple of heartbeats and then it came again, urgent this time. "Bravo 1 to Base."

I looked at Greg. Ben was calling us, but Greg was still talking on the phone. Just as I was wondering if I should try to do something – God knows what I thought I could do – his call terminated and Greg responded.

"Base to Bravo 1: Med evac dispatched. ETA ground zero is one minute."

Did I detect a triumphant note in Greg's response? I certainly detected a relieved note in Ben's reply. "Thanks, Base. Nice work."

Silence descended. There were no more images on the screen, no sounds from the radio. There was just Greg adding more notes to his sheets of paper ... and me, staring at the now dead console, as I tried to comprehend all that had happened. The room was eerily quiet after the noise that so recently filled it. Greg finished his notes, sat back in his chair, and joined me in silently staring at the console for a few moments. When he finally spoke, his voice and demeanour had returned to normal.

"I could do with a cup of coffee about now. How about you?"

"Good idea. I'll see what I can rustle up."

I left Greg still sitting at the desk, and went to investigate the kitchen's coffee-making resources. It presented no challenges: a small capsule-type coffee machine, a variety of capsules, sugar, and fresh milk in the fridge. I called out to Greg to find out what sort of coffee he'd like and how he took it. We both settled for long blacks – no sugar for either of us – and I managed to work out how to make it happen. By the time the coffee was ready, Greg had joined me in the kitchen. He retrieved a packet of savoury crackers from a cupboard and collected his coffee. I ferreted a small bowl out of a cupboard and, coffee in hand, followed him into the small sitting room.

We settled down with our coffee and crackers, but conversation did not come immediately. I couldn't tell whether Greg remained hyped after all that happened, or if he was mentally analysing the night's events. He stared into space as he silently sipped his coffee. Obviously, I want all the details – chapter and verse please – of tonight's operation, but my thinking is so incoherent, I can't even work out what questions to ask. Greg eventually broke the silence that had settled over us.

"Did you manage to survive tonight all right?"

"Yeah, no problems." If he hadn't notice already, there's no point in letting him know I'm a wimp. "I'm amazed at how well orchestrated the whole operation was, and even more surprised that there were no hiccups. Well, none that I detected anyway."

"You've every right to be amazed. I can't believe how quickly Ben pulled it all together, and how well planned it was. I was only on the periphery of the whole thing, so I don't know all the details. I'm sure Ben will fill you in though." In my mind, a more accurate substitute word for that last comment is 'might'. If I'm lucky, and he is feeling generous, he might fill me in.

"Speaking of Ben, how long before the others get back here do you think?" I asked.

"Hard to say; I don't think they will do the interrogations tonight. Probably just charge them all and leave them in the cells overnight."

Charge them with what, I thought but didn't dare ask – not yet. "That surprises me. I thought he would want to question them straight away – the ones that weren't wounded at least – especially that older bloke who looked like he might be the boss."

"Ah, you mean Mr Green."

"Yes, I suppose that's who he was."

"Normally, you would interrogate key prisoners as soon as possible. Ben knows he is not going to get anything out of that bloke tonight, or probably even tomorrow. He's also probably aware by now that he doesn't need to in order to be able to hold him. There would be no fewer than at least six outstanding warrants for his arrest."

"Oh, so you recognised him from the images we saw? I take it from the way you said 'Mr Green' that isn't his real name."

Greg chuckled as he told me he believed every Police Officer across at least three States would recognise 'Mr Green'. I almost had to rescue my eyebrows from the ceiling when he said the man's real name. It was one of the two scary names I looked up on the internet this afternoon. Should I tell Greg about the man's appearance on the phone list? Something suggested 'probably not' was the better option for the moment, so I said nothing. After all, Greg had a copy of the list and could discover it for himself.

With surprising ease, we slipped into general conversation completely unrelated to tonight's operation or Therese's case. Conversation rambled on, exploring a range of less than exciting topics including his job, how I got into private investigating, and where my home base was located. Somehow, in this way, we managed to while away over an hour. I began to feel in danger of outliving my welcome, and started thinking of ways to take my leave without appearing uninterested in the night's outcomes. We heard the main door open.

Greg stood and made to exit the sitting room. I watched on from my chair, not sure whether to be apprehensive or excited. My doubts were short lived. David met Greg at the doorway to the sitting room. They shook hands and Greg stood aside to let David enter. David nodded to me as he lowered himself into a chair. I smiled back in reply.

Not a lot of conversation happening so far, but Greg came to the rescue again. "Would you like a coffee?" he asked David.

"Yeah, that would be good, but I might have a quick shower first. I've been scrambling around in the bushes and the dunes all night."

"With that gorgeous blonde, no doubt," I commented and received a dismissive look for my trouble. I must be tired. There was no need for the bitchy comment.

David still wore the biker boots and leathers he had worn into the resort lobby. The only evidence of his Police connection was his navy blue cap with the reflective blue and white chequered band now lying on the end of the coffee table. True to his word, it was a quick shower.

Now wearing lightweight casual slacks and polo shirt, he returned to the sitting room. Greg handed him a mug of coffee as he walked past the kitchen.

"Any likelihood Ben will be joining us at a respectable hour?" Greg enquired.

"I don't think he'll be much longer. He saw the three locked in their cells for the night, and then was going to check on the officer that was wounded, before coming back here."

"It's never good when of one of your own is wounded. Ben will be upset about that. How bad was it?"

"Not serious; just a flesh wound to the upper arm. I think a ricochet got him, and not a direct hit. They might put a suture or two in it but, more likely, they'll just pull it together with those plaster strip things."

"Your 'Cityslickers' didn't have much to do tonight."

"No, and I was happy about that when I heard that AK47 going off. I didn't really want to fly them up here just to get them shot. It was good experience for them though, and being a part of any operation helps keep them sharp."

"I notice you didn't spare yourself. It must have been tough riding around on a monster bike with that blonde pillion passenger." Greg tried to remain straight-faced as he spoke but didn't quite succeed in hiding the grin.

"She is a knock out, isn't she?" I added.

"Oh, yes, that was some bike – and the blonde wasn't too bad either. You're right. Tough job, but someone had to do it."

The light-hearted banter eased the atmosphere in the room. David checked his watch and commented that he thought Ben would be here by now. We all checked our watches and there was unanimous murmured agreement. There wasn't much else to do to fill in time. A few moments later, the main door opened. The unmistakable smell of fish and chips preceded Ben into the complex.

"We're in here," Greg called out.

Ben stuck his head around the door, but didn't come in.

"… 'Evening all. I brought food. There's nothing like a bit of excitement to bring on the hunger pangs."

We heard him rattle plates in the kitchen before, armed with a tray loaded with crumbed fish bits and chips, he joined us in the sitting room. As Ben entered the room, Greg exited it. He soon returned armed with frosty beers for everyone.

"Can't have fish and chips without a good cold beer to wash it down," he announced as he distributed the beers to those gathered around the table.

"Congratulations," David and Greg said almost simultaneously, and we three raised our beers to Ben.

"Yeah, it was a good night's work. Apart from one of my blokes getting in the way of a shell, everything went to plan – like clockwork."

"How is your officer?" I asked.

"He's fine. It was nothing serious – not much more than a Band-Aid job – but he'll have something to brag about for a day or two."

I couldn't control my curiosity any longer. Although I had witnessed the actual event, I wanted to know all the details. When and how did he plan it at such short notice? How did he know where they would be? What about the damage to the resort? I spewed out a long list of questions without stopping to draw breath. By the time I'd finished, the other three were just about rolling on the floor with laughter. Ben recovered first and conceded it probably would be good to go over the operation.

"That's good. I witnessed most of the operation from the ops room, so I think I have my head around most of that part. My questions mainly relate to before the actual operation. For example, how did you know where they would be and how did you get everything in place so quickly? It seemed like there were quite a number of people involved, so they all needed to be briefed on their roles, vehicles organised, and whatever."

Flapping his hand dismissively at me, David answered condescendingly, "Just solid Police work."

I fixed David with a stony stare. "You supercilious arse!" I retorted and shuffled forward in my chair so I could stand up to leave. Greg snorted with laughter and Ben looked crestfallen.

This was Ben's night and he didn't need it overshadowed by a slanging match between David and me. On the other hand, I wasn't going to stay and put up with David's attitude. Disappointment fuelled my resentment. I thought their attitude towards me had changed. Greg's certainly had.

Ben looked reproachfully at me and opened his mouth to speak, but David cut across him. Holding up both hands to silence Ben, he turned to me.

"Accurate assessment, Ma'am," he said looking contrite. "Sincere apologies; why don't we talk it through from the beginning as Ben suggests?"

An uneasy truce descended upon the group. Conversation, stilted initially as people tried to resume normal communication, gradually returned to normal, although it took me a minute or two to cool down sufficiently to speak without snapping. However, talk we all did and, surprisingly soon, there was an animated post-mortem in progress.

Ben explained how he followed up on the SUV with Barney from the hire car place. Barney told him of some gadget he fitted to all his vehicles a few months previously. After a couple of his more expensive vehicles went missing and, after some time, eventually were found wrecked at interstate locations, he decided to outlay the expense and fit the devices to all of his vehicles. The device allowed Barney's office to monitor the location of any of his vehicles out on hire. Ben explained that, about three months earlier, they had trouble with a case. It seems the major case proved difficult to break for a while. Finally, it was information from Barney – and one of his tracking devices – that led the police to the culprits.

This morning, Barney was on the verge of ringing Ben when Ben called him to enquire about the SUV. Barney provided the hirers' details but also added his concern. The hirers' address while in Ralston, as provided on the hire contracts, was not where the vehicles had been located since they left Barney's premises. He admitted it could be innocent enough, but he was a little uneasy about it. Ben took the devices' co-ordinates and sent an officer to check on it. He found the SUV at the resort where the tracker gadget indicated it was located, as well as a second vehicle hired by the same group. Because of our interest in the black SUV, Ben wanted information on the hirer and his party. A 'watcher' placed in the resort was able to relay information throughout the day on any movement of the vehicles or their hirers. Ben stopped speaking. The rest of us silently nodded our understanding.

Ben then murmured softly, thinking aloud rather than speaking to us, "…Must talk to Barney again tomorrow after we chat with the ones we brought in tonight," and he pulled out his notebook and scribbled a note to himself.

David then took up the story and explained how he came to have his team of 'Cityslickers' in Ralston. "When we met for our session this morning, Ben told us about the SUV and how he was trying to put in place an operation for tonight. With his Special Task Force out at the Army base, his main concern was having enough men to cover everything properly. I made some calls, pulled some strings, and got four of my Special Ops guys on the lunchtime plane."

"Couldn't you bring your Special Task Force blokes back for the operation?" I asked Ben. To me, that seemed like the logical thing to do.

Ben considered the question for a moment before carefully wording his reply. "Yes, under other circumstances, I might have done that. But, you do remember why they are out at the Army base at the moment, don't you?"

I knew he wasn't talking about the ruse of giving them some specialist first response training, so I just nodded and indicated I knew what he meant. Our exchange didn't attract any attention from the others, and David took up the story again.

"It didn't matter that my blokes didn't arrive till this afternoon. Our role was to guard the rear perimeter in case anyone decided to do a runner out the back door, so to speak. It didn't take too much to brief them and have them ready to go. I had my special extra role to play, but the rest of the time I would be out the back with my team."

Ben took up the story again after Greg returned with another beer for everyone. Just as well they were only light strength, or I was likely to end up under the table if this kept up.

"Even with David's guys, I was still short of manpower to cover all the contingencies. I'd borrowed everyone I could from this precinct and a couple extra from suburban stations. That still left me with no one to cover the front perimeter. I was – reluctantly – considering pulling my Special Task Force back in, when I thought of the Officer in Charge at the Army base who I had been dealing with recently. I gave him a call and he offered to send five of his tactical response group to help. They were the 'Renegades' that covered the front area."

The niggling question in the back of my mind was how he managed to get everything in place in such a short timeframe. He didn't have a clue this was going to happen until he spoke to Barney this morning and after that, he spent large slabs of time in my apartment during the day, as well as meeting with David and Greg. Ben chuckled at the question.

"I had the information early this morning. I rang Barney at 5.30."

"I'll bet you were popular," Greg mused.

"No, it wasn't a problem. I know that ever Saturday morning Barney is on the golf course by six o'clock so, by 5.30, he would have to be up and ready to go to golf. After that, I sat in my office and roughed out a plan until seven o'clock, when I had four senior officers join me. We worked until about eight o'clock on getting the plan nailed down. Then I left them to get on with it and I came up here to meet with you two as planned." Then he added an extra comment especially for me. "I told these two what had transpired and what I was planning. That's when David started making calls to get his guys up here."

"It's amazing that the whole thing came off without a hitch," Greg said shaking his head in disbelief.

"…Without a hitch, until they started shooting up the place," Ben responded. "We were lucky there weren't more serious injuries."

"How serious were the other mob's injuries?" Greg asked. "From what we could see on the screen, it looked like a couple of them had fairly decent wounds."

"Yeah, two of them were wounded. One only needed patching up, but the other needed surgery. It wasn't serious though. By the way, thanks for getting the Ambulances in so quickly."

Greg smiled as he replied. "Once I heard the firing and screaming start, I moved the Ambulances up as close as I could to Ground Zero. I was concerned that, if any of ours got hit, we needed to be able to get them out as quickly as possible."

"I am with Greg on this one," I said. "I still can't believe the whole operation was pulled together in such short time and was so successful."

"Towards the end of the day, it almost looked like it wasn't going to go ahead. The black SUV and most of their crew went out and didn't seem in a hurry to return to the resort. We needed all the mob together for it to work. While I was with you late this afternoon, I got a call telling me the SUV was back in the district and headed back into town. I took a punt and decided we'd go ahead as planned. It worked out perfectly. After tracking the SUV's movements around after it returned to the city, we were able to pick it up and follow it back to the resort this evening."

"So, it was the 'watcher' you placed in the resort that recorded the footage in the resort lobby?" I asked.

"Yes, he was at a table just off the lobby with a drink and the weekend's racing form guide."

My turn again. "How's the resort reacting to having its top floor shot up? It looked like there was a fair bit of damage from the shooting and doors being kicked in."

"Ah, yes. They weren't too impressed. However, it's the offseason for tourists so they are not busy. They have been renovating the place, systematically attacking it floor by floor. That's why the few guests they have are all on the second floor. That floor's renovation is complete and the third floor is just about finished. The Department will be contributing to the renovation costs when they get around to refurbishing the top floor. Actually, all round, it's been a fairly expensive day for the Department, given the repairs and all the overtime to be paid." The last comment seemed to amuse all three men who enjoyed a bit of a giggle at the prospect.

Ben stretched back in his chair clasped his hands behind his head, and contemplated the ceiling as he spoke. "Tomorrow looks like being another busy day. The three downstairs need interviewing. We'll need to look at outstanding warrants for their leader, and maybe look at initiating extradition proceedings if needed. And I have what I expect to be an interesting meeting at eight in the morning."

David queried what the meeting was about, but Ben sidestepped the question. I saw Greg yawn and managed to stifle one myself. Then Ben stood up and looked around the room. "I don't know about you guys, but I have had a long day. I'm ready for a shower and bed, so I think I'll bid you all good night."

We all agreed that sleep would be good. Ben disappeared and the three of us cleared away the debris we had created before Greg walked me out of the Special Task Force area and down to my door. It wasn't until I was inside and sitting on the edge of my bed to take my shoes off that I realised how tired I was.

I checked my watch on the bedside table. It was now well and truly tomorrow.

# Chapter Eleven

Sunday morning saw me out of bed at my normal time, but doughy from lack of sleep. After last night, I want to make a major effort on the phone list today, before I mention to anyone about our 'Mr Green' having made a frequent appearance on the list. So, after a quick breakfast of cereal and coffee, I got down to work.

I didn't expect any interruptions today, and none came. By the end of three hours of hard slog, my caffeine levels were at low ebb, but I had all but completed work on the list. There remained only three department staff names still causing me an uneasy feeling. These I need to investigate further, as my gut instinct kept suggesting there was no logical reason for Therese to call them. I resolved to tackle them with a clear head after taking a break, so I took a break and put coffee on to brew. After washing my face to wake myself up, I headed to the kitchen to make my coffee.

Just as I picked up the pot to pour the coffee, Ben called from outside the closed door causing an interruption to the process and making me reach for another mug. "Any chance of a coffee this morning?"

"Come in. I've just made fresh coffee and, yes, I have two mugs lined up. I am surprised to see you. What with everything you had going on today, I didn't think you would have time to breathe let alone come up here for coffee."

While he didn't look so great, he seemed brighter than I was feeling. He told me they had completed interviewing the three they brought in last night, but didn't seem keen to elaborate any further. I didn't push for more information. That aside, curiosity nagged me about the meeting he had scheduled for early this morning. I guessed it might be with the internal investigators. I was sure it had something to do with the work they were doing for Ben. He had spoken about an investigation resulting from his concerns about a possible 'rotten apple' in his Special Task Force. I moved the conversation in that direction by asking when the Task Force members were likely to return from the Army base.

"They are due to come back sometime late on Tuesday, so it's unlikely we will see any of them in the office before Wednesday. That's probably a good thing. David and Greg have decided to stay on for a couple of extra days, and it will be good if they continue to stay down in the Task Force area. However, I don't want them there once my guys get back."

"Are you any the wiser yet on whether you do have a rotten apple in the group, and who it might be?"

"Yeah, that's what we met about this morning, and the answers to your questions are 'yes' and 'yes'. That's something else I'll have to deal with this afternoon. I'm just waiting for a couple of phone calls to finalise arrangements before I make a move."

"Were there any surprises, or were your suspicions confirmed?"

"Unfortunately, there were no surprises."

His tone suggested he considered the subject closed. There didn't seem much point in trying to press him to expand on what he shared with me already. How frustrating. That person had jeopardised my safety, so I felt I had some right to know which team member it was.

We barely finished speaking when David and Greg arrived. More coffee required all round. When everyone had coffee, we moved to the lounge and the discussions turned serious. Not surprisingly, perhaps, the main topic was this morning's interviews. Everyone was keen to know if the interviews produced any new information that might help progress any of their ongoing major investigations. At that point, Ben consulted his notebook before continuing the discussion. As expected, 'Mr Green' chose to be uncooperative and refused to answer any questions. However, two of his minions were more forthcoming.

Ben assessed them as possibly new to Green's group, and new to being so seriously on the wrong side of the law. They weren't exactly fine upstanding members of the community, but he believed that last night's shootings unnerved them. He guessed they were rethinking their rash move of having thrown their lot in with Mr Green. They were keen to explore whatever opportunities existed to extricate themselves from their current situation, any options that didn't involve incurring serious risk to their ongoing well-being.

It proved beneficial for the detectives to have the interviewees unsettled by the previous night's activities. Both men provided useful information on other shady associates in the Ralston area. They also provided other names they had heard mentioned, but they were unaware of the nature of the association of those named or their location. Based on this information, Ben organised a handful of officers to try bringing in a couple of the locals whose names received mention. He didn't think it would prove fruitful, but considered it worth a try.

However, the real gem that came out of the interviews was the reason for Mr Green and his merry men's presence in Ralston. It was a long trip from their home base in a southern State just to take in the beautiful weather up here. The two new members of the group didn't have all the details, but knew the key points. Mr Green wanted to meet up with some people – identities unknown – in Queensland, so the group moved north. They spent a few days in the south-east corner while Mr Green tried to establish exactly where in Queensland he was likely to meet up with whoever they were. It seems the people they were to meet were arriving in the State from somewhere else. One of the interviewees thought the people in question might be internationals, but couldn't explain why he thought that.

"If they're internationals we're talking about," Greg began slowly, "It strongly suggests what the trip might have been about."

Ben nodded in agreement and continued. "Anyway, a week or so ago, Mr Green received information that the people he wanted to see were going to be up this way somewhere. He moved his team up to a small town not too far from here. They spent a few days there under the guise of southerners on a fishing holiday. However, they started to attract unwanted attention. Then, information came through that Ralston was where these people would be sometime in the next week. That's when they relocated to here. The interviewees' information was a bit sketchy, but I estimate their arrival in Ralston just prior to that horror weekend a week ago."

I could feel a headache coming on from trying to keep track of who, where and timings details of Ben's story and, at the same time, deal with a major question that was in the forefront of my mind. At the risk of making a fool of myself, I asked the question. "Were all those things that happened that weekend – including Therese – Mr Green and his group's handiwork?"

Greg shrugged and murmured, 'maybe', while David, in keeping with his usual brash approach, demanded, "Who else?"

Ben had the final word. "Possibly… there's a bit more information that suggests there might be some association with at least one of those incidents." Everyone seemed to come to attention when Ben threw in that nugget.

With us all now sitting upright and fully focused, Ben continued. "Well, the meeting planned for Ralston was a fizzer. The people in question, who were believed to be on a boat heading for the harbour at Ralston, didn't arrive. They supposedly chose to head for Darwin instead. However, the particularly interesting news is that Mr Green was having a bit of clean-up of his operation, including his contacts and associates. It seems that somewhere along the way, one of his foot soldiers blotted his copybook in some way. Mr Green generously gave him the opportunity to make amends. He set the man a task – or a test if you prefer to think of it that way. Successful completion of the test allowed the bloke to re-enter the ranks. Failure attracted fatal consequences. The test appears to have required fixing a problem of some sort for the boss. Word is that the bloke must have been success-ful as he seems to be back in favour."

"What does 'fixing a problem' mean...? Does it mean what I think it means?" I blurted out.

"W-e-l-l, it could mean anything," Ben replied, "But I think we are all able to guess what it entailed."

"Do you think… Therese?" I asked cautiously.

"Don't know, and I'm not prepared to speculate until I get more information. My interviewees did suggest that, while they were in the Ralston area, Mr Green saw it as an opportunity to sort out some of the 'mess' that existed here."

Ben might want to be cautious, but my mind was firmly inclined to believe Therese was a part of that sorting out process. Still, sometimes it is good to keep one's thoughts to one's self. I decided this was one of those times. I forced myself back to the conversation continuing around me. Ben had harked back to something he mentioned earlier.

"…So, as I said, we will follow-up on those shady associates they named. Some of my officers will try to bring in a couple of the locals mentioned. I don't think it will prove fruitful, but it's worth a try, and it might unsettle others enough to prove useful for us."

One of the other names mentioned in the interviews, but about which the interviewees couldn't provide any information, created a spark of interest for David. He thought he had encountered the same name somewhere previously, and intended checking his files when he returned to their rooms. The two prisoners did not provide the names of any 'significant players', so it was assumed those named were among the ranks of the foot soldiers rather than being part of the hierarchy.

After indulging in a few moments of self-deliberation, I decided this to be the right time to produce the work I had done on the phone list. I qualified the work as 'not quite finished' as I spread the list out along the kitchen bench. There followed a brief overview and explanation of the methodology I employed, and the information I had scribbled all over the list. Then I turned to the first of the scary names and the associated notes I made about its owner. Grunts and murmurs from the three men acknowledged my efforts, and Greg let out a low whistle.

"That's one really heavy dude she's been talking to, a *real* bad dude. I've recently come across something else that I think points to an association with him; haven't had a chance to dig any deeper yet though," Greg shared.

David scanned the page. "Some others on this page are recognisable too. They are more in the 'middle weight' class, not 'heavy weight' like the one you're looking at there, Greg."

Ben returned to the start of the list and worked his way slowly through the names. After a couple of pages, he voiced his thoughts.

"There are a lot of department staff names on the list. I accept that's expected, but your comments against some of them are interesting – like this one stationed out at that small western operation, for example. I don't know much about the operation of that department – don't even know much about how the Police Department works much of the time! – but, at first glance, it is difficult to know why Therese would be calling him. It's not until you look at their history that their earlier association starts bells ringing."

"It might be too premature to mention this, but I am getting a whiff of western connection tied up somehow in Melrose's death." As I spoke, I hoped sharing this thought at this early stage wasn't going to leave me with egg on my face.

"Go on," encouraged David. "You can't jump to that conclusion just because of this one name that appears on the list. What else have you got?"

"No, I sort of have more but, at this stage, it remains a shadowy thing lurking at the edge of my thinking." I turned to address Ben directly. "This is why I need to spend time with Kate and Emily. I have asked them both to think about life before Ralston – you know, about names, places, events, that kind of thing."

Ben looked surprised. "I didn't think Emily had been out west."

"No, well, yes. While her father was out there for a few years, she visited him a number of times. Her father, Therese, that name on the list we were just discussing, and Kate and Ken were all out there during the same time span."

"I see. Whereabouts were they exactly, do you know?"

"I don't really know. I only have ideas from vaguely remembered conversations. I would be guessing, until I get more information from the women. Do you think there might be a connection with your plane crash?"

The other two examined the phone list while Ben and I carried on our conversation. With the mention of the plane crash, they both stopped reading and turned expectantly to Ben. "What plane crash?" they chorused.

"We haven't had a chance to go through my stuff yet. There have been too many other things going on to finish the things that you came here to do. However, when we get around to it, included in my list of 'funny things that happened' is a suspect plane crash out west."

"If we keep turning up new stuff like this, we might have to keep extending our stay and never leave Ralston," Greg suggested.

Ben's phone rang. He moved to the far end of the sitting room to take the call while the rest of us continued discussing the phone list. I watched Ben out of the corner of my eye, bent over the coffee table, writing in his notebook as he spoke. He read the notes he had taken as he made his way back to the kitchen area. Everyone looked up expectantly, but he stood for a moment, deep in thought, before speaking.

"We will have to work out how you can get together with Kate and Emily."

I was surprised and the others looked confused by his statement. We expected him to pass on something from his phone call. He appeared privately to continue mulling over his phone call. A few seconds later, he did enlighten us.

"That call was from Barney; Barney Fellowes from the hire car place. He tried to contact me last night and again earlier this morning but couldn't get me. He's only just found time to try again. It seems our gang of miscreants hired three cars, not only the two we know about that were at the resort last night. One of the cars, the one we didn't know about, is now a long way from Ralston."

"Do go on…," Greg encouraged him. "I have a sneaking suspicion I know where it is heading."

"It appears two vehicles were hired on one credit card transaction, while the other vehicle was a transaction on a different card. It wasn't until Barney was finalising the day's paperwork last night that he realised something looked a bit odd. The two transactions were under different names. However, the cards used belonged to the same business entity."

"Not a unique or suspicious manoeuvre in itself," David commented.

"No, that's true. However, it got Barney's antennae twitching and, given our interest in the other two vehicles, he checked the third vehicle's tracking information. It was then a long way from Ralston and heading north, although it had been hired for 'Ralston environs' only. It went a long way north overnight, and is now heading west."

"There's that word again: west," I said.

"Funny that; it's exactly the word I was expecting to hear," Greg announced triumphantly.

Before there was any further discussion, Ben's phone rang again. He checked the caller ID and announced he would take the call outside. We three looked at each other expectantly. Everyone shrugged. None of us knew what was happening. This Sunday morning's coffee break had taken on interesting dimensions. Ben was gone for a few minutes. As he re-entered the room, he stuffed his notebook back into his pocket.

"I've got to go and make some phone calls," he announced. "It might take a while, say, half an hour. By then it will be time for lunch. Could one of you organise some lunch for us all to have here when I get back?"

Everyone nodded, and David said, "I noticed a kebab place down the far end of Byron Street. We might sample their wares if they are open today." Everyone nodded and murmured agreement.

"In the meantime, feel free to work on your own stuff or continue with the phone list, if you like," Ben suggested. He shot me a look, which I didn't understand, before leaving us. Now that attention had focused elsewhere, I decided I wouldn't mention that other scary name that appeared frequently on the phone list: Mr Green's real name.

Following Ben's departure, nobody made to leave, so we stayed at the kitchen counter and continued to pore over the phone list for a few more minutes until David decided it was time to go in search of lunch. Greg disappeared back to their kitchen at the other end of the complex to find something to drink with lunch, and I cleared away after the morning's coffee. The review of the phone list after Ben left was superficial at best. My trump card didn't attract any attention. I would reveal it to Ben when we were alone. In the meantime, it didn't seem worthwhile starting anything else while I waited for lunch and Ben to arrive.

David arrived first, laden with lunch, and complaining about the multitude of choices that confronted him at the kebab place. He had stuck his head into Ben's office before coming upstairs, and assured me Ben would join us shortly. I scurried about organising crockery and cutlery and, for want of anywhere else, set them out on the kitchen counter. Designed to serve as a breakfast bar, it could accommodate us all reasonably comfortably for lunch. Greg arrived with beers and apologised for the lack of choice of what to drink with lunch. Ben followed him in. Then we endured the usual brief period of filling plates and glasses before conversation of any import commenced. Ben led the way with an update on the situation with last night's prisoners.

As they thought, Mr Green (nobody bothered to refer to him as anything else) did have a string of outstanding warrants for his arrest. "His future is being handled by another officer now, but it looks as though extradition will be to Victoria. Proceedings have been initiated I believe." David, his brow furrowed, pondered Ben's information for a moment before speaking.

"It occurs to me that, whatever was going down here must have been big to lure Mr Green himself to Ralston. He avoided arrest for so long; he was like a ghost. It would have required something significant for him to get involved personally. His normal mode of operation is to stay well-hidden and to send in one of his lieutenants to run the operation. Whatever he wanted to meet with those mysterious people about must have been really big."

David's observation prompted nodding and murmured support for the notion from everyone. Without any details of Mr Green's history other than what I gained from the internet, I felt a little ill-informed compared to my present company. A question niggled at me since Ben's comments on this morning's prisoner interviews so, at the risk yet again of appearing naïve, I aired it.

"We've heard why the interviewees thought they were in Ralston, but not the 'who or what' details of the events that were supposed to occur when they met up with 'those people'. So, what was their objective... and why did they decide to take an interest in me?"

"Good questions," Greg conceded. "Are we any the wiser now, Ben?"

"I have nothing definite, but it appears this lot only arrived a few days before Sonny noticed them tailing her. However, I gained an inference that others had preceded them and, most likely, they – or a local recruit – nobbled your car, Sonny."

"Speaking of my car…"

"I'll talk to you later about that," Ben cut in, leaving me in no doubt the topic was off limits in present company. "They are interviewing the two wounded members this afternoon," Ben advised. "Let's see how co-operative they choose to be."

Lunch over, everyone moved to the more comfortable lounge chairs. Conversation returned to information collected from the prisoners this morning, and Ben elected to be a bit more expansive. He elaborated on the names of those locals they were hoping to bring in this afternoon for questioning. Reluctant to interrupt the flow of information and conversation generally between the three detectives, I sat quietly, making mental notes to myself, until all went quiet for a moment. Not wanting to be intrusive, I wasn't taking notes and was relying on my memory to retain everything I heard. I felt brain-fade setting in as I tried to remember all of the details. Time for something positive.

"As I was listening to the names of those locals that were of interest, it occurred to me that most of those – could even be all of those – feature on that phone list," I said, nodding to the list on the coffee table. "There might be a couple I didn't recognise. Could you give me them again please. I'll check the list as you call them."

Ben read out eight or nine names from his notes. Only three did not appear on the phone list. Of those on the list, there had been heavy call traffic to two of the names, with fewer calls recorded to the others. All three men bent forward over the low coffee table in an effort to follow what I was saying as I ran down the list. I sat back. The others continued to examine the list. My mind was approaching breakneck speed. I needed a white board, or paper and pencil, or something – anything – to write on. I needed to mind-map the vague connections my mind struggled to put together.

I slipped away unnoticed and went to the bedroom. In an effort to keep the living area tidy, I had stacked most of my office-type stuff in a corner of the bedroom. I dug through everything to find a small flip chart. Loaded up with the chart and coloured marker pens, I returned to the living area. The three men had moved around a bit during my absence and now spread themselves across most of the lounge area including the space I had recently vacated. I set my flipchart up near the kitchen bench, sat on a kitchen stool, spread my pens out on the counter, and blanked out everything to do with the other end of the room. No one appeared to notice, so I remained undisturbed while I worked.

I needed to get my mind organised and my thoughts in some sort of logical order. On the first sheet of the flip chart, using my own peculiar cryptic shorthand, I noted all the facts as I knew them. This always worked for me in unscrambling my thought processes. It also allowed me to see immediately where interconnections occurred. I tore the page off and spread it out on the counter so I could refer to it easily as I started the mind-mapping exercise. Different coloured markers were used to identify known facts and confirmed connections, probable connections still unconfirmed, and what I saw as (or deduced to be) possible connections.

Working quickly, it did not take me long to create the map of what I knew to be true, probably was true, and possibly could be true. Once I laid it all out visually, potential lines of enquiry became obvious – to me at least. I sat contemplating my handiwork for a couple of minutes. A lull in the drone of conversation from the other end of the room penetrated my thought processes and brought me back to reality. The others had ceased speaking and now sat looking at me expectantly.

Bugger! Am I ready to share all this yet, or does it need more work before I dare show it to them? It proved a rhetorical question. All three men stood up and moved in my direction. They gathered round and peered over my shoulders.

"What's this then?" asked David.

"It's called mind-mapping," I answered with a shrug. "When your mind is trying to hang onto too many threads, it's difficult to get a clear picture of everything that's going on. Once it's available visually, it becomes easier to see connections and make assumptions about future directions. It also frees up some head space to enable logical deductions."

I know I am babbling. No doubt because I feel self-conscious about them examining something that I haven't yet had time to look at closely myself. I saw Greg and David exchange a look. Then David gestured towards the flipchart.

"How do you add more on to it?"

"I'm not sure what you are asking," I answered slowly. "As more information becomes available, you simply extend the connections, or start new ones, if it's completely new information."

"There's nothing to do with our cases on there." David's observation sounded almost accusatory.

"I don't know anything about your cases." I glanced quickly at Ben. It wasn't exactly a lie. I didn't know details of their cases, although Ben had given me basic stuff about the 'funny' cases they were investigating.

"Oh, yeah, okay." David backed off. He glanced from Greg to Ben before resuming. "Straight away, I can see what look like possible connections with our stuff. How do you add to this; I mean, how do we get our info added to it?"

"Without knowing anything about your cases, I think it probably would be best to start them as separate maps. If you identify a common connection, it would create the link between the separate maps. That way, all of the maps that connect become like a group of satellites, all with common links."

"What are we waiting for?" Greg said, looking expectantly at David. "This is what we all got together for, and this is way better than the approach we adopted."

Ben nodded in agreement. The building excitement became almost palpable. I couldn't work out where it was all heading, and thought it a good idea to make my position clear. "Look, I'm not sure how much you two know, but Ben is aware, my only interest is in the murder of my client's mother, Therese Melrose. I don't know about any of the other cases the three of you might have open now... and I don't know that I need to know. If I can help, that's fine, but Melrose's death is my focus."

They all nodded their understanding. Ben excused himself, citing 'stuff going on downstairs' as needing his attention, and stood up to leave. David and Greg followed his example, claiming they had work to do, and disappeared off to the other end of the hallway. They beat Ben out of the room. I took advantage of the brief time while just the two of us remained together.

"Ben, there are a few things I need to talk through with you. I know you're busy, but I do need some time with you."

"Yes, I know. Maybe tonight; see how things go."

"...And what happened to that third car? Do we know where it is?" I called after him as he walked out the door.

He waved and responded over his shoulder, "Catch you later."

Alone at last. Yet again, I cleaned up, straightened the place up a bit, and moved my flipchart and markers to the far end of the room. Was there anything else that I knew but had omitted to add to the map? I settled back with my notes and the flipchart for a contemplative interlude. After about an hour, I made coffee before returning to my deliberations.

Disappointed, I put aside my notes. They provided no further information for the map. However, on a positive note, the map provides clear indications of where further investigation is required. It clearly suggests lines of enquiry, including questions I should pose to Kate and Emily. I am not sure how useful Emily will be but, if I asked the right questions, she might be able to pump her mother for answers. Of course, how possible that might be will depend on how successfully she manages to re-establish communications with her mother.

I retrieved the notebook from my bag, and spent the next half hour or so listing the questions I was going to ask the two women at our next meetings, whenever they might be. That done, I spent some time thinking about the questions I needed to put to Ben. Foremost is, when can I go home? I promised clients I would be back in Millhaven by tomorrow to commence work on their cases. Unless Ben surprises me, it looks as though I will be putting them off for a bit longer yet. I thought I had a strong argument to put to Ben though. With the 'SUV gang' rounded up, surely it was safe for me to go out now, even to go home.

What do you do on a Sunday afternoon when there are so many things to follow up, and no way for you to do any of it? My mind was still too actively engaged on the case to be able to settle down with my half read book. The only option appears to be to turn on TV and find a show that allows me to switch off for a while. Surfing the channels provided live coverage of every code of football imaginable, a couple of lame movies and a 24-hour news service. I was about to abandon the exercise when one of the movies finished and was followed by an episode of Midsomer Murders. Although an old episode – and one I already had seen a couple of times – it was the best on offer. Besides, John Nettles is always worth watching.

By the time the show ended, much of the afternoon had disappeared but it was still too early to think about dinner. I might as well fill in some time looking at those few remaining names that bothered me on the phone list. It's amazing what a fresh look at something reveals. The first thing to jump out at me was that there appeared to be two different people with the surname Fanning. One had the initial N, while the other's initial was B. Mr and Mrs? …Maybe not. They had different phone numbers.

They probably were not important but they aroused my curiosity. I thought it worthwhile digging around a bit to see if anything turned up. I chose the first entry on the list for that surname – N Fanning – and asked Google about it. It came up with more entries than I expected. Two of them screamed at me. One Norman Fanning was a public servant of Central Queensland now retired. More interestingly, what appeared to be the same Norman Fanning, retired public servant of Ralston, featured in an article on a tragic road accident. A check on the date revealed the accident happened on that fateful weekend a week ago. A vague recollection of the name from some distant time tried unsuccessfully to wriggle its way to the fore. Liz Cranston might know why the name was familiar.

The thought of Liz reminded me I had intended to ring her sometime this weekend. I checked the TV for the time. An early edition of local news had just started. It offered mainly sports results, but no mention of last night's operation or anything else of interest. It was a bit early to ring Liz. She would still be out walking the dog. In the meantime, I might as well move on to the next challenge: what to organise myself for dinner. As I rummaged in the fridge and freezer for inspiration, I found myself again rueing the fact that my life now seems to revolve around nothing more than food and coffee.

Eureka! There was a tray of frozen croissants, and I remembered there is cheese and – I think – a packet of ham in the fridge. Once the croissants were in the oven, I took a break from domesticity and rang Liz Cranston. She had been Therese's assistant for many years, and was an astute operator. If anyone noticed anything different in Therese's behaviour in recent time, it would be Liz. She also had an amazing knowledge of who was who in the Public Service.

I half expected Liz not to answer. It was Sunday evening. Liz and her 'good friend' Jim, the security officer, probably had better things to do than be sitting at home. I smiled to myself as I listened to her phone ringing. After a relationship that had lasted all these years, I would expect her to be comfortable enough to admit to their being more than 'good friends'. I told myself, one more ring and I'll hang up. Then she answered.

"Hi Liz, have I caught you at a bad time?"

"Sonny. No, I've just come back from walking the dog. I heard the phone ringing as I opened the gate."

"Are you okay to talk, or would you rather I rang you back later."

"No, now is good. I've been dying to hear from you. At work, we all seem to be operating in a parallel universe. It's as though we are isolated from the rest of the world. We don't know anything. What's been happening? Is there anything new regarding Therese?"

…And I thought I was going to ask the questions! "That's interesting. I did ring to talk about Therese. What do you mean when you say you don't know anything? Surely, Ken has been talking to people, and I would have expected him to be talking to you in particular. The pair of you often used to share a chat and a joke."

"Our great white leader …"

"Your what?"

"The Director… has forbidden anyone to speak about Therese or speculate on what might have happened to her. He singled Ken and me out for special attention, and not particularly pleasant that was too. I don't know what he said to Ken, but I do know it ended in a heated exchange."

"That's ridiculous. What the hell's he playing at? Who exactly are you not to discuss it with?"

"Everyone and anyone – both internal and external. There hasn't been anything said officially about her death. The official line is that she is away and may be away for some time."

"Yeah, for a bloody long time. Geez, it looks like I've put you in an untenable position. I'm sorry, Liz. I wouldn't have called if…"

"Don't be silly. Discuss away, I'm all ears."

"So, who is filling in while she is 'away'?"

"No one; everything has to go through to the Director. It makes my job difficult I can tell you."

Now that is interesting, and there was a brief pause while I tried to digest that nugget of information and its implications.

# Chapter Twelve

After Liz's revelation about the Director taking direct control, I had difficulty pulling my thoughts together. I would have thought Geoff had more to do than get involved in the day-to-day running of a School and the campus. It took me a few moments – spent making rude comments about the Director to fill the hiatus – before I asked Liz if she noticed any change in Therese's behaviour over the last month or so.

"Since I first spoke to you, I've spent hours going over everything in my mind, looking for anything that might be a clue. There were changes. Her work pattern changed for one thing and she seemed distracted. She made mistakes and forgot a few things, like appointments even though they were in her calendar. She blamed me for those. I knew they had been in her calendar. I put them there, and I always print out a couple of weeks in advance so I know what to have ready for her meetings. The missed meetings appear on my printouts. When she accused me of forgetting to add them, I checked her calendar. They were gone."

"Who has access to her calendar?"

"Just the two of us: Therese and me."

I pictured the indignation and hurt Therese must have caused Liz. Liz was one of the best PAs around and Therese knew that. They had a funny working relationship, one based on mutual respect. As Liz tells it, Therese's behaviour seems way out of character. It sounded to me like she had tried to cover up something, and probably removed those entries from her calendar herself. Who else could have done it?

We chatted for a couple of minutes about staff and the department; nothing of any importance. I was edging the conversation towards asking about Norman Fanning when she suddenly returned to the original topic of Therese's behaviour.

"You know, now that I think about it, there was something else. She was away a lot more. She was always out of the office a fair bit but, suddenly, it seemed like she was *never* here."

141

"Was there something happening within the department that might account for it? You know what I mean, some new crisis or something?" I prompted her.

"No, and some of the absences were substantial. Some of them I didn't know anything about. She would just announce she wouldn't be in for the next couple of days. On other occasions, she would mark out slabs of time in her calendar as 'out of office' but never say where she was going or why she would be absent. I always asked if she wanted something prepared to take with her – photocopying, files or whatever – but the answer generally was 'no'." That certainly was a departure from the norm for the Therese I had known.

The opportunity to ask about Norman Fanning finally arrived. I swear I could hear down the phone line Liz's mind working overtime as she searched her memory banks for the information I wanted.

"I don't know much about him. He wasn't with our department and moved to Ralston from somewhere up north. Not too long after he arrived here, he retired. I remember him as being old – past the normal retirement age – but, this being the Public Service, there couldn't be forced retirement. Anyway, retire he did after only a short while in Ralston. I only remember him because of his connection to Therese."

"What sort of connection?"

"There were a lot of phone calls between them in the early days. I think his arrival in Ralston was not long before you left us. Contact with Therese dropped off after he retired but I think there were still a few phone calls after that. I have the feeling they knew each other – or worked together or something – sometime in the past. Norman stayed in Ralston after he retired. I think he had family here. Don't know much more than that, I'm afraid."

"Thanks, Liz, that's great. I came across his name somewhere recently and I recognised the name but didn't know why." It would pass for a 'white' lie.

I was winding up the conversation when Liz remembered something else.

"It's funny you should mention that name: Fanning, I mean. When I was trying to gather that information to email to Therese in those few days she was missing, I was scratching around in the piles of stuff she accumulates on her desk. I came across a scrap of paper covered in scribble and doodles – the sort of thing you do when you are on the phone. I looked at it to make sure there was nothing important before I threw it out. The Fanning son's name was on it. Now what was his name?... Brett ... no ... Brenton ... Yes, Brenton Fanning, That's it. I'd guess she had spoken to the son sometime recently."

My guess would be much the same. After promising to keep her informed, the phone call finally ended. By then, I could smell my croissants were ready. I plonked myself at the kitchen counter with a croissant and a mineral water, and went over my notes from my conversation with Liz. I returned to Google and searched for information on the road accident the previous weekend that involved Norman Fanning. Norman, his wife and two grandchildren were killed when their car ran off the highway just south of Ralston and ended up at the bottom of a deep gully.

Somehow, during all that I managed to polish off two croissants. I wrapped the other two in foil and stashed them in the fridge. I was deep in thought as I cleaned up, when Greg's voice brought me back to earth.

"May the three musketeers enter?"

All three marched in, David and Greg each clutching a bundle of paper. Ben, empty handed, gave me an apologetic look as he passed. It didn't take me long to work out what that was all about. David took the lead.

"We've put together – sort of listed might be more accurate – all the information on our two major cases. Not sure what to do next, we thought we would bring it here to see if you could do one of those map things with what we've got."

After a couple of heartbeats, and none too enthusiastically, I said, "Show me what you've got. It's not difficult to do. Even you two could do it. This will not be the same as producing my own map. I already knew all the information for that. The connections were already firmly in my mind. I've been living with that case for over a week now. All I can do for you is map exactly what you have on these pages. I don't know all the nuances, all the grey areas that might relate."

They both sat smiling at me, hands in laps and nodding enthusiastically.

"Right; well bugger off and let me get on with it... and don't expect anything tonight."

All three stood and started to move off.

"Not you, Ben. I want to talk to you."

"I thought you might." He sighed and sat back down.

I was tired and a bit cranky. No doubt, he was tired too, but I was not in a mood to make concessions. Answers were wanted, and I was going to get them before he left tonight. The interrogation began and a quick-fire staccato question and answer session followed. "What is the status of my car and where is it?

"It's okay but it's locked up in the workshop."

"Can I now go out and about to be able to do my job?"

"Possibly; I'll let you know tomorrow."

"When can I go home? I've clients to see, a business to run."

"Maybe in a couple of days."

"What happened to that third hire car?"

"It hung around Normanton for a while but now seems to be stationary at Burketown."

"What tipped the SUV gang off about my involvement in looking into Therese Melrose's death?"

"I'm not sure yet, but I am still asking questions."

Playing 20 questions lost its appeal, especially as the answers hadn't been all that helpful.

"Can I go now?" Ben asked with a hint of pleading.

"Yeah, okay. You're not being much use anyway." I resigned myself to that fact that was all I was going to get. "Oh, no, hang on. Why haven't you mentioned Norman Fanning's accident to me?"

There was a blank look and a slight pause. "Who the hell is Norman Fanning… and what does his accident have to do with anything?"

"I was hoping you were going to tell me."

"Look, I'm tired and not in the mood for playing silly games. Tell me what you're on about or I'm leaving now."

"Okay, if you genuinely don't know about Norman Fanning, perhaps you had better look into his road accident last weekend. My gut tells me you might have another 'funny' death on your hands – four of them to be precise."

"Christ, not more."

I gave him as much as I had been able to glean from the internet and the bit from Liz about a possible connection to Therese."

"It would have been one of Pete Messell's cases, and still an open case. Pete's been off all week. He caught the same flu bug as the coroner had. He'll be back tomorrow. I'll try to catch him first thing. Your thinking on this one might be right."

One last question – well, two actually – and I would then have run out of things to ask. "When is the Special Task mob back? What about the 'rotten apple', is that going to be an ongoing problem?"

"They were going to come back on Tuesday afternoon, but I might bring them back earlier. The rotten apple issue will cease to exist after tomorrow morning."

We said goodnight, and I almost immediately became acutely aware of being very weary. I managed to get myself into bed in something approaching warp speed.

*****

Monday morning had me feeling less than enthusiastic about everything. In Ralston for over a week now, I found myself increasingly fed-up with being virtually under house arrest. I watched an early morning news broadcast while I ate breakfast, and dawdled around in the kitchen afterwards. Any procrastination rather than get started on what I had to do.

What did I have to do today? Only those blasted maps for David and Greg. Now, those two did present as an interesting team. David was a bit aloof; bright enough but a bit superior in his approach. Something of a show pony disposition perhaps. I felt there was some deeper current running through David. My subconscious likened him to an iceberg: only some part of him was visible. Greg, on the other hand, was down to earth, open and the more astute of the two. Nevertheless, they were a good pairing, as each of their strengths and weaknesses was a perfect foil for the other's. Although based at different stations in the metropolitan area, recent circumstances brought them together, and now with Ben involved as well, the three of them made a formidable team.

I settled myself at the flipchart, stacked up David and Greg's respective paperwork on the coffee table, and prepared to attack the mapping task. The first bundle of paper randomly selected turned out to be David's notes. Might as well read it all first before I try to map it. It was a lot more detailed than I expected. I offered him a half-hearted mental apology. When I reached the end, I went back to the beginning and started again. I was hooked. Some things immediately suggested possible connections to the periphery of my map. With my pulse rate now slightly elevated, I launched with gusto into mapping David's information.

When I finished mapping all of David's information, I took a moment to sit back and study his chart. It had been frustrating work. Just about every fact I recorded seemed to throw an unanswered question at me. I decided to jot down those questions. You never

145

know, maybe it will help open up some new lines of enquiry for them, I told myself. That's when my phone rang.

It was Kate. She was dropping the kids off at school when her solicitor called to ask her to come and see him first thing. She phoned while waiting to see him.

"It can only be about that stuff I asked him to do on Friday," she said excitedly. "I'll let you know as soon as I'm finished here."

"Don't get your hopes up too high," I counselled. "It's too soon yet for him to have uncovered very much."

With the long list of questions for David completed, I prowled around the living area for a while to clear my head and stretch a bit before tackling Greg's information. I hesitated by the kitchen. Was it too early for another coffee? While pondering this important question, my phone rang again. This time it was Emily.

She sounded a bit concerned, but had information to share. "I rang my mother as soon as I thought it was safe to do so this morning. Our conversation started out quite stilted, but she loosened up after a while; gave me all these excuses for not ringing me. Some of them might have been true, but somehow I could detect my father behind it all. Anyway, the long and short of it is, I lost it and told her she was expecting me to believe a load of rubbish. If she was telling me the truth, wasn't it strange she was able to ring my sister a few times but not me?"

"Ooh, I don't imagine that went down too well."

"Well, no. It was a bit harsh I suppose. She started sniffling and got upset. I was right about my father being involved. He had forbidden her to contact me. She didn't seem to know why exactly, but said it had something to do with us – her and I or, more particularly, me – having gotten involved in Therese's death in some way."

"Did she explain what that was all about?"

"She didn't know I don't think. She was upset and confused, not by my call, but by my father's attitude to her – and his attitude generally over this whole Therese thing. Can we meet up somehow somewhere? We ended up having a good chat and I asked her a few things. I'd rather discuss it with you face to face if we could."

"Sounds like the right way to go. Give me a few minutes to see if I can organise parole or a leave pass or something to get out of this place. I'll call you back."

I tried Ben's number: no answer. I gathered up a few things I wanted to take with me and stowed them in my bag. Still no response from Ben's phone. Desperation was setting in. I didn't like venturing downstairs, but I was determined to meet with Emily and Kate today. I took the elevator to the ground floor and went down to Ben's office. No sign of him. On my way back to the elevator, I was mulling over what to do next, when I rounded the corner and ran headlong into that stunning blonde police woman.

She extended her hand, "Hi again, I'm Sam. Is everything okay?"

"I was looking for Ben but he appears not to be around at the moment."

"No, I think he is out on a case right now. Can I help at all?"

An idea occurred to me as she was speaking. "You passed yourself off as me for my 'relocation' the other night?"

"Yes, there wasn't terribly much involved in that." She gave a small, embarrassed smile.

"No, maybe not, but I am wondering if the Station has a collection of props – disguises – for use in, say, undercover operations."

"Not really, but I've collected a few bits and pieces from jobs I've worked on. I keep them in a cupboard out the back. Would you like to have a look?"

I nodded and she led me through to a storage area and unlocked a cupboard. The first thing to catch my attention was a hat. It was a pale yellow straw number with a wide floppy brim, and a plaited ribbon hatband held in place by a bunch of oversized artificial daisies that created a riot of colour against the pale straw.

"Where did you get that hat? It looks like a relic of the '70s."

"Do you mind? I only bought it a couple of weeks ago."

"Could I borrow some of this stuff?" She hesitated for the length of a couple of heartbeats.

"Hmm, I suppose so; as long as it doesn't get me fired. What would you like?"

"Definitely that hat and I rather like that long red wig."

Sam pulled them out and placed them on top of a nearby filing cabinet. "There's a large tote bag in here somewhere that would go with that hat. Ah, here it is. What are you going to wear with all this?"

"What you see. I was only coming to Ralston for a couple days, so I didn't pack much of a wardrobe. This is about the extent of my resources."

She looked me up and down and went back to rummaging in the cupboard. "No, that won't do. This will work better than what you've got on."

She handed me a colourful, wildly pattern caftan looking … er, shirt? Dress?

"It's a beach cover-up. You know, it's something you wear over your bathers to maintain some degree of decency while you parade along the beach."

Made of light gauzy material, I couldn't see myself parading along a beach in it. I tried it on over my shirt. It was loose and mid-thigh length. On Sam, it probably looked like a tent. As I bundled everything into the large tote bag, Sam voiced her concern.

"Whatever it is you're planning to do, I'd prefer Ben didn't know I had a hand in it."

"Understood; he won't find out from me. The sisterhood is strong."

I rang Emily while on my way up in the elevator and arranged a meeting at her apartment, and gave her information about the laneway behind the Italian restaurant where we had eaten a couple of nights ago. "Pick me up outside the Precinct's side door that opens into the laneway. I'll be waiting inside. Sound your horn when you arrive."

That done, I tried on my newly acquired disguise. In the midst of trying various hairstyles with the red wig, my phone rang: Kate again. "Sonny, I have to talk to you. I don't know what to make of anything anymore. Can we meet now somewhere? I need to talk to you about the stuff the solicitor has found out."

"Emily is in town at the moment and I've just arranged to meet her at her apartment. Do you need to talk to me privately, or would you like to join us at the apartment?"

She elected to come to the apartment. I gave her the address and she said she would be there in about 20 minutes. Time was getting away. Emily would be waiting. I grabbed my bag, intending to empty its contents into the tote bag. Then I realised my whole bag would fit into the tote. I shoved the bag into the tote, slammed on the hat and my sunglasses, and headed for the elevator again.

There weren't many people around on the ground floor. I walked quickly out the back door of the station and through the courtyard to the door in the perimeter wall of the precinct. I opened the door a crack and peered out into the lane: no sign of Emily yet. While I waited to hear her car horn, I checked what I could see of my outfit. Sandals replaced my runners. They looked okay, but I decided the jeans spoiled the effect and needed a bit of adjustment. I bent down and rolled them up a few turns, exposing a bit of bare calf. There, that looks more in keeping with the rest of the outfit.

While admiring my handiwork, I heard the car horn. I peered out cautiously – just in case! Then rushed through the gate and dived into the car. Emily drove off as soon as my door closed. With eyes focused straight ahead, she drove – a little too fast perhaps – the length of the lane before speaking.

"It is Sonny, I presume? If I hadn't known I was picking you up there, I probably would have locked the doors the moment you tried to get into the car."

We both giggled as she drove out of the lane and onto Byron Street. She offered to drop me at the front door of the apartment block before going to park the car. I needed some exercise, so opted to walk back from the car with her. Once we got out of the car, instinct replaced bravado. On high alert, we walked quickly through the carpark and into the apartment block. I broke our silence on the way up in the elevator.

"Emily, I hope you don't mind, but I have asked Kate to join us here. Her solicitor has given her some information this morning that I think I'm going to want to know about – and as soon as possible."

I briefly explained my meeting with Kate last Friday and the list of things I asked her to see if her solicitor could pursue for us. Emily let us into her apartment and I dumped the heavy tote on the nearest chair.

"I'm fine with Kate coming. I too want to know what she has to add to the story. I was going to make coffee. Do you know how long Kate will be? Should I wait till she arrives?"

"She should be here in a few minutes, so maybe we should wait. This is a nice apartment. It even has a view. With the way tariffs are in the city at the moment, it must be costing you a packet."

"No, it's really cheap. The mining company I work for leased the whole building some time ago. Staff who have to come into the city for business, medical or whatever could never get accommodation. Everywhere always was booked out. It's all due to the mining boom in this area. So, the company acquired this place and only lets it out to staff. We book apartments through our HR department and only pay a pittance. I stayed here once before, but I prefer to pay and stay somewhere else, away from the people I work with."

Kate's arrival ended the conducted tour of the apartment. She looked awful, even more haggard than the last time I saw her, if that was possible. Her eyes were almost lost in deep smudgy shadows, and her dress hung off her to the extent that she looked like she was wearing one of her mother's oversized frocks. Emily made coffee while the three of us kept up idle chatter about nothing in particular.

It was obvious Kate was anxious to start telling her story and, as soon as the coffee arrived, she launched into her commentary.

"I don't know what to make of it, Sonny. The more information we uncover, the murkier everything looks. I just cannot take it all in. My mother owns two very large buildings, here in Ralston."

Okay, that is interesting, but if I don't get some direction happening in Kate's report, I am in danger of ending up in a state of complete confusion. "Suppose you start from when the solicitor called you this morning and then work through your meeting step by step."

"As I told you, I went to his office as soon as I dropped the kids off at school. First up, he explained to me how, in estate matters, he appoints one of his staff to monitor bank accounts. The job of this person – the monitor – is to identify regular debtors and creditors who might need contacting if they don't respond to the advertisement the solicitor places in the newspaper. The person attached to Mum's estate was away for a couple of days at the end of last week, so she came in a little earlier this morning to make the routine checks on all the accounts she is looking after. The checks she would normally have run at the end of last week. As soon as her boss arrived, she showed him a printout of the KLN Trading account. I've got a copy here."

She handed me a sheet of paper from her bag. Emily leaned over so she could read it as well. "I can see there was a deposit last Friday made by what looks like a real estate firm. There doesn't seem to have been any other by them during the period covered by this printout," I said.

"No. That's what caused all the fuss. The solicitor rang the firm straight away thinking they might have made a mistake and deposited it in the wrong account somehow. They assured him the deposit was correct and told him about the two buildings Therese owned, and how all the rent has been going to paying off their purchase loans."

"Do we know anything about the buildings?"

"Turns out, I drive past one of them fairly often without knowing anything about it. It's a multi-storey apartment block. I think it has five floors. It's huge. Apparently it comprises a mixture of one, two and three bedroom apartments."

"Given current rental prices in Ralston, it must bring in a packet each week. Do you know how many apartments there are?" Emily asked.

Kate dug in her bag again. "I've got some details here somewhere."

"Have a look for it later. Keep going with the story for now," I encouraged her.

"Right, where was I? Oh yes, apparently the real estate firm looks after letting the apartments but is also the property manager. They look after cleaning, any maintenance and pay any bills. The strange thing is, the top floor is never rented out. Its only access is with a special key for the elevator. The real estate mob doesn't have a key. A privately hired cleaner comes periodically. They don't know who she is, but she always parks in one of the parking spaces allocated to that top floor."

"If there is a cleaner it must mean someone lives there, or at least visits occasionally," Emily ventured, and looked expectantly at me for support for her theory.

"A reasonable assumption, thanks Emily. The question then is who hires her? Presumably that's the tenant of the top floor."

While we spoke, Kate removed more photocopies from her bag and pushed them across to me. "Here's the information on the apartments that I was looking for. While I was with the solicitor, his contact in the Titles Office sent through the Real Property information for the two buildings owned by KLN Trading."

"Thanks, Kate. What do we know about the second building? Do we have any information on that?"

"Yes, I was just going to start telling you about that one. It's right here in the city. It's multi-storey again, with shops on the ground floor and office accommodation on the one above. The top two floors are apartments. It's also huge. I had a look at it as I drove in. Located right in the city heart like it is, it must bring in an enormous rental."

Emily's brow furrowed. "If these places are bringing in considerable income, why haven't there been other deposits into that account? I don't understanding how there wasn't anything until last week to create an awareness of these buildings."

"The real estate person explained that. She – Mum – bought the apartment block first. Paid a considerable amount off the purchase price and took out a loan to cover the rest. Any rental money left over after expenses went towards paying off the loan. Then, a couple of years ago, she went through the same process to buy the second building, extending the original loan to cover the balance of the price on this second building. The rental income from both buildings then went towards paying off the substantial loan. That deposit made last week was to go into the account the previous week. However, they were finalising the loan repayment and that took a bit longer than expected."

"So the loans are now paid out?" I checked my understanding of what she had said.

"So it seems. The real estate people were aware there would be a surplus of funds in the trust account, but they had to wait until they finalised everything to do with the loan before they could work out how much remained to deposit into the KLN Trading account. That one deposit that led to uncovering details of the two buildings was the balance of the rental trust account."

"I know this must have been going on over a period of years but, even so, either the loans were very small, relatively speaking, or there was an incredible income stream available to pay them off so soon," I suggested.

"While I was with the solicitor, one of the staff made a few calls and tracked down the loan. She had them send a copy of the transaction file and brought it into us just as we were about to wind up the meeting. You can see that the regular repayments are all there. In addition, every so often, there is an extra payment of a large sum of money from outside the rental trust account."

Kate thrust more photocopies at me. Emily moved around to sit beside me so it was easier for her to read anything Kate gave me, as she did now. Her eyebrows rose slightly and she gave a low whistle. Kate and I swung round to look at Emily.

"Those extra repayments are big. Could it have been a build-up of left over rental funds over a period of time getting to a point where they needed to be cleared out?" Emily asked.

"How do you mean?" Kate responded. "The excess funds every month went towards the loan."

Emily thought for a moment before replying. "Yes, but I was thinking that the real estate mob would have withheld a certain amount each month to cover anticipated expenses and contingencies. There probably were months when expenditure was less than provided for, allowing a surplus to remain in a 'working account' or something similar. Eventually, that would need to be cleared out I imagine, or reduced to some extent. What's your take on the extra payments, Sonny?"

"I don't know, and I'm not prepared to speculate at this stage. However, if the information you received is that it came from an outside source, then I don't think it came from any account the real estate people handled."

Tears trickled down Kate's cheeks. "How could she do this? How could my mother do this to us? She charged us rent every week when we could ill afford it and were struggling to make ends meet ... but she needed the money 'to help pay off the house we were all living in'. What a lie," Kate spat venomously.

We allowed her a moment to compose herself before, while still sniffling, she continued.

"The real estate people also said she had taken out a 30-days option on another property. She was looking at buying some building off the plan in that new beach suburb development. There are still a couple of weeks to go on the option. They expected her to take up the option before she paid out the existing loan. If she chose to do that, in much the same way as before, she could extend the existing loan to cover the new purchase and roll it over. When nothing eventuated, they had to make the final loan repayment."

Silence reigned for a few moments while we digested Kate's revelations. Emily broke the silence. "Obviously she wasn't short of cash if she was planning to buy more property."

"I don't understand why she seems obsessed with acquiring buildings. Why couldn't she at least tell us about what she was doing?"

Both women were looking at me as though I had the answers to their questions. I was still struggling with my own questions. "Kate, I'm not sure you are ready for some of those answers. Some may not be what you want to hear," I warned.

"I need to know, Sonny. So, if you have any ideas, please share them. I know I'm a mess at the moment but I can deal with anything – if I know what it is."

"Okay, but this is merely speculation on my part. My preliminary thinking is that KLN Trading was a shelf company that your mother was using to 'lose' money coming in from unknown sources."

"Are you talking about money laundering?" Emily blurted out, and then bit her lip when she realised it was not the most tactful comment.

"I suppose that is what I am thinking. You can't keep accumulating vast amounts of money without eventually attracting attention.

By buying real estate in a company name instead of her own, she managed to avoid attracting any attention – so far. In reality, she didn't lose anything as her shelf company retains some valuable property. However, I suspect she didn't realise that, at some point in time, a company that acquired considerable valuable property, also would come under scrutiny."

"Sonny, what am I supposed to do?"

My heart went out to her. She looked totally defeated. "Nothing; go home. Try to get on with life as normally as possible. We still have some other things we asked your solicitor to look into for us. Let's wait and see what comes from that."

It was late and we hadn't had lunch. Emily offered to slip out and get something. Kate shook her head, said she wasn't hungry, and should go as she had things to do before she picked the kids up from school. She left. Emily and I decided we were starving.

# Chapter Thirteen

Having regained some of our bravado, we walked to a cafeteria across from the carpark, ordered toasted sandwiches and sat down. Emily was nervous. So was I, but I selected a seat that allowed a good view of the street while keeping me relatively hidden. I was putting a lot of trust in my disguise, and the belief that the round-up on Friday night had netted the entire SUV mob. We despatched our lunch without anything untoward happening and walked back to Emily's apartment. Although we heard and dealt with Kate's news as much as possible, there was still Emily's news to hear.

I opened the conversation as soon as we were back in her apartment. "Right, how did you go with the call to your mother?"

She reiterated the points she gave me over the phone before reporting the key points from what her mother had said. "Her main concern is my father. He is cranky and distant. She can't even have a conversation with him, and he has been away a lot. She says he is hardly ever home. She thinks he is working on special projects for the Director General; doesn't know details though. From something she found in his pocket – I think it might have been a boarding pass – she knows he has been out west and up to Burketown."

"Burketown…?" I echoed. I could hear that little bell ringing – no, clanging loudly more like.

"Yeah, Burketown; she can't understand why he would need to go there. Overall, I don't think her life is too good right now, and she's talking about spending a week or two with my sister. We put in place an arrangement whereby I could call her when dad wasn't around. I didn't ask any questions about the time out west because I didn't think it worthwhile right then."

"I didn't ask Kate about their time pre-Ralston either. I doubt she has thought about it anyway. She certainly wasn't in any state to cope with anything else today, but I am going to have to follow up with her. There is something else too that I need to ask her about that happened out there." Liz Cranston's comments about Therese having a problem with someone from out there were stuck in my mind.

155

It was three o'clock and I needed to get back to the precinct. We spent a few minutes going over Kate's information, but it was time to go. Emily drove me back and dropped me off in the lane at the same place she collected me from this morning. I slipped in through the side door and into the station.

The duty officer did a slight double take as I walked past on my way to the elevator. I barely had time to dump my bag and pour myself a cold drink when Ben burst in, without knocking and, as I discovered, with no intention of wasting time on niceties.

"Where the hell have you been all day?" he demanded loudly. "And what's with the get-up?"

I groaned inwardly. The duty officer, told to keep an eye out for me, probably informed Ben the moment I returned. I couldn't get a word in to answer his questions, so I let him rant for a while. I could see his point of view – to some degree. At last, he seemed to be running out of steam. He ceased bawling me out, threw his hands in the air and shook his head. "I can't work you out. Have you got nothing to say?"

"Oh, I've got plenty to say… as soon as I get a chance to speak. And, for your information, I did try to talk to you before I left this morning but you weren't around and weren't answering your phone. Both Kate and Emily had information they wanted to deliver face to face." I shoved a sheaf of papers at him. "Make photocopies of these and I'll share that information with you."

He opened his mouth to protest, thought better of it, turned on his heel and strode off down the hallway to return a few minutes later with a sheaf of paper in each hand. I sorted them into order and gave him back one set. We settled ourselves on the lounge chairs, each of us with our pile of paper on the coffee table in front of us. I started with Kate's information about the buildings, working my way through the relevant documents as I went.

"Ben, the thing that's been bugging me about Therese's case from the start was the absolute lack of anything personal in her flat. There were no bills, no bank statements, no mail of any descript. Like most normal humans, she would have accumulated photos and other personal bits and pieces but they weren't there in the flat. There was nothing. It was like a motel room with only an overnight occupant just stopping over on their way through to somewhere else."

"I wasn't aware. Langborne's report didn't mention anything like that."

"I don't think Langborne investigated the granny flat. He immediately accepted it as a domestic accident and his investigation didn't go any further. The flat was sterile, Ben. I've been wracking my brain for the last week trying to work out where she might keep such things. We checked everywhere in the flat. Kate said she didn't store anything upstairs, and her PA couldn't find anything at work. I think the top floor of that apartment block might be her bolt hole. It might be where she really *lives*. If not, some other very interesting person must be the tenant." I finished with a shrug.

He looked off into the distance for a moment before replying. "You know, I think we might just have to get a warrant for a bit of a look around up there. Do we know anything about the cleaning lady?"

"Not a thing other than, according to the contract cleaners for the rest of the building, there is one and she parks in a top floor parking space when she comes."

With Kate's information dealt with, I moved onto what I had gleaned from Emily. Nothing nearly so significant or substantial in this, but it did provide something else to think about. With nothing more to gain from talking to me, Ben left, but not till after a few more admonishments about staying put and doing as he asked. Huh, fat chance!

The rest of the afternoon I spent typing up my notes and working on mapping the information for David and Greg. My stomach rumbled. I realised lunch had been light and a few hours ago; time to think about dinner. For want of anything more exciting, I unwrapped the remaining two croissants and popped them in the oven. I was contemplating whether to turn TV on when my phone rang.

"Hi Kate, what …."

"Sonny, there's been a shooting. They shot the dog and Ken's been hurt. Everything downstairs is a mess," she screamed down the phone.

Before she had finished speaking, I was pounding on the door at the other end of the hallway, my phone still gripped to my ear. Greg opened it. He stepped back, startled as I rushed past him. Ben was speaking on his phone. He held up a hand to stop me. After a few more words, he terminated the call and I started to speak.

"There's been a shooting at…," but he was already on his way out the door.

"Stay here!" he shouted at me. "Do not let her leave," he barked at the other two men.

He was gone, and there were three stunned people left standing in the Special Task Force office. David regained the power of speech first. "You look like you need a stiff drink. What's happened? What new disaster has occurred?"

He thrust a tumbler with about two-fingers of Scotch into my free hand. With my other hand, I was searching my speed dial for Emily's number.

"Emily, are you okay? Look, there's been an incident at Kate's place. I don't think it's associated with our meeting today but, just to be on the safe side, don't go out if you can avoid it."

"Is she all right? I wasn't going out. I was watching TV."

"Yes, she's all right. Please stay put if you can until I know what's happening."

I ended the call as Greg began shepherding me through to their small sitting room. David took command.

"Sit down. Drink up. The question still stands: what's happening? You and Ben look as though Armageddon is about to arrive."

I told them about Kate's call and the shooting. Now my conscience was prickling. I was concerned that today's meeting with me might have been the trigger."

"Was anyone shot?"

"No, I don't think so... oh yes, the dog. She said Ken had been hurt. She didn't say 'shot'. The kids are terrified. I could hear them screaming in the background. I think our crime scene came in for some special attention."

There was silence as we sipped our drinks and tried to take it all in.

Oh, shit! I forgot the croissants." I made a beeline for the door.

"Where the hell do you think you're going?" Greg queried as he blocked my exit.

"I've got croissants in the oven. They'll be cinders by now."

They both followed me down to my kitchen. The croissants were a sorry sight.

"We had just decided we were having fish and chips for dinner and ordered enough for three large blokes," Greg announced. "That was before all the excitement broke loose. It should arrive downstairs shortly. I'm sure there will be enough for two burly blokes and one not so burly female."

David retrieved the bottle of Scotch from their quarters and I consigned the croissants to the bin while Greg, summoned by the duty officer, went downstairs to collect our dinner. While we waited for

Greg to return, it occurred to me that I should alert Ben to something. However, I had a sneaking suspicion he would not take my call, either thinking I was interfering or because he was too busy. There's always more than one way to do things.

"David, do you have your phone with you?" He held it out to me and I dialled Ben's number.

"Ben, don't hang up. There's something I think might be important."

"Okay, but make it quick."

"How badly hurt is Ken?"

"Lacerations from flying glass; a couple of them will need suturing so they've taken him off for attention. What is so important?"

"Ken has been acting strangely, inconsistent with 'normal' and inconsistent with what might be expected given recent circumstances. Kate and I both shared some concerns about him. I have not yet managed to convince myself he is not involved in whatever Therese was involved in." I didn't mention my troubling thought. The moment I heard what had happened, my mind flashed back to the comment by the SUV interviewee about cleaning up the mess in Ralston. Was Ken part of that mess? It was beginning to look increasingly likely.

"Hmm, thank you. That ties in with something else. As soon as we arrived, we loaded Kate and the kids into a van to take them away from the scene. As they were trying to get them into the vehicle, Kate started yelling at Ken: 'why were they trying to shoot you? What have you been up to? Why would they want to kill you too?' I didn't give it too much thought at the time, thinking it was just shock and reaction to the incident. There might be more to it though. I've got to go."

As I handed David his phone, he looked at me expectantly.

"...Everything okay?"

I grimaced. "I don't know, but I'm beginning to doubt that it is."

Very little conversation intruded on the despatch of the fish and chips. As I cleared away, David was deep in thought. When I returned to my lounge chair, he voiced those thoughts.

"The information you've fed Ben certainly is significant to his investigation. I doubt it would have been easy for his team to gather the same information as quickly."

Before responding to his comment, I searched his face for signs of a hidden agenda but found none.

"I had the advantage of being on the scene earlier than Ben but, also, I used to be a Public Servant for many years and worked in this particular department. In a sense, that gives me some sort of insider knowledge of how things work; makes it easier to identify when things look abnormal. I've also traded heavily on past friendships to get some of that information."

"Don't misunderstand the comment," Greg cut in hurriedly. "It's envy. We would love to have someone feeding us that kind of information on the cases we are dealing with."

"Looks like Ben is in for another very late night," David mused.

"Look guys, I'm not going to go anywhere. It is late and I don't think we are going to see Ben tonight. Why don't we all call it quits and turn in for the night?"

I had expected some degree of resistance, but there was no argument. The night's events left me unsettled. I knew I would not be able to sleep, so I curled up in a lounge chair with the book I had been trying to read all week. Shortly after midnight, the sound of soft footsteps leading to my door made me abandon my book. There was a gentle – perhaps tentative – knock. I snagged my bag off the nearby chair and crossed the room quickly to stand just inside the darkened bedroom doorway. A key rattled in the lock. My hand slid into my bag and gripped the Glock. I held my breath as I heard the gentle swish as the door opened and then closed.

Then Ben's voice was calling softly, "Sonny. Sonny, are you still awake?"

My hand came out of the bag. The gun remained in its resting place. The less Ben knows about the contents of my bag the better. I stepped out of the bedroom and into the living area. "Could be a bit risky breaking into someone's place at this hour of the night don't you think?"

"I didn't know if you'd still be awake or not but I noticed your light was on. I thought you might want a report back on your client and the Tirandi Street incident."

"I do, I do. Would you like a coffee, or a drink? David left his bottle of scotch here."

I was relieved when he refused. I wasn't inclined to play hostess right now. We sat and Ben delivered his concise report. I asked questions, but most of them would remain unanswered until at least tomorrow. The only real information he had to offer was that they had the shooter in custody. He was one of the locals they had interviewed on Sunday. Kate and her children were now in safer accommodation with Police guards.

My mind went into overdrive. I need to speak to Kate. Because of the relationship we have developed, I believe I will be able to get more of the finer details about tonight out of her than Ben will, and I need to be able to sort out in my own mind whether our meeting today precipitated or contributed in some way to tonight's events. More importantly, I need to know about their lives, all of their lives before Ralston.

I definitely need to talk to her first thing tomorrow morning – no, this morning, some of which has already elapsed. Now, the question is, how do I convince Ben that's what needs to happen.

*****

Not surprisingly, the morning came round much too soon. There wasn't much of it left when I finally went to bed. God, I look a wreck. These late nights are not doing me any favours. No time to waste worrying about it, I need to catch Ben before he disappears, and to persuade him I need to talk to Kate.

I was surprised to find Ben sitting in his office going through a thick file. He looked worse than I did. I received something of a distracted greeting and realised just how weary he was. So far, nothing boded well for a positive reaction to my pitch to see Kate. The KISS principle was probably the best approach I decided. Concise and to the point but, if that failed, pleading might work.

As I anticipated, I got a negative initial response, but he made the mistake of querying everything I said, allowing me to strengthen and build my case. And then, success. Kate and the kids were coming to the Station early this morning so a counsellor could spend some time with the children. Ben intended to interview Kate while this occurred.

He agreed I could talk to Kate, but he would observe and listen from the next room. He would step in at any time he felt it warranted. On the understanding that he would call me when they arrived at the Station, I retreated to my quarters to prepare for the interview. I didn't know how much time I would have with her, and I needed to find out a hell of a lot. With so many questions to ask, I couldn't waste time on irrelevancies or by not asking the right ones.

Ben's call came just after ten o'clock. Kate's appearance shocked me. Ben and I looked wrecked, but Kate was something else. She looked older and more haggard than she did yesterday. How much worse can she get before her health caves in? A small wry smile was the only greeting she could manage. After a few polite questions about how the children were and how she was coping, I got down to business.

"Kate, I know it's going to be difficult, but I want to know everything that happened last night. No, I want to know everything that happened from when you left Emily's apartment. I'll ask questions when I need to, but you should feel free to talk. Just tell it as it comes to you as you run it all back through your mind. Do you feel up to it?"

She nodded, biting her lip. "More than ever, I need to know what it's all about and now, particularly, if Ken was involved."

"Okay. When you left our meeting yesterday, you said you had things to do before picking up the kids. What did you have to do? Where did you go?"

"I was going to buy a birthday card for Poppy to give one of her friends, I needed some elastic to fix one of Poppy's dance outfits, and I was going to pick up bread and milk. As it happened, I didn't do any of that. Once I got to my car, I realised I didn't feel like going shopping. I needed to let the school know I would be taking next week off work in addition to this week, and I wanted to speak to the teachers to see how the kids were going, how much impact this last week has had on them. I had about an hour before classes were over for the day, so I went straight to the school and spent the time speaking to the people I needed to see."

"Did you notice anything out of the ordinary – anything suspicious – in the carpark or on the drive to the school?"

"No, nothing at all; I wasn't followed. I do keep my eyes open after our experience the other day. It wasn't busy when I left the carpark, and I drove directly to the school and parked in the pick-up area beside the road in front of the school but I didn't … Oh, I did notice …. aw no, it was nothing really."

"Let me be the judge. It might have been nothing, but I need to know everything and anything. Think of it as giving me a running commentary, something like: Walked to the car (no one paying any attentions to me), drove to the exit gate and paid, drove onto High Street (no sign of anyone paying me attention), drove down Broad Street (no apparent follower). Try that sort of approach. Start from when you drove up to the school pick-up area."

"I'll give it a go. Okay, I'm driving up to the pick-up area. There is a large dark blue van parked in the wrong place."

"What do you mean by 'in the wrong place'? I don't know the first thing about picking up kids from school, so you need to explain."

"There are all these unwritten rules about how to use the short-term pick-up area. You learn all about them by getting it wrong and having other parents correct you. For instance, you have to enter the lay-by

162

from the western end and drive through until you come to the furthest vacant parking space. You are only supposed to be there for a couple of minutes. The teacher on duty has all the kids marshalled behind the fence and, when a parent pulls up, they let the relevant kids out the gate to go home. The van had parked at the western entrance to the lay-by. I smiled to myself thinking, once the parents start arriving, someone is going to walk down and sort you out. The driver actually parked half in the last bay (western end) of the pick-up area and half outside the area. He came close to blocking the driveway of the house next door to the school. I didn't give the van too much thought. I guessed it was either making deliveries or was lost and pulled in there to check a map."

"How many people in the van and what were they doing?"

"Uhmm, just the driver and he was reading something."

"So, at that time of day, you would have been the first car and would have driven up to the furthest bay at the eastern end. What happens if your child is kept back on detention or, on sports day, their match goes a bit longer?"

"No, I didn't park in the pick-up area. It was just after two o'clock. It would be an hour or so before the kids came out. There's a long-term pick-up area just inside the school's western gate. If you have to come in to talk to teachers or whatever, or your child is likely to be late getting out, you park in the long-term pick-up area and wait. I drove through the first part of the short-term pick-up area and through the gate into the school grounds."

"Okay. You parked in the long-term area. What next?"

"I spoke to everyone I needed to see and went back to wait in the car. Poppy came out a few minutes later and the boys were only a couple of minutes behind her. There's a circular driveway. It exits the grounds at the eastern gate and exiting traffic merges with cars leaving the short term area to enter the roadway."

"No problems so far?"

"No. You have to turn left onto the roadway. That's the wrong direction for us to go home, so I have to drive to the end of the street, turn right and then right again into the street running parallel to the school. It involves driving halfway around the block before I end up heading in the right direction. I checked the rear vision mirror repeatedly. When I left the school, I think the van might have been some cars back behind me. Cars drop away at various points along the street so, by the time I got to the end of the street, I could see the top of the blue van above the sedan immediately behind me. It followed us into Tirandi Street and the sedan between us turned into a driveway shortly after. The van kept following us up the street."

"Did it speed up, pull up, did it do anything different at all?"

"No, I became nervous and was going to drive straight past our place and keep on driving down the street. I don't know where I thought I was going to go, but one of the kids was telling me to hurry up because he needed to go to the toilet, so I turned into our driveway. The kids piled out and raced upstairs. I sat in the car and watched for a moment. The van drove past and disappeared, but I was concerned it might have been checking out where we lived."

"You're sure that van wasn't anywhere around when you left the carpark after the meeting at Emily's apartment?"

"I'm sure. I checked regularly and I would have noticed it."

"What happened next?"

"I stood at the kitchen bench and made the kids a snack. The kitchen window overlooks Tirandi Street, so I kept one eye out for the van. I stayed leaning on the bench while the kids had their snack and we discussed their day. Then they went off to their rooms to do their homework. We were having a stew for dinner, so I got everything out and started chopping vegetables and stuff at the bench while I continued to keep an eye on the street. There was no further sign of the van. I decided I was jumping at shadows, put the stew on to cook, and went and took the clothes in off the clothesline."

"So you were feeling a bit more relaxed. Had Ken come home by then?"

"No, lately Ken hasn't been coming home until about six o'clock, but on Mondays we eat early. We don't sit down to dinner normally until about half six but, on Monday nights, there's a TV program the children watch that comes on at that time. Therefore, on Mondays we try to sit down by six o'clock so dinner is over and they can watch the show until seven o'clock."

"Then they have about half an hour before lights out at half seven. Ken came home at 5.30 or maybe a few minutes later. He didn't have much time to relax before we sat down to dinner."

"What happened after dinner?"

"Dinner was uneventful; nothing unusual happened. At the end of it, Ken and I sat and had a cup of tea together and chatted about nothing important. At half six, the kids settled down to watch their program. Ken gave me a hand to clear the table. I packed the dishwasher and Ken went downstairs to feed the dog. He usually feeds the dog and is back upstairs to watch the news broadcast that comes on at seven o'clock, straight after the children's program."

"Was there anything different last night?"

"Yes, now I think about it, there was. It took Ken longer than usual to feed the dog, but sometimes he has a bit of a play with the dog before feeding it, and that takes extra time. It was a couple of minutes before seven o'clock, when I noticed he hadn't come back upstairs. I was about to call out to him that he was going to miss the start of the news when the shooting started."

Kate stopped and took a few deep breaths. I saw her swallowing hard to fight back tears. After a few moments, she continued.

"At first I didn't realise the shooting was at our place. I raced over to the kitchen window. It was dark outside. The nearest street light is too far away. I thought I could make out the shape of a van. The neighbours turned on their outside lights. They light up their front courtyard. It helped make the van more visible. I rushed to our front door and turned on our driveway light. It's one of those floodlight things that take ages to light up. I saw Ken run from the yard and crouch in front of Mum's car. The shots followed him. Ken pulled out his phone and made a call. He stayed there, crouched down, for quite a while. They shot up Mum's car and all down the side of her flat. Ken made a dash for safety and dived in through the open laundry door. Thank God, I had left the laundry door open. My bag was on a chair near the front door. I grabbed my phone out of it and called you, Sonny."

"Did they fire at the upstairs part of the house at all?"

"No, just the downstairs area; *they were trying to shoot Ken.* The kids were terrified. They were screaming. I kept yelling at them to stay in their rooms."

She propped her elbows on the table and dropped her head into her hands. Her breathing reflected her stress level at having to relive the shooting. I sat silently until she managed to collect herself. She had been weeping, tears still visible on her cheeks. I offered her a small packet of tissues I had in one of my pockets. She nodded her thanks and wiped her face, took a deep breath and then looked at me with all the resolve she could muster.

"They were trying to shoot Ken. Why? What's his involvement in whatever this is, Sonny? I've tried asking him about a few things. He just gets angry."

"I don't know the answer to that yet, but what you tell us can help us find out. If you're up to it, can we return to the shooting?"

She sniffed and bit her lip. "I'm fine. What do you want to know?"

I asked her how she knew about Ken's injury already when she spoke to me, and about the shooting of the dog.

"I saw blood trickling down Ken's arm while he was crouched in front of the car, and another piece of flying glass cut his leg as he ran for the laundry. That was while I was talking to you. Now, about the dog …uhmm … oh, yes, after Ken dived into the laundry, there were more shots along the side of the flat. By then, the driveway light was nearly fully lit. The dog was still in the yard. It was terrified and carrying on something terrible. The firing stopped, probably only for a second, but there was a bit of a pause. Then there was a single shot that killed the dog; one single deliberate shot. The van sped off. By then I had seen it more clearly. I'm sure it was the same dark blue van."

"That's great. You're doing a fantastic job. Now I want you to thinks about the shots you heard fired. What can you tell me about them?"

She looked at me blankly. Okay, reword the question, Sonny. Ask exactly what you want to know, I chided myself.

"What about the sound… what did the shots sound like?"

She looked into the distance. Her brow furrowed as she searched her memory bank for the sound of the shots. Having located what she was looking for, she became a bit embarrassed.

"I don't know how to do this. It's going to sound a bit ridiculous. Here goes. When the boys are playing cowboys, they have toy pistols and shout at each other: bang, bang, bang-bang. When they are playing soldiers, they have different toy guns and they imitate the sounds you hear in war movies. It's more like 'rat-a-tat-tat' or 'ack-ack-ack' and, except for the one that killed the dog, that's what the shots sounded like. The one that killed the dog was just a single bang. Does that make any sense?"

"Yes, that's exactly what I wanted to know. How many people do you think were in the van?"

"I could only make out one: just the driver."

I explained that, in a drive-by shooting, the shooter usually sits next to an open window so they can shoot out of it. In this case, the van was facing the wrong way. It was on the same side of the road as the house. That put the driver on the wrong side of the vehicle to be shooting at the house. He was on the other side of the car, too

166

far away from the vehicle's passenger window, which was nearest to the house. I asked her to think about whether there was anything to suggest someone was sitting next to the passenger side window. She stared at her hands for a few moments before answering.

"No. I don't think so. There was like a little flash every time the gun fired. If someone were firing from the passenger seat, that flash would have come from near that window, or even outside of it. That's not how it was. The flashes were inside the van, more towards the middle of the cabin."

I queried her memory of it, and asked her to go over the bit about the flashes again. She remained adamant her recollection was correct. I took a few moments to consider whether there was anything else to ask her. A knock at the door broke my train of thought. I looked up as police woman Sam, entered the room.

"Sorry about interrupting, but the children have finished with the counsellor," she said and then, looking at Kate, she added, "I thought you might want to join them."

Kate stood up and moved towards the door. I spoke to her before she reached the door. She stopped but didn't turn around to face me. "Kate, I'm going to have to organise another meeting with you as soon as possible. I asked you to think about life before Ralston. We need to take a close look at that. I think the answers we're looking for are most likely to be found in that time and not so much here in Ralston." Then, in barely a whisper, "I might give you a ring about something specific about that time, if that's okay."

Still with her back to me, she just nodded and left the room. I went back and slumped at the table. I was mentally exhausted, but I needed to digest everything Kate said while it was still fresh in my mind. I had recorded the whole session and madly scribbled notes as we spoke, but I needed to think about any instances where I should have asked for more detail. Were there any hesitations or verbal cues I should have noticed? I had been so engrossed in my thoughts I didn't hear Ben enter the room. He startled me when he spoke.

"That was fantastic. You did a great job of getting her to recall every detail, even down to the weapon and how it was used." That was high praise indeed from someone like Ben.

"If it was an automatic weapon and he used it from the driver's position, he wouldn't have had much control. His accuracy would have been off. That probably saved Ken's life," I suggested. "How is he, by the way? Where is he?"

"I think the response is: he's helping us with our enquiries. He spent the night under guard in hospital – not because of his wounds. He was suffering from shock and, while he is in there, we can keep an eye on him."

"Has he been holding out on us, Ben? Is he involved up to his ears in whatever this mess is that got Therese killed?"

"I don't know yet. Maybe he will be more forthcoming today, especially after last night's scare. By the way, everything is in place for us to look at the top floor of that apartment block at one o'clock. Want to come with us?"

Did I want to go? What a silly question. "Yes, if that's possible. Would it create a problem?"

"No problem, there's only Greg and David coming with me – and you, if you want to. I've ordered sandwiches for us all to have an early lunch and then we will go."

"Okay, count me in, and thanks."

# Chapter Fourteen

After the long session with Kate, I went back to my rooms and made coffee in the hope it would revive me. Emily swam into my thoughts. Oh God, I should ring her. I think she is safe enough. Last night's incident doesn't appear related to our earlier meeting. Still it won't hurt for her to be extra vigilant. I would be a lot happier if she wasn't in Ralston at this time. Although I intended it would be a brief call, Emily had other ideas.

She wanted to know why I rang last night and told her not to go out. I had to tell her about the shooting that occurred, but I wasn't prepared to share any more than that with her just yet. Anyway, I was too brain-dead to go into detail, although she certainly was asking for more. The call ended with Emily in a bit of a huff because she didn't get what she wanted. I would have to work on squaring that away later.

Ben arrived with sandwiches. The others would join us shortly. It was obvious he had engineered it for us to have a few minutes alone.

"I'm working on how you and Kate might meet again – safely. I can't quite work out why you are so interested in their lives before they came to Ralston. Care to share your theory with me?"

"I don't know that it's a theory as such. It's more of a hunch, a gut feeling, that something was going on long before they all moved to Ralston. Whatever it was continued to grow and develop here, culminating in Therese's death and the attempt on Ken's life. I think it has its roots, its genesis, long before Ralston, and a long way from Ralston."

At that point, David and Greg joined us for lunch. Ben and I allowed our conversation to lapse, and started a new all-inclusive discussion on what this afternoon's visit to the apartment block might uncover. The temptation to ask Ben about what 'assistance' Ken was able to give with his case was almost overwhelming. He knew I would be dying to find out. Keeping in good with Ben was important. I needed that follow up meeting with Kate and I wasn't going to do anything to jeopardise that … at least not until another meeting was confirmed.

A man from the company that maintained the elevator met us at the apartment block. He confirmed only two electronic keycards existed. Both issued to Therese. He overrode the code to allow us to reach the top floor. Ben asked him to change the code and issue a new keycard to him so only the Police were able to access the top floor in the future. After a brief phone call, the man confirmed the change of code and that someone from his office was bringing over two new keycards. Ben asked for the courier to wait on the ground floor and to give the keycards to the officer Ben stationed there. The officer would bring them up to Ben when they arrived.

The four of us stood in the silent foyer area of the top floor. Beyond the small entrance foyer, a carpeted hallway bisected the area. Large sculptural pieces produced from various materials dotted the length of the hallway. Doors opened into the hallway from both sides. The anticipation was almost palpable. The real question was whether what lay beyond the apartment's doors would help unravel the mysteries of the past week… behind those locked doors. Getting into the apartment posed no problem for Greg and he soon swung the first door open. I looked enquiringly at Ben.

He just shrugged and said, "It's covered by the warrant."

It was as I imagined entering Aladdin's Cave might be like. I was sure we had made a mistake. This was nothing like Therese's flat. It didn't look like her style at all, and I quietly commented accordingly to Ben.

"If it is her place – and we'll find out soon enough – it shouldn't look like her flat. It should look like somewhere she liked to live, not like somewhere she kept for a specific purpose."

Decorated beautifully in neutral shades, there was the occasional splash of bright colour here and there throughout. The furnishings were modern but comfortable and very expensive by the look of them. We were standing in the right hand segment of the floor, now converted to one large open-plan living area. We entered at the lounge end of the room, which then progressed through a dining area to a well-appointed kitchen.

It came as a surprise to find a door just prior to the kitchen area didn't open into the main hallway. It opened into a small sitting room. That room doubled as a walkway through to the left hand segment of the floor. The left hand side contained two large ensuite bedrooms and an enormous office. Both bedrooms had doors opening onto the main hallway. The office did not. Its only access was from the living area via the small sitting room or through a door from what I assumed to be the main bedroom.

I stood transfixed surveying the office: its furniture, technology, artworks and (sharp intake of breath) its security camera and motion detector. Ben heard the intake of breath and spun round to face me.

"What?"

"Look at the security hardware up there. This place is probably being monitored by some security outfit as we stand here."

"I hope so," he replied with a grin, "and I hope they send over someone to investigate. They won't be able to access the place even if they have a keycard since we changed the code. However, the nice Policeman on duty downstairs will be happy to bring them up using one of our new keycards. Maybe they could tell us something useful about this place and its occupant."

We walked along the main hallway, opening doors and peering inside, and confirmed there were only two bedrooms. In addition to the ensuite, the room I decided was the main bedroom also had a walk-in wardrobe/dressing room. Lots of clothes in the hanging space and shoes in the shoe rack. I removed a hanger from the hanging space and inspected the dress on it.

"Not your colour," Ben quipped as he peered into the dressing room.

"Not my colour, but about Therese's size," I responded.

She was a large woman and this dress looked about the right size to fit her. I worked my way down the row of hanging garments checking labels as I went. All top brand stuff, and the shoes all looked expensive as well. Still, large size clothing in the wardrobe didn't necessarily mean it was Therese's apartment. We needed something more concrete before we could be sure. I left the three men drooling over the black polished granite tiles and bench tops in the ensuite and went back to the office.

It was a wonderful room, dominated by a magnificent timber desk. There were a couple of comfortable looking visitors' chairs in front of the desk, a small round table and a couple of lounge chairs adjacent to one wall, good quality original artworks on the walls and a couple of small bronze sculptural pieces on what looked like marble plinths. The desk was devoid of paper, with only a lamp, computer screen, keyboard and mouse occupying its surface. It was far tidier than any desk of Therese's I'd seen before. A matching credenza was along the wall behind the desk. The lack of filing cabinets anywhere in the room was curious. There were none at all.

I reasoned that the identity of the apartment's occupant was most likely to be found in the desk, so I went directly to it and sat in the chair that was drawn up to it. The chair, enormous and overstuffed, enveloped me, and I found myself having to wriggle forward and perch on the front edge of it to reach the desk comfortably. Drawers extended down both sides of the desk, three on each side, with the bottom drawer on each side deep enough to be a files drawer.

Only the shallow top drawer on the right hand side of the desk was unlocked. It had a built-in tray containing pens, pencils, paperclips and the like, but nothing of any interest. There was no sign of a key for the other drawers; understandable I suppose. You wouldn't lock up and then leave the key within easy reach. I looked at the locks; no problems there. How to deal with locked drawers was something a Public Servant learnt early in their career.

Part of life for a Public Servant was clearing your desk of paperwork and locking desks and filing cabinets before leaving each day. The problem was, keys were lost or left at home. Anyone worth their salt learnt how to overcome that problem rather than have to admit to a supervisor having been less than careful with keys. There were a couple of letter openers in the unlocked drawer, one decorative flimsy looking number, and a more robust looking one. I inserted the robust letter opener and popped the lock on the second drawer on the right-hand side.

The drawer contained a number of folders. As I removed the top one, I noticed a cheque book against the side of the drawer. Heart pounding, I grabbed the cheque book and flipped open the cover. Mixed feelings surged as I read the name printed on each blank cheque: KLN Trading Pty Ltd. This was good but, as we hadn't yet proved Therese's connection to KLN Trading, it wasn't enough. I turned my attention to the bottom drawer. As expected, it contained hanging files. I'll come back to those later, after I've discovered what other prizes the desk has to offer.

My attention turned to the top left-hand drawer. It was shallow and mirrored the top drawer on the other side. The drawer contained recent mail – possibly accounts to be paid – and another cheque book. I snatched up the book and flipped it open. This was a personal account cheque book. Printed below the signature line on each blank leaf was Therese's name.

"Yes," I yelled and, with the cheque book held aloft, I jumped up from the chair.

"Did I just miss a Eureka moment?" My yelp brought Ben to the office door. "Share the moment. What have you found?"

Too excited to bother explaining, I simply thrust the cheque book at him. He flipped it open. "O-o-h, yes. That is worth getting excited about."

Ben called David and Greg to join us. Greg arrived immediately and David a few seconds later. After checking where I found the cheque book, Ben tried to open the next drawer down. He grunted.

"Bugger, it's locked."

"So were the others. I'm sure it's covered by the warrant but, if you don't want to know how they got unlocked, I suggest you go over there and help David examine that wall for whatever it is he's looking for," I told them both.

"Ignorance is bliss and, in this case, safest. David, what is it you're doing over here? Sonny suggested I should help you," Ben said. Greg decided he was more interested in what I was doing.

Ben went over to David while I, with my trusty letter opener, opened the remaining two drawers, while Greg looked over my shoulder. When Greg and I stood up behind the desk, an intriguing view greeted us: two blokes on their knees, with backsides in the air and pointing in our direction.

"Have you got your phone, Greg? It's probably worth a picture… and I'll have a copy thanks. I doubt you're looking for termites, so what are you two up to over there?"

Ben stood up. He gave us a wry grin when we assured him it wasn't his best view. David remained on his hands and knees, closely examining the bottom of the stained timber panels that lined the length of the opposite wall.

"Gotcha," he exclaimed and stood up.

David applied the toe of his boot to an area of the bottom corner of one of the timber panels and it silently swung open, revealing a bank of three filing cabinets. He applied the same procedure to the other three panels along the same wall. The second panel he opened revealed more filing cabinets. The third revealed a space lined with shelves that looked like a mini walk-in pantry. He had to apply his boot to the fourth panel a couple of times before finding the right spot. It swung open to reveal more shelves arranged around a substantial safe that was about a metre square.

With all four panels now open, we stood staring, dumbstruck as we tried to take it all in. David recovered quickest and spoke first, telling us he had seen something similar once before and thought it worth a try.

"It could be just that she was a very tidy bunny and couldn't stand filing cabinets cluttering up a room," I volunteered lamely. That brought a giggle from everyone, and normalcy once more descended on the room. Ben sprang into action.

"This is going to take forever to go through. I'll have to pull in everyone I have. I'd better start making some phone calls."

The three blokes went into a huddle to discuss strategies for attacking the massive job that lay ahead. I decided to inspect the kitchen and was on my way through the adjoining sitting room when a voice startled me. "Sir? Sir?" I heard it call and I made my way out into the hallway to investigate.

A uniformed officer made his way tentatively down the hallway. The three men left the office and went to meet him. He had been questioning other tenants in the block. One 'old bird' (his words) wasn't too impressed that a strange car often parked in the space allocated to the top floor. She recorded the registration number 'just in case there was ever a problem'. The officer ran a check on the registration and gave Ben details of the woman who was the registered owner.

The three men returned to the office and I continued with my quest to explore the kitchen. My target was the huge two-door fridge. It contained milk, butter, cheese, several bottle of fruit juice, a couple of oranges, tomatoes and a lettuce, but no meat. The reason for no meat was evident in the freezer. It was packed with frozen meals, mainly frozen pies and pizzas. Everything in the fridge was fresh but the milk was close to being out of date.

Ben joined me in the kitchen, and I gave him a report on the fridge contents.

"So it looks like she had been using the place right up to her death. We're going to head back to the station, unless there is something else you need to look at. Others will arrive shortly to start going through everything. The cleaning lady is being brought in for questioning."

"I'm right to go whenever you are. One thing has me curious though. Why was there no response to our being here from somebody from a security firm? It looks like an expensive system. Surely it must be monitored – or raise an alarm of some sort – if it's not deactivated when someone is here."

"Good question, but one I don't have an answer to yet. Let's see what the cleaning lady knows before we worry about it too much."

We all went upstairs as soon as we arrived back at the station. Greg and David went to their end of the hallway while Ben walked me to my rooms.

"Can you come in for a few minutes, Ben? There are a couple of things I wanted to talk to you about."

"Yes, no problem. Oh, I meant to tell you, that meeting with Kate is set for tonight; about eight o'clock."

"Thanks, that was one of the things I wanted to talk to you about, but I'll come back to that. Ben, this whole thing – the wealth, the cash, everything – it has to be about drugs doesn't it? I can't think of anything else that would involve so much money."

"It could be about any number of things, most of them illegal but yes, unfortunately it is likely that drugs are a big part of it. The question is, what was Melrose's role in this thing? How big a part did she play and how did she get involved in the first place?"

"That's three questions, but I know they are at the bottom of all this. I have some ideas about the when and where it all started. That's why I want to have this next meeting with Kate."

"Yeah, well, I've set it up for you for tonight. We'll see what that brings. You seem a bit hesitant. What's the problem?"

"It's just with everything that has happened over the last 24 hours or so, I wonder whether I should go ahead with that meeting now, or wait until we see what comes out of the search of the apartment. You've had a chance to talk to Ken. Is it possible that, between any information Ken has given you and what they find at the apartment, we'll have the answers we have been looking for without having to put Kate through anything more?"

"Nice thought, but no. Ken has given us nothing so far. In fact, he's been what some might describe as downright uncooperative. So, he will remain not well enough to join Kate and the kids for a bit longer." An exaggerated wink and firm nod accompanied that last comment.

"Damn, I was hoping it wouldn't be necessary for Kate to go through another session. She's been through too much already. I assume you will give me details of tonight's meeting sometime this afternoon."

"...Just as soon as I get the last of the details in place. I've a mountain of things to do in my office. I'll catch up with you later."

He was gone, alone at last. I took out my phone. Although I was meeting with Kate tonight, I wanted to ask her about something Liz mentioned, and I wanted to keep it to myself until I explored it further. No point in looking a fool if there was no need for it, particularly if another might be observing that conversation. I keyed in Kate's mobile number.

She answered almost immediately and sounded tired. God I hate myself for disturbing her again. "Kate, I'll try to keep this as brief as possible. Do you remember your mother having a problem with some bloke just before she moved to Ralston? I think the problem might have followed her here and been serious enough for her to involve a solicitor."

"Hmm, yeah, I think I know the issue you're talking about. I think she copped a hard time for a while before she moved here. She never spoke to me about it and I don't really know what was happening. It was clear something was wrong, although I didn't know what, and I overheard a bit of a conversation she had with Ken one day. I asked Ken about it later. He just lied; said he didn't know what I was talking about. We were packing up to move to Ralston at the time, so there was plenty happening and I didn't get a chance to do anything about it."

"What about the bit of conversation you heard, what was said?"

"Mum was upset. It sounded like the bloke involved was accusing her of ruining his son's life. She was talking about needing to take legal action but, for some reason, Ken was saying not to. Whatever it was must have continued after we were here in Ralston, if it followed her here when she came later."

"Do you have any ideas on who the bloke was that was giving her grief or why?"

"Yes; it's funny you should be asking about all this. He was here just recently."

"Here... Where?"

"At the house; actually, I think I saw him twice. I didn't know the bloke. I just knew who he was. Uhmm ... Bawden ... no, that's someone else. What was his name? ... Baldwin. Yes, Baldwin was his name. Tony, I think was his first name. You know all the properties out west are big, and some are extremely big. He owned a property, but it was just an average sized one. He had a son. I can't think of the son's name, but I'm not sure if I ever knew it. What the fuss was about I don't know except that Mum told Ken the father blamed her for ruining his son's life."

"What did you take that to mean?"

"I just thought it had something to do with Mum's job. You know, maybe the lad had his apprenticeship cancelled for some reason and his unhappy father blamed Mum for it. I just assumed it had something to do with something involving the institute and the son's training which had gone sour for whatever reason."

"Your mother taught community service and childcare courses. It was more likely the lad was doing an engineering type course. In which case, your mother wouldn't have been involved. It would have been in Ken's area of studies."

"I suppose you're right, but I never thought of that."

"How did you come to see this Tony Baldwin recently?"

"The first time – I'm almost sure it was him – he was sitting in his car parked across the street from the house when I brought the kids home. When I got out of the car, I made a point of standing, looking at him. For a few seconds, he made a great show of making a phone call and then drove off. At the end of that week, he turned up at the house. I wasn't feeling well and got a lift home at lunchtime. My car was getting some work done to it. Only Mum's car was at home. Anyway, I took a couple of pills and went to sleep. It was nearly five o'clock when I woke up. There was loud banging coming from downstairs. I crept over to the door and, careful not to be seen, had a look. A man hammered on Mum's door and hurled abuse: 'come out you bitch; come out and face me; you know you are responsible', that sort of thing. The terrible abusive language went on for a while. It was Tony Baldwin, I'm sure of it, although it did take me a while to remember his name."

She paused for a moment and I let the silence linger. After a few moments, she continued.

"Anyway, I was concerned and decided to phone the Police. I don't know whether he heard me move to get my phone or whether he just gave up, but the next thing I heard was the crunching of the gravel in the driveway. I rushed over to the kitchen window. He walked out of the driveway and down the street to his car parked a couple of houses further along. He drove off. A few minutes later the Andersons dropped the kids off."

"When was this?"

"The incident at the house was on Friday; the Friday before ..."

"...A week before your mother's death? Was she home at the time?

"No, her car was there but I saw her leave in a taxi early that morning. She had her usual computer bag and a small overnight bag. I assumed she was going to the airport but it was unusual for her to call a cab. On other occasions, she either drove to work and Liz took her to the airport, or Liz picked her up from the house and took her."

"Did you know she was going away?"

"No, but lately we didn't always know what she was doing. I went to the supermarket next morning. On my way home, as I turned into the lower end of Tirandi Street, I saw a taxi drive away from the house. Mum must have come home and gone inside. She didn't come out to see me when I arrived."

The phone call lasted longer than I anticipated and I was feeling guilty about having grilled her for so long. I needed her to be rested and refreshed before our meeting later this evening. I reminded her of the meeting and suggested she try for a nap before then. I also stressed how I would not revisit our conversation about Tony Baldwin when we met later.

I felt myself succumbing to tiredness, or was it just sheer exhaustion. Whichever it was, I gave in and took myself off for a nap. Well, what else could I do? There was plenty I should do – like piles of notes needing transcribing. The thought of that was too overwhelming. I gave in to temptation and hit the bed.

My phone's persistent ringing brought me some way back to the land of the living. I crawled out of the blackness of a deep sleep. So much for my intended nap, I had been dead to the world. I struggled to sound even half intelligent as I answered the phone. I mumbled 'hello', and was jolted fully awake by Ben's reply.

"Did I wake you?"

"No. No, I ... er ... I was reading something. Sorry if I sounded distracted. What news has you ringing me?"

"I said I'd let you know about arrangements for the meeting tonight. It's set for eight o'clock. Dinner is arranged. I'll come up there a bit before seven o'clock; be ready to go if you can. Oh, and best try not to go back to sleep again."

He rang off and I sat blinking at my watch on the bedside table while trying to get my brain into fully functional mode again. It was almost six o'clock. Bearing in mind my instructions to be ready to go when Ben arrived, I dashed off to shower and change accordingly. There was still a little time before I expected Ben to arrive, so I booted up my computer. Might as well use the time to see if the internet has anything of interest to say about Tony Baldwin or his son. My search brought up a scant handful of entries. I didn't have a chance to open any of them. It was just after 6:30 and Ben had arrived with Sam in tow.

"Hi Sam, we seem to be running into each other all over the place lately. I am ready to go as instructed," I said as I picked up my bag ready to move out.

"If we keep this up, we'll end up on each other's speed dial and become besties. Anyway, you are not quite ready yet. Do you still have that red wig?" Sam had a cardboard box perched on her hip as she spoke. "Come on, we need to get you ready." She began propelling me towards the bedroom.

As she dragged me along, I looked over my shoulder at Ben who appeared to be enjoying the situation immensely. Sam emptied the box, spreading an outfit out on the bed and dropping a pair of shoes on the floor.

"I think – I hope – the shoes are the right size. I think everything else will be okay, and here's a bag to go with it all. I really didn't think that wild looking tote you borrowed would look too flash with this outfit."

The outfit she chose for me comprised a biscuit coloured maxi skirt in some soft flowing fabric a long sleeved knitted top with the same biscuit-coloured stripes on a white background. To complete the outfit, there was a pair of tanned leather wedge-heeled sandals and a small leather shoulder bag. She had good taste. I loved the outfit and it would go well with the red wig.

I changed obediently, and she fussed a bit with the wig to achieve what she considered an appropriate hairdo for the outfit and the evening. When she was satisfied, and with me appropriately attired, we returned to Ben who had been whiling away the time in front of TV. There was little conversation as the three of us rode the elevator to the ground floor.

Greg waited for us at the back door. Together, all four of us trouped out to an unmarked car in the courtyard and made the short journey, in what turned out to be Sam's personal vehicle, to a multi-storey hotel a few streets back from the precinct.

As we piled out of the vehicle in the hotel carpark, Ben said quietly, "We are just a group of friends – coppers, if someone recognises any of us – having dinner together in the hotel's brasserie after work."

In keeping with the ruse, we walked in chatting and laughing, as we made our way towards the bar.

Sam lightly took my arm to hold me back a bit behind the men. She leaned in to me and giggled as if sharing some girlie secret.

"We don't know David tonight. He's our lookout," she whispered.

I know how to play this game, so I dredged up my best shocked expression and gasped, "I didn't know that!" … and we both giggled some more as we sped up to join the men who were already at the bar. They had ordered their drinks when we reached them. We added our requests to the order and, when they arrived, carried them through to our table in the brasserie.

The food was good, but a keen observer might have discerned that perhaps it was eaten a trifle too quickly. We maintained the charade through dinner: animated conversation interspersed with laughter that bore no relevance to the topic of conversation in most instances. Amongst other conversation, everyone was familiarised with the plan for this evening's meeting with Kate. She and her children were in a suite on the sixth floor. Nobody else was on that floor except the Police officers guarding them.

As Ben explained, the plan was that, by eight o'clock, the children would be in bed. With Sam keeping an eye on them, Kate would be free to talk with me in another room on that floor. Audio-visual technology installed in the meeting room during the day allowed Ben and Greg to follow the interview from an adjoining room. I was pleased I had phoned Kate discreetly earlier. David would remain downstairs initially, watching for anyone displaying an interest in our group.

Just before the appointed hour, Sam announced that she and I were off to find a 'Ladies'. We slung our bags over our shoulders and sauntered out of the brasserie, making a show of looking for the toilets as we moved through the lobby area. The lifts were located down a side corridor and just prior to where the toilets were located at the far end of that corridor. We stopped a couple of metres before reaching the lifts and Sam scratched round in her bag on the pretext of looking for something. She faced down the corridor towards the toilets and I faced her, which allowed me to look back up the corridor along the way we had come.

"Nobody watching from the lobby," I announced.

"… And nobody watching from down there either," Sam replied as she summoned the lift. It was already on the ground floor. The doors opened immediately and almost silently. We dived inside and hit the button for the fifth floor. When we exited the lift at the fifth floor, the hallway was deserted. We located the staircase and climbed the stairs to the sixth floor.

It was show time, and I was not feeling good about what I was about to subject Kate to yet again. I hoped with all my heart that she was stronger than she looked.

# Chapter Fifteen

Our pace relaxed and casual, we chatted as we climbed the stairs to the sixth floor and our meeting with Kate. The officer on guard showed us to the suite where Kate and the children were waiting. After the usual greetings, Sam walked Kate and I across the hallway to the interview room, then returned to the room where we first met them to stay with the children until Kate returned. As we entered the interview room, I glimpsed Ben and Greg arriving on the sixth floor via the staircase.

Not being sure how long it would take the two men to be in position to monitor the interview, I quickly reminded Kate we were not going to mention our earlier phone conversation to avoid any distraction from the topics we were going to discuss this evening. It was only another small white lie. Then I spent a little time enquiring after Kate and the children's wellbeing and how beneficial or otherwise she thought the earlier counselling session had been for the children.

To prevent her becoming inhibited or guarded in any way, Kate remained unaware our meeting was being monitored by others. We reached the point where any further stalling initiatives would become obvious as such, so I trusted to luck that the others were now in place and launched into the interview. "Thanks for agreeing to this interview, Kate. If you start to feel stressed, tired or overwhelmed in any way, please say so. We can stop. This isn't meant to be an ordeal."

She nodded her understanding, said nothing and continued twisting her wedding ring on her finger.

"I am trying to get an understanding of where you were and what you were doing before you all moved to Ralston. By 'you', I mean you, your mother and Ken. If I remember correctly from my early days of working with Therese, you were all living at Normanton prior to moving here. Is that right?"

"Yes, we were there for a number of years but, although Mum was actually based there, she travelled a lot throughout the western area and also out to the coast and down to the capital."

"Roughly how long were you at Normanton and what made you move there in the first place?"

"It was about eight years – or closer to nine maybe – we were there." She paused to gather her thoughts before continuing. "We – my family – were living in the main regional city out west from before I was born. I grew up out west. Then Mum finally got her qualification in community work and, after a while, got a job teaching with the department. Not too long after that, I managed to get an administration job in the institute's office. There wasn't a lot of work available out there outside the department, so I was happy to get the job even though it wasn't the most exciting work. That's where I met Ken. He was teaching there too, and it wasn't long before we started going out together. So, you see, I spent all my life out west until we moved to Normanton, and then to Ralston."

"I'm surprised you got away with it, you and Ken getting together, I mean. I didn't think the department approved of such relationships."

"No, it doesn't. You would never get away with it here in Ralston but, out there, things are a lot more relaxed. Besides, as the department is the biggest show in town, it's a bit hard to meet anyone worthwhile from outside the department. That's probably why they tend to turn a blind eye to such things out there."

"So what precipitated the move to Normanton?"

"The department had small training facilities at places like Normanton and Mornington Island, and Ken had regular scheduled visits to those places to deliver classes. Mum was doing much the same thing, but her situation was a bit different. She was teaching at the institute, but she also had a few students at various locations in the Gulf country. Like Ken, she had to travel every so often to visit those students. Then the department was awarded some grant funding – a substantial amount of money – to undertake work in the Indigenous communities in that area. They initiated a project to spend the funding. It started with Mum going into the Indigenous communities up there to teach the women about hygiene, childcare, healthy eating and all that sort of stuff."

"I remember all the publicity that followed the award of that grant. There were lots of big ideas on how it would be spent, but I don't remember any follow-up about how it eventually was spent."

"It seems the project was a hit with the locals, and the need for them – Ken and Mum, that is – to be in that area increased. The department decided to station them permanently in the area. It all happened quickly, probably because, prior to receiving the grant funding, the department had been kicking around the idea of building a proper training facility with attached residential accommodation at Normanton. Mum's role was expanded to include overseeing the construction work and setting up of the facility, including the residential hostel."

"What was the idea of the residential hostel? The department didn't usually go down that track. It didn't go in for live-in students."

"You probably appreciate that most of the potential students up there are Indigenous. Some might come from around the town, but most would come from outlying communities. Part of the Government's initiative to make education and training available to those students meant somehow making the training accessible to them. Their solution was to build a small residential complex as an adjunct to the new training facility. Designed to hold a maximum of 16 students, it had a separate small cottage to accommodate visiting staff. Problems always arose if members were away from their communities for any length of time. The initial idea behind this project was for students to live-in during the week, and spend weekends back in their communities with their families. Some students would go on to get qualifications, but most would simply receive training in those skills that would enhance their employment chances on the properties around that area. You know the sorts of skills: a bit of welding, basic vehicle maintenance, use of power tools; that sort of thing."

"Okay. So your mother and Ken moved to Normanton?"

"Yes. The department provided two small demountable houses for them to rent from the department. There was no furniture or anything else provided. Ken and I had been seeing each other for a while. We decided I should go too and move in with him. I managed to transfer my office job to the new Normanton office. They thought I was moving up with Mum, not Ken, so it didn't create any problems. It was interesting for quite a while after we got there. We had no furniture, nothing much in the way of kitchen stuff, except for the stove already installed in the cottage. Apart from that, Ken's camping gear was all we had. We slept in our swags on the floor. Food and everything else up there was so expensive, and we were broke; absolutely broke. Ken bought a new SUV just before all this happened, and I hadn't been working very long and didn't get much of a pay packet anyway."

"How did your mother manage? Did the department help her out in any way?"

"Mum was a bit better off. She brought some of the excess bits and pieces from home but, because she had no fridge, she was using an Esky, the same as we were. Then, after a few months, things improved: a fridge arrived and, shortly after that, a bed. It was wonderful, but I knew we didn't have the money to buy these things. The cost of living was so high up there we hadn't been able to save very much at all. I had it out with Ken. I thought he must have taken out a loan or gone into debt somehow."

"I can understand how you might have been a bit concerned. So how did he manage to afford it?"

"He said they – he and Mum – managed to get some good deals on the purchase prices and on the freight on material for the complex. They were starting to bring up stuff for the residential complex. Although the first intake of students wasn't until the start of the next academic year, it was critical to get everything on-site before the wet season set in. The buildings weren't ready yet when stuff started arriving. Mum was doing all the ordering, and Ken said she managed to include some bits and pieces for us at the same time and at the same bulk corporate prices as the department was paying. It sounded like a great arrangement but, later when I thought about it, I still couldn't see how we were going to afford to pay for it."

She paused and examined her nails a moment or two before continuing. I took advantage of the break to catch my notes up to the same point as the conversation.

"More stuff kept arriving: dining suite – more of basic kitchen setting really; a washing machine; a couple of lounge chairs and a TV. Look, if I have to be honest, deep down I knew something wasn't right. We just simply couldn't afford any of that stuff. At the rate it kept turning up, I wasn't game to think about how deeply in debt we were going to be. Things became tense between Ken and I, and a lot of it was down to my concern about our finances. In an effort to shut me up I guess, eventually he told me he arranged with the department not to take his annual pay increase. They were to withhold it every fortnight and put it towards paying off the debt for all the stuff we acquired. I wasn't happy, but I accepted his explanation and decided that, we had the stuff so we might as well enjoy it."

"Did you speak to your mother about your concerns or the arrangements that were in place?"

"Oh yes, I spoke to her on several occasions, but she just laughed at me. She gave me much the same story as Ken gave me. Her situation was much better than ours was, of course. Her classification was middle management, even though she still did some teaching, and her salary exceeded Ken's mine put together."

"In your conversations with Therese, did you feel you were being given the truth? Was there anything that made you feel more concerned or, seeing how it corroborated Ken's explanation, were you satisfied that your concerns were unjustified?"

"I don't think I ever really believed it. Sometimes, somethings seem just too good to be true. Every time I tried to talk to her about it, she evaded the questions. If she had been a little less dismissive of the whole thing – and me – I might have felt a bit more comfortable with it."

"For how long did this 'manna from Heaven' continue to arrive? Was it only over a few months or did it extend over a longer period?"

"A lot of it, all that first stuff, arrived over a short period of time before the end of that first year. At the start of first term the next year, a computer and small desk arrived. I queried Ken about it. He said it was all above board, and that the department approved it so that he could catch up on work at home from time to time. That seemed reasonable and made sense to me, so I accepted it. A few more things might have arrived during the remainder of that year but, if they did, they were only small and probably insignificant in the overall scale of things."

"Was that the end of it then?"

"No, it turned out to be just a lull. It all started again in a big way the following year when I got pregnant. We had to turn one of the bedrooms into a nursery, and I was getting pretty excited about how I was going to do it and what I would have. However, I was quite sick with all sorts of complications that required me to fly out to the coast often for specialist medical attention. Anything we'd saved was fast disappearing on plane tickets. I was getting concerned about how we were going to afford the basic things, like cot, pram and all those other things you need for a first child. Then furniture started turning up again out of the blue."

"What sort of things turned up? I assume they were for the nursery."

"A top-of-the-line cot and changing table and a chest of drawers that looked like basic department issue arrived. I challenged Ken and Mum over this stuff, as I couldn't see how this could possibly be part of some bulk order for the facility. However, I was wrong. Mum was setting up an area on campus where she could teach childcare to the girls and some of the older women. She purchased a number of these pieces of furniture to set up that teaching space. So again, the story was that a big order for the department had our stuff included and, therefore, attracted the very best discounted price. A couple of years later, when the next child was on the way, a single bed and cupboard arrived for the older child. By the time we left Normanton to move to Ralston, we were set up. Each of the kids had their own well-furnished room."

"That's great, you're doing well. Now, can we leave all that for a moment and talk about what life was like up there? What sorts of things did you do? For instance, Burketown is a bigger place. Did you go across to Burketown very often?"

"No, not often; I went there only two or three times. Ken went more often though. He had some mates over there. They used to go fishing and crabbing together, so he often went over for the weekend. He also used to have to visit every so often to check on students. Some of the students obtained employment around the Burketown area as part of their studies, and Ken had to go to talk to their supervisors about how they were progressing. Most of the time, those trips usually meant he was away for more than one day. When that was the case, he usually stayed at the Burketown pub."

"What about Therese, did she get to Burketown very often?"

"Yeah, Mum was over there quite a bit, not necessarily in the town itself, but in the communities around the town. She was running those workshops for the women, but she also was chasing up students."

"Chasing up students? Was she recruiting students or something?"

"No. Students staying in the residential complex initially went home on weekends. The trouble was, some of them forgot to come back on Monday – or Tuesday, or at all for the week. If they didn't turn up on Monday, Mum would go and track them down and bring them back. It didn't take too long for the department to work out that the arrangement was a dud. They changed the live-in arrangements so that students were allowed to go home only once in the middle of term for a week and then at the end of term for the normal term break."

She laughed, the first time I had seen her laugh since I was in Ralston. It caught me by surprise but I tried to hide it. It was great to see, but she quickly continued her story.

"The department just didn't understand the student cohort. They, the Indigenous students, can't stay somewhere for so long removed from their families. The students absconded and went bush, never to be found again – not by us anyway – and never to be dobbed in by their own mob. Not surprising perhaps, the student residential aspect of the place slowly died. Only a dedicated handful ever stayed there after that."

187

"Did your mother do much travelling further afield than Burketown?"

"A fair bit; she went back to our family home fairly often. Well, in the early days she did. She used to try to go home every second weekend. She would work up extra hours during the fortnight and then make a long weekend of it. Over time though, it slipped back to once a month and then maybe not for six weeks. That's how she found out dad was playing away, so to speak."

"That's when the marriage broke up?"

"Yes. She often had to go back to the main centre for meetings or whatever and, she would back-fill their positions if any of the management staff were on leave. She was in charge there for quite a few months at one stage while the boss took extended leave. I think it was medical leave, or something to do with health."

"Geoff was the boss at that time?" She nodded. "Okay, so Geoff took extended leave and Therese back-filled his position. Go on."

Anyway, she always used to let dad know when she was coming home next – usually about once every six weeks by then. On one occasion, she had to go back for a meeting in the middle of the week. On a spur of the moment impulse, she decided to stay and not come back to Normanton until the following Monday. It was a week earlier than when she intended to come home. She went to the house after work but dad wasn't there. She waited until it got late and she decided to ring him. She asked him what he was doing and he told her he was just sitting around at home with a beer waiting for the football to start on TV. You can work the rest out for yourself."

"Oh dear; a prime example of how to drop yourself right in it without really trying."

"Yeah, anyway, with him gone, the house was empty while she was at Normanton. After that, she made a point of going home every week or two to make sure everything was okay. A bit later, her job changed to include liaising with other centres throughout the region. She didn't spend much time in Normanton after that."

"Ken's fishing mates, were they from Burketown?"

"I think some were from around Burketown. Some were staff from other centres and some were off properties from all over the region."

"How did they all manage to get to Burketown just for a weekend's fishing?"

"They didn't all turn up at the same time. Ken used to go over almost every weekend, but the same ones didn't arrive every time.

Most of them used to fly in on Friday evening and fly out again early on Monday morning to be back in time to start work. A couple of Ken's mates who lived at Burketown had boats and they looked forward to having someone to go fishing with every weekend."

"They'd fly in? That would work out fairly expensive if they did it on any sort of regular basis."

"I suppose fuel for the planes was expensive but it wasn't like they were paying for commercial flights." She saw my brow furrow and explained. "All of the properties have their own light planes and all the young blokes have a pilot's license. A couple of the department staff had their own planes. They often brought a mate with them, and another couple of the staff who used to come had licenses but no planes. They hired a local aero club's plane for the weekend."

"Did you know any of the ones he went fishing with, or even their names?"

"No, I don't think he ever told me who they were and, as I didn't have anything to do with them, I wasn't particularly interested. I did hear him use sort of nicknames when he rang people a couple of times, but I don't remember what they were. I just remember they caught my attention because they sounded strange."

I nodded and then changed tack again. "Geoff, Emily's father, was the boss out there for a number of years. Did you see much of him at Normanton?"

"Uhmm, yes, a bit I suppose. He visited all of his outlying centres on some sort of regular scheduled basis. He would visit Normanton as part of his run, although he only stayed at the residential complex once or twice. I suppose he must have stayed in Burketown on other occasions. He seemed to spend most of his time there, or over that way somewhere. I have a feeling he might have spent one week each month travelling around the centres."

It was getting late and I was beginning to feel exhausted. To end the interview, I made excuses about her needing to get back to her kids and me needing my beauty sleep. She agreed to give me a call if she thought of anything else that might be important. I gathered up my notebook and other bits and pieces I had spread across the table and stood to leave. She remained seated, staring at her hands in her lap.

"Sonny, where's Ken? Is he all right? Why can't I see him, or why hasn't he joined us? I want to know what's going on. Is he involved?" She looked up at me. The look of anguish on her face made me desperately wish I had answers for her.

189

"I don't know, Kate – truly. I haven't seen him either. I believe they kept him sedated in hospital because he went into shock after the shooting. His wounds weren't serious, but that's all I know. I haven't seen him either, and I'm not sure where he is."

After promising to see what I could find out for her, I held out my hand to help her to her feet. She looked so worn out and frail and willingly took my hand. I delivered Kate to the officer outside the door. He walked her back to her suite while I waited in the hallway for Sam to come out and join me.

Ben and Greg emerged from their room and we made our way down the stairs to the fifth floor where David sprawled in a lounge chair near the lifts. He spent the duration of the interview in that chair reading a magazine while keeping an eye out for anyone showing any interest in where we had gone. As soon as we joined him, he took the lift to the ground floor, while we idled around outside the lifts on the fifth floor until Ben received a phone call. David's call advised that nobody appeared to be looking for us, so we followed him down to the ground level and left him standing at the bar as we headed for Sam's car in the parking lot.

Back at the station, we assembled in the Special Task Force area. Curious; the Task Force officers who normally inhabit this area still haven't returned. Note to self: ask Ben about that at the first appropriate moment. On our arrival, the first port of call was the kitchen to rustle up coffee, and crisps and nuts for nibbles. Then, armed with sustenance, we straggled into the meeting room. Ben took the seat at the head of the table, eliminating any doubt as to who was in charge.

"Okay, post mortem time: how do we think tonight went, folks? Thoughts, comments, anything at all would be useful."

Two of us started flicking through our notebooks while Sam looked as though she was mulling over what Ben said. At this point David wandered into the meeting room, quickly retreated to the kitchen, and returned a couple of minutes later with a coffee.

Sam led off. "I'm not sure I have anything to contribute. I think the bit I was involved in went well, but I don't know about the interview itself because I wasn't involved. More importantly, Sonny, how do you think it went? What ..." Greg interrupted before she could finish.

"I agree with Sam on this one. I was involved but I'm not sure about what we gained, if anything. You asked a lot of questions and covered a lot of ground, Sonny, but I don't see how the exercise was useful."

"I'm very happy with what came out of it. It confirmed a few things that were kicking around in my mind for a while, and confirmed suspicions I had." I glanced around the table and noted the hint of a wry smile flit across Ben's face.

Greg persisted. "Maybe you would like to share some of that with us because I'm totally in the dark on this one."

"Look, I'm not being funny about this. I just think it might be a bit premature to be sharing my thoughts at this moment. Tonight's interview settled some things in my mind. As all interviews tend to do, I suppose it also raised a few other questions. I think it would be premature of me to lay it all out until I'm a bit more confident about some things. If I try to explain it all now, I suspect I would only succeed in further confusing everyone." Ben was enjoying my discomfort. His slight smile was now a wide grin.

"I don't think it would be premature at all," he said. "I think now would be a good time to share your thoughts, even if they do turn out to be wide of the mark in the long run. You never know, we might not be as thick as you think we are, and what you tell us might trigger some new thinking on our part."

Bugger! "Okay, if you insist. I'm not sure how to tell it, but here goes. For some time, there has been something about some sort of western connection niggling away in the back of my mind. Don't ask me why. Just accept that there has been. That's why I've been asking Emily and Kate about what went on out there. Emily couldn't give me much information because she only visited a couple of times. Over the years that her father was out there, her mother only spent, cumulatively, about half a year at most visiting him. Again, for reasons I can't explain, I felt that, on top of everything else that points to the west, there was something important connecting everything with a common place: with the Gulf area. That's why I was asking about life in Normanton."

There didn't seem to be much enthusiasm for what I was saying so far. Greg had taken to flicking through pages in his notebook as I spoke. Nevertheless, they had asked for my thoughts, so they were going to get them.

"I was still a public servant working in the Department when the Normanton 'great initiative' – the one that Therese and Ken were involved with – was happening, so we all knew about it. Some of the questions I put to Kate about it were only reality checks to give me an idea of how straight her answers were. In the end, the Normanton stuff didn't give me all that much. It was the Burketown stuff that was really important."

Brows furrowed, Greg and Sam looked at each other and then back at me. It fell to Greg to seek clarification. "I'm hoping there's more to the story because I still can't see how any of it was really useful."

"Ben, how good is your relationship with the drugs squad, or more importantly the Federal police?"

"Sonny, you know I get on well with everyone. I think my credibility is still intact with all of them. Why do you ask?"

"I'm just checking at the moment. Your contacts within the Federal Police could become important after I've had more time to think about what came out of tonight's meeting."

David was interrupting the process by demanding to know what I was thinking. I stammered and stalled for a few moments while I tried to get it all straight in my head. He didn't allow me that luxury. "That's lovely, but an explanation of why you think Ben will need to talk to Feds would be helpful at this time. Is there a bottom line to this story? Perhaps fantasy is a more accurate description." he growled.

"Okay, before I try explaining my theory, a brief history lesson might be in order." Everyone groaned.

"Make it brief, please," Greg pleaded. I noticed Sam trying to stifle a yawn, so I launched into the background story.

"Back in the earliest days of settlement, some intended Normanton would become the main town in the Gulf area. Somehow, Burketown slipped in under its collar and wrestled that honour away from Normanton. The significance of being the main town was that it also became the port of entry for supplies for the whole of the Gulf region. However, in the earliest days, before Burketown became properly established and Normanton wasn't much more than a few shacks, the port was actually located on Sweers Island. It's in the Gulf, not far out from Burketown. Ships unloaded cargo at the facility developed at Sweers, not just for the Gulf area, but also for much of the settled northern areas of east coast of the state. Long before any of that, Matthew Flinders discovered Sweers and his crew established a well on the island. Once the island became an important port, establishment of a settlement to support port operations happened. Then, over a period – a relatively short time, in fact – most of the people who were living on the island died of some fever or other. As a result, as soon as Burketown became established, they abandoned Sweers Island as the port in favour of Burketown. Over time, all trace of the early facility on the island disappeared. No one lives on the island now, but there is a fishing resort that operates for a few months of the year."

"That's interesting, but how is it relevant?" Greg asked.

"When the resort is operating, there are only about four or five staff and a small number of guests on the island at any given time. All guests arrive by light plane from Burketown."

I glanced around the table as I tried to formulate in my head the rest of what I had to say. I could see Ben had made the connection. He was leaning forward on the table and I could see the excitement on his face. However, I knew something didn't quite fit with my theory, and could demolish it. I opted to have Ben clarify it for me if possible before I continued.

"Ben, a few months ago, the Feds intercepted a major drug haul on a boat off the coast, somewhere near Cairns or Townsville I think. What do you know about that?"

"Oh, as I recall, that was pure luck. After receiving a tip-off, they were waiting to intercept a yacht when it arrived from Indonesia, but they intercepted the wrong boat. The one they were supposed to intercept didn't come down the east coast. It went to Darwin. When they found drugs on board the boat that they –wrongly – did intercept, it raised a whole raft of questions, about their intelligence sources, apart from anything else. The boat they searched wasn't foreign, and had never been outside Australian waters. It tended to shoot down the Feds' theory that foreign yachts coming into the top end were bringing in the drugs."

Fantastic; Ben's information might seem a bit unrelated, but it helped confirm the germ of an idea that had been trying to develop since we arrived back at the Precinct. I still hadn't teased it out completely. Premature or not, my gut instinct was telling me I was on the right track.

Sam saved me from having to go public with any more of my speculations when she suddenly pushed her chair back and stood up. "I'm sorry, guys, I can't keep my eyes open. If I don't go now, I'll be an accident waiting to happen on the drive home."

"You could always spend the night in the crash room instead of driving home," David suggested.

"Ha ha ha, good one, David. Spend the night in the same room as you lot; you must think I'm naïve."

"I have to admit I can hear my bed calling me too," Greg said. "It's not that your story isn't fascinating, Sonny. I've simply had a long day and I'm ready for bed.

"Yeah, I agree. It's been a long day. Let's call it a night and pick it up again sometime tomorrow," Ben said as he stood up as well. "I might just check on a couple of things and then I'm off home as well." Ben departed, phone in hand, and Sam made the most of the opportunity and followed him out.

Greg insisted on walking me to my door and his gallantry provided me with the opportunity I'd been searching for, I just needed to think about how to take advantage of it. I had worked out my approach by the time we reached my door.

"Greg, do the officers guarding Ken know you?"

"Yes, I've been in to see him a couple of times with Ben."

"I need to get in to talk to Ken. I know there is not a chance Ben would arrange it, and I think he has more to do than worry about what I might think is important. It appears Ken hasn't been forthcoming with any information and I don't think he is about to talk to you blokes. If I can get in to see him alone, there might be a chance he will talk to me. There is another agenda in there somewhere and I don't think it's just about him protecting his own hide."

"What do you think this 'other agenda' might be, and what makes you think he will talk to you?"

"Put it down to gut feeling if you must, but he gave me a lot of stuff when I first took on this case. Stuff he didn't share with anyone else. I have the feeling that he wants Therese's murder solved, but can't do it himself, and he needs to be very cautious about how he helps engineer it for someone else to achieve."

"Let me think about it. I'll give you a call in the morning. In the meantime, let's see if we can't get some sleep in what's left of this night." He smiled and said goodnight.

I sat in the dark in my lounge room for quite a long time. I knew sleep would evade me tonight. There was too much going on in my mind and the adrenaline rush that accompanied the prospect of closing this case would ensure I remained awake for quite a bit longer yet.

# Chapter Sixteen

I awoke in the lounge chair – again – and headed for the shower immediately to bring myself back to life once more. I had not done much more than make coffee for breakfast when Greg called from outside my door. He started explaining as I opened the door, but he didn't make any move to come in.

"Ben is going to be tied up all morning at least, so I thought it was a good time for us to try to see Ken. If you're right to go, we could head off now."

Breakfast suddenly lost importance. I turned off the coffee, snagged my bag as I walked past the kitchen bench and exited to meet Greg in the hallway. I spent the drive to the hospital trying to get my head around how the conversation with Ken might go. It was early, so the hospital was relatively quiet. The guard outside Ken's room stood up as we approached. He looked hesitantly at Greg who allayed his concerns by flashing his badge. Greg assured him I was only going to speak to Ken for a few minutes, but the officer seemed reluctant for me to enter the room until Greg reassured him that he was coming in with me. That arrangement didn't suit me. I was about to say so when a hard look from Greg silenced me.

Ken was dozing when we entered. I sat down beside the bed, while Greg remained standing just inside the door. After a few seconds, Greg left the room and spoke to the officer on guard. I saw the officer disappear off down the corridor and Greg take his place outside the door. I spoke quietly to Ken who immediately opened one eye and struggled to focus on me. He blinked a few times as he gradually joined me in the real world. Not detecting any adverse reaction to my presence, I gently eased into my interview with him. Before I had a chance to say much, he was asking about Kate and the kids.

"They're okay. The police have them in some safe accommodation until they can figure all this out and they are confident it is safe for them to go home. The other night's events stressed the kids badly. A counsellor had a couple of sessions with them and they seem to be settling down okay. Kids are pretty resilient, but the shooting really did frighten them."

"What about Kate? How is she coping?"

"Ah well, Kate is a different story. I met with her last night. I can honestly say that I have never seen anyone look so haggard and wrung out. This whole thing has taken a heavy toll on her and I don't just mean her mother's death. I think the shooting the other night just about tipped her over the edge. It's not about just the death and the shooting. It's not knowing what it's all about, why they are being put through this, and what it's going to take to make it all go away again."

Ken looked away and continued to avoid my eyes for some time. I didn't know how much time I would have with him. Although I wanted to gain his trust and get him to feel comfortable about talking to me, I couldn't afford to waste too much time. I decided to take a gamble and push my assumptions to see what reaction I got.

"Ken, we know the basics of what was going on up in the Gulf. You need to talk to people. You need to tell them what you know. We believe a number of people who were involved have met with strange deaths lately, and the incident the other night could well have added you to the list. More importantly, if the police don't get the whole story and can't work out how to shut it down, then not only your life but also those of Kate and the kids might be the next in line. I'm sure you know, or, at least, have a good idea, why someone was trying to shoot you the other night. You need to share that information with others. If you don't want to talk to the police, tell me the story, as much as you feel comfortable with, and between me and the police, we will try to work out the whole story and what action can be taken."

He became very agitated and angrily snarled his response. "I can't talk about it. Anyone I've talked to is now dead. The only way I can stop the killing is not to talk to anyone, and that way it's only me that's in danger."

"You are wrong, Ken. Kate and the kids are in danger, but I know you probably don't want to believe it's your fault. Okay Ken, here's what we're going to do. I'm going to tell you how I think the story goes. You don't have to say anything, but feel free to correct me if I get it wrong."

He didn't argue or agree, but I thought I detected a softening in his attitude. It suited me to think that might constitute some form of agreement, so I ploughed on with my assumptions.

"I believe all this started long before Ralston. It goes back to your days at Normanton or, more correctly, your association with

Burketown. I believe the worst thing you're guilty of is acquiring a whole lot of furniture, appliances other bits and pieces for your own use at the government's expense. However, somewhere in amongst all that, you somehow became involved in what we believe is a very lucrative and long-standing drugs trafficking operation. My suspicion is that you were something of a bystander rather than a true participant. I also believe it was that bystander role you had then, that now puts you – and your family – at risk. My thinking is that Therese was a major player in a public service based network that facilitated the distribution of the drugs and that, for whatever her reasons, she could not extricate herself from that situation. I'm not sure she even wanted to but, regardless, she couldn't."

I paused for a moment to see if I had generated any reaction from Ken. No, no change detected. His eyes remained averted and his hands fiercely continued to worry an area of the bedsheet. I decided there was nothing to do but continue in the hope of hitting a nerve that would bring a response.

"What did Therese do? What did she say, and to whom? What did she do that broke the rules of this business and got her killed? The police need to know. Kate needs to know. I need to know. The only person who isn't looking for answers is you, because you already have the answers. This won't go away on its own. You won't stop the bad things happening by not talking to anyone. The only way forward, the only way out of this is for you to man up, bite the bullet and tell people what you know."

I saw anguish etched deeply into his face as he looked up at me pleadingly, silently begging me not to continue. The sight of him almost weakened my resolve. I took a few seconds to think about how to progress the interview. I had not prepared well for this. However, I knew much of how I progressed from here would involve responding to whatever Ken's reactions were. As I fumbled around in my mind for what to say next, an entirely new idea came to me from out of nowhere and I decided it was worth using it for one last hard-hitting attempt.

"Who was holding you to ransom, Ken?" The startled look from Ken was my hoped for response.

"What do you mean by 'holding me to ransom'?"

"Aarrgh, come on, Ken, someone is holding something over you. Who is it and what have they got on you?"

He just pressed his lips together and shook his head violently. Okay, that was a reasonably solid response in itself, so let's push it a little harder and see what else we can make happen.

"As I said before, Ken, the most I think you might be found guilty of is misappropriation of government property, but I think someone has a hold over you. A hold that says, if you don't play the game their way, they could incriminate you in this other ugly trafficking business, simply because you were there when it was happening. You weren't a participant, but you could be made to look like one."

My left-field idea had taken on a life of its own. It was in danger of becoming the stuff of fiction novels. Ken hadn't disputed anything I said so far, so I felt game enough for another major dose of imagination.

"While we are examining this hypothetical story, I might as well tell you what my major theory is. I think whoever has a hold over you is involved in the drugs trade. Further, I believe they are a person in authority."

Ah hah! Oh yes, that found a nerve, just as I desperately hoped it would. I was running out of ideas. His reaction was one of pure fright. His eyes darted around the room, returning to check the door a couple of times. Having not spied anyone hiding behind the curtains, he turned back to me, his face reflecting a cavalcade of emotions: fear, anger, doubt. Now I had found the sore point, I needed to hit it again – hard. Think, Sonny, take that last point a bit further. What's the extension of that thought? It was a no holds barred situation, and probably make or break time for me, as my time with Ken must be running out. So why not indulge in something fanciful – way-out-there fanciful?

"Let's take my hypothesis a little further. I think the person we're talking about is probably involved in the investigation, but has a foot in both camps. They are actually involved in the trafficking, perhaps even helping to facilitate its ongoing operation. Let's not beat about the bush. Let's call it like it is. I think the person who has a hold over you is a law enforcement officer."

Ken responded with an almost imperceptible nod of his head but kept his downcast eyes fixed firmly on the piece of bedsheet he'd been attacking for most of our meeting.

"Federal...?" I asked quietly.

Again, an almost imperceptible nod, but now he looked directly at me. I couldn't tell whether his face reflected relief or defeat. It was time to wind up the meeting, but I wanted to give him a chance to add information if he felt inclined.

"I guess I would be pushing my luck if I asked you for a name," I said quietly, and he nodded his agreement with my statement. "Okay, is there anything else that you can tell me... will tell me?"

"Sonny, I can't tell you anymore. Anyway, I think you've probably worked out most of the story already. I tried to warn Therese. I tried to get her to pull out of the whole thing. I don't know if she tried to do something or not, but all I did was get her killed. I'll do whatever it takes to make sure the same thing doesn't happen to Kate and the kids."

It was my turn to nod. Bit by tiny bit, Ken had provided enough detail to create a solid lead. I had what I came for, and the process now had us both exhausted. I quickly took my leave and slipped out to join Greg in the corridor while the officer on guard duty chatted to a nurse at the nearby nurses' station. I gave Greg a nod to signify I was done, before turning left and heading for the exit. Greg waited a few seconds and then turned right and sauntered down to the nurses' station to tell the officer he was leaving. We drove back to the station in silence although, in my peripheral vision, I saw Greg glance anxiously at me a few times during the short trip.

As we drove into the station, Greg asked me whether I had breakfast before going to the hospital. I just shook my head. He told me to go up to the apartment while he went and found something to eat. I did as he suggested. I felt drained and some time alone would be good right now. It seemed like only a few minutes before Greg arrived with croissants and raisin toast from the coffee shop a bit further down the street. I put a batch of coffee on as soon as I came upstairs, and the aroma of freshly brewed coffee and hot croissants convinced me I was hungry. Over our breakfast, Greg cautiously initiated conversation about my meeting with Ken.

"How did it go this morning? Was it worthwhile?"

"Yes. Yes, it went well. I'm still trying to get my head around all the information, maybe when I get it all typed up it'll be easier to take it all in."

"Look, Sonny, we do need to tell Ben about the meeting with Ken this morning."

"Yeah, I know. I'll do it myself. I need to talk to him about a few things, including when I might be able to go home. By the way, how much longer are you and David going to be around? I thought you would have gone by now."

"I thought we were going home early this week as well. I made plans for this coming weekend, but now I'm not sure I'm going to be home in time."

"What's David up to this morning? I haven't seen him around."

"I don't know. He didn't say he had any plans for today. I expect he's doing something with Ben. He was gone when I got up this morning."

We didn't discuss my meeting with Ken, although I knew Greg was anxious to know what came out of it. Nothing more than light conversation accompanied our breakfast. Soon after we finished eating, Greg excused himself saying he needed to ring his office to check up on progress on his outstanding cases. As soon as he left, I rang Ben, fully expecting the call to go through to voicemail. To my surprise, he answered on the second ring. Damn, now I can't avoid telling him any longer.

"I know you're busy, Ben, but I need to talk to you. It should only take a few minutes. I've got a confession and information that I think you need to hear."

"Is it urgent?"

"Yes, you need to know about it as soon as possible."

"How about if I come up and see you at lunchtime: probably around noon?"

That gave me a little time to type up my recording of the meeting with Ken. The recorder I used works with my voice transcription program. It records everything but only transcribes my part of the conversation because that's the only voice it understands. Then you have to go along and fill in the 'gaps' by actually typing in what everyone else said. As Ken had not said much until the very end of the meeting, I didn't have many gaps to fill in. However, I did have to indicate where he had responded with a gesture of some sort, otherwise it wouldn't make any sense.

Ben rang shortly before noon to say he would be a bit later than arranged. It suited me, as transcription took longer than I expected. I was waiting for the second copy of the transcript to finish printing when Ben arrived shortly after one o'clock, complete with very large salad rolls for lunch. He didn't waste any time in getting the conversation going.

"Okay what's so urgent?"

"Well, confession first: I went to see Ken this morning."

"You did what?"

"Hear me out and then you can snort and yell much as you feel inclined. When I arrived in Ralston to look into Therese's death, Ken was very helpful. He had the presence of mind to take photos when they first found her and he gave me a number of bits of information that were useful. He didn't give any of that to the Police. I don't think he gave it to me just to help my case, I think he was hoping I would pass it on to the 'right people', which I did. I gave it to you ... after Langborne wasn't interested. I thought I might be able to get him to talk to me, seeing as how the police weren't making much progress with him."

"I'm assuming you had some success."

"Yes, it was worthwhile. He gave me ..."

Great, just when I was getting into my stride, Ben's phone rang. He took one look at the caller ID and strode to the far end of the room. An animated conversation lasted a couple of minutes or so, and then he was telling me he would catch up with me later as he rushed for the door. When he reached the door, he stopped and turned to face me, and explained apologetically, "Gotta go. I have a million things on the boil that I need to keep an eye on. Sorry. I will come back to you later on, as soon as I can, but it might not be till this evening."

For want of inspiration and lack of enthusiasm, after reading through the transcript of my meeting with Ken, I frittered away the rest of the afternoon on various bits and pieces but mainly spent time on trying to refine and crystallise my concept of everything that had happened. There were new bits to add to my mind map of the case, and I wanted to document my hypothesis before I met with Ben again.

It was eight o'clock before Ben reappeared. He held aloft a couple of carrier bags to greet me when I opened the door. "Dinner has arrived. I thought we would eat in the Task Force area. There's more room."

I couldn't argue with that and the smell of the food in those carrier bags would convince me to follow him anywhere. Tonight's fare was a selection of pasta dishes accompanied by sides of bruschetta and garlic bread. Sam joined us again. I couldn't work out whether she was now officially part of the investigation or she was around so much because the blokes were smitten with her.

We dealt with the food as soon as we were all seated; didn't want it to go cold. After that, there was some general talk about what people had done during the day. All three men receiving phone calls they couldn't ignore at different times punctuated those discussions. Ben reminded me that I still needed to bring him up to speed on my interview with Ken. David was unaware of my early morning visit to the hospital and wanted to know the details. I explained why I thought Ken might talk to me rather than the Police and how I hadn't had a chance yet to share that information with Ben. Then it was as if the clock had turned back to yesterday. Ben seamlessly picked up the thread of the final discussion from last night.

"I remember the last thing before we called it a night, Sonny, was you asking me how good my relationship was with some of our other law enforcement agencies. Let's continue that conversation. Why did you ask?"

"Is there someone, probably in Federal Police, whom you could ask about the supply? I'm talking about drugs of course, and I'm interested in whether they have identified the source of the stuff that is coming in, and whether there are any peak periods for arrivals."

Ben looked at me hard for a moment before answering. "Yeah, there is someone I can call." He checked his watch. It was already after 11 o'clock. "Don't know that he will be real happy about me ringing him at this hour." He shrugged and began flicking through his contacts list as he left the room to make the call.

While Ben was gone, we chatted about the western region and the Gulf area, with the other three all admitting that they knew very little about that part of the country and how my 'history lesson' was a bit of an eye-opener. Ben was not gone very long before he returned looking decidedly grim.

"I was right, he wasn't terribly impressed about being rung at this hour, but he soon got over it and became interested. He needs to check on something and will call be back as soon as he has the information he needs."

Greg harked back to the part of our previous discussion regarding the Feds' good luck in intercepting the wrong boat but still coming up with the drugs haul they were expecting. He suggested that finding the drugs on a boat that had never left Australian water tended to shoot down the Feds theory that foreign yachts coming into the top end were bringing the drugs in."

"Ah hah, the boat they intercepted didn't have to leave Australian waters. It could have rendezvoused with the incoming yacht somewhere behind Sweers Island. An alternative scenario might be that the drugs are dropped off somewhere on Sweers for later collection, while the incoming foreign yacht carried on to Darwin. When it arrived in Darwin, Customs would find nothing of interest on board that boat. There are a couple of frightening places when you sail a boat through Torres Strait and over the tip of Cape York. Unless they are skilled yachtsmen and know the way through there very well, most would avoid making the trip. That's why ingress through Burketown makes a lot of sense, and those flying in for 'fishing weekends' provide an excellent network for distribution. However, I don't think the main story lies with property owners' sons and whatever distribution networks they might have developed. Their distribution is likely to be a minor part of the problem. I am convinced – no, almost convinced – the big story is about public servants and a potentially much wider distribution set-up."

"Are you kidding?" David and Greg said in unison.

"I see where you're coming from," Ben said slowly, "But proving the connections might be difficult."

"Yes, you could be right but, if we work on the hypothesis that they are involved, then some of the details we gathered today go a long way towards giving us a pretty good overview of the front end of the operation. If you accept my scenario might be a possibility, Ben, it gives you a new slant on your plane crash case. It also gives our southern colleagues here something to think about in relation to their 'funny' deaths cases. In the meantime, while we are all thinking about that, perhaps there's some work for a government fraud investigator." I raised an eyebrow enquiringly at Ben after this last comment.

The room went silent for some time as each of us examined our own thoughts. Ben was first to speak.

"If there's an airstrip on Sweers Island, it seems that for more than half of the year there is no one around to monitor air traffic to the place. With so many boats and planes flitting around from that Burketown area, your scenario that has Sweers central to drug trafficking is very credible. I think I need to go and wake up a Fed again – right now – although I am supposed to be waiting for him to call me back." I don't know why, but the prospect of waking up the Fed again seemed to amuse him no end and he chuckled loudly as he stood up. He paused before walking away.

"It's already late, and I think we have all had enough late nights for one week. I suggest we call it a night now and pick it up again sometime tomorrow. I might be tied up for a while first thing in the morning so, if we can get together as soon as I'm free…"

There was unanimous support for his suggestion and Sam and I followed Ben as he left the Task Force area, leaving Greg and David to clean up. I had no difficulty falling asleep tonight… and in bed for a nice change.

*****

After breakfast, I wasn't sure what to do next. I didn't want to start something in case Ben arrived. What did I have to do anyway? A load of washing taken care of, I sat in the lounge with the book I had been attempting to read since I arrived in Ralston. It looked like being a slow day if it continued in this fashion. The only relief was Greg who dropped in around 9.30 to see if I'd heard from Ben about when we might be meeting. I was surprised he came alone. Where one goes, the other usually follows. Greg stayed for coffee. Before he left, I had to satisfy my curiosity.

"What's David up to this morning? I haven't seen him around."

"I don't know. He didn't say he had any plans for today. I expect he's found something else to do with Ben. He was gone again when I got up this morning. He doesn't usually surface as early as he has done the last couple of mornings." The he was gone and I was left wondering what to do with myself once more.

It was almost 11 o'clock when Ben arrived. He announced he had ordered lunch for 12 o'clock and suggested we get straight down to business. I asked about letting the others know and received a one-word answer, "Later." Coffee was high on his agenda, so I made a fresh brew and had yet another cup to keep him company. Seated in the lounge area with our coffees, he picked up things from where we left off the previous night.

"I already knew they identified the source of the drugs as mainly from Asia, and that hasn't changed, except now all of the supply seems to be coming in from there. Supply comes in all year round, but the heaviest traffic appears to be between November and May, even though this includes the wet season part of the year. New supplies tend to come in throughout the rest of the year but in smaller quantities. So, Sonny, how is this relevant?"

A burst of excitement surged through me as I tried to digest the information Ben provided. Things are starting to fall into place. I just need to finalise a couple more connections but that fits with my thinking.

"I need you to answer one question for me first, please. How sure are you of the person you rang last night after we met with Kate?"

"I'm sure."

"Are you confident they can be trusted? Can you be sure …?"

"Completely sure and completely trustworthy; for God's sake, Sonny, he's my brother." Well, that got that question out of the way. "So, instead of messing about, how about you tell me what came out of your talk with Ken."

"Okay, the short version is that Ken was not a participant in the drugs trafficking but he was leant upon to maintain his association with the Burketown mob and pass information back to another person. That person threatened to make it look as though Ken was involved if he didn't comply. Ken tried to warn a couple of the other people he was close to, including Therese, that he suspected something nasty was about to happen and that they could be caught up in it. They all ended up dead. Whatever those people did, regardless of whether it resulted from of something Ken did or not, the person that's intimidating Ken blamed him for it. Ken believes the shooting incident the other night was about eliminating something that was becoming a problem: Ken. I'm not sure what Ken's future looks like, but I am concerned about retribution being directed at Kate and/or the kids."

"Do we have any information on who this person might be?"

"No names, just that he is one of the Feds who has been involved in 'investigating' the importation of drugs through the northern areas. Hence, my question about how far you could trust the person you rang last night. Here's a copy of a transcript of my meeting with Ken. You can listen to the electronic recording if you want or I could copy it onto something if that's what you need to do."

"I can feel another call to the Feds coming on. By the way, was David with you this morning?"

"No, Greg thought he was with you. Neither of us has seen him today. Is that important?"

"No, just asking…"

Now that was curious, and I wanted to know why he was asking, but his phone rang and the moment was lost.

"Now, where were we?" he asked distractedly when the call ended.

"I think we had covered everything. The only other thing I would like to go over with you at some time soon is my list of who 'might have done it'. We seem to have accumulated a reasonable amount of information about a possible network operation, but don't seem to be any closer to sorting out the 'who' involved in the various cases."

Ben's phone rang again. As his call progressed, he slowly made his way towards the door. He opened the door, turned and said, "Thanks. Good work," and then was off down the hallway with this phone to his ear.

Damn, we never seem to finish anything before Ben dashes off somewhere. It would be nice to know if he planned anything for dinner, or if I had to escape from incarceration again to avoid starvation. Fed up with everything in general and not having anything pressing to be getting on with, I took myself off for a nap. Late nights were starting to take their toll – or maybe it was frustration and boredom taking over.

# Chapter Seventeen

It was almost five o'clock when I woke. The snooze left me feeling sluggish and disconnected. Coffee might fix it. Ben arrived as I sat down with my mug. He was alone, which was something of a blessing given my current lack of intelligence. After helping himself to coffee, Ben sat with me – and grinned. I suspect the fact that I had just woken up was no secret.

"You said you wanted to talk about potential 'who done its'. Are you up to that now, or do you need more time to join the real world first?"

"I am fine to discuss my thoughts now," I replied a little too sharply, and then amended my tone before continuing. "A number of names emerged in the course of my discussions with various people. Some I dismissed outright at the time, while others were more interesting. Even some of the interesting ones I think have a slim chance of being real suspects."

"Okay, that's the way it usually works in my line of work so I don't see why it would be different for you."

"The first one I think worth a look is a western property owner named Tony Baldwin. At least, that's the name I was given. There was an incident involving his son, presumably, it happened in the gulf area or at the family's western property. Somehow, Therese was involved. I don't know how. However, the father blames Therese for ruining his son's life. His harassment of her followed her to Ralston. I think she took legal action against him soon after her arrival here. That suggests it all happened some years ago, but Mr Baldwin was in town about a week before Therese's death … and he still harboured a truckload of hatred."

I reiterated Kate's story of Tony Baldwin's interest in the house and visiting the flat looking for Therese, and suggested Ben see if he could dig up anything on what happened to the son. Ben asked for approximate dates and scribbled himself a few notes.

"Okay, who else?"

There was a bloke named Poole who lost his job in a shoot-out with Therese." I saw Ben's eyebrows lift. "Not literally; it happened as part of a restructure. Two equal positions with different Schools reduced to one position over a combined School. The existing incumbents had to reapply for the resulting single position. Therese got the job. The other bloke lost his job and, subsequently, his marriage. He was bitter, took to alcohol for comfort, and seemed to have no luck finding another job. He went broke and blames Therese for his sorry state. A lot of his staff supporters believed Therese's appointment was another example of the favoured child getting all the sweets ... so did Mr Poole."

"You think he is a firm possibility?"

"No, not really, but I didn't feel I could discount him entirely." Ben scribbled himself more notes.

"Who's next on your list?"

"W-e-l-l, obviously I think the Federal Police Officer who has been holding Ken to ransom for so long might be involved in the episode with Ken. I don't mean I think he was the shooter. You have already arrested him, but I wonder if the Fed might have issued the order for the hit."

"I suspect so, but we are still looking into that one. Any others got your attention?"

"Persons unknown..."

"Oh, great; go on tell me about them." Ben heaved a deep sigh as he said it. He hates when I hypothesise, but that's how investigations proceed in my world. I must explain that to him one day, but not right now.

"You have established that Mr Green was here specifically to deal with Therese. He was to meet a boat that didn't come. Suggestion was that, seeing his business with the boat couldn't happen, he might have a 'clean up' here instead while he was in town. It sounds, according to your interviewee, that a foot soldier guilty of some transgression had to redeem himself by carrying out some task. I'm wondering whether that task might have involved Therese, the travel agent bloke or Norman Fanning – or even Ken. Perhaps it was a different foot soldier altogether in Ken's instance, or perhaps it was the same one involved with one or more of the others."

"You don't believe in making life easy, do you? Any further complications you would like to add while you're about it?"

"Just one, a question really: what about your 'rotten apple', is it likely he could be involved in any of this in any way?"

"Not that we are aware of... yet? Investigations are ongoing. Is that it then, there's no more?"

I smiled sweetly and shook my head. "No, I think that's it... for the moment. Have you anything to add to any of this. Oh, I just thought of something. What about Norman Fanning? Did you find out any more about his 'accident', and why was his son contacting Therese?"

"No ..." Ben's phone rang. He took the call in the hallway. It lasted a few minutes.

With the call ended, he resumed his seat. He flicked through his notebook and I waited expectantly for him to share with me. If Ben was going to offer anything, a knock on my door ended it. It was about six o'clock when Greg came in followed by no one. I looked past him to see if David was tagging along. He was nowhere in sight. I looked enquiringly at Ben and was about to ask about David. The look I received in return silenced me.

"I've organised an early dinner for us. It's on its way. I thought we might dine down the other end in the meeting room where there is a decent sized table to spread things out." Ben's appearance changed. He now looked tense, his face stony as he issued the invitation. His demeanour didn't encourage me to argue. Not that I wanted to, and Greg didn't look as though he would object either.

Greg and I followed him down to the Task Force area. Sam arrived almost at the same time. She was laden with food. The bags and boxes indicated we were eating Italian again – from Dominic's Italian Restaurant this time. Greg took the food through to the meeting room while I sourced plates and cutlery, and Ben spoke briefly to Sam. Ben took his now customary position at the head of the table and we began filling our plates from the range of pasta dishes provided. I had barely taken my first mouthful when Greg asked the question that took the edge off the rest of the meal.

"Is David not joining us tonight, Ben? I haven't seen him all day. I assume you've had him gainfully employed."

Ben's voice was flat when he replied without as much as a glance in Greg's direction. "David flew out of Ralston in a private light plane at six o'clock this morning."

"This morning...!"

Greg and I shared a startled glance across the table before turning to Ben expectantly.

"Has there been a breakthrough or something, or a problem, at home. He never said anything to me about going," Greg said.

"No," Ben replied sharply. "Look, it's a long and involved story. You both need to hear it and I think I need to tell it from the beginning." He paused for a moment and glanced from Greg to Sam, as he gathered his thoughts before continuing.

"Sonny, you remember I started an internal investigation into one of my Task Force officers who we dubbed the 'rotten apple'? I was concerned about security of information within the group, so I arranged for the group to spend a few days out of the Army base undergoing first response training. That's why this whole area is vacant at the moment and, Greg, you and David were able to take over the place. The investigation turned up some damning evidence. I arranged for him – the 'rotten apple' – to be redeployed to the special force they are putting together and training for the G20 summit later in the year when all the heads of government will be on the Gold Coast."

Ben's move confused me, and I noticed Greg seemed to struggle with the news as well. "Why would you choose to give someone like that opportunity to be involved in something special," I asked.

"It wasn't that sort of opportunity. Let me finish and it might make more sense. Now, where was I? Oh yes, I rang him, the rotten apple, that is, on the Sunday afternoon and gave him a major serve of BS about how he'd been selected and how, if he did well, it was likely to mean big things for him immediately after the Summit. I did the bit about not wanting to lose him, but this was a great career opportunity for him, blah, blah. I told him there was a vehicle coming back in from the Army base early the next morning. If he took up the offer, he needed to be in that vehicle and go straight to his place and pack. I had arranged for a car to pick him up from his unit at 11 o'clock to take him to the airport for his lunchtime flight to join the training camp."

"You were taking a gamble he would jump at the opportunity. He might have turned it down," Greg commented.

"I figured I knew this bloke fairly well. He is a bit of a 'show pony'; loves to be important. I knew dangling the 'something big after G20' carrot would be an irresistible lure. Anyway, it wasn't an issue. He jumped at the opportunity. From my point of view, this move effectively isolated him for the duration of the training and allowed the investigators more time to keep digging while he was there. They found he had a phone we knew nothing about..."

"Surely having a personal phone your workplace doesn't know about isn't an indictment in itself. I suspect the majority of people have a personal phone that is just that: personal and private. They don't necessarily hand that number out at their workplace," Greg argued.

"True, and there isn't a problem as long as the phone isn't involved in activities contrary to the aims and aspirations of the person's employer and, in particular, those of this department."

Ben's irritation at the interruptions built to the point where there was now a distinct edge to his voice. Greg and I squirmed uncomfortably on our chairs. I shot Greg a hard look, hoping he would get the message to shut up and let Ben get on with the story. I wanted to hear what the outcome of all this was. I didn't want Ben getting so exasperated that he gave up and walked out before delivering the punch line. Whether Greg got my message or whether he worked it out by himself wasn't clear, but he held up his hands to signal he would desist and then gestured for Ben to continue.

"Thank you. The problem in this case was that the phone in question frequently called a Federal Police number, as well as another number somewhere in the metropolitan area."

"I am assuming those numbers proved to be relevant to the stuff we determined from Kate and Ken?" I suggested quietly, and almost bit my tongue immediately for interrupting. It was a relief when there was no negative reaction and Ben continued his story.

"My Fed contact held suspicions about one of their guys and, like me, had been digging around to convince himself one way or the other. When I rang him after our meeting with Kate, we both spent the night swapping notes and digging a little deeper. Suffice to say, the connections become apparent when you know what you're looking for. As soon as my rotten apple left the Army base, the rest of my special task force packed up their gear and headed to the Gulf country. They are staying on a private property, venturing into town in singles and pairs and posing as tourists while they keep an eye on things. Today was a very busy day for them."

Ben went on to explain about the rogue Federal police officer. The evidence against him was damning. That included those comments from Ken, with whom we discovered the officer had maintained contact. The officer was taken into custody early this morning. The Feds also managed to round up another 10 or 12 people from the Burketown area. Ben expected that number to have increased by now, and there would be more arrests across that western area tomorrow. He anticipated quite a few well-positioned public servants might suddenly disappear from their jobs in the very near future. The story then moved to the Ralston area.

"The guys going through Therese's secret apartment uncovered a whole world of information. She kept records of all sorts of stuff. Presumably, she thought it might provide some sort of safeguard but, in the end, maybe it contributed to her death. In addition, the shooter from Tirandi Street, the one who tried to take out Ken, decided it might be worth his while to assist us with our investigation and has been singing sweetly. Based on the names he provided and information from Therese's apartment, a major roundup happened in this area as well. Our correctional institution's population swelled significantly today."

"Damn! I feel as though I've been sitting on the sideline while it has all be going on around me. I've missed all the action. I'll bet David managed to get involved up to his neck. So, what was his role in all this?" Greg demanded with a hint of peeve apparent in his delivery.

"You could say that," Ben sighed. "That phone in the metropolitan area involved in heavy call traffic to and from that arrested Federal officer and my 'rotten apple' was eventually identified as belonging to a woman."

"A woman! I hadn't expected that," Greg said.

"No reason a woman should be excluded from the picture. Therese wasn't – and it seems she was a major player." I retorted. Ben gave me a look. I got the message and nodded I understood.

"Further investigation found that the phone was actually in the woman's maiden name and she had changed her name when she married quite a few years ago. Officers called on the woman before she went to work this morning. She knew nothing about the phone. She never owned it. She genuinely knew nothing about that phone which was bought in her name and used without her knowledge. It was in the maiden name of David's ex-wife."

I saw Greg's jaw drop in disbelief. "Charlotte?" Greg blurted out. "What are you saying, Ben?"

"Okay, hang on a minute, I'll get to that. Once we established that connection and realised David had disappeared, we did some investigating here in Ralston and found that he caught a cab early this morning. It took him to the aero club's airfield. He then flew in a private light plane down to the metropolitan area with the plane's owner, a person of interest to me for some time now. We found out where the plane landed and we tracked its owner's mobile phone. Therefore, we also knew where to find him. However, we were much more interested in what David was doing. It took us a while initially, as he had turned off all his phones that we knew about. It wasn't until sometime later that we got lucky when he made a call from his hotel using the phone in his ex-wife's name. We tracked him for a short while after he left the apartment, so we knew the general direction he was heading, but he turned the phone off again."

"He's no fool and he knows standard Police practice," Greg mused.

"Yeah, but I thought I knew where he was heading, and that he too might be looking to 'clean up' a bit. I contacted the bloke in charge of training the G20 Summit force and explained my concern. He set up a special exercise for another team. Fortunately, David turned his phone on again just before I came up here this afternoon. He rang my rotten apple."

"So there was a continuing connection," I murmured, but it passed unnoticed and Ben continued.

Those in the training camp must leave their phones in their lockers during the day but, at the end of the day's training, they are free to use them. David knew that, and he waited until the appropriate time to call to set up a meeting near the perimeter fence tonight. We monitored the call. The training camp team apprehended David as he attempted to shoot my rotten apple with a non-Police issue weapon. My rotten apple, by the way, has a non-life threatening wound and is also now in custody."

"Shit! I'm having trouble taking in all this. How could I be so blind to what David was doing? What he was really like?" Greg, sitting with his head in his hands, slowly lifted his head and looked from Ben to me.

"Christ!" I exclaimed. "Never mind about that; what about Kate and the kids? David knows where they are, and probably where Ken is being kept as well."

"Relax, Sonny. When I left here last night, I was talking to my Fed contact, and Sam followed me out. With the information he gave me, I realised we might have endangered them. I caught Sam before she drove off. I sent her and three other officers to the hotel to move Kate and the kids and to guard them overnight. I left four officers on the sixth floor where the family had been staying so it would look normal if anyone came snooping around. They did; two of them. There was something of a set-to. One of the officers was wounded – knife wound, not serious – although he will be off work for a while. The two 'visitors' were taken into custody."

"Did David know where Ken was being kept?" I asked.

"I'm not sure but I had him moved, to be on the safe side, probably not long after you left him after your interview. Surprise, surprise, someone did come looking for him too. That person is now helping us with our enquiries, as they say."

I felt a little relieved by Ben's quick thinking. However, the revelation about David was all too much for Greg. He sat with his head in his hands again, shaking his head from side to side, as if everything he heard about David was beyond comprehension.

Then there were a few sporadic bursts of questions and answers spread across the next half hour or so. Much of the pasta hadn't been touched when Ben began his story. Much of it remained that way after the gathering broke up. I was first to make a move. I thought Ben might want some time alone with Greg. As I stood to depart, Ben spoke quietly to me.

"How close are you to Emily?"

"Close…? I wouldn't say we were close at all. I first met her years ago but I've not had much contact with her. I've had more to do with her in the last couple of weeks than the rest of the time put together. Of course, her mother has always kept me up to date with what the girls were doing. You don't think Emily is involved in all this in any way?"

"No, but you should know they took her father into custody late this afternoon."

"Oh, bloody hell, it will rock that family. Do Sandra and the girls know?"

"Patience, Sonny. They were going to bring him in for questioning tomorrow morning, but they discovered he made a last minute booking on the five o'clock flight out of Millhaven. They arrested him at the airport – with his passport in his bag. His wife doesn't know yet and she probably won't know until sometime late tomorrow, unless they raise a warrant to search the house before then. What you choose to do with that information is up to you, but feel free to alert Emily if you think it might help for her to be with her mother."

I just nodded, thanked him, and left the two men alone. After wrestling with my conscience all the way back to my apartment, I phoned Emily as soon as I was inside. Not an easy call, but one I felt obliged to make. In spite of her feelings towards her father, the news shocked her. As I anticipated, she elected not to tell her mother yet, but to drive up to Millhaven first thing in the morning. Her aim was somehow to prepare her mother for whatever the news ultimately might be.

With slightly more than two fingers of scotch, I sat sipping it in semi-darkness as I struggled to comprehend all Ben shared with us tonight. About an hour later, Ben came to see me. He thought that, by Friday at the latest, it should be safe for me to return home. I should pack as much as possible beforehand to be able to leave at short notice if necessary. I wasn't sure what 'if necessary' meant but I assured him it would take me five minutes to be ready when the time came.

I didn't think sleep was going to come easily, so I busied myself packing up my computer and other office paraphernalia I had managed to spread about the place over the last couple of days. Then the wardrobe came in for attention and any 'unnecessary' items went into my case. I rounded up all the bits and pieces in the bathroom and corralled them beside the hand basin. With nothing left to do except go to bed and read my book, that's what I did ... and fell asleep after about one page.

*****

Thursday morning saw me out of bed at my normal time and wondering over breakfast how I was going to fill in my day with everything now packed away in readiness for the trip home. I was likely to be reduced to reading my book all day, but I wondered if I might be able to sneak out to a supermarket if there was one close by to stock up on a few things for when I arrived home. I tossed the supermarket idea around for a while and had almost abandoned the idea when Ben rang. He thought it would be a good idea for us to go and have a chat to Ken. He asked me to meet him downstairs. On the way to the hospital, he gave me a broad overview of the information I should share with Ken.

Ken looked a bit wary when I arrived and I could understand why. Straight off, I mentioned the name of the Federal officer who was now in custody. I noted his reaction to the name. Good, it was the right bloke. That was the person intimidated him for so long. It was only a short visit but, by the end of it, I convinced him to tell Kate everything, and assured him he would be joining Kate and the kids soon.

We left the hospital and I noticed Ben wasn't driving back towards the station. He was taking me to see Kate and, again, he suggested what information to consider passing on to her. As it was with Ken, my visit to the hotel was short. I gave Kate a very brief version of finding Therese's secret apartment and the little I knew of what they found there. She seemed remarkably unmoved when I told her of the number of arrests made and their probable connection to her mother. I explained I would probably be leaving Ralston within the next day or so, gave her another one of my business cards, and told her to ring me at any time if she felt the need.

"What's gnawing at you?" Ben demanded as we drove away from the hotel. "You've been sitting there worrying the strap on your bag to death since we got in the car."

"Eh? Oh, sorry. I was miles away."

"I don't think so. I think you were still here in Ralston. So, what issue with this case still preoccupies you?"

"I can't help thinking I really haven't closed the case. I haven't given Kate closure."

"What do you mean by 'closure'? ... and it wasn't your case to solve; it was ours."

"Yes, I know. My brief was 'to look into Therese's death', whatever that meant. I suppose, if I apply logical extrapolation to that, it really meant establishing that Therese's death wasn't an accident."

"You did all that. So, where's the problem?"

"I don't know how to put it into words. I feel that, to give Kate 'closure', as I'm calling it, she would need to know who killed her mother, details of the situation that eventually led to her death, and probably all the rotten details of her mother's involvement in that drugs network. All that information would be hard to take on board but, I feel that without it, Kate will spend some part of the rest of her life wondering about it."

"We will give her some information when we close the case, but it will be restricted. However, remember that Ken knows probably more than any of us does about Therese and her involvement. I'd be surprised if he doesn't share that with Kate, once he feels safe."

"There have been so many deaths; so many public servant's deaths. I wonder how many more there would have been if the whole thing hadn't ended. I don't know that I feel any sorrow for the public servants that died, including Therese, but I feel for their families and the others they left behind who trusted them ... and that includes Greg." I found myself teetering on the brink of a fit of depression. Ben brought me back to reality.

"Yes, there is that aspect of it, but only those of us who have been closely associated with those deaths will have those thoughts. The majority of the population would not mourn the loss of a public servant, let alone a bent one. Many would see one less bureaucrat as a

Godsend. However, in this case, most will see their deaths as a public service."

"Death as a public service…?" I queried the concept.

"Yes, I suppose you could put it that way. Someone – albeit other bad guys – providing a public service by eliminating rogue public servants who betrayed the trust of the community. However many of those public servants there were, they actively contributed in some way to the destruction of so many lives in our community. They were providing a deadly service that ruined many lives."

I sighed and looked out of the window at nothing in particular as we drove along. With my case wrapped up, I should be looking forward to going home and getting on with other cases. I was looking forward to going home but, for me, this case felt 'unfinished'.

Ben sounded exasperated. "Now what's wrong with you? What's all the sighing and long face about?" It was difficult to explain the 'unfinished' feeling, but he nodded and seemed to understand.

We arrived back at the Precinct and I expected Ben to leave me to my own devices while he went off to do his job. Instead, he insisted in coming up to my rooms with me. It was obvious he wasn't just seeing me safely to my door. He followed me in and marched straight through to the lounge area. From the comfort of a lounge chair he demanded, "Coffee."

I joined him and we sipped our coffees for a few moments before he spoke. "Now, let's deal with this unfinished stuff that seems to be bothering you."

I sat upright; I hadn't expected this. Not wanting to say anything in case I changed his mind, I nodded and said nothing.

"Right; where to start…? Let's deal with your potential suspects. Pete Messell is back at work, and his investigation of the Norman Fanning accident has added it to the list of 'funny' deaths. He is now exploring what business the younger Mr Fanning might have had with Therese. Our accommodating travel agent had a good set-up for distribution of drugs and a number of friends in the Public Service at various centres around the State. We added him to that list as well. The bloke we arrested for the shooting at Tirandi Street was another sad case that a certain Fed officer – now in custody – had an interesting hold over. So, that makes the shooting a separate matter, although it was associated with the drugs network. My talkative informant identified the foot soldier who had to 'redeem himself', as you put it, and that person is 'helping us with our enquiries'. No, he wasn't responsible for Therese's demise."

He stopped speaking and consulted his notebook, then closed it and returned it to his pocket. I thought he might be getting ready to leave. I still had a couple of unanswered questions. "What about Tony Baldwin?" I blurted out.

"Oh yes, Tony Baldwin; a bit of a sad case, that one. His son became a drug addict and became a dealer for the network in order to pay for his supply. Things went bad for the lad and he fell foul of the main players. I think he was skimming. They threatened to take their revenge on his family, suggesting that his disabled sister would come in for 'special treatment'. The lad committed suicide but left a letter for his father detailing the whole story ... and implicating Therese. Hence, Tony Baldwin's belief that Therese ruined his son's life. Before you ask, Tony Baldwin was not in Ralston when Therese died and has a solid alibi for the time in question."

"Thank you for that. He was probably right though about Therese ruining his son's life, along with a lot of others I suspect. As I understand you though, Therese's killer remains a mystery."

"For the moment... Now, I do have things to attend to, so you are going to have to entertain yourself."

After Ben left, I didn't quite feel up to curling up with my book, so I retrieved the notebook from my bag and spent some time writing up notes from memory on yesterday's events and this morning's meetings with Ken and Kate ... and Ben's information on my 'potential suspects'. Then the pace of the day stepped up a notch.

I had barely finished my notes when Ben arrived with salad rolls and announced we were having an early lunch, and that I should be ready to leave Ralston by one o'clock. I would be driving my own car, and Sam and another officer, Brett, would follow in an unmarked police vehicle. My argument against the need for an escort went unheeded. We disposed of lunch quickly. I left Ben making phone calls in the kitchen while I dumped the last of my stuff into my case. When I returned to the kitchen, Ben was still making phone calls, so I busied myself tidying up the kitchen and the rest of the living area. At the end of his last call, Ben said it was time to go and helped me get all my bits and pieces downstairs.

As we rode down in the elevator, he explained that the original intention was for Sam and Brett to escort me for only the first half of the journey, and that a car from Millhaven station would provide the escort for the remainder of the trip. However, Millhaven had arrested four or five people, including the director (Emily's father), and several of their officers were involved in transferring the men to a prison about five hours drive north of Millhaven. As that station already had a number of officers assisting with arrests out west, it left them shorthanded and unable to provide an escort vehicle. Therefore, Sam and Brett would follow me all the way home.

No time was wasted in getting our cavalcade under way. The drive was just as long and boring as ever. I selected a favourite blues album from the CD stacker. I turned it up loud and sang along equally loudly.

As we reached the outskirts of Millhaven, I saw what I needed. I veered off the highway and pulled into the parking lot of a small general store. My escort vehicle screeched to a stop behind me, sending a spray of loose gravel flying. The two officers were out of their car and running towards me, their hands on their weapons. A quick defuse of the situation required.

"Whoa, relax. I just need to pick up a few things. You know, milk, bread, and other bits and pieces, so I've got something to see me through until I can get to a supermarket tomorrow." I was relieved when they elected to remain on guard outside the shop rather than follow me around inside the store.

The shopping done, we got back into our cars and drove sedately to my house.

# Chapter Eighteen

Security system disarmed, I parked in the garage and walked around to open the front door. My escort, delayed by a set of traffic lights a few blocks prior to my street, finally arrived at my house a couple of minutes later. It was a relief that all those neighbours who could see into my yard worked during the day. By the time we arrived, it was late afternoon but the neighbours hadn't arrived home from work yet. My arrival back home with a police escort probably wouldn't do much for my standing in the neighbourhood.

The two officers promptly went into search mode, searching the house inside from top to bottom and then all of the yard and the shed before declaring the place safe. About the only place they didn't search was under the carpet. Confident there was no one lurking anywhere, the officers joined me in the kitchen for coffee accompanied by the cupcakes I'd picked up at the little store.

As it would be too late for them to head back to Ralston after seeing me safely home, Brett and Sam were booked into a motel only a few blocks away for the night. It was getting dark. Brett started making noises about checking into the motel. Sam seemed reluctant to leave, but Brett became insistent. They walked out to the police car together. I started to relax. I was home and alone at last. The feeling of freedom only lasted a few moments. Sam returned with her case. She decided she was staying the night with me and nothing would persuade her otherwise.

I made omelettes for dinner, using more of the meagre supplies purchase on my way home. Afterwards, Sam sat in my office chatting to me as I unpacked my computer and other office gear. With the spare bed made up ready for Sam, we did a bit of channel surfing before deciding there was nothing worth watching on TV. We headed off to bed just before ten o'clock. As I was drifting off to sleep, I heard Sam wandering around. I eased my door open a fraction for a discreet look at what she was doing.

She had taken bedclothes and the pillow off the spare bed and set herself up on the sofa in the lounge room. I hadn't known Sam very long but I knew that, if this was what she was determined to do, I should just let her get on with it. She wouldn't find it easy to sleep in the lounge room. Even a stranger could wander around out there at night without turning on light. There was already so much light provided by all the LEDs on the equipment in the living area of the house.

Back in bed, I tried to doze off again. Sleep evaded me. I realised I wasn't completely relaxed and felt as though I was trying to sleep with one eye open. My bag was in the cupboard at the far end of the bedroom where I normally stored it overnight. Out of bed again, I retrieved my bag, and placed it on the bedside table... and immediately fell asleep.

A soft, almost imperceptible noise woke me. A light sleeper all my life, the slightest noise out of the ordinary usually does that. I lay quite still, barely breathing, waiting to hear if the noise – or some other noise – happened again. Nothing heard for a few moments. I slid the covers off and sat up. I was trying to decide whether to get up and investigate, or if I was just being unduly nervous as a result of recent events. That's when I heard Sam shouting something. Decision made. I was out of bed and grabbed the gun out of my bag in the one move. The bedroom door remained partially ajar after I opened it earlier. I peered round the door and into the dimly illuminated lounge room.

Sam struggled with somebody. She screamed. I heard a thump as she hit the floor. Her assailant almost lost his footing. Arms flailing, he quickly regained it. With his arm lifted high above his head, he leant over Sam's inert body. The light from the motion sensor in the corner of the lounge room glinted off the blade in his hand. Instinctive reaction; I fired on the rise. Not fussing about careful aim, I just fired in the general direction of the body mass. I didn't care what happened as long as it prevented that blade going anywhere near Sam again. There was another thump. The assailant joined Sam on the floor.

I ran to the lounge room and turned on the light. Neither of the people on the floor moved. I kicked the assailant: no reaction. Sam was bleeding heavily. She was unconscious. I checked the assailant. He was alive – barely – and bleeding, but not likely to cause a problem in his present condition. My phone was on the small table near the hallway. I covered the distance in a couple of heartbeats and dialled 000. I used the magic words 'officer down', gave them my name and address and requested urgent medical evacuation for Sam.

Brett's mobile phone number was where he left it earlier that evening: on the table next to my phone. I keyed in the number. "Brett; it's Sonny. Sam's been stabbed. It's bad. I've called it in."

"I'm on my way."

The local Ambulance Centre is only five streets away. A chorus of sirens sounded in the distance as I keyed in Ben's number. I relayed much the same message to Ben as I had given Brett, except that I remembered to add the bit about me shooting the assailant and the fact that he was still bleeding into the rug on my lounge room floor.

The sirens became louder and would arrive at any minute. After ending my call to Ben, using my phone, I clicked off half a dozen shots of the crime scene, including the front door, especially the area of damage caused by the forced entry. That's what I was doing when I heard a vehicle coming up the driveway. I rushed to the centre of the lounge room from where I could get a clear shot at anyone coming through the front door.

Brett arrived first, rushed through the door and skidded to a standstill when he came face to face with my Glock. I heaved a huge sigh of relief as I lowered the weapon and gave him a weak grin of welcome. Then the paramedics arrived. Brett directed them to deal with 'the officer' (Sam) first, but they were concerned about compromising the scene before the police arrived. I told Brett I had already photographed the scene. Brett flashed his credentials and told them to get on with dealing with Sam's wounds.

Two police vehicles arrived and four local officers swarmed in. Brett introduced himself and explained who Sam was. They didn't need the explanations. They received a briefing earlier about our arrival in their town. My knees were decidedly weak and wobbly. If I wanted to retain any sense of dignity, I needed to sit down before I collapsed. A thought occurred to me. I interrupted Brett's conversation with someone who appeared to be the officer in charge of the local group.

"I don't know if this bloke was a lone warrior, or whether he has mates lurking about the place somewhere, but there's been no evidence of anyone else so far," I told the officers.

"Three of my men are combing the outside areas. They brought the dog with them."

Brett looked pensive for a moment before commenting. "I think this bloke might have been working alone. There was an off-road motor bike parked at the entrance to your driveway when I arrived. It's the kind of bike that doesn't provide for a passenger."

"Yeah, I saw that as we drove in. Obviously didn't want to announce his arrival so he walked up from the street," the officer agreed. "Do we know who he is?"

"We haven't looked," Brett answered, "But it's probably time we did."

The assailant was dressed all in black: jeans, biker's jacket (no colour patches), rubber-soled suede boots and a woollen ski mask. Brett reached down and hauled the ski mask off. I gasped.

"Really...? This bloke's an all-time loser, but he has the balls to break into my house and stab a police officer?" I couldn't believe my eyes. When I looked up, I found I was the centre of attention.

"You know him?" the officer queried.

"I wouldn't say I *know* him. I recognise him from my days with the Department." I gave them his name. "I don't know much else about him or what he's been up to lately. A couple of years before I left the Public Service, he was employed by the Department as a storeman – or maybe a groundsman or odd job person, something like that anyway – but he didn't last long."

"What happened to him? Did he jump or was he pushed?" The officer's pen was poised above his notebook.

"He jumped just before he was about to be pushed, and that was in the days when it was almost impossible for the Public Service to get rid of anyone. He wasn't too fond of work; wouldn't expend energy on breathing if it weren't necessary for survival. I never saw him again, but I heard he had about 20 jobs over the next two or three years. None of them ever lasted long. He talked well and wrote a good story, but had nothing to back it up. Then about two years ago, some dumb rookie recruitment officer in the Department hired him again. I don't know if he was still there."

While Brett and the officer examined the assailant, I surreptitiously managed to take a couple of photos of him. A second Ambulance vehicle arrived and they readied the assailant for transport to hospital. They were just leaving with Sam as the second vehicle arrived. It had taken them some time to control her bleeding and get an IV line inserted.

"By the way," speaking to no one in particular, I gestured across the room, "His weapon is over there by that chair. He dropped it when I shot him. It skidded across the floor and came to rest against the chair."

They took my statement and asked me to come into the station later to sign it. Brett chatted to a couple of the officers as they packed up to leave. I walked over and stood ruefully examining the rug that so recently had held both victim and her assailant. The loose rug in front of the sofa was a bloody mess but, miraculously, it had contained all the bleeding and not a drop escaped onto the floor.

"Don't worry about it. We'll be taking it with us." Brett and the officer rolled the rug up and slid it into a large bag that another officer brought in. The second officer carried it out to their vehicle.

Brett and the lead officer headed for the door. As they were about to step outside, the officer turned and said, "Oh, just to put your mind at rest, my men found no one lurking in the bushes, and a vehicle will be coming to pick up that bike that's parked down at the end of the driveway."

I nodded, and then took myself off to my office, leaving Brett and the officer standing chatting beside the police vehicle. I booted my desktop computer back to life and connected my phone to it. All of the photos I took tonight I emailed to Ben. With nothing else to do, I wandered back to the kitchen and stood staring out of the window. The house was now deathly silent (unhappy choice of words perhaps) and the sun was more than half up. Birds found something to sing about, and the scent of rosemary and mint wafted through the now open window as a neighbour's dog ran through my herb garden.

When Brett came back inside, I suggested he go back to the motel for a couple of hours sleep before he had to check out and head back to Ralston. He just laughed and said he wasn't going anywhere, but that I should try to get a bit more sleep.

"There is no chance of that happening. Besides, it's daylight already."

"You have an alternative suggestion then?"

"I don't know what you do but, about this time of the day, I usually have breakfast."

I found a loaf of raisin bread in the freezer and managed to prise off a few slices. Today's fare would be raisin toast and coffee. If Brett wanted anything else, there were eggs, but he would be cooking them himself. I was not inclined to any culinary activity beyond toast. Breakfast was a long, drawn-out process that morning. There was plenty to discuss, starting with my quizzing Brett about what had prompted Sam to stay the night instead of going to the motel. He didn't know, but he did want to go over all the night's details again, although I already been through it all with the other officers.

We had almost finished breakfast when I was startled to hear a car pull up. Brett motioned me to stay where I was. He stood up, hand on weapon. Ben strode in. For him to get here so early, he must have left Ralston immediately after I phoned him. He marched straight up to me and wrapped me in a bear hug.

"Are you all right?"

"A bit weak kneed still but, apart from that, I'm fine."

"Good. Do you think you might find a bit more of that loaf for me?" I smiled and set about making him toast, as I struggled to hold back tears. I knew it was just shock setting in, but having Ben here was somehow comforting.

When Ben finished eating and asking questions, we all trooped into the office where I brought the photos up on the big screen for him. He hadn't had time to view the ones I emailed him before he left for Millhaven. The photos only precipitated more questions. Eventually, the questioning ended. It was already nine o'clock. I had to go to the station to sign my statement and we all wanted to go to the hospital to check on Sam. We went to the hospital first because Ben wanted Brett to be on the road back to Ralston as soon as possible.

Sam was groggy and pale looking but happy to see us. After a minute or so, Ben left Brett and me to talk with Sam while he went off in search of her doctor. He was gone for about ten minutes. Some way through that time, Brett said his goodbyes and left. He had to call in at the Police Station and check out of the motel before setting off for Ralston. His departure left me making light conversation with Sam until Ben returned. I made some inane comment about how it had been so long since she had been in uniform that, by the time she was back on the job, she would have forgotten how it all went together.

She looked a bit confused and then the truth dawned on her. "He hasn't told you, has he? I'm not in uniform any more. I made detective a week ago… about the same time as a vacancy in the Ralston team opened up."

"No he hadn't told me. Congratulations – or maybe commiserations – about your new boss," I said with a nod towards Ben.

"Geez, she's only been with me a week and already I'll have all the paperwork to do for a commendation."

"Commendation…?" Sam and I queried in unison.

"Seriously injured while engaged on protection detail."

That caused a spate of light banter, but Sam was beginning to look exhausted, so we left her to rest. As we were leaving, Ben told her he had arranged for her transfer back to Ralston where specialists would check out her injuries. He expected the transfer to happen later that day if the doctors assessed her condition as fit enough to travel.

Next stop was the Millhaven Police Station. I signed my statement and answered a few more questions while Ben was in a huddle with the station's top brass. That left us with nothing else to do in town, so we went back to my place for Ben to collect Sam's things before leaving for Ralston. It was nearly lunchtime. I made a salad and opened the packet of ham I bought the previous day.

I had questions for Ben. Over lunch was a good time to ask them. Foremost in my mind was what prompted Sam to stay with me last night. It was supposed to be safe. That's why they allowed me to come home. She must have had some concerns about how safe it really was. Initially, his answers were evasive. I was losing patience with the lack of straight answers. I clearly and succinctly acquainted him with that fact. He considered his options briefly before answering.

"The investigations that identified the other Millhaven participants in the network also uncovered another phone number. It received only a few calls. There were no calls to it for some time. It seemed probable its owner was a minor player. We couldn't trace the owner of the phone and didn't know if they were still involved. Of course, they might have been using another phone that we hadn't discovered yet. We didn't know if the person was still in Millhaven or even if they were still alive."

"So, I was the bait to lure him out."

"No, that wasn't the case. We really didn't think that person was still around; didn't think he would show up. In fact, we thought that, if he was still around and knew about the rounding up of the others, he would head for the hills rather than hang around. Sam always had some doubts about that line of thinking, and it was just as well. She is astute, and highly intuitive. She is going to make a great detective."

Well, I guess that answered the question of why Sam wouldn't go to the motel. "How is Greg holding up?"

"He's devastated by the betrayal – of him and the job. At least, that's how he sees it. He and David were friends for a long time. They were at the academy together, and were dating sisters at one time. David married Charlotte, but Greg's romance with the other sister eventually died a natural death. The two guys played a round of golf together every so often and, most Fridays after work, met up for drinks somewhere. He never suspected anything, and can't believe all the stuff that has come out about David's involvement."

"He wasn't the only one who didn't suspect anything. Having him involved in that operation to take down Mr Green and his gang could have been a disaster. I can't understand why he risked being involved. What if one of the gang had seen him; recognised him?"

"I don't think any of Mr Green's gang would recognise him. They wouldn't have known him. Whatever else David was, he was a good detective. I think, in his own mind, he isolated what he was doing as just some little cash-earning scheme on the side. He was relatively small fry in the network. I don't think he saw it as part of the bigger picture, not initially anyway. He developed something of a high lifestyle during his marriage and, after the divorce, found it difficult to maintain it on a copper's salary."

"Yeah, I can understand what you're saying, but wasn't his being involved in the takedown of Mr Green something of a conflict of interest, for want of a better way of putting it?"

"Yes, I can see how it does look that way but, remember he was still a good detective, and he enjoyed the thrill of the operation. The other thing to think about is how taking down Mr Green and his gang could have twofold benefit for David. In the first instance, his involvement in the operation certainly helped allay any suspicions anyone might have had about his involvement in the network and, secondly, having Mr Green and his men out of action improved the chances of his involvement remaining undiscovered."

"When you put it like that, it does make sense. I didn't really like David very much but, like Greg, I am still having difficulty reconciling the David I knew with the David we uncovered."

"His involvement came as a shock to all of us, and it certainly caused me some anguish. I brought him into the precinct. Think of what the consequences might have been if he had chosen to spread the word about who else was resident in that part of the precinct at the time. I don't think I need to tell you the chances were we would not be sitting here having this conversation." Ben looked hard at me to make sure I understood what he was saying. I simply nodded in reply, being incapable of any other comment as his inference hit home.

"If we are talking about what might have been, think back to that first night I spent at the Precinct. The 'someone' who tried to pick the lock on the door of that secure unit was probably your 'rotten apple'. Think about the connection between that person, David and the network. We might not be sitting here chatting if he had been successful with the lock that night."

Ben grimaced. "I wasn't going to mention that."

"I didn't have a chance to say goodbye to Greg. Would you thank him for everything he did for me? I have a lot of time for him, and I really feel for him at the moment."

We had exhausted the topic, and Ben needed to head off. I had the afternoon to myself. After straightening up a bit, I spent the rest of the day in my office completing my case notes on Therese's murder, and compiling and emailing my account to Kate's solicitor. I wasn't sure how Kate would come out of this. I thought she and Ken would be okay, but how much of Therese's cash she would end up with was another matter. There was the possibility the Law would deem the properties and cash to be proceeds of crime, and confiscate them. However, I think the house at Tirandi Street should be safe. Somehow, I think that would be good enough for Kate.

There finally was time to go to the supermarket to restock my pantry and fridge. The milk I left in the fridge when I left for Ralston – I was only going to be gone for a couple of days! – had turned into something resembling custard and the remnants of a head of lettuce bore no resemblance to any vegetable by now. While I was out, I called at my office and checked the mail. Nothing too exciting amongst it, but there were a couple of potential job enquiries. I spent the rest of the day on domestic chores out of necessity and in the hope of regaining some normalcy in my life.

I sat in front of TV surfing channels until quite late before going to bed. In spite of reassurances, I spent most of the night in fitful sleep. It wasn't until the early hours of the morning that deep sleep finally arrived ... and then I slept late.

*****

After that, I made a lazy start to the day: checked my emails, did some filing. By mid-morning, I had time for pure indulgence. With coffee made, I retrieved that book I had been trying to read for the past two weeks, and settled myself on the sofa. I decided to start reading from the beginning yet again, as I now had no idea where I was up to or what the story was about.

I had read about two pages when the phone rang. I glared at the phone. No, no! *No!* The last time I was like this on a weekend morning and the phone rang, I ended up spending two weeks in Ralston. I let it ring. However, I do have a business to run and I can't really afford to ignore potential clients. Will I or won't I answer it? I was still procrastinating when the answering machine clicked on and I heard the heavy English accent of the only person I knew who still used my full name.

"Good morning Sonoma. This is Edward Drysdale. My firm has the contract to investigate issues – er, what one might call irregularities – in the Public Service in this State. I am putting together a team to undertake the work and thought of you immediately. We have had an excellent working relationship in the past and I value your expertise and professionalism. Of course, your knowledge of the Public Service would also be invaluable. I hope you will give this offer favourable consideration and will be available to join my team. I shall be pleased to have your response by the middle of next week at the latest. Bye for now."

Drysdale's firm had put a number of lucrative contracts my way over the years, and he paid well. Aarrgh, a whole raft of questions attacked me. Did I want to do this? Did I need to take this contract? Did I want to be a part of what I knew this would involve? Did I want anything to do with the Public Service again so soon … or ever again?

Oh well, no point in rushing. I had a few days to think it over.

*The End*

# About The Author

NEIVE DENIS is the creator of the series featuring the Private Investigator, Sonoma Whittington. Neive Denis is the pen name of a writer who was lured from her usual genre to focus on the mystery and excitement that are a part of Sonoma Whittington's world. Neive came into being specifically for this series and, for the moment at least, intends remaining faithful to only Sonny's stories.

This series of stories tells of the intrigue and scrapes – some on occasion life threatening – that are part of the life of Sonoma Whittington, an Australian Private Investigator based in a Central Queensland coastal city. However, Sonny doesn't confine her escapades to Australia, and that provides Neive with an opportunity to weave some of her other areas of interest into Sonny's hair-raising adventures.

See more about Neive Denis and her work at
www.neivedenis.com
or contact her at
contact@neivedenis.com

www.ingramcontent.com/pod-product-compliance
Lightning Source LLC
Chambersburg PA
CBHW031238120726
47905CB00002B/644